"Roger, Green House," Lopez said, "we got a real problem here." He outlined their air and tank situation. "If we're not out of here by ten tomorrow, we're dead meat."

"Spunky, Green House Six. Here is the situation. The weather is full down and forecast to remain so for twenty-four hours. Further, we have been denied air assets. Cougar assets are to handle the situation. Right now this is his show." Bull Dall's voice was heavy.

"His show!" Lopez shouted into the microphone. "God almighty, we've got Americans dying here. Does COMUSMACV know about this?"

"Affirmative. I've been on the horn to him all day and half the night." The voice of Green House vibrated with anger. "Hang on, I'm going down . . ." The bunker quivered under a muffled explosion and the radio went dead. Lopez tried another radio. No answer.

"They got the antenna," he said. There was momentary silence in the bunker, then, with muffled curses the diggers went back to work. Toby helped pass the dirt out to the Vietnamese, who packed it by the door. Lopez drummed his fingers on the radio table, then started passing sandbags.

Overhead, two tanks crisscrossed the bunker, working on the corners, stopping and spinning on a tread, diesels roaring, slowly grinding the bunker down.

About the author

Mark Berent served in the Air Force for more than twenty years, first as an enlisted man and then as an officer. He has logged 4,350 hours of flying time, over 1,000 of them in combat. During his three Vietnam tours, Berent earned not only the Silver Star but two Distinguished Flying Crosses, air medals, a Bronze Star, a Vietnamese Cross of Gallantry, and a Legion of Merit. Now a pilot-reporter and the aviation editor for the *Asian Defense Journal*, he lives on a farm in Virginia, where he has just completed a sequel to *Phantom Leader* called *Eagle Station*.

Phantom Leader

Mark Berent

CORONET BOOKS
Hodder and Stoughton

Copyright © 1991 by Mark Berent

First published in the USA in 1991 by G.P. Putnam's Sons

First published in Great Britain in 1992
by Hodder and Stoughton Paperbacks

Coronet edition 1994

Map illustration copyright © 1989 by Lisa Amoroso

This is a work of fiction. All of the characters in this book are fictional
and bear no resemblance to real-life personages either living or dead.
(Sometimes I think the Vietnam war bore no resemblance to real life.)
However, in striving for authenticity, some of the organizations and
public figures exist or existed at the time. Note that not all actual
events occurred in the exact chronology presented.

The right of Mark Berent to be identified as the Author of
the Work has been asserted by him in accordance with the
Copyright, Designs and Patents Act 1988.

10 9 8 7 6 5 4 3

British Library C.I.P.

A catalogue record for this title is available from
the British Library.

ISBN 0 340 56918 2

Typeset by Phoenix Typesetting, Burley-in-Wharfedale, West Yorks.
Printed and bound in Great Britain by
Cox & Wyman Ltd, Reading, Berkshire

Hodder and Stoughton Ltd
A Division of Hodder Headline PLC
338 Euston Road
London NW1 3BH

This book is dedicated to the KIA, MIA, and POW aircrew from Air America, the U.S. Air Force, the U.S. Army, the U.S. Coast Guard, Continental Air Service, the U.S. Marine Corps, the U.S. Navy, the Royal Australian Air Force, and to the men of the U.S. Army Special Forces.

And to MiG-Killer USAF Colonel Phil Combies: RIP. "We stand to our glasses ready."

And to MB.

"I would think if you understood what communism was, you would hope, you would pray on your knees, that we would someday become communists."

> — Jane Fonda speech at Michigan State
> University to raise money for the Black Panthers,
> *Detroit Free Press*, 22 November 1969

"My position on the POW issue has been widely misquoted and taken out of context. What I originally said and have continued to say is that the POW's are lying if they assert it was North Vietnamese policy to torture American prisoners."

> — Jane Fonda, "Who is Being Brainwashed?"
> *An Indochina Peace Campaign Report*
> Santa Monica: Indochina Peace Campaign 1973

"We have no reason to believe that US Air Force officers tell the truth. They are professional killers."

> — Jane Fonda, *Washington Star*, April 19, 1973

"I am the Vietcong. We are everywhere! We are all Vietcong."

> — Tom Hayden, Bratislava, Czechoslovakia, 1967

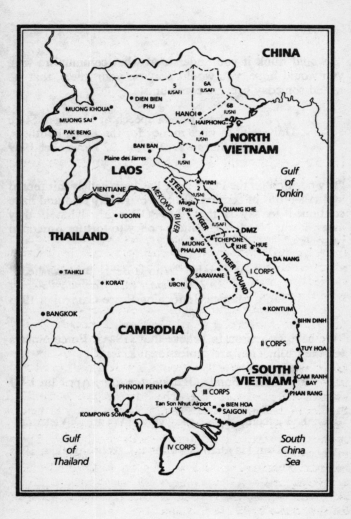

PROLOGUE

1015 Hours Local, Wednesday 22 November 1967
Near Vinh,
Democratic Republic of Vietnam

He was a big man. He hung in his parachute harness three hundred feet above the men crouched in the rice paddy who wanted to kill him. They were small men who carried long poles. He stared down, and realized the poles were sharpened bamboo lances.

"Oh dear God," he breathed. There was nothing he could do. His left arm hung numb, not responding to signals from his brain. Broken, he knew. Or worse. His helmet had been blown off and he could not see out of his left eye. Heart pounding, he jerked frantically with his right hand at the shroud lines in a vain effort to steer away. The men shifted and positioned themselves, running, then holding the lances butt-down like Masai warriors ready to spit a charging lion. He drew his feet up to kick away the deadly spears as he drifted into them with alarming speed. Three miles away, his shot-up F-4 jet fighter carrying his dead backseater crashed into a low green hill, and exploded into a towering red-and-black fireball. He was Major Algernon A. "Flak" Apple, the first black Air Force fighter pilot to be shot down in North Vietnam.

1

0630 Hours Local, Wednesday 24 January 1968
In an O-2 over the Ho Chi Minh Trail
Royalty of Laos

In the early Laotian dawn, USAF Captain Toby Parker balanced his tiny airplane on a wing and stared down at what could only be an enemy tank partially hidden under the jungle canopy. He was positive it was a tank. He was elated. Finally he could get clear proof that the North Vietnamese were moving Russian PT-76 tanks down the Ho Chi Minh Trail.

The first time Parker had reported seeing a PT-76 on the Trail, he had not been believed. "Impossible," the intelligence officers at MACV had said when he reported his second sighting. MACV, the Military Advisory Command to Vietnam in Saigon, ran the war in South Vietnam and Laos. Their disbelief, coupled with Parker's reputation as a moody drinker who had already lost a pilot by allowing himself to be sucked into a flak trap, resulted in a TWX being sent to his commander suggesting he at least counsel Parker, if not reassign him to nonflying duties.

Parker's commander, Lieutenant Colonel Charles Annillo, had done neither. He knew Parker as a young man who had grown up too quickly after abruptly suffering losses during an earlier tour in Vietnam, a tour in which he had performed heroic actions. Further, Annillo didn't necessarily subscribe to the MACV theory that the North Vietnamese wouldn't or couldn't send tanks down the Ho Chi Minh Trail. He had seen too much of this Asian war to dismiss any theory out of hand, regardless of how improbable it might seem. So he had told Toby Parker to furnish hard evidence, such as a photograph. For a week now Parker had been flying with a government-issue 35mm Nikon. He didn't know it leaked light.

Parker pulled his Cessna 0-2 around in one more tight turn, and raised the camera hanging from the strap around his neck. In the camera was a roll of Kodak Plus-X film. Toby stared at the partially hidden tank.

As a FAC – Forward Air Controller – Toby Parker's job was to fly his prop-driven observation plane along the enemy routes in northern South Vietnam and portions of Laos to ferret out targets. To mark the targets – usually supply trucks, sometimes the guns that guarded them – his plane carried two underwing pods, each with seven 2.75-inch rockets with explosive heads of white phosphorus to send up billowing clouds of smoke. He was given – "fragged" was the word – fighters for preplanned missions on specific targets. Or he could call Hillsboro, a C-130 airborne command post, to request fighters if he found a lucrative target of opportunity. With his bad reputation, he knew better than to call Hillsboro this morning for some diverted fighters to hit tanks everybody knew didn't exist.

Parker, call sign Covey 41, was based at Da Nang, the air base on the coast of the South China Sea in I Corps, South Vietnam. Now he was at 4,500 feet over the Ho Chi Minh supply trail that ran from the wide highways in North Vietnam through the mountain passes into Laos at Mu Gia and Ban Karai. At the passes, the Trail became a twisting network of rough paths and carved-out dirt roads through the Laotian jungle into South Vietnam. So far American Air Force and Navy fighters had been doing a creditable job of demolishing the daytime flow of truck supplies destined for the North Vietnamese Army and the Viet Cong in South Vietnam.

From altitude – nearly a mile above its hiding place – the tank didn't even show in the viewing lens of Parker's camera. With disgust, he wondered why in hell Supply couldn't issue a telephoto lens. Toby Parker knew there was only one way to get a sure shot and that was to get down in the weeds. His slow banger of an 0-2, commonly called the Oscar Pig, was not built, designed, powered, armored, or fast enough to be over Laos at *any* altitude, much less in the weeds. It was a stubby, twin-boomed, push-pull prop job whose cruise speed was 125 knots. And Parker was deep in Indian territory, where the bad guys had quad-barrel ZSU-23mm guns that could saw a low-flying 500-knot F-4 Phantom in half with barely a twitch of the trigger pedal. But hell, he thought, no one believed his two previous reports about sighting the Russian tanks. So, nothing for it. Got to do something. He let the camera hang from the strap and slammed the throttles full up.

Engines roaring, he headed away from the PT-76 as if he were leaving the area. As soon as he topped a karst ridge that put him out of sight of the tank, he racked the 0-2 into a tight 180-degree turn, pulled out the carburetor heat knobs, pulled the throttles back, pushed the pitch-control levers forward, and shoved the nose down to point just over the peak of the karst. Maybe everybody in the gun pits was asleep this morning, and he could at least come down the side of the karst to the deck silently, with no engine noise, snap a shot or two, then scoot away at a breathtaking 150 knots, dodging and twisting among the karst ridges. He swallowed hard and felt his heart rate increase. Time slowed, and engine noise and the whine of the power inverter behind his head faded out. His concentration had narrowed to the task at hand.

Nobody had been seriously shooting at him for the past hour. There had been a few desultory 37mm bursts over his head from a new gunpit location, but they had quickly ceased. Parker surmised that the local air defense commander had jumped all over the apparent novice 37-gunner for giving away his position to a FAC. Parker had noted the new site and planned to destroy it when he next called in fighters.

He easily topped the 2,500-foot ridgeline and zoomed down the 60-degree face of the black karst. Holding the control wheel forward, he felt the airplane buzz and vibrate from the increasing speed. The wind noise through the struts and rocket pods increased from a low rushing noise to a shriek. He could see the exact clump of tall baseline trees and brush where the tank protruded from the other side. As he came to the bottom of his plunge, he aimed to the right of where he knew the tank to be and propped his left arm with the camera on the left window. He removed his right hand from the control yoke for an instant and slammed the throttles forward.

The engines coughed, then caught with a roar as he cleared the trees at twenty feet. He threw the left wing down and began to snap as rapidly as he could while sighting over the top of the camera, unable to risk the time and concentration to peer into the viewing lens. During the few seconds he had as he flashed by, he saw several green-clad figures scrambling in the brush near the tank and, farther back, he saw the outline of several more PT-76 tanks. Then everybody on the ground opened fire on him.

He pulled back on the control yoke and banked hard left, seeking safety over the tops of the triple-canopy jungle trees. A tableau formed in his eyes as he got a last glance. Several figures were shooting AK-47s at him, smoke streaming from the barrels, and a man on top of one of the tanks was frantically swinging a turret-mounted gun toward him. Then he was out of their sight, but he knew all hell would soon break loose as the chief fire controller for the sector realized that the pilot of the little plane had seen one of their secrets. He flew low over the top of the jungle canopy as he headed for the karst face and comparative safety. He let his airspeed build up as fast as it could, but the engines didn't sound or feel right. He pulled his eyes away from the approaching karst to scan his instruments. The manifold pressure and RPMs were low. With a start, he realized he hadn't pushed the carburetor heat knobs off. When he did, the engines picked up.

Suddenly a cherry string of tracers tore past his canopy from his left and above him on the karst. His heart jumped, and he started jinking – random and abrupt turns to spoil the gunners' aim – as he climbed the karst face. He had a thousand feet to go before topping the ridgeline. Agonizing seconds became hours. Climb, CLIMB, Toby yelled, and pushed again on throttles that could go no farther forward. He was steadily losing airspeed as he both climbed and jinked. He heard tinks and thuds as slugs tore into the skin and frame of his airplane.

Thank God, he gasped, nothing vital hit – yet. Ahead, he saw tracers erupting from a gun site. He could see the muzzle flashes coming from inside the mouth of a cave that he would have to overfly to reach safety. Without looking, he reached down and armed his marking-rocket switch. His arm jerked as if with an electric shock when a slug smashed a hole in the right side of his windscreen and embedded itself in the rear of the cockpit. He banked slightly to aim at the black of the cave mouth that looked like a giant spider hole. He stabbed the firing button twice. Two rockets cracked out from under each wing and drew sharp trails of white smoke and flame as they darted toward the gunner's hole. Toby saw one impact just outside to the left, the other slammed directly into the cave. Immediately, thick white phosphorus smoke gushed out, giving Toby a few more precious seconds to clear the karst ridge looming over his head.

A few heartbeats later, he cleared the ridge and throttled back. Calming, he took a drink of water from his canteen and set about the task of navigating back to Da Nang. He called Hillsboro. He didn't mention the tanks or the film. He told them he was outbound and had suffered some combat damage. Hillsboro wanted to know more.

"Covey Four One, what's the extent of your damage? Are you declaring an emergency?"

"Negative emergency. I've taken a few rounds through the windscreen and into the avionics. My engines are okay,

15

gages in the green. Some of my nav gear is out, but I'm VFR and the weather looks good." He wanted to get to Da Nang and get the film developed. VFR meant visual flight rules.

There was a pause, then Hillsboro transmitted, "Covey Four One, Hillsboro. The senior controller directs you to do a one-eighty and pick up a heading for NKP. Contact Invert on 354.3 for steers to NKP. You copy, Four One?" NKP was the identifier for Nakhon Phanom, the USAF base in Thailand directly across the Mekong River from Laos. Invert was the call sign of the local USAF radar station that swept the Steel Tiger portion of Laos.

"Roger, I copy," Toby said, "but why?"

"Covey Four One, the senior controller wants you to divert to the closest friendly base because of your condition."

"I can't do a one-eighty or I'll fly right over the guns that shot me up in the first place."

There was another pause, then an older voice came on. "Covey Four One, Hillsboro."

"Hillsboro, Four One, go."

"Parker, get your ass over to NKP. You're too shot-up to stay on course. The weather might look good where you are now, but it's down along your course line and at Da Nang. Duck north around Delta Sixty-nine. No reported triple-A there. Acknowledge."

Most of the old heads in SEA knew who Toby Parker was. They also knew he was gold-plated by 7th Air Force and, although he could fly dangerous combat missions, he wasn't allowed to hang it out *too* far. Too many highly visible fighter pilots like the USAF's Korean aces Risner and Kasler, and the Navy's McCain, were POWs. Risner had made the cover of *Time* just before he had been shot down; the rescue attempt for Kasler had been the largest ever; and Navy Lieutenant Commander John McCain had been the son of a four-star admiral. So it simply wouldn't do to lose Toby Parker.

Parker had received a lot of notoriety on his first tour in Vietnam as the nonpilot who had taken over the controls of an 0-1 FAC plane when the pilot had been killed and rescued what was left of a Special Forces unit. He had received the Air Force Cross, the Vietnamese Cross of Gallantry, the Purple Heart, and an immediate appointment to a flying training class. Although he was back in combat, the USAF didn't want their genuine, boyish, aw-shucks young captain to buy the farm for *any* reason, much less a foolish one.

"Roger, Hillsboro, diverting to NKP," Parker transmitted. After Parker consulted his FAC book, he turned northwest until he picked up a curve in the river that looked like a rooster tail. From there, his TACAN navigational receiver told him NKP (also known as Naked Fanny) was 268 degrees for 35 nautical miles. He cruised in the cool air at 10,000 feet. Although the slipstream whistled and hissed through the holes in his plane, nothing vital had been hit by the groundfire. Soon he spotted NKP through the broken cloud layer. When he called the 23rd TASS command post on 128.0 on his VHF radio to say he was inbound, they said they would have someone pick him up. He called the tower and was cleared to land. The base looked hot and dusty, like an old airfield in Texas scrub country. Even the Mekong River looked brown and muddy. Small patches of green paralleled the Mekong, where low thickets grew in the festering backwash of the great river. Toby throttled back and zoomed down, careful to remember the carburetor heat.

The control tower called when he was on final approach. "Covey Four One, are you declaring an emergency?"

For an instant Toby was startled. Then he remembered why he had been told to divert in the first place.

"Ah, negative, NKP. Everything is under control." He checked his landing gear and flaps down, and put his plane smoothly on the runway. In the distance, air base buildings of redwood stood clustered like a small town. He opened the left window after he turned off the runway. Steamy air swept in as if from a hot bath. Following the directions of an airman from the Transient Alert squadron,

17

he parked across from the camouflaged Base Operations building, unstrapped, and climbed out. He took his helmet off and rubbed his hand through his blond hair. It was short-cropped and matted with sweat. Toby Parker had clear blue, slightly oval eyes, a well-formed face, strong jaw, good shoulders tapering to a narrow waist. He stood just under six feet in height. He stretched and rolled his shoulders as he watched the airman put chocks around the wheels. Toby told him he had some battle damage. Together they walked around the airplane, while the airman made notes. Then the man climbed in the airplane. In a minute he was back out.

"It's gonna be a while before you get this bird back in the air, Cap'n. We got skin to patch, plexiglass to replace, and some busted instruments. Who knows what damage there is I can't see?" He held out a form for Toby to sign. Toby signed and looked around the air base.

The ramp area was partially asphalt and PSP – pierced steel planking laid down in linking strips that stretched off in the distance like a ribbed bridge. There were no jet airplanes on the base. NKP was a flying museum of World War Two airplanes adapted to fly and fight over the Ho Chi Minh Trail and in support of friendly troops within Laos and South Vietnam. B-26s, C-119s, C-47s, and the big A-1 fighters with fourteen-foot, four-bladed props covered the base. Dust hung in the air as heat waves shimmered. Two A-1Es roared down the runway, one after the other, their big radial engines thundering a deep bass. A jeep with its top and windscreen down swept around the ops building headed toward Toby.

A sandy-haired captain wearing USAF fatigues and an old, billed Air Force hat waved as he drew up to the twin-boomed 0-1.

"Jump in. I'm Mel Brackett from Intell. Heard you were coming in. Always wanted to meet you. I'll take you to Ops so you can close out, then over to our shack for a debrief."

"You got a photo lab?" Toby asked.

An hour later Toby Parker sat next to Brackett's desk. They had just finished Toby's standard USAF debrief: the what, where, when results of his mission. The who and why were left to the analysts. FACs just reported the facts. Now they looked at the results of the pictures Toby had taken under fire.

Brackett fingered some photos. "If those are PT-76 tanks, they must be preparing for Arctic operations. These pictures look like white frosting on a black cake." All the pictures showed the effect of the light leak. Toby picked them up, shuffled them like playing cards, and flipped them into the trash can with an exasperated sigh.

Brackett brought out the enemy armor book. "Which tank did you see?"

Toby searched through the book and stopped at the photos and diagrams of the PT-76. "These."

The Piavaiuschiij Tank was a 15-ton tank with a thin welded hull, steering vanes, and twin hydrojet propulsors that made it amphibious. It had a 76mm main gun and a 7.62mm coaxial machine gun. Its primary mission was listed as reconnaissance, not heavy combat.

Toby tapped the page. "The tanks are there. I've seen them three times now," he said. "But nobody believes me."

"I do," Brackett said.

"Why?"

"Nobody would get as shot up as you did just to take pictures of the jungle. You were down there, you saw the tanks. I believe you." He paused. "Besides, I've heard noise on our acoustic sensors that sounds like tank treads. My boss says that can't be, because there *are* no tanks on the Ho Chi Minh Trail. C'mon. I'll show you what I mean." Toby followed him to another, larger building with no windows. "This is the ISC," he said, "the Infiltration Surveillance Center."

F-4 Phantom jets from the 25th Fighter Squadron at Ubon had been for some time scattering acoustic and seismic sensors in carefully laid strings across and around the Ho Chi Minh Trail. The devices reported coded telemetry data to orbiting aircraft that relayed the information to the analysts and their big IBM 360-65 computers at Nakhon Phanom. The idea was to track supplies and troops headed down the Trail by listening to their noise or sensing the vibration of the big trucks. Since the precise location of each string was known, the analysts would make the plots, then send them up the line to the 7th Air Force Director of Operations. Seventh would make up the frag order sending strike planes to drop bombs on the points the analysts determined were the most lucrative targets. The program was called Igloo White.

The sensors were long, camouflaged devices shaped like thin bombs. They would hit the ground and plunge in, after which their transmitting antennae would stick up like a long blade of elephant grass. Some of the listening devices would snag a tree and hang in the air like some metallic twig, their electronic ears alert and listening.

Inside the heavily instrumented and air-conditioned ISC building, Brackett gave Toby the whole briefing. He showed him the assessment officer's position where "traffic" on the Trail could be monitored on a big screen. An illuminated line of light they called "the worm" would show a convoy's progress. Then he took him to a small room, where he set up a tape recorder.

"Besides truck and troop passage," he said, "we hear some interesting things." He threaded the tape. "Listen to this. Gives us the laugh of the week."

They heard the sound of a man climbing a tree, the rasp of a saw (presumably on the limb the sensor hangs from, Brackett said), then the crack of the limb breaking and the cry as the man fell to the ground. He had cleverly sawn through the limb inboard of where he sat. In another, the undiscovered sensor recorded the entreaty and final success of a gunner courting a female road-crew worker. Parker had a good chuckle and Brackett shut off the recorder.

"Humor aside, I think the whole program is a waste," he said.

"Why is that?" Toby asked.

"This is an extension of McNamara's so-called electronic wall. Nothing is supposed to get past it without our knowing about it. But what's to prevent the bad guys from making a lot of fake noises or from running a truck several times past the same spot once they discover one of our sensors?"

Toby shrugged. Brackett continued.

"We spend a lot of money laying these things, and a few lives, too. The delivering airplane, the F-4, has to fly straight and level at a low altitude to get these strings in just right. We lose a few on this project."

The black phone on the desk rang. Brackett picked it up. "Intell, Captain Brackett speaking, sir." He listened for a few seconds, then spoke. "That very man is right here, sir." He handed the phone to Toby.

"Captain Parker," he said.

"This is Colonel Annillo, Toby. Are you okay? I understand you took a few rounds." His voice faded in and out as the microwave transmissions suffered heatwave anomalies.

"I'm just fine, Colonel. Ah, I saw some tanks again. PT-76s."

"Did you get any pictures?"

"No, sir. The camera leaked light. But there's a guy here who believes me. A captain. He says he's heard tread noise on a sensor string."

"Is the noise verified as produced by a tank?" Annillo sounded wary.

"Well, actually, no, it isn't," Toby said.

"Did you report your sightings?"

"Yes, sir."

"Well, that's all you can do. Meanwhile, Maintenance says your airplane is too full of holes to fly for a few days. They'll fix it up for a one-time escorted flight under VFR conditions only. Should get back here next week some time. So I'm having an early-go Covey divert into NKP tomorrow after he works the Trail to pick you up. Be there about ten. See you when you get back." Annillo rang off.

Toby told Brackett he had to spend the night.

21

"Great," Brackett said. "I'll get you fixed up."

Like all good FACs, Toby had a shaving kit in his FAC bag. One never knew when one had to divert. Brackett got him a room at the BOQ, then took him to the Officer's Club.

As they ate cheeseburgers in the dining side of the club, Toby marveled at the cute Thai waitresses.

"They're different than the Vietnamese women," he said. "Fuller, more, ah, *rounded*." He put his fork down, remembering his days in Saigon during his first tour.

Toby had loved a Vietnamese girl, a *métisse*. Her mother had been Vietnamese, her father a German in the Foreign Legion. The girl, Tui, had been a Viet Cong. She had been killed in front of Toby during an attack on the Bien Hoa Air Base. Toby still had nightmares of her death, although less frequently now. After she'd died, he and an American girl, Tiffy Berg, who flew for Braniff, had seen each other off and on, but it hadn't worked. There had been no magic, mainly because Toby was drinking too much by then. Finally, after a humiliating arrest in Florida for drunken driving, Toby had stopped drinking. Although his heroic deeds performed during his first tour in Vietnam had preceded him, so had his reputation. Only the people at Da Nang, where he was stationed, knew he had shaped up and no longer drank.

The men moved to the barroom, where Toby ordered a Coke and Brackett had a beer. The ceiling of the room had giant green footsteps across it to symbolize the rescue of many downed pilots by the helicopter crews who flew with the call sign Jolly Green Giant. The long wooden bar was crowded with men in flight suits, most with short sleeves. For some reason the pilots and air crew of nonfighter aircraft had started having their sleeves shortened. The wiser ones said, "Nothing doing – in case of fire I want whatever protection I can get."

Toby and Brackett pushed their way through the crowd to the outside patio, shaded from the setting sun. A breeze started that, if not cool, at least wasn't from a blast furnace.

Toby and Brackett talked quietly of home. Brackett was an Air Force Academy graduate; Toby had received his commission from ROTC at a college in Virginia where his parents were big in real estate.

"I've read a lot about you, Toby. You had some great writeups about that job you did rescuing the Special Forces team." Toby nodded.

They talked aimlessly. Then Toby said, "You're an intelligence officer. What do you think is going on with those tanks, and why doesn't Seventh believe us?"

Brackett thought for a moment. "What I think is going to go on is a big push by the VC and the NVA. All the indicators are there. The Disums are full of them. From captured documents all the way down to the Marines seeing an unusual amount of young men on the streets in Hue, the indicators say something is going to happen. Now, the guys at MACV are very aware of all this. They just are not sure where and when the push will start. Sounds crazy, but I think tanks are tied in with the whole scheme, at least in South Vietnam just below the DMZ. I know that most of South Vietnam is all jungle and narrow trails, and certainly almost all water in the Delta. But there are some hard trails and roads south of the DMZ around Lang Tri and Khe Sanh. And Route 9 runs from Laos smack into South Vietnam, right from the Tchepone River by Lang Tri and Khe Sanh on to Cam Lo and Dong Ha. Maybe it's no big deal, but I think there are tanks out there regardless of what the wheels in Saigon think. They want realities to fit the concept, and the concept at Seventh says there are no tanks coming down the Trail."

Toby nodded. "Damn," he said. "I had it all in sight and the damn camera was busted. Those pictures would have convinced them."

Brackett leaned forward. He was a lean man, and his pale blue eyes were intense. "I've got a great camera with a telephoto lens."

"And I've got an airplane," Toby said. "A little bent, but it works. And I know where the tanks are."

"How about an oh-dark-thirty takeoff?" Brackett said. "Hit 'em at first light."

"Sounds good to me." Toby Parker flashed a rare smile.

After an intense and convincing talk with the transient maintenance people, Toby and Mel Brackett lumbered off the runway at Nakhon Phanom at 0545 the next morning. A staff sergeant had reluctantly provided Brackett with a headset and boom mike, but no helmet like Toby wore. It mattered little ... unless they crashed and he received a blow to the head. Toby had given Brackett a quick briefing on the right seat, the parachute, and what to do if they were hit – "Bail out and pull this thing" (the silver D handle). Brackett wore his two-piece USAF fatigues. By 0615 they were over the Rooster's Tail, where Toby swung south-easterly toward the spot where he had seen the tanks the day before. He checked in with Invert.

"Roger Covey Four One, what's your mission number? I don't have you on today's frag."

Toby thought fast. "Ah ... Invert, we don't have a mission number. This is a test hop."

"Covey Four One, be advised you're getting pretty far east into Indian country for a test hop."

"Roger, Invert. We're doing a little recce also. Four One listening out."

Toby grinned at Brackett, and pulled out his 1:50,000 map and pointed out where the tanks were, eight kilometers northwest of Lang Tri at XD 672387. "I won't come down the karst this time," he said on the intercom. "I want to come from the other direction, from up along the Tchepone River. I don't think they have any big guns pointed down on the river, so all we have to worry about is small arms from the guys taking an early dunk."

"Just give me a two-minute warning," Brackett said. He carried his own Minolta single-lens reflex camera with a 135 mm telephoto lens. He had put in a roll of thirty-six prints at 400 ASA. Toby glanced over as Brackett estimated what the light would be, and dialed in settings of f8 for the lens, and 500th of a second for the speed. He hoped it would be enough to counteract the wobble of the long-range lens from a bouncing airplane.

The morning coolness swept through the cockpit as Toby descended from his cruise altitude of 8,000 feet down to skim just above the surface of the muddy river. A high overcast blocked the morning sunrise. The banks were still partially hidden in the gray dawn.

"Two minutes," Toby yelled.

"Shit, it's too dark," Brackett yelled back.

Toby immediately threw the twin-boomed airplane up on a wing and hauled it around to fly back up the river. His wingtip was five feet from the water's surface during the turn. Toby glanced at Brackett. He looked green.

"You okay?"

"I may barf, but press on."

"We're not quite in the bad area yet," Toby said. "How much more time do you need?"

In answer, Brackett turned his head out the window on his right and threw up. The slipstream splashed the effluvium along the sides and bottom of the craft. Some of it flew back in to splatter the radio equipment in the rear. The stench twisted Toby's stomach for a second. Mel Brackett gripped the sill of the window and retched until nothing more came up, then reached under his parachute harness and pulled out a bandanna from an upper pocket of his fatigues. He wiped his face and mouth.

"I'm okay now," he said on the intercom. He looked out of the airplane, then checked his Seiko watch. "Shit – about fifteen, twenty more minutes. I should have calculated the sunrise over the karst peaks as being much later than on the flatland."

"There's a place down here, just east of the Razor karst, where I'll pull inland and we'll orbit for a few minutes. This is a fairly safe area. I don't want to climb back up and alert all the gunners."

The Razor karst, like the Rooster Tail and the Dog's Head, were well-known projections, highly visible from the air. "It doesn't make any difference. They probably already know somebody is down here stooging around."

Toby held the plane in an easy bank while Brackett wiped the perspiration from his forehead and checked the light. A few minutes before seven, he judged it bright enough.

"Okay," Brackett said. "Let's go find those tanks."

Toby headed back up the river. Just before the turn where he judged the tanks to be, he pushed the pitch and mixture full up, then both throttles. There was no surge. The airspeed crept up to 165 knots. Brackett looked at Toby, a big question mark on his face.

"That's it," Toby said. "There isn't any more airspeed. This is as fast as it goes. You still want to try it?"

"Press on," Brackett said.

Toby flew the smooth bathtub shape of the push-pull aircraft barely five feet off the river water.

"Get ready," Toby yelled, and pulled around the last turn. Brackett hung out the right window, his camera poised.

The NVA Trail infantry were ready for them. An entire four-squad platoon lined the east bank. All forty-eight men started shooting with AK-47 assault rifles and SKS repeating rifles at the little gray aircraft. Spumes of water like scores of tiny white fountains erupted from the river short of the airplane and behind it. The shooters weren't leading their target enough.

"The tanks should be over there," Toby yelled. "Hurry up. We gotta get out of here." The spumes crept closer to the airplane.

"I don't see them," Brackett yelled back.

"Over there." Toby pointed just ahead of a large clump of trees. "Hurry up, start snapping."

All at once the spumes caught up with the airplane. Bullets peppered the right-hand boom and rear engine cowling with tinks and thuds. Several spangs sounded from the right rocket pod. It tore loose to hang crazily from its rear mount. More hits. Brackett yelled something. The rear engine missed a beat and the RPMs started to fall. Toby banked away from the treeline and struggled to keep the plane in the air. It pulled to the right and the nose wanted to drop. He held in left aileron and left rudder while pulling back slightly on the control column, then banked left, away from the river and the tanks, and the shooting men, clearing the scrub growth at the river's edge by a bare six feet. The airspeed needle dropped ten knots.

"Didja get them?" Toby yelled. He was too busy steering for a low hill to hide behind, to look at his passenger. He jerked as the rear engine dropped another 100 RPM, tore his eyes from the approaching hill, and looked at the instrument panel.

"Oh my God," he yelled at Brackett. The oil gage was dropping for the rear engine, and the cylinder-head temperature was climbing. "We're going to lose that engine, and she won't fly on one. We haven't got enough power to get home." Brackett didn't answer. Toby pulled the airplane around the hill, safe from the gunners for the moment, and started to climb. Then he looked over at Brackett. He was slumped back in his seat, right arm dangling out the window. Blood stained his parachute harness and the camera dangling from his neck. His eyes were closed and a thin trickle of red ran from one corner of his mouth. Toby couldn't tell if he was unconscious or dead.

He flew with his left hand and reached over to shake Mel Brackett. There was no reaction. The rear engine dropped another 100 RPM and started to clatter. Toby had to grasp the wheel with both hands. When he had the plane under control, he snatched a map from his FAC case. Brackett's blood smeared it as he spread it on his right knee and traced where they were with his finger. The closest friendly location was the Special Forces camp at Lang Tri. Toby took up a heading for the camp.

He tried all his radios. There was no response. He put his transponder on emergency in the vain hope it was still transmitting, but he had no way of knowing if the signal was being received. He took out his emergency radio from his leg pocket and called for anybody on Guard channel to answer. There was no response. He transmitted in the blind.

"Mayday, Mayday, Mayday. This is Covey Four One in an Oscar Deuce with one passenger. We're hit and trying for Lang Tri. My passenger is badly wounded. Covey Four One going to Lang Tri." The plane started to fall off on a wing and he couldn't hold it with one hand. He slid the radio under his right leg, and with an effort, righted the 0-2.

He was at 1,500 feet now, but could claw for altitude at a rate of only one or two hundred feet per minute. When the rear engine let go, he would be descending at the same rate, because the underpowered 0-2 could not hold altitude with the weight of the radio equipment and two people with parachutes, and the drag of the two rocket pods – one shot almost off and hanging crazily. The engine clattered on. At this rate, Toby estimated, it would take twenty minutes to get to Lang Tri. There was no airstrip; he would have to crash-land in an area he hoped wasn't mined.

Again Toby looked at Brackett. There was absolutely nothing he could do. He needed both hands to fly the airplane. For an instant he felt curiously detached, as if Brackett wasn't real, or the scene wasn't real. He felt no fear, just apprehension that he might not find the Lang Tri camp. Then they would crash in some out-of-the-way place that no one knew about. And probably die. He and this man Mel Brackett, that he had known less than one day, would die together. Or perhaps Brackett was already dead.

He risked a hand from the wheel to fumble at Brackett's chest. Maybe he was alive. Maybe there was a bleeding wound that needed a tourniquet. He awkwardly unfastened the man's chest harness and fumbled around under his fatigue blouse. He couldn't feel a thing. Then Brackett's hand came up and patted his wrist. He moved his head slightly and moaned, but did not open his eyes.

Toby hastily withdrew his hand to right the airplane. "Hey, Mel, hey man, it's going to be okay. You're going

28

to be just fine," he said with as much conviction as he could muster.

He looked below. They were off the Trail now. There were no gunners, no people, no river. Just mile after mile of triple-canopy jungle and steep karst rising up like grotesque ships on a green sea. The engine lost another 100 RPMs and Toby found not only could he no longer climb, he could barely maintain his altitude, which was now 2,000 feet. He looked toward Lang Tri. The weather looked ominous in that direction. Rainsqualls were dropping from bulbous gray buildups and sweeping through the valleys and over the mountaintops. He checked his map. Outside of an airstrip at Khe Sanh, there was no other place to go, and he could not go there. The 1,500-foot Khe Sanh plateau was farther away, and, Toby saw, rose up into the cloud base over the Annamite mountain range.

It had to be Lang Tri, a Special Forces camp with an A Team and a contingent of Vietnamese. It fronted Route 9 west of the Khe Sanh plateau. The purpose of the base was to surveil, and, if possible, block VC and NVA movement along the east-west Route 9 that ran from Tchepone in Laos to Dong Ha in South Vietnam. It was also a base for harassing patrols and a surveillance point for Ho Chi Minh Trail activities. A year ago, in December 1966, COMUSMACV, General Westmoreland, had decided to make Khe Sanh a U.S. Marine base. A colonel had moved in, the Seabees had lengthened the runway from 1,500 to 3,900 feet, and the SF contingent had taken their mission to Lang Tri. There had been some animosity. The Marine colonel was a ramrod-stiff man who did not like the unconventional Green Beret methodology.

Then, the following March, two USAF F-4 Phantoms had mistakenly bombed the nearby Bru Montagnard village, killing 125 and wounding 400 tribesmen. This had placed the Special Forces men at Lang Tri at further disadvantage. Up to the bombing, the Bru had been, if not friendly, at least not adversarial. After the bombing they had stopped providing patrols and intelligence information about the

29

Viet Cong. Had this not occurred, and had there been tanks across the Tchepone River, they would have seen and reported them.

Toby had to try for Lang Tri. He threaded his 0-2 between the two hills just as his rear engine shuddered to a clanking halt. He quickly threw the propeller to the pitch position, where it would create the least amount of drag. Even with the front engine at full RPM, he was losing altitude. Ahead of him was Route 9. Just to the north of the road, he saw the Lang Tri SF camp. Its concertina wire perimeter and crowded construction, with the many gun pits, defensive firing positions, and bunkers, made it stand out in contrast to the dilapidated French buildings and the rough huts of the Lang Tri village just south of the road. A light rain was falling on the camp.

He concentrated on his airspeed and aligning his plane to land on the road. He tore his right hand free from the wheel for an instant to check that Brackett's harness was locked, then looked straight ahead. He estimated the width of the road to be 15 feet. The main wheels of the 0-2 landing gear were 6 feet apart, but the wingspan was 38 feet and would overlap the ditches on each side. The surface of the road looked like hardened mud with deep ox-cart ruts. From previous study Toby knew the crumbled asphalt of the road was under several layers of red mud made thick and sturdy by ox and water buffalo excrement. The road had not been maintained since the French had been defeated in 1954.

He held steady pressure as the right wing of the plane wanted to dip. At 500 feet he threw his landing-gear lever down. Hydraulic power from the front engine locked the two mains and the nose gear in place. At 300 feet he eased the flap lever down. The plane immediately tried to roll to the right. He slapped the lever up and rolled the wings level. He experimented and found he had to hold his airspeed at 95 knots, 20 more than required for an undamaged airplane. He came down, down, then flared over the road's surface and slowly eased the throttle of the front engine back to idle. He held the plane twelve inches above the road's surface and, nose high, carefully felt for the ground with the main gear.

When the main wheels touched down, the right main – its tire shredded by groundfire – dug into a rut and collapsed, spinning the 0-2 sharply to the right. The right wing dug in and ripped off as the plane continued lurching farther to the right. Thinking of fire, Toby turned the magnetos off and grabbed the underside of the instrument panel to brace himself as the plane bucked and tore across the road and into a ditch. The propeller bit the ground once, throwing up a clod of dirt before it bent back. Then the left wheel and strut tore off, and Toby and Brackett were flung back and forth as the crashing plane skidded to a stop, nose down, leaning at a 45-degree angle to the right. The wreckage rested on its torn right wing stub; dirt and debris had been flung into the cabin after the plexiglass windows had broken. As if in a dream, Toby saw his hand reach up and turn the master electrical switch off. He marveled at the hand. It worked. He turned it this way and that, flexed the fingers, made a fist. Then he heard a noise outside the wreck.

Feeling and reality returned. "Hey," Toby yelled. "Hey. In here. Help my friend. He's wounded." He was at such an angle he couldn't see out the windows. A figure appeared, and squatted to look in the cracked and mud-splattered windscreen. Toby tried to unbuckle his harness with hands that started to tremble and shake. The figure in front of the airplane began to pull away the pieces of the broken windscreen. Slowly and carefully, Toby undid his harness and braced himself so as to not fall on Brackett.

"Hurry," he said to the people outside. "Hurry. I don't know if he's still alive." He balanced and kicked out the remaining piece of the front windscreen. Then he went to his hands and knees and crawled out of the wreckage. He looked up.

The plane was surrounded by soldiers wearing the green uniforms and khaki pith helmets of the North Vietnamese Army. They all had their rifles pointed at Toby. One man

31

jerked his rifle in an upward motion. Still kneeling, Toby raised his hands. The Vietnamese butt-stroked Toby across the back with his rifle and yelled something Toby didn't understand. Two men grabbed Toby, emptied his pockets and tore the boots from his feet.

Another man crawled into the wrecked airplane. He called out something in Vietnamese to the leader, who barked one word, *Giet*. There was a shot, and the man crawled out, clutching Mel Brackett's dog tags. Two soldiers ripped through the skin of the aircraft with bayonets until they found a fuel tank. They stood back and one man fired a round into it. They lit some brush with a match and tossed it into the trickling aviation gasoline. It lit with a roar, singeing the two closest men, who leaped back, causing the others to laugh and yell out words of derision.

Yellow-and-red flames engulfed the smashed airplane, and the blistering heat forced the Vietnamese to back farther away. The plane burned quickly and noisily with loud pops and crackles punctuating the hissing roar. Black smoke created by the oil and rubber and the petroleum billowed hundreds of feet into the air. Toby tried without success to force the picture from his mind of Mel Brackett's body cooking and blackening.

The leader spoke again. The troops gathered their gear and started up a hill. In the rear, two men grabbed Toby. One tied his elbows together behind his back so tight Toby felt as if his chest would rip in half, the other slung a noose around his neck, jerked it, and started running up a hill after the departing column. Toby fell to his knees, then had to scramble sideways while the two soldiers screamed *Di di mau len, di di mau len*. He got to his feet by bracing his back against a tree, and stumbled after them. He went down immediately as a sharp rock punctured his left instep. The man holding the rope stopped. The other came back with a rifle and jammed it against Toby's head so hard it ripped the skin on the side of his skull. He snarled something and pulled the trigger.

32

2

1030 Hours Local, Wednesday 24 January 1968
F-4 Phantoms Near Kep Air Base
Democratic Republic of Vietnam

The heavy flak started before they were even in the target area, and the SAMs came up soon after. The first plane torn out of the sky was an F-105. Three miles above the earth, it exploded in a flash of white light. An antiaircraft shell had burst its belly, simultaneously detonating its bombs and fuel. Seconds later, all that remained was a vast black cloud, from which pieces of airplane rained down. The remaining seven planes dashed toward their target along the railroad northeast of Hanoi. Below, SAMs exploded off the ground in huge balls of dust and rocket smoke to streak toward them. Then MiG warning calls sounded from the Red Crown controller on a Navy radar ship.

"Bandits, Bandits. East of the Bullseye for ten miles."

"Okay, Buick, let's get 'em," USAF Major Court Bannister transmitted as he turned his flight of four F-4D Phantoms toward the MiGs. The Bullseye was code for Hanoi. North Vietnamese tactics were to attack the strike force from low and behind. Defending F-4s, the MiG Cap (combat air patrol), had to interpose themselves successfully if they were to save the F-105 and F-4 bombers from being shot down.

"Contact, twenty port for nine. About a dozen," Bannister's backseater said over the intercom. He saw twelve blips on his radarscope bearing to the left of their aircraft at nine nautical miles.

"Tallyho, Buick, bandits eleven o'clock low. Three, take the ones to the left," Bannister ordered as he drove his aircraft toward the enemy fighters. Buick Three, Captain Tom Partin, shifted himself and his wingman more to the port. Court Bannister leaned forward in his harness, nerve ends tingling. He never took his eyes off the flights of climbing MiGs.

"They're Nineteens," he said to his backseater, Pete Stein. The MiG-19 was a smaller, more maneuverable aircraft than the F-4, but not as fast.

"Roger, Boss. I got a lock on the number-four bird. Go get him."

"I'll get him," Bannister said in a tight voice. I'll get him, he repeated to himself. He was high scorer in Southeast Asia, with four MiG shootdowns to his credit. Only one other man – Robin Olds – had as many, and he was back in the States. Bannister also had a possible and a probable to his credit. He fixed the MiG's position on his canopy, took one last look around the sky above and behind his plane to clear himself, noted the position of his wingman, and returned his attention to the MiGs. Court Bannister had positioned his flight to put the glaring sun behind him, and the MiGs had not seen them yet. This would be an easy kill. With it, he would become the first Ace of the Vietnam war.

Bannister rechecked his switches. The big fighter carried eight air-to-air missiles and a 20mm cannon. Because he was approaching the enemy fighters from the front, he had selected the radar missiles rather than the heat-seekers, which needed a hot engine on which to home. He placed his gunsight pipper directly on the number-four MiG-19. The enemy fighter grew larger as they approached at 95 percent of the speed of sound, nearly 700mph. An easy kill. The first Ace. Behind the visor of his helmet, Bannister's eyes had a feverish glint.

An electronic ring in his gunsight showed he was well in

range. His finger tightened on the trigger of his stick grip.

"Shoot, Boss," Pete Stein said eagerly, "we've got a lock-on."

Bannister didn't answer. Not yet, he said to himself, not yet. I want this missile to fly right up his nose. Then it was time to shoot, and still the MiG hadn't seen him. He felt a flush of victory in the split second before he was about to squeeze the trigger.

Suddenly, out of the corner of his eye, he saw two fighters closing from the right. They were F-105s that would pass between him and the MiGs. He estimated time and speed, and realized with an angry wrench that he dare not launch the missile. Buick Three and Four were still clear to fire, so was his number Two, a young captain. He could make a shot.

"Buick Lead aborting the run, Two take the kill," Bannister said rapidly over the radio. Buick Two fired immediately. He was a great wingman who, besides protecting his lead's tail, kept track of what was going on in front. Two AIM-7 missiles dropped from under his Phantom; their rocket engines ignited one after the other and drew vivid white trails to the MiG. The first missile blew the right wing off, the second streaked into the wreckage and exploded.

At the same time, Buick Three, Tom Partin, fired a missile that tore the tail from another MiG.

The sky exploded with activity. Buick flight pulled up and away to position for a re-attack from above, and the MiGs dove down to form a defensive circle. Court checked his wingman. He was still in position.

"Nice shots, Two, Three," he transmitted, careful to keep the acid of envy from his voice. "Now let's get some more."

"Yeah, yeah," Two said, in an excited and panting voice. "More, more," transmitted Three.

Court cleared the sky. There was no flak or SAMs firing now, because they were in the area where the MiGs flew. Yet he saw no other MiGs except for those in the defensive circle turning below. The MiGs were level and circling at

5,000 feet, one behind the other, in a Lufbery maneuver, each protecting the other's tail. They could wait until the American airplanes became low on fuel and had to leave the area, then they would break out and land safely.

In the distance Court could see black-and-white smoke from the marshaling yard on the northeast railroad that the F-105 Thuds had hit. The last of the big fighters were leaving at tremendous speed out over the Tonkin Gulf. Radio chatter had died out. Bannister estimated his flight had about four more minutes of fuel to use for fighting before the low man would call Bingo. He looked down at the tempting circle of MiG fighters.

"Lead's in," Court transmitted as calmly as if he were rolling in on a stateside gunnery range. "Going IR," he told Pete Stein as he selected a tail shot at one of the MiGs that was slightly out of position. Low puffy clouds were forming to one side of their circle.

Court dove down from 10,000 feet. As he lined up on the MiG, another from across the circle pulled his plane up toward him and shot off several rounds of 30mm cherry balls. At the same time, Court heard the tone in his headset indicating one of his AIM-9 infrared missile had a tentative lock on something. Court hoped it was the MiG, but shooting downward could be deceptive with IR. The ground played tricks with the heat-seeking head.

Time was running out. When one of the cherry balls banged into an outer panel of his left wing, he knew he had to shoot and get out of there. He fired one IR missile, and another, then fired two radar missiles like giant bullets with radar interlocks out, and zoomed for altitude, his wingman following. He grunted under the G-load, and his ribs hurt. The radar missiles were fired manually before the fire control system had completed its computations.

"We took a hit, Major," Pete Stein said in a tense voice. Court checked the tip of the slablike wing, and then his cockpit gages. "Nothing serious," he said. His blood was pounding now. He looked back at the MiG to see his missile explode a few feet behind its tail. Immediately, a tongue of flame erupted from the tailpipe. His other two missiles, without radar to guide them, streaked harmlessly through the formation.

"Hot shit," Court yelled into the microphone in his mask, "I got him. Watch him go in, Two." Unless the gun camera recorded it, there had to be a second ship to confirm a shootdown before 7th Air Force would award credit. Gun cameras could record a gun kill because the plane was so close and pointed at the enemy while the shells impacted. But the camera rarely caught a missile kill because the nose of the killer airplane wasn't always pointed at the one killed at the time of missile impact.

"Watch him go in," Court said again, his voice taut with excitement. This was it. Not only Ace, but the first, the very first Ace in SEA.

Court had to take his eyes away for a moment to maneuver his airplane back up to altitude, away from the probing cherry balls that were coming now from two of the other MiGs. Their defensive circle was working very well. Somebody always had their guns trained on an attacker. He checked his fuel. Two minutes remaining. He rolled left and looked down at the circle. One MiG was missing, but there was no fireball on the ground.

"Where did he go in, Two?" Court asked.

"Couldn't tell, Lead."

"WHAT?"

"Ah, lost him when we climbed out. He went into a cloud or something. My GIB didn't see him either." There was genuine anguish in the pilot's voice. GIB was pilot slang for "guy in back."

"Pete, did you see anything?" Court asked his backseater.

"No, Major. I was on the scope and the gages. Didn't see a thing."

"Jesus H. Christ," Court blurted. "You bastards all blind? I got him. You mean to say no one saw him go down?"

"Hey, Major," Pete Stein said from the backseat, "you want to try again? I'm game."

Court forced his voice to be calm. "You are one shit hot

guy, Stein. But jumping into that circle jerk down there is out of the question. We'll just keep turning like we are now and in another ninety degrees we'll be headed home." Yeah, right, Court thought to himself. What a calm and reasonable thing to do. I WANT TO ATTACK . . . but I can't. Got my flight to think about, got my backseater to think about.

Court was still steaming at the two missed opportunities. The MiG he had just hit would be his third probable or possible, but not a positive. To attack the MiG Lufbery again would be too reckless and he knew it.

"Buick Four, Bingo," Buick Four transmitted, announcing he had only the minimum fuel necessary to get to a tanker for aerial refueling. The number-four man in a flight of four, like the tip of a whip, always had to travel the farthest to stay in position, causing him to run out of fuel first. Generally, Two was next, followed by Three.

"Roger, Four. Three, close it up. We're outbound." Double shit damn fuck, he said under his breath.

"Hey, Court," Pete Stein yelled from the backseat, forgetting military protocol. "Look down there, ten o'clock low."

Down on the left was Kep, a North Vietnamese MiG base. They could see several silver MiGs flying low and slow in the landing pattern. The Rules of Engagement said a pilot could not attack a MiG base, only the MiGs from that base that flew up to attack him. Hundreds of American airmen – Navy, Air Force, and Marines – had died or been captured because of that crippling "don't strike until you've been struck" restriction.

If I were flying a single-seater, I'd roll in and attack in a heartbeat, Court Bannister said to himself. But with a second man on board, a pilot couldn't always do what he wanted. Court squinted at the airfield as it blurred for an instant. His head felt full now, and his eyes burned. He blinked and popped his eyes, trying to clear them. His ribs throbbed with a dull pain.

"We've got the fuel. Let's get one," Pete Stein said on

the intercom, as if he had read Bannister's thoughts.

Bannister quickly made up his mind. "Okay, we'll do it. Going guns," he told Stein in happy answer. "Tom," he transmitted to Buick Three, "take the lead, make one orbit, if we're not back up, take the flight home." Court rolled his Phantom up and over and pulled it down to dive in on the airfield even as he transmitted.

From his position at 12,000 feet, Court unloaded the G forces and let the twenty-five-ton fighter build up airspeed to avoid using the afterburner until climb-out. He needed to save all the fuel he could. When he eased the nose up out of the dive at 4,000 feet, he was nearly supersonic.

The concrete runway at Kep airfield was dead ahead. Clouds formed a gray and towering backdrop. A half dozen MiG-19s were in the landing pattern or approaching the pattern. Court and Pete were head-on to two of them flying on downwind, gear and flaps hanging.

Then the groundfire began. Muzzle flashes erupted, making the base look like a firefly nest. Puffs of black-and-white 23mm and 37mm shells began filling the sky in front of the Phantom. In between were cherry and green tracers from the 14.5mm and 12.7mm barrels. Court quickly switched from guns to his last remaining missile, an AIM-9 infrared. Without waiting for a lock-on tone, he hosed it off in the general direction of the MiG base, then switched back to guns. He was breathing very fast now.

"Just to keep their heads down," he told Pete to keep him informed. On a gun attack, all the GIB could do was make sure the radar and fire control system was automatically feeding range information into the frontseater's gunsight, look around for enemy fighters, check the gages, and keep track of where they were, both from home base and from the target. He had to do all that while making sure his pilot's altitude, airspeed, and attitude were proper for the conditions.

Court sighted on the lead ship on the downwind and headed toward him. Their combined closing speed was over 1,000 miles per hour. He couldn't hold his heading for too long or he would pass over the center of the base. Scores of AAA puffs suddenly dotted the sky in front of him. He had to shoot now. At the moment, he was out of range, but in split seconds would be in range. He squeezed and held the trigger. The M61 Gatling gun, electrically firing 20mm shells at 6,000 rounds per minute, held 1,200 rounds. Court had 12 seconds of trigger time.

He came into range, held the pipper steady, and placed a stream of cannon shells on the first airplane, which frantically wallowed and ducked to one side, then he changed heading a few degrees and opened fire on the second MiG, which caught fire immediately.

"Hey, they've stopped shooting," Stein yelled as they neared the base. There were no more basketball puffs or tracers in the air.

"They don't want to hit their own birds. We're safe as long as we're in the pattern," Court said. He banked to the right and pulled directly over the base, hosing now at two other MiGs that were bringing their gear and flaps up, furiously trying to escape across the runway. Court chased them, still shooting. He saw several flashes and sparkles when his shells impacted, then his gun wound down. He was out of ammunition.

"We gotta get outta this place," he sang nasally to Pete Stein. He knew he finally had his fifth MiG, maybe – hot shit – a sixth, a seventh, who knows. The second ring of gunners outside the perimeter opened up as he exited the Kep base confines. He slammed the throttles outboard and, burners roaring, pulled up and away from Kep, turning and twisting in mighty jinks to spoil their aim, slamming him and Pete Stein around in their cockpits, humming a tuneless victory song.

"Head outbound, Buick Three," he transmitted. "I'll catch up. And you backseaters watch for the splashes." He risked a glance over his shoulder down at the base, searching for the red flames and greasy black smoke marking a crashed jet fighter. There were none. In minutes he drew parallel to the flight and regained the lead. Over the water, he steered them south toward the KC-135 tankers that would give them enough fuel to fly home to Ubon, their base in northeast Thailand.

"Okay, anybody see anything?" he asked. He suddenly realized he was sweating heavily, and felt feverish. His adrenaline was draining away.

There was a long silence before they answered.

"Two, negative."

"Three, negative."

"Four, negative."

Court cursed. Empty again.

Pete Stein spoke from the backseat. "I guess that makes you the Ivory Ace, boss."

"What do you mean?"

"Ninety-nine-point-forty-four-percent pure. Sorry."

Court said nothing. His eyes ached.

An hour later Buick flight was strung out, one behind the other, in the Ground Controlled Approach pattern for Runway 27 at Ubon Royal Thai Air Force base, home of the 8th Tactical Fighter Wing. There were thunderstorms in the area, and the base of the cloud layer was at 800 feet above the ground. As flight leader, Court Bannister was first in the pattern. The controller spoke.

"Buick Lead, Ubon GCA. You are now eight miles from touchdown, on course, on glide path. Check gear and flaps down."

Court reached up and threw the gear handle down. The nose gear and the two mains dropped from their wells and thudded into place. He placed the flap handle down and absently corrected the nose rise as the flaps slid into place on the trailing edge of the wing. He squinted at his instruments. The small numbers were swimming. He wiped his gloved hand over his forehead. It came away stained dark with sweat.

"Buick Lead, Ubon. You are below glide path. Decrease your rate of descent." Court corrected by adding a small amount of power.

"Buick Lead, you are now six miles from touchdown, cleared to land. You are drifting off course. Turn right five degrees to two seven five." Court made the correction. He shook his head. The instruments on his panel were wavering in and out of focus. He felt sweat course down his body.

"Pete," he said, "something's wrong."

1945 Hours Local, Thursday 25 January 1968
Hoa Lo Prison, Hanoi
Democratic Republic of Vietnam

They opened the door and pushed him in. He tried not to groan from the pain in his left arm and leg. He wore blue shorts of a rough material tied by a drawstring. He was slick with sweat, urine, and vomit. The cell was dark and damp, about 7 feet long, Major Algernon A. "Flak" Apple automatically estimated, and 8 feet wide. The floor and the walls were concrete. A 5 × 2 concrete slab was attached to each side wall. The ceiling was of wood laths. A light bulb attached to bare wires hung from the ceiling. A rusty and dirty can with sharp edges used as a wastebucket was placed in one corner.

"Down, down," a Vietnamese guard screamed, punching at his back. Flak fell sideways onto the concrete slab on the right. It was stained with body fluids and dried waste matter. Rusty metal leg stocks were attached to the dirty wall at the foot of the slab next to the door. Flak struggled to get up, but the guard pushed him flat on the slab. Another guard came in the room and sat on him while the first put his ankles, one by one, into the U-shaped metal stocks and pushed a heavy metal bar across the tops of the stocks and across his ankles. The U-shaped bar extended through the wall to the outside corridor. The bar pressed so tight Flak thought it would cut him to the bone. They left

42

the room after admonishing him, "No sleep, no sleep." The door slammed and he heard and felt the metal bar locked into place from outside the cell.

For an hour he lay in the red fuzz of pain and exhaustion. His arm and leg wounds throbbed deeply and continually. Then he became aware of the sharp pain of the leg stocks. It was almost a relief to play his mind back and forth between the two pains. Emphasis *this* one, and *that* one fades to the background. Emphasis ankle, and arm is okay. Emphasis arm, and ankle is okay. Then the two merged, and he was on fire from the waist down and his arm throbbed with a mighty pulse of pain. Another hour went by, then another. He fell into a twisted and gritty sleep.

"NO SLEEP, NO SLEEP." A guard had flipped open the cover to a six-by-eight-inch opening in the thick wooden door and screamed again, "NO SLEEP, NO SLEEP."

Flak fought to keep his eyes open as long as the Vietnamese was looking at him. He played one of the mind games he had devised. One, two, four, eight, sixteen, thirty-two, sixty-four, one twenty-eight, two fifty-six, five twelve, ten twenty-four. He went on doubling the numbers, remembering the story of the canny beggar and the wealthy curmudgeon king. One penny salary on the first day, two on the second, four on the third, and so on for a month. By the thirtieth day, Flak reckoned the king owed the beggar five million, three hundred sixty-eight thousand, seven hundred nine dollars and twelve cents. Someday he would calculate a whole year. Kings should study their math.

He started the mantra again, eyes open and unfocused. One, two, four, eight, eight . . . eight. The guard slammed the flipper and strode away. Sixteen, thirty-two, sixty . . . sixty . . . he thought he heard a tapping or a scratching from the wall next to him. All his senses went on alert. Yes, he heard taps. They were rhythmic, and repeated at short intervals.

Tap, tap, ti-tap tap, pause . . . Then again, Tap, tap, ti-tap tap, pause . . . Tap, tap, ti-tap tap, pause . . .

Suddenly he got it. "Shave and a haircut," pause . . .

"Shave and a haircut," pause . . . "Shave and a haircut," pause . . .

He answered. Tap, tap. "Two bits."

The cadence sounded quicker this time. Shave and a haircut . . .

Two bits, he rapped. They did it again.

Shave and a haircut, two bits. And again.

Shave and a haircut, two bits. Flak was ecstatic. This was human contact. For two months he had heard only Vietnamese screaming at him, or cajoling him, playing on his pain, his blackness. They told him one day he was the white man's lackey, and the next day he was a war criminal. They had tied him in ropes and straps that brought unbelievable electric pain, and broken his arm again. He had screamed and cried, and finally wrote and signed a statement. "I intenshunly bombered a Vietmese hospittle," he wrote. That gained him an hour's respite, then they put him back in the ropes until he printed "I intentionally bombered a hospital." He had some satisfaction in "bombered," but not much. He was terribly ashamed he had caved in. He was weak. He was less than a man. Real men wouldn't have signed *anything*.

He knew the Fighting Man's Code of Conduct had been drawn up in 1955, because the horrors of the North Korean prison camps had caused not only the deaths of many POWs, but also serious collaboration and the defection of twenty-one American soldiers to the other side. Flak particularly knew the fifth paragraph: "I will give only name, rank, serial number, and date of birth, and evade answering further questions to the utmost of my ability. I will make no oral or written statements disloyal to my country and its allies or harmful to their cause." But he had caved in, couldn't take it. He had castigated himself in shame and dishonor. Oh God, even women tortured by the Gestapo didn't cave in. But he had.

Ever since his capture he had been alone. There had been no Americans. Then they had broken him three weeks ago. He had lived with his guilt ever since.

44

But now . . . oh joy, oh joy.

Shave and a haircut, two bits.

Shave and a haircut, two bits.

Shave and a haircut, two bits.

Then he got serious. They had to talk. He started Morse code, tapping out the dits and dahs with his knuckles.

Dit dah, A. Dah dit dit dit, B.

The man answered. A, B. They used two quick raps for a dot, two spaced raps for a dash. It was a lengthy and unwieldy process. All flyers have to learn Morse code to identify radio navigation beacons that transmit their station letters in dots and dashes.

Then Flak tapped out words: A-P-P-L-E-U-S-A-F, and listened. Tears sprang to his eyes when he heard: F-R-E-D-E-R-I-C-U-S-A-F. There was a pause, then Frederick continued in Morse code: I-T-E-A-C-H-U-T-A-P-C-O-D-E.

They labored through the night, teacher and pupil. Flak almost forgot his pain in the joy of contact. He wrapped a rag around his raw and bleeding knuckles so as to not mark the wall. Once the guard almost caught them, but the canny Frederick had heard him coming. A quick thumping by the heel of a hand meant break it off. Frederick taught him to form a cube matrix of the alphabet, five letters to a side with the K omitted.

```
A  B  C  D  E
F  G  H  I  J
L  M  N  O  P
Q  R  S  T  U
V  W  X  Y  Z
```

The first taps refer to the number of the row reading across, Frederick rapped. The second taps refer to the column reading down. Tap tap . . . is the F row, tap tap tap tap is the fourth letter in the F row, I, because it is in the fourth column. I-T-E-D, Frederick rapped out.

Flak caught on to the sequence immediately. His mind

saw the matrix, and the tap sequence; two-four, two-one, three-one, one-one, one-three. I FLAC, he quickly tapped out, using a C for the nonexistent K.

WELCOME TO HOA LO PRISON, Frederick rapped back. WE CALL IT HANOI HILTON. THIS PARTICULAR AREA CALLED LAS VEGAS. DIFFERENT CELL BLOCS CALLED BY HOTEL NAMES. THUNDERBIRD. STARDUST. DESERT INN. WE ARE IN THE MINT. Frederick stopped tapping.

WHAT IS MINT, Flak questioned.

MINT HOTEL. YOU NOT IN LAS VEGAS RECENTLY.

NO, Flak responded. He had been an instructor in the testpilot school at Edwards Air Force Base in California and hadn't been to Nellis, the fighter school located outside Las Vegas, for some time, so he hadn't heard of the Mint Hotel. Before being stationed at Ubon in Thailand to fly combat, he had upgraded into the F-4 at George Air Force Base, also in California.

WHEN U SHOT DOWN.

Flak wanted to tap out 22 Nov, but didn't know how to signal numbers. WHAT R NUMBERS, he tapped.

NUMBERS R QUIC TAPS TO NINE. ZERO IS Z.

2 2 NOV 6 7.

NOTED. WE CALL THE VIETS THE V. WHAT YOU LOOC LICE. NEED TO PASS ON SO WE NOW WHO TAKEN WHERE N WHEN BY THE V.

AM 6 2. HUSCY. SHORT BLAC HAIR. BLAC EYES. IM BLAC.

ME TOO. BLAC AND BLUE.

NO. IM BLAC N BLAC. It occurred to Flak that the term "black" might not have made the POW lexicon yet. BLAC AS IN NEGRO.

ARE THERE ANY OTHER CIND. YOU WANT MAYBE A MEDAL. SO. ANY WOUNDS. ANY TORTURE.

BURNS, BROCEN ARM. BAD LEG. Flak lay back for a moment. Wounds, oh yeah. Torture, oh my God yes. His eyes flooded and he started to cry. He had to tell someone. ROPE

TORTURE. I SIGN STATEMENT. OH GOD I SIGNED.

ME TOO. IN ROPES ALL SIGN. WE BOUNCE BAC. U GOT TO BOUNCE BAC.

Flak bowed his head, his mind feeling the first relief since the beginning of the awful torture. Oh God in heaven. Maybe he wasn't alone.

BUT WHAT ABOUT CODE OF CONDUCT, he asked.

HOLD WHAT YOU CAN. THEN BOUNCE BAC. EACH GUY DIFFERENT.

Flak lay back for a moment. He was more alert than at any time since his shootdown. The light from the small bulb cast the cell in gray. He felt so much better. He slapped at a mosquito and rolled toward the wall to tap again.

WHEN U SHOT DOWN. HOW MANY HERE. WHO SRO. SRO meant Senior Ranking Officer. All aircrew were taught in survival school that POWs should try to align themselves in order of descending rank to maintain a military chain of command. POWs were expected to resist by every means available and to carry the war to the enemy.

18 DEC 6 6. OVER 3 5 0 POW. SRO BE DENTON GUARINO RISNER STOCDALE OR TUNNER. DEPENDS. V CATCH SRO PUT IN SOLITARY FOR MONTHS YEARS. Frederick had tapped slowly so Flak could learn the code and absorb the words.

Flak remembered Major Ted Frederick as the F-105 pilot from Tahkli who had been court-martialed for supposedly strafing an unarmed Russian trawler in Haiphong Harbor. He had beaten the charge when it had turned out the trawler was armed and had shot at Frederick two days in a row while he had been leaving the target area.

WHAT U LOOC LICE, he asked Frederick.

SHORT, SQUATTY. THIC SHOULDERS. BLAC HAIR. BROWN EYES. SORT OF APEY.

Flak paused and formed a picture in his mind. He was having a hard time keeping the mosquitoes off him. The pain was returning to his body as his initial flush of adrenaline wore off. He asked Ted Frederick what clothes and goods he was supposed to have.

PJS SHITCAN MOSQ NET CUP SPOON STRAW
MAT, Frederick tapped.

NO HAVE NET CUP SPOON MAT OR PJS.

THEY NO LICE U.

Flak digested that bit of information. So far he had
always had to eat with his fingers from a bowl, and at
no time was he protected from the mosquitoes. He found
some solace that this was the cool time of the year and the
mosquitoes were not too thick. The only clothes he had
now were the rough blue shorts he wore, and at night he
was often cold. He had been issued some maroon-and-gray
pajama-style shirt and pants. He wasn't sure what had
happened to them. He had a vague memory of their being
blood soaked and torn from his body.

Maybe they *didn't* "like" him. His interrogation had
taken many zigs and zags. At first he had been treated with
incredulity as he had been trekked up to Hanoi through
every village along the route from Vinh. The soldiers had
led him by a rope around his neck. The peasants had spent a
lot of time touching and rubbing him as if he had something
on his skin that would rub off. Flak Apple had figured it
out. The only black men they had ever seen before, if any,
were the Senegalese in the French Foreign Legion that had
fought their Indochina war thirteen years before.

At each village, after Flak had been exhibited, one of
the men in the entourage – a political officer, Flak finally
reasoned – would begin speaking to the peasants. Beginning
with normal cadence and gestures, the man would build up
to a frenzy of words and wild gestures. Under his guidance,
the crowd would become a screaming mass that would then
begin hitting Flak with sticks and stones and pummeling
him with their fists. As it would almost always happen, the
soldiers would have to hustle him away so he wouldn't be
killed.

The soldiers couldn't believe that Flak was an officer
and a pilot. They knew the blacks were downtrodden and
used as slaves in America. Once he was in Hanoi, the more
sophisticated Vietnamese probed him for anti-white and

hence anti-American sentiments. He made it abundantly clear he came from a country that believed in meritocracy. White or black, work your ass off and you will profit.

At first they were easy on him as they assessed his potential as a propaganda tool. They presented stilted antiwar statements they wanted him to sign, and said he could make a tape recording to his loved ones at home if he did as they wanted. Certainly he could get better medical attention for his arm and leg, and burnt face. (They had made the most perfunctory attempt to doctor his wounds. The result was he had thick scabs on his arms and leg. He had no mirror so he didn't know about his face, but it hurt, felt puffy, and was terribly tender.) They told him he could meet with various American and European "peace groups." They even hinted at letting him go home if he was "cooperative." When he was not "cooperative" by his third week in captivity, that was the end of their assessment. He was a hard nose, so they put him in a dark hole for three more weeks, and started progressive torture that culminated in the ropes and his signed "confession."

He had broken in the ropes. To even think of the torture brought sweat to his body and curdling fear to his stomach. A torturer with small pig eyes had used ropes and straps to tie and stretch him into a ball of shrieking pain. He had been fed his own toes while his arms were tied flat together behind him, nearly dislocating his shoulders and causing his sternum to feel broken. He doubted if he could take it again without losing his sanity.

He rolled to the wall and tapped to Ted Frederick.

ANYBODY ESCAPE. Before he could hear an answer, his cell door burst open.

"No talk, no·talk," a guard screamed at him. He ran to Flak and grabbed him by his badly healed broken arm and shook it.

Flak roared in agony. "AHHH. STOP, AH GOD, STOP."

A Vietnamese in civilian black pants and white shirt entered behind the guard. After he spoke a few fast words, the guard stiffened and went out the door. The man stood next to the slab, looking down at Flak Apple.

"Did you enjoy your conversation with that criminal Frederick?" he asked.

Flak lay sweating and trying to stifle his moans. He looked up at the man in the dim light and said nothing. He could see the Vietnamese had prominent front teeth and a pulled-up nose. He looked like a rabbit. The rabbit spoke again.

"Oh, yes. I know you knock on wall to each other. He will be punished because of you. You are new, so I make special privilege for you. You want talk, I have someone for you to talk." He stopped and pulled his lips back, exposing his yellow teeth in a grotesque smile. "Someone is here from United States and they want talk to you. You will like. They have black skin just like you."

3

Army Lieutenant Colonel Wolf Lochert stood in front of the Catholic Cathedral in John F. Kennedy Square in Saigon. In his late thirties, Lochert, whose christened name was Wolfgang Xavier, was a broad-shouldered, stocky man of medium height, with dark hair shaved so close to his skull it looked like a dusting of black powder. The sleeves on his blue sports shirt were rolled up sausage-tight on his thick biceps. His muscled forearms were matted with dark hair. Next to him was a thin Vietnamese man named Buey Dan. He wore a white shirt and baggy black pants. The twin spires of the red-brick cathedral rose high in the heavy dawn air behind them, pointing like fingers to the low black clouds scudding furiously across downtown Saigon. The morning wind had picked up, and blew bits of papers and leaves around in tiny cyclones. Thunder over the city muttered nearby.

"What did you want to show me, Bee Dee?" Wolf Lochert said, his bushy brows knotted. Both men were gaunt and hollow-eyed. They had returned the day before from a long-range patrol in Laos that had lasted four weeks: a patrol that had been more harsh than productive. Good men had been killed; a main mission objective to set up a pilot-rescue net in the mountains and on the plains of

51

Laos had not been accomplished. There had been too much fighting with the enemy when there should have been contacts and arrangements made with the friendlies. Wolf Lochert wasn't used to failure, and he was raging and searching inside himself for the clues as to why. Was his leadership at fault? Was he losing his trail craft?

Wolf had been on many operations with Buey Dan, a former Viet Cong soldier who had rallied to the Saigon Government under the *Chieu Hoi* program years before. Wolf had judged him intelligent, loyal, and extremely competent. Buey Dan had saved his life on their first patrol. Another time the two of them had served together as altar boys at a Catholic Mass held in a Special Forces camp. But the Vietnamese had been acting increasingly strange as of late. On the patrol just ended, he had been less than cooperative, and had once disappeared for several hours. Several critical hours, it had turned out. A North Vietnamese patrol had savagely mauled Wolf's team before they could escape. His team, call sign Dakota, had been there to find downed American crewmen, as well as try to set up a rescue net. They had not been on a search-and-destroy mission; they were to fight only if cornered. Buey Dan had returned after the attack, saying he had been cut off. It was this incident that had started the uncomfortable feeling in Wolf about Buey Dan. Or was he suffering paranoia and blaming external forces for his own failure? Wolf didn't know. He only knew that under no circumstances would he allow a man he could no longer trust to be on patrol with him.

Immediately upon return from the mission yesterday, Wolf had been debriefed by his boss, Colonel Al Charles, a barrel-chested black man with a square face. Several others had listened in a small room at the rue Pasteur headquarters of the Special Forces unit called by the innocuous name Military Advisory Command, Vietnam, Studies and Observation Group, or simply MACSOG. Wolf, standing over his map, had concluded his debrief with his reservations about Buey Dan. An older man in civilian clothes who had not spoken nodded as if familiar with the case. Although Wolf had never seen him before, he had been treated with deference by Al Charles. After a nod from the man, Charles told Wolf to terminate Buey Dan's contract, that his services were no longer required. No explanation was given. Wolf – an eyebrow raised – nodded, and said, "Yessir."

Late that afternoon Wolf had told the Vietnamese Buey Dan he no longer had a job with the United States Studies and Observation Group. Buey Dan had nodded, said he understood, and had quietly asked Wolf to meet him for seven o'clock Mass the next day at the big Catholic church in Saigon, that he had something interesting to show him.

"What do you want to show me?" Wolf repeated. The first spatterings of heavy raindrops stained the pavement.

Buey Dan motioned with his head and started across the square to one of the many trees lining the sidewalk. Wolf thought Buey Dan walked as if he were on a patrol about to be ambushed. "Over here, Trung Si," Buey Dan said, his eyes as expressionless as gutter water at midnight. Wolf caught up to him by one of the large tamarind trees that lined the sidewalks.

Buey Dan pointed to the base of the tree. "There," he said. "Down there." The rain started to fall with increasing power.

Wolf bent over to get a better look, then abruptly twisted sideways as he sensed rather than felt a quick movement made by Buey Dan. He turned his head to see the Vietnamese thrust a stiletto directly toward his groin. Reaction based on his years of combat tensed Wolf's entire body, and jolted his system with a rush of adrenaline. He whirled to face the attack, trapped Buey Dan's outthrust arm against his body with his right arm, and threw his left knee into his groin as he tried to lever the Vietnamese against the tree. In a flash Buey Dan ducked out of the hold and, rising like a striking snake, thrust up again with the rapier-thin blade. Wolf leaped to one side, slammed into the tree, and fell off-balance as Buey Dan's lunge continued. As he fell, Lochert deflected the thrust with a sideswipe of his left hand, slid his right hand over Buey Dan's outthrust arm, clamped onto his wrist, and pulled the Vietnamese down with him. As Wolf hit the ground, he twisted out of the way – still holding Buey Dan's slender wrist – and plunged the stiletto into the falling man's stomach. The force of the impact was so great, the point of the stiletto protruded from the back of the Vietnamese as he slammed to the ground.

In one motion Wolf rolled to his feet. He stood for a moment, panting. Hard rain smashed the streets, and the trees and the leaves, and water ran down his face. With his toe he turned the man over and looked at his face. He squatted next to him and slowly pulled the bloody stiletto from Buey Dan's stomach. He nodded slowly as he remembered he had been told over a year ago that Buey Dan had picked up a knife near Wolf, just before they had ridden out of an ambush zone on a rescue helicopter.

"You took this from me on that first mission, didn't you?" He looked at the tree, and back into the face of the dying man, comprehension dawning. Buey Dan's eyes slowly focused on him, and flickered with hatred and loathing. He spoke with effort. "You will die by that knife. Someday you will die by that knife. I, *Than Lan*, the Lizard, say this."

Suddenly Wolf knew. A year earlier he had killed a young man who had just exploded a bomb in the Catholic church. He had killed him with the same stiletto and at very nearly the same spot on this street. "What was he to you?" Wolf demanded.

The black eyes flared. "My seed," he whispered, "my son." Slowly his mouth collapsed and went slack, and his eyes became dusty. His body seemed to flatten and shrink into the ground. The eye sockets started pooling with liquid, distorting the pupils, making them look alive and flickering.

Wolf Lochert glared at the stiletto, then at the dead face. He savagely wiped the blade on the grass and tucked it into

54

his sock. It all became clear. The death of Menuez on that first patrol, the failed missions, the deaths of others, maybe even the C-130 that had disappeared after flying the Dakota team to a night drop zone in Laos.

Comprehension turned Wolf Lochert's face into a raging mask as the rain pelted him with stinging fury. Thunder detonated in his ears and crashed in his head.

"You killed my men," he said slowly, Then louder, "*You killed my men.*" In a frenzy he snatched the body from the ground and held it over his head with both hands, then crashed it into the tree. "YOU KILLED MY MEN," he roared. The body fell to the ground like a half-filled sack, head and arms at impossible angles, legs doubled over, a huge red circle in the center of the white shirt that clung wetly to the thin body.

A movement caught the corner of his eye. He spun and crouched, hands up as claws, ready to kill again. A terrible grimace had transformed his face into that of a predator who has just made a blood-lust kill. He focused, and glared into the narrow eyes of an older Caucasian man in a safari suit who stood next to a Vietnamese who was framing Wolf in the lens of a whirring movie camera. Behind them at the curb stood a tan Land-Rover with the International Telecasting Company sunrise logo, and a third man behind the wheel.

Wolf started toward the two men, perception flooding his mind.

"Get in the truck, quick," the Caucasian yelled to the cameraman, never taking his eyes off the advancing Wolf Lochert. Rain ran off the man's crumpled, floppy jungle hat. He had small eyes that peered out from under bushy eyebrows and from over a red nose that had been broken once too many times. He was thick around the middle. Ignoring the rain, he thrust a horny hand at Wolf Lochert. The cameraman jumped into the truck.

"Mal Hemms, ITC," he said in an articulate but rumbling voice. The Land-Rover engine started.

Wolf ignored his hand and brushed past him toward

the Land-Rover. Hemms signaled the driver of the Land-Rover, who immediately let the clutch out and sped off into the heavy rain, sending up a silver bow wave.

"Let's talk about you," Hemms said. "What is your name?"

When Wolf made a move to grab him by the lapels of his safari suit, Hemms ducked and popped up outside of Wolf's arm reach. When Wolf advanced, hands flexing and moving in front of him like two fighting snakes ready to strike, Hemms ducked, bobbed, and weaved, but did not retreat. He did not swing or try to fight. The rain had turned his safari suit into a sodden mass. He started to dance around Lochert.

"You won't tag me," Hemms said. "Believe me. Fifteen years in the ring, Golden Gloves to light-heavy semi-pro. Rarely tagged, never bagged. Just tell me your name." His eyes lit up as he stepped in close, then away from Wolf Lochert in a daring pass. "Just tell me your name."

Wolf Lochert stopped dead and stood flatfooted, rain streaming down his face. He put his hands at his sides, then suddenly brought his palms together in front of him with a clap as crisp and as loud as a rifle shot. When Hemms' eyes involuntarily followed the motion, Wolf aimed a kick at his crotch. Hemms caught the movement and turned sideways just in time to deflect the kick off his left outer thigh. As he absorbed the blow, Lochert closed on him, grabbed his right wrist, and, turning, brought it up to a sharp angle behind Hemms' back. Hemms did not resist and seemed strangely slack. His upper torso was bent nearly parallel to the ground under the painful pressure. He managed to keep his head up, looking at something. Wolf followed his gaze. The ITC truck was back at the curb, the Vietnamese was filming the action through the open window. Wolf flung the man to one side and turned away. He wasn't sure if the film had caught his face or not.

He scanned the area. He saw small groups of Vietnamese, huddled under umbrellas, watching. He looked back over his shoulder. Two *Quan Canh*, Vietnamese policemen, were bent over the body of Buey Dan. A third QC was flagging an American Military Police jeep splashing through the Square.

"So then what happened?" Al Charles said an hour later, his face tense with concentration. They were sitting in his office at MACSOG. He and Wolf Lochert had been pals since their time together in the 10th SFG at Bad Tölz.

Wolf Lochert shook his head slightly. "I couldn't refuse to show the MPs my identification. They picked me up and here I am."

"Could you have run away?"

"Never occurred to me."

"What happened after the MPs picked you up?" Charles asked. He turned to a fresh page on his yellow legal pad where he had been taking notes.

"We went to their post, where I told them exactly what had happened. I guess they knew who I was. All they did was fill out an incident sheet, called it self-defense against a terrorist attack. They drove me back to my jeep."

The white telephone on the desk of Al Charles rang. He picked it up, said "yessir" twice, listened some more, then said, "No, not exactly, Colonel Dall, but I have Wolf Lochert right here ready to go back with you. He has a relief plan all worked out." Wolf heard some words crackle through the receiver. Charles said, "Yes, sir, right away," and hung up. Colonel Bull Dall was the commander of the 5th Special Forces Group at Nha Trang. The 5th was in charge of all the SF men in Vietnam.

"That was Bull Dall from MACV. He just flew down from Nha Trang. There's some bad news about our troops at Lang Tri. They need help bad. The camp is being ground down and those goddamn jarheads won't do anything about it. Bull has an Air America Beech ready to run him back up north. He's been arguing with General Westmoreland about not getting relief for Lang Tri. He wanted to know if we have any assets in the area. I told him no, but you were all set with a relief plan." He looked at his watch.

"It's nine o'clock. Bull is holding his airplane for you to go back with him and brief him on your plan."

"*My* relief plan?" Wolf echoed. "What relief plan?"

Al Charles stood up and grabbed his green beret. His black face split in a beatific smile. "I'll run you out to Tan Son Nhut. We'll cook up your plan on the way out."

The rain had stopped as the two men piled into a jeep and splashed out the gate and turned up rue Pasteur toward Tan Son Nhut Air Base.

1845 Hours Local, Sunday 28 January 1968
NVA Bivouac West of Lang Tri
Republic of South Vietnam

It was not quite dark in the craggy hill country around Khe Sanh and Lang Tri. Rocket, mortar, and artillery fire had been booming and thudding in the distance for the last twenty-four hours. Toby Parker sat with his back grating against the rough bark of a tree. His arms were bent behind him around the circumference of the tree and tied with a loop of rope. He was conscious but felt a raging thirst. His head still ached and he felt partially deaf from the explosion when the soldier had pulled the trigger of his AK-47 assault rifle next to his ear three days ago at the crash site. His feet were swollen and bloody. Both big toenails had been ripped off while walking barefoot through the jungle. Between his legs was a bowl of thin gruel. For an hour he had been trying to shimmy his arms down the tree far enough to shift his whole body to one side of the bowl, then bend down, hanging from his arms, to place his face in the bowl. For each of the last three nights he had faced the same problem.

At first, when he had been captured, the squad had seemed in a hurry. Toby had been dragged and pulled up and down the rugged hills until his knees were buckling with exhaustion. Then, on the second day, after some words on a backpack radio, the Viet Cong had slowed down. The lead man had checked a map frequently, as if he had a rendezvous. Toby was treated somewhat better. He was given a pair of Ho Chi Minh rubber sandals to put on his ravaged feet, and more water.

At night they liked to watch him struggle to eat. They seemed to find just the right-diameter tree to make him strive for his food each evening. The first night he tried to bend his body down so that he could place his head between his knees. He had had no luck. Even if he could get his arms down, he knew it would be impossible to flatten his body down between his knees. Then he realized that if he could shift to one side, placing his legs to one side of the bowl, he could bend down and put his face in it. It was only last night that he had been able to stress his body down far enough to get his face into the liquid. When he had, it had been sour, with lumps that had made him retch. But he had sucked it up and swallowed because he knew he had to, or die.

Tonight was one of his lucky nights. He got his face into the bowl and slowly sucked up the liquid. It was slow going, for he was bent in such a way he could not easily swallow. At the end, there was a layer of liquid he could not get to, and two chunks of something rubbery. He picked up one chunk with his lips and sat back. He worked it into his mouth. It was cold and the gristly texture caused waves of painful retching. He swallowed it whole and bent over for the second piece and forced it down. Then he picked the bowl up in his teeth and let the remaining fluid slide down his throat. When it had, he dropped the bowl and leaned back against the tree. His flight suit was torn and caked with mud, there was dried blood on his face, and his hair was matted and wild.

He watched the twelve-man VC patrol prepare the camp for nightfall. Under triple canopy, there was no gradual dimming of the sunlight. Rather, it was a sudden grayness as the sun angled down to the far treetops, then quick blackness as it set beyond the trees. Their uniforms consisted of green baggy shirts with two pockets, floppy slacks, and black rubber sandals made from old truck tires. Toby could see no rank badges, though one man was clearly in charge. They wore green pith helmets and floppy rucksacks on their backs. Each man removed the branches and leaves he had cut that morning to attach to his helmet and backpack for camouflage, and threw them into a central place where the soldier who prepared the one meal a day lit a small smokeless fire. The fire was short-lived. Just long enough to boil water for tea, then doused before complete darkness. Each man contributed a pinch of tea to the main pot that, Toby estimated, couldn't have held more than four quarts of water. Sometimes if a soldier caught a tree toad or a lizard, he would spit it on a stick and hold it in the flames until roasted. Their main staple came from the rice they carried in their packs or in cloth tubes slung round their necks.

Toby felt an ache in his bladder. During the days he was unbound long enough to use his hands to urinate, but at night he was on his own. He had worked out a system so that at least he didn't have to sleep in the liquid. He had managed to pull the bottom zipper of his flight suit up a few inches. Now he squirmed a few degrees around the tree and twisted his body to one side. He swung one leg over the other and propped himself up with that foot. Then he jiggled and shook his torso until his penis – acorn size now – was close to the opening. Then he let the dribble fall to the ground. Due to his dehydration, there wasn't much. As before, most of it went into his flight suit and Boxer shorts that were rancid and putrid with sweat and urine. He had had no urge for a bowel movement the entire three days. Yet he knew it was but a matter of time until his bowels erupted in protest at the water and food he had ingested. When he finished, he twisted back to his former position.

The soldiers had finished their meal and strung their hammocks. They were gathered in a semicircle around a man other than the leader. He seemed to be lecturing and exhorting them about something. Toby heard his voice rise and fall, saw his arms wave to emphasize a topic, even point at him once. This was the last event of each evening, so Toby guessed it was the political officer expounding on the joys of communism. Then it was dark. The perimeter guards were in place; the patrol was bivouacked for the night.

Toby fell in and out of a fitful sleep. Crawling insects investigated all parts of him, twigs became hot spots under his buttocks; when he moved his swollen arms and hands, needles of pain shot up through his shoulders. His thoughts drifted from his takeoff last Friday morning to the shot he had heard inside the airplane. On one hand he was glad Mel Brackett was dead and didn't have to go through this torture. Then he would curse himself for agreeing to the flight, and blame himself for Brackett's death. There was no moon, no breeze, no sounds except of the night animals. Distant gunfire erupted sporadically.

Shortly after two in the morning Toby awoke to feel he was being strangled. Something clasped the back of his head and pushed his face into a thick padding of cloth. He struggled, then lay still as he heard a whispering in his ear. Whoever it was touched his ear with his lips, actually had his lips inside Toby's ear. He listened to the words.

"Lie still; I am an American. Lie still; I am an American. If you understand, nod your head twice. Nod your head twice. Make no noise when I release you. I am an American. Nod your head twice."

Toby nodded twice against the cloth, which immediately was pulled away. He realized he was being cradled in the arms of someone behind him. He felt a sawing motion, then his hands were free. He slowly pulled them in front of himself. The man spoke into his ear again.

"You are doing just fine, just fine. I am an American. This is a rescue, do you understand?" Toby lay back in the man's arms like a woman encircled by her lover. He nodded his head. He saw absolutely nothing in front of him or over his head.

The man whispered again. "Nod your head twice if you

61

can walk." Toby nodded twice. "Good," the man said. "Now I am going to give you some water. Take three sips, then hand it back, only three sips." Toby felt a movement, then a plastic water bag was put into his hands. His hands felt numb and thick, and prickly, as if on fire. He had difficulty, but he managed three sips of the purest water he had ever tasted in his life and handed the bag back.

"Very good, very good. You're doing just fine. Do not talk to me. Now listen to what we are going to do. Do not talk. We want to get you safely away from this camp without waking them up or alerting the guards. We are just here to get you, not to blow them away." The man whispered in Toby's ear very slowly, and with careful enunciation, as if talking to a young child. "Nod twice if you understand." Toby nodded.

"Very good. Outstanding. You are doing just fine. When I tap your leg, I want you to crawl very slowly, very slowly to your left around the tree. Take ten minutes, take an hour, but go so slow you make no noise. Someone will be there, laying flat. Tap his shoulder three times. He will tap back twice, then reverse himself and start to crawl away. You crawl behind him, holding on to his boot. This will all take time, much time. Pretend you are in a slow-motion movie. We must make no noise. I think you can do all this, don't you? I'm going to put my ear next to your mouth. Whisper to me what I just told you."

Slowly, as if in molasses, the man moved his head around Toby and positioned his ear next to Toby's mouth. He smelled faintly of pine or lemon, Toby wasn't sure which. Then he realized the man's odor was the same as that of some of the plant leaves he had brushed by. The man's head felt greasy. Toby repeated the instructions. The man nodded, then put his lips back in Toby's ear. "If something goes wrong, and the place lights up, one of us will grab you and lead you away. We are all wearing black pajamas and we have camo stick on our faces. There are three of us, all Americans. You seem very sharp. Prepare yourself. You will do just fine. Here is more water. This time slowly take

three medium swallows. There will be plenty more later."
Toby realized that the man was rationing him so he would
not gulp down the water then throw it right back up.

Toby drank – ah God it was like no water he had ever
tasted before – and handed back the bag to the unseen
figure. When the man tapped his knee, he moved an inch
at a time up from the man's body where he had been
lying. Big hands helped push him up. He felt around for
his sandals and slipped them into a front pocket, then
crawled around the tree. He tapped the shoulder of the
figure lying there, waited while he reversed himself, then
crawled behind him. It seemed like an hour before they
were at what he estimated to be the camp's perimeter. He
heard no noise behind or in front of him. His knees hurt,
but feeling was coming back to his hands.

The man he was following stopped and rose to his knees.
Toby could feel steel and webbing on his torso. From
behind came a shout in Vietnamese, then a shot. In seconds
there were more shots, then the beams of several flashlights
waved about the area. More shots sounded, then rippling
bursts of assault rifles. The man in front of Toby turned and
gripped Toby's arm like a vise. He spoke in a low, hurried
voice. "Okay, stick with me. We got to make tracks to the
rendezvous point. Grab the back of my harness and hang
on."

Toby slipped the sandals on his feet and started after the
man, who walked crouched, elbowing his way among the
growth, stopping every few minutes to peel back the cover
of his fluorescent compass face and check his heading.

Back at the campsite the shots were scattered and not
concentrated. Then an explosion that sounded to Toby
like a hand grenade. There was silence for a while, then
a huge explosion followed by cries and shouts. "Hah,"
said the man Toby followed. "That was Ryder's Claymore. That means he's okay. Just a little while longer
and we'll be at the rendezvous."

Toby's legs felt rubbery, and sweat was gushing from
every pore in his body. His hands and arms had a dull

63

ache, yet he felt totally exhilarated. The adrenaline of relief was flowing and he felt every milligram. They made the rendezvous, a point on a narrow stream bed, and waited. There was no jungle canopy directly over the stream. Toby was able to see the bulk of the man by the faint glow of starlight.

"I'm Sergeant Lopez, Captain Parker, from the Special Forces Detachment at Lang Tri."

Toby was startled. "How do you know who I am?"

"You might not have known it at the time, but Hillsboro heard all your transmissions. They triangulated you to your crash site and notified us. Three of us went out in the bush and saw you come down and get captured. Nothing we could do against the patrol in the daylight. We restocked and have been tracking you almost from the beginning. Right now we're barely five klicks from Lang Tri. We'll hole up here for the night and make it to camp at first light."

"How about some more water?" Toby said.

"Sure. Finish it off. You earned it." Lopez handed him the water bag. Toby drank half, slowly and with great relish, and handed it back. He felt a wave of relief and gratitude, and something else. Hot tears sprang to his eyes. He didn't know why, they just did.

"Better take these," Lopez said, giving Toby some pills. "They're antimalaria and real stoppers for dysentery. You're bound to get the trots after what you've been drinking." Toby gulped the pills, took another slug of water, and made himself as comfortable as he could. Then he remembered why he was out there.

"Do you have a map, Sergeant Lopez?"

"Of course. But if you want to see it, we got to get under my poncho before I'll put a flashlight on. What do you want to know?"

"It's not what I want to know. It's what I want to show you. There are PT-76 tanks less than ten klicks from here, and I'll bet they are headed for Lang Tri and Khe Sanh."

"Wait until the other guys get here. I don't want us under a poncho without a guard. Make yourself comfortable. I'll keep an eye out and wake you when they show. Then we gotta make tracks back to camp. Those guys were just waiting to hand you over to a bigger NVA unit that was going to run you up through the DMZ into North Vietnam. There are other big units all over the place. A big push is mounting and we're right in the middle of it."

Toby was keyed up. He had to talk. In quiet whispers he told Lopez the whole story of the tanks, the camera flight with Brackett, and the shootdown. "Yeah," Lopez said. "We searched the wreckage. We got your pal out." Lopez didn't tell him they just had time to break the burned head loose from the body. There had been no dog tags. They had thrown the head in a body bag and sent it to Da Nang on a resupply helicopter, along with a piece of paper giving the location and type of aircraft in which it had been found. That was standard practice on jungle-patrol body recoveries behind the lines. Generally there wasn't enough of a body to recover from crashed airplanes, not even the head. But when there was, they took only the head to save time and space. The teeth were all that could provide positive identification.

Toby finally wound down. When Lopez handed him a poncho, he rolled up, blinked once, and went out like he had been pole-axed.

Lopez shook him awake at first light, cautioning him to be quiet. Toby sat up. The poncho was wet with dew. Fog was overhead and hung in keep wisps in the trees. Lopez was hunkered down next to him. He was a broad-shouldered man, with a big square face showing generations of Hispanic bloodlines. His dark eyes matched his dark hair. He wore black pajamas and a floppy jungle hat. He carried an AK-47 slung under his right arm. In the early dawn he looked like a giant Viet Cong.

"God, you look good to me," Toby said with a wide grin.

Lopez grinned back. "Aw, I'll bet you say that to all your rescuers. Do you feel up to a bit of a trek?"

Toby slowly crawled out of the poncho. The swelling in

his arms and hands had gone down, but his feet were like two open wounds, bloated and full of pus.

"Got to show you where the tanks are," he said.

Lopez spread out his 1:50,000 map. Toby pointed to XD67253875, a spot barely three kilometers from where the two of them sat.

"There have never been any tanks on the Trail before," Lopez said in a voice just short of total skepticism.

"There are now," Toby answered. "What's all that shooting I've been hearing the last days?"

"Nothing to worry about, just a major attack against the Marines at Khe Sanh," Lopez said.

"Well, hell. Isn't Lang Tri just down the road toward Laos from Khe Sanh?"

"Yeah," Lopez said. "But we have a deal with the grunts. They get attacked, we help them. We get attacked, they help us. If this wasn't a pilot-rescue mission we'd be out scouting the rear ranks of the NVA, seeing what they've got."

Toby nodded and tried to stand up. He sank back with a groan as pain arced up from his feet.

Lopez knelt and examined them, then pulled a medical kit from his pack and went to work. He cut away the dead tissue, lanced swollen parts full of pus, finally sprinkled sulfa powder on the bottoms of Toby's feet and bound them in bandages. Then he took a pair of canvas Bata boots from his pack and, by slicing them just right and using parachute cord, he fashioned a covering for Toby's swollen feet.

"Just before we start out," he said, "I'll give you a local shot to dull the pain so you can walk. If we hustle we can make the camp before noon." He gave a low, whistling warble. It was answered twice from opposite directions. "That's Ryder and Dickson. Ryder's the guy who cut you loose last night. He'll be point. Dickson will follow up as tail-end charlie. Sorry we can't get you out of here by chopper, but first off, we're right in the middle of Indian territory. Secondly, the weather's gone apeshit. The clouds are down to the deck and will be for a few days." He pulled a syringe from his pack and gave Toby a shot in each ankle.

"You'll have damn little feeling. It'll be like walking on two stumps, so watch yourself. You could tear a foot open and never know it." He waited a few minutes for the shots to take effect, then stood up. "So let's make like cowboys and hit the trail." He gave one more low whistle, then moved into the brush, as silent as smoke. Toby lurched after him and immediately fell as he misjudged his footing. Lopez turned back and helped him to his feet.

"Captain Parker," he said, "you will just have to do better than that or I will personally jam this AK up your ass and pull the trigger on full auto."

4

1815 Hours Local, Sunday 28 January 1968
Room 27, BOQ T12, Tan Son Nhut Air Base
Saigon, Republic of Vietnam

Major Court Bannister stood at the window of his second-storey BOQ room and stared through the night rain at the lights of the crowded Tan Son Nhut Air Base. He stood 6'2" and weighed a dehydrated 175, down from his normal 190. His crew-cut brown hair had been bleached blond by the sun. He was dressed in red athletic shorts and a white T-shirt with the faded letters SOS 17 on it. Four days had passed since he had awakened in the Ubon hospital.

Outside, the lights hanging from crossbars on poles bathed the streets in a yellow glow. It was early evening, not quite seven on Sunday, and the traffic was still heavy. Jeeps with their tops up and heavy trucks splashed water as they hissed by in both directions. Blue USAF buses carried men to and from work. A few bicycles ridden by airmen in ponchos threaded their way along the roads. Fronting the thoroughfares of the busy Air Base, all the rows of windows of the two- and three-storey camouflaged office buildings were lit up. Inside, all was a bustle. Logistics, maintenance, administration, intelligence, communications, and operations people were on their usual twenty-four-hour schedule. The fact that it was Sunday meant nothing. Somebody, somewhere in this war needed something, be it orders or supplies, people or airplanes, boots or bombs.

Bannister absently massaged his sore ribs as he thought back to a few days earlier, when he had had to get his backseater to help him land his F-4.

He remembered waking up in a hospital bed with an IV bottle hanging from a metal stand next to him, a rubber tube leading to a needle in his left arm. He had slowly focused his eyes on a man who stood at the foot of the bed reading his medical chart. He was a plump man, with a smooth baby face and wisps of blond hair on a balding scalp. He looked remarkably like Baby Huey in the cartoons. He wore a green smock. Court finally recognized his old flight-surgeon friend, Lieutenant Colonel Conrad Russell, MD.

"In addition to dehydration, a temperature of 102, and a case of mild malaria," Russell had said, "your ribs have not healed properly."

"Did I get my fifth MiG?" Bannister had croaked.

"Not so much as an hello, or a good to see you again do I get," Dr. Russell had sighed. He and Bannister had been close friends at Bien Hoa Air Base two years earlier, during Bannister's first combat tour. "Lad, I am your friendly flight surgeon, not your wing commander." He thumbed toward the door. "You'll have to ask him. He and a few others are at this very minute hovering outside, anxiously waiting to hear about your condition."

"Damn, Doc, it is good to see you. When did you get in? Are you here PCS?" He held up a hand.

"Noon. Yes," Doc Russell said in clipped tones, and managed a look of exaggerated indignation. They shook hands.

"Sorry, Doc. I'm kind of fuzzy. What did you say was wrong with me?"

"What it is, you're all poohed out." Doc Russell grinned.

"Next you'll say I need a rest."

"You need a rest."

"Come off it, Doc. You know what I have to do."

"Something about making Ace, I understand. Your backseater told me all about it. Said you're an Ivory Ace.

But you've got to forget that for a while. As of immediately you are DNIF until I say you are not."

DNIF, pronounced duh-niff, was "Duty Not Involving Flying." Court Bannister was grounded for medical reasons. "I read your medical records." Doc Russell tapped the folder in his hand. "I see where you were shot down a few months ago and had to E&E for a few days in the wilds of Laos. When you were picked up, you had cracked ribs, a mild concussion, malaria, and dysentery from intestinal parasites. You were back flying in one week. Oh yes, you picked up a few medals at the same time."

Bannister took a deep breath. "Give me just one more flight."

"No. Enn Oh, no. You've got to take care of yourself. Keep this up and I'll recommend you for permanent DNIF with duty as commissary inventory officer. You never should have been allowed to fly so soon after your shootdown. I know the guy you bamboozled into releasing you. He doesn't know a spatula from a spit stick."

Bannister threw up his hands.

"Watch that IV," Doc Russell warned.

"What do I have to do?"

"Three days' bed rest, lots of fluids and antibiotics, retape your ribs, followed by two weeks' convalescent leave and upper-body-muscle therapy, that's what you have to do. Then we'll see."

"No flying? Not even in the backseat?"

"Not even in the backseat."

Bannister sighed and lay back. "Dammit. You know, I gave up an attack pass on a MiG and let my wingman have it. Wish now I'd gone ahead, then I'd have five."

"Why didn't you?" Doc Russell asked.

"It just didn't look right. I might have hit an F-105 that was in the way."

"Court, you just answered your own thoughts. It was doubtful, so you didn't do it."

Court gave a bitter laugh. "Maybe I should have tried that one . . . well, hell, if it went like my last flight, I'd have

70

missed anyway. I am some snake-bit." He lay back. "Who did you say was outside the door?"

Doc Russell became serious. "It's Colonel Stan Bryce. I understand he's the wing king around here. He doesn't look pleased. Actually, he is not exactly just outside the door. He's at the end of the hall in the conference room in deep conversation with Major Somebody-or-other, an Intell officer. The other guys outside the door were your backseater and other members of your flight. I told them to bug off for the O'Club, that you'd be okay, that I'd brief them later. You sure you feel up to seeing Bryce? I can put it off, you know."

"Doc, I'm just a major. He's a colonel. He can see me anytime he wants. Colonels are eight-hundred-pound gorillas. You say sir to them and salute a lot."

Doc Russell ushered in Colonel Stanley D. Bryce, the Commander of the 8th Tactical Fighter Wing.

Stan the Man, as he liked to be called, was six feet even, with sharp gray eyes, wore his black hair in a crew cut, and had powerful shoulders and a square, pleasant Slavic face. He was popular, played a vicious game of handball, and flew missions about twice a week, usually leading a flight or an element, but never the entire strike force. He flew only with men of experience.

Two months ago he had stood by Court Bannister's side at a ceremony at Tan Son Nhut when the Commander of 7th Air Force, a four-star general, had pinned a Silver Star, a DFC, and a Purple Heart on Bannister. The medals were for Court's heroism in shooting down a North Vietnamese MiG-21 piloted by a Russian, and his subsequent escape and evasion from North Vietnamese troops in the Steel Tiger area of Laos after being shot down himself on the same flight. On that mission, Bannister's close friend, Flak Apple, had been shot down over North Vietnam and was missing. Court's backseater that day, Ev Stern, though badly wounded, had saved Court's life. After the bailout, Stern had fallen unconscious in his parachute among enemy troops.

71

Court Bannister had not been the soul of cooperation for that day of ceremony in November. Whereas Colonel Stan Bryce had been exuberant and thrown his arms around Court and called him Ace (which he had not been), Court had been brooding and morose. He owed his freedom to the Russian fighter pilot – Vladimir Chernov he had said his name was – who had refused to turn him over to the searching enemy troops. "The bastards torture," Chernov had said by way of explanation. Then Chernov had gone down, a bullet in his chest fired by the attacking communists who had thought him an American. As yet Court had not told anyone of the loss he felt for the man who had set him free, or what the blue scarf he carried meant to him. The scarf had belonged to Chernov.

In his BOQ room now, Court made a face as he remembered the day after his rescue. He and Bryce had been flown down from Ubon to Tan Son Nhut in a T-39, a small USAF passenger jet. When the plane had taxied to a halt, Court had looked out and seen a red carpet leading to a four-star general standing at a podium. Civilian and military news cameras were in position. The door of Court's T-39 was opened and the military band struck up a cheerful martial air. All eyes were on the door, but Court Bannister had made up his mind he wasn't getting out of that damned airplane to go through all that hero horseshit. His head still hurt from a blow he had received in the jungle, his ribs ached, and his mouth felt full of old socks from a big drunk the night before celebrating his rescue. So nothing doing on the hero stuff. He was over here to fight, not mess around with the wheels. Then his bowels had betrayed him. The T-39 he was in was a five-window model, not the seven-window that had a head. His stomach had rumbled and boiled. The jungle water he had had to drink during his trek without chlorine purifying pills had finally caught up with him. He bolted out of the door, held himself ramrod stiff for the ceremony, dodged the press, whispered something into a line chief's ear, and was whisked away in a maintenance van. It had been a near, near, thing. He had found the sergeant later and had given him a case of beer.

After that, Colonel Stan the Man Bryce had not been as solicitous. He had, in fact, become rather cool since Court had never really responded to his friendly overtures. It had been made clear to Bryce that Court Bannister had been foreordained by the USAF to become the first Ace of the Vietnam war. In such a case, not only would the Air Force be a big one-up on the Navy, the USAF would garner a lot of favorable (they hoped) publicity, because Court Bannister was the son of movie star Sam Bannister. Because of that official placing of hands, Bryce had tried to be Court's buddy, not his commander. Court's missing pal, Flak Apple, had also been so foreordained, not because he was the son of anybody famous, but because he was black.

Things hadn't worked out quite the way Court Bannister, the USAF – and Colonel Stan Bryce – had wished. And certainly not for Flak Apple, who was carried on the books as MIA – Missing in Action. But the war ground on. If the MiGs weren't up, you couldn't shoot them down. If you shot one down and it wasn't recorded, you didn't shoot one down. (If a tree fell and no one was in audio range . . .) Time was passing, and Stan the Man had places to go. If Court Bannister became a liability, then he had to be jettisoned. Historically, the commander of the 8th Tactical Fighter Wing went on to become a brigadier general – unless he got fired, as Bryce's predecessor had. Stan the Man's mind was never far from that fact. But he could only go so far. And the Air Force could only go so far.

"The Air Force can only go so far, Bannister," Stan Bryce had said as he walked in the hospital room with Major Richard "George" Hostettler, his intelligence officer. Bryce carried a green, brick-sized Motorola HT-20 radio to keep him in touch with the command post. He was not smiling.

"You're in deep kimchi," the colonel continued. "Not only were you flying when you were sick and damn near lost an airplane because of it, you violated the Rules of Engagement by attacking the MiG base at Kep."

"Sir," Bannister had said, "I didn't attack the *base*, I

attacked the MiGs flying around the *base*. It's not the same thing."

"You're quibbling, Bannister. You are allowed only to attack MiGs that attack you."

Bannister's head throbbed. He felt reckless and out of control. "Yeah, Colonel, just like the SAM sites. We can't hit them until they shoot at us, then it's too late. What the hell kind of a war is this, anyway? A hell of a lot of guys are gone because of those goddamned ROE."

"You think I like it, Major?" Bryce had flared. "You think I don't know what's going on out there? I fly too, you know. I've seen the shit up there. I've been hit, and I've seen others go down. But that's what we get paid to do. So you listen to me. We are in the military and we do what we are told. You, me, and every other guy that wears a uniform swears to follow the lawful orders of his superiors. And that's just what we do, and that includes you. Maybe there are those in Seventh that want to see you become an Ace. But I'll tell you, not at the expense of breaking the Rolling Thunder ROE."

Rolling Thunder was the code name for the bombing and interdiction campaign in North Vietnam that had the twofold purpose of convincing Ho Chi Minh the U.S. was serious and stopping the flow of supplies into South Vietnam. Rolling Thunder was an on-again, off-again campaign run from the White House. Because it was not sustained, because it was on targets chosen for political, not military reasons, it was not effective. But its cost in pilots and airplanes was criminally tragic.

At the same time, North Vietnam was also the only place the MiGs flew, the only place where a fighter pilot could become an Ace. The skies of North Vietnam was where the action was. Bryce had continued.

"Anybody that breaks the rules gets into big trouble, Ace or no Ace. There's a big plan and the ROE are a vital part of that big plan. You copy?"

"Big plan, Colonel? You really think there's a big plan?" Bannister could not keep the sarcasm from his voice. He was going too far and he knew it. But he didn't care. Doc Russell and Major Hostettler stood quietly to one side.

"I sure as hell do, Bannister. We may not yet be privy to it, but it exists." His voice did not convey the conviction of his words. "And you are going to have to do some answering to somebody about your actions up North. Read this." He threw a message on the bed. Court picked it up and read it.

```
= = = = = = = = = = = = = = = = = = = = = = = = =
TO: CMDR/8TFW/UBON RTAFB THAI
FM: DIRECTOR OPERATIONS/7AF/TAN SON NHUT AB RVN
INFO: N/A
MSG: 240945ZJAN68
QQQQ
UNCLASS EFTO
SUBJ: MAJ COURTLAND EDM BANNISTER, FV3021953
1. REF OUR TELECON 1645L THIS DATE,BANNISTER
TO REPORT DO/7AF ASAP.
SIGNED ADMIN OFFICER FOR 7THAF/DO
= = = = = = = = = = = = = = = = = = = = = = = = =
```

"I have a hunch your days of going north to hunt MiGs are over," Bryce had said and left the room.

Hostettler had stayed behind. He had been grinning.

"Tell ya how it is, Court," he had said. "I'm reviewing your gun-camera film . . ."

"Did I get my fifth MiG?" Court Bannister interrupted.

"No, nothing conclusive there. Hits, yes, but no flamer. What I'm telling you is this. I'm trying to break out the big numbers those MiG drivers have painted on the nose of their airplanes. It's just possible the very MiGs you fought with were the ones in the traffic pattern at Kep. Small consolation, don'cha know, but since they are trying to hang an ROE violation on you, it's just possible we might be able to prove you were merely attacking the MiGs that were attacking you. I'll go over the photo negatives in the Lab myself. The angles and the sun cause some problems, but I'll see what I can do." Court thanked him, and he went out.

Doc Russell nodded. "Well, Court, I see you haven't changed one whit."

Court Bannister had studied him for a moment, then shook his head. "I've changed, Doc," he had said in a quiet voice. "Oh how I've changed."

"How's that?"

"First off, I no longer think Washington wants to win this war. Secondly, I may never fly over North Vietnam again."

Dr. Russell drew up a chair. "What brought all this on? You don't sound like the eager-beaver Court Bannister I knew back at Bien Hoa."

"I'm not. Isn't the reason obvious? Here I am, trying to do my job and damned if I'm not in trouble. Trouble so high up it looks like I'm being called upon to bypass my own wing commander to find out what it is. And I wouldn't be in any trouble if it weren't for some damn fool politicians who can't make up their mind what they want us to do over here." He tried to sit up but only made it to rest on his elbows.

Doc Russell pursed his lips. "You're just mad because you might not be the first Ace. There's plenty of war to go around. Besides, many a man would be happy not to fly north again."

"Not if he's a real fighter pilot, he wouldn't." Bannister lay back. Down deep, down where the thoughts he didn't always want to admit were carefully stored in the back rooms of his mind, he had felt a stirring of relief. He put it away. Court knew fear and knew how to control it, to convert it to alert apprehension that tuned his body and mind to be a more effective fighting man. It almost always worked . . .

He stared out the window at the rain. Here now, in this BOQ room at Tan Son Nhut, he still felt some measure of relief, but it was completely outweighed by his desire to make Ace. You never found the edge of the envelope until you pushed at it. Or, as Colonel Boots Blesse had written about tactics at the fighter school at Nellis, "No Guts, No Glory."

He turned from the window and pulled a can of beer from a paper bag on the bed. He popped the top, took a deep swallow, then lit a Lucky Strike cigarette.

Court Bannister's BOQ room at Tan Son Nhut was small, ten by twelve, with a bare wooden floor and walls painted a sickly green. It was sparsely furnished with a wooden-frame bed, a small night table and lamp, a desk, and a straight-back chair. An air conditioner mounted on the wall chugged and dripped moisture from its base.

Yesterday he had tried to report as ordered to the Director of Operations as soon as he arrived. When he had presented himself to the DO's outer office, he had been told the DO, Major General Milton Berzin, was busy and would send for him as soon as he could.

This morning, a written invitation for dinner with the Chief of Intelligence for 7th Air Force had been delivered to his BOQ room. *Here I am, trying to report to some general for, as implied by Bryce, probable violations of the Rules of Engagement, and I get invited to dinner with some other general. This doesn't happen to majors.* He checked his watch. It was time to go.

On the bed was his B-4 bag. Hanging from a hook on the door were his khaki uniform pants. His shirt, the fruity-collared 1505 kind, was draped over a chair in front of the desk. Silver senior pilot wings and Army parachute wings were pinned to the left breast. Beneath them were Silver Star, Distinguished Flying Cross, and Purple Heart ribbons – each with an oak leaf cluster denoting two awards, and several other ribbons denoting military service in and out of Vietnam. Under the shirt was a lightweight rib-cage harness issued by the hospital to support his sore ribs.

On the desk were his wallet, Seiko watch, and a packet containing his red passport and a first-class round-trip ticket between Saigon and Singapore. The red passport was issued to military in Vietnam to differentiate them from the civilians with their green passports. Clipped to the

77

packet was a note confirming a reservation for two suites at the Raffles Hotel for ten days. Next to the packet was a small brass folding photograph holder with a picture of a tall blonde woman poised on a large sailboat. She grasped the forward lines with one hand and waved with the other, golden hair streaming in the wind. Her eyes were alive and sparkling, her smile infectious and full. *To my very own*, was written on it, and the signature, *Your Susan*.

Court picked up the picture and stared into Susan Boyle's eyes. He had been writing and calling her for several months. Her return letters had been warm and humorous. She sent him pictures of herself on the beach, and in the chair of her living room, and by her car. She sent pictures of the people at Donkin's, and showed how they had put a huge picture of him and his airplane, the F-4 he had called Donkin's Wallbanger, on the wall. Always her smile was warm, and her mouth wide and generous and inviting. Her eyes were clear and looked straight into his. She was beginning to fill a void, and become a greater warmth in his life than any other woman before. Even his former wife, Charmaine, for all her happy, bubbly ways, had not filled him as full, or made him as content and happy. Maybe now, he said, maybe now. He put the picture down and tapped the bundle of letters from her. Maybe it was time. Maybe he was in love. Just maybe it was time to quit the Air Force and settle down. All of a sudden, a quiet life with her seemed reasonable and desirable, maybe necessary.

Next to the travel packet was a series of cablegrams from international magazines requesting interviews. The magazines ranged from the lurid *Gossip International*, called by its acronym GI, to one with serious aviation articles, *Aviation Week*. In between were the weeklies, with *U.S. News & World Report* being the most balanced. The egregious GI magazine had been after him for weeks to respond to a headline they had run a month before proclaiming in two-inch-high letters: SAM'S SONS: ONE KILLS VC, ONE SPIES FOR VC. *AvWeek* had just picked up on the Ivory Ace title and wanted to interview him about his four MiG kills.

Even the *Stars and Stripes* and the *Air Force Magazine* wanted to talk to him. He had not responded to any of them.

A subheadline on one story repeated the ditty that had followed his father, Sam Bannister, around since before World War Two, when his international sexual exploits had been legion.

> *Silk Screen Sam, the ladies' man.*
> *If he can't get in, no one can*

Court tightened up. Until his half-brother Shawn had been taken into custody by the OSI last fall, he had been leading a quiet life as a fighter pilot in the USAF, rising to fame quite on his own.

Centered on the cover of another magazine was an old movie photo of Sam Bannister, flanking him were current photos of his two sons, Courtland and Shawn. Sam was sword-fighting on the deck of a pirate ship in a 1939 movie. Court was in pilot's gear, Shawn was shown wearing a safari suit in a photo taken in Vietnam. The caption was big and clear: SILK SCREEN SAM'S SONS: ONE AN ACE, ONE A SPY. The feature story inside profiled all three men.

In the late 1930s, at the age of twenty-five, Sam had been a world idol. Just before World War Two he had fallen deeply in love with and married Monique D'Avignon de Montségur of France, who had given birth to Courtland. Sam had been devastated when Monique had died when Court was two years old. During the war, wild and lonely, Sam Bannister had been a B-17 gunner with the 8th Air Force. After the war, the de Montségurs had helped raise Court, schooling him in France during his early years. It was during that time that Sam had married Mary McDougal, who had become Shawn's mother. Sam had picked up his acting career, made several highly successful adventure movies, and invested his money in movies for TV and in California and Nevada desert real estate. Except for Mary McDougal, it had all worked out. Sam had divorced her. He now lived in the penthouse over his hotel, the Silver Screen, in Las Vegas.

A picture inside the magazine of Court showed him as a teenager in cowboy garb in one of the few movies in which he had worked as an extra. The magazine writer described at length his combat career, first as an F-100 pilot flying from Bien Hoa Air Base in South Vietnam, then as an F-4 pilot at Ubon.

The inside picture of Shawn Bannister showed him in Las Vegas with a dazzling smile and a show girl on each arm. The article chronicled his rise as a correspondent in Vietnam for the liberal *California Sun*. Several articles he had written had made him famous in the antiwar crowd. The first to gain him national notoriety had detailed how his brother, Court, had shot up a civilian bus with his F-100, then napalmed the passengers. That the story had not been true seemed to have made no difference to Shawn or the readers of the *Sun*. But the story that had guaranteed his international fame had been his report of an interview with Viet Cong Colonel Tung in a tunnel complex under Cholon, a section of Saigon. The article had stated in depth why the American imperialists could not win their war of aggression against the peace-loving people of Vietnam.

The main story in the magazine explained how Shawn had been apprehended by the USAF Office of Special Investigation in a bar in the village of Ubon Ratchithani, soliciting information from airmen assigned to the fighter base. In his defense he had produced copies of his articles in the North Vietnamese newspaper Nhan Dan and said he was a newsman on assignment, legitimately collecting material. He had pointed to articles in *Aviation Week* and *Flight International* detailing similar stories. Shawn Bannister had then been released by an embarrassed USAF.

It had not been good, that day in Ubon, when Court had accompanied Shawn after his release from the base. His half-brother had railed about fascist police, violations of his civil rights, and his responsibility as a journalist to get at the truth regardless of the cost. Court had had the distinct impression Shawn wanted to remain in custody so he could gather more scathing material for attacks on the U.S. military in general and the United States Air Force in particular.

Court had taken his half-brother to Shawn's shabby room that overlooked the runways of the military air base. Two Thai policemen had been waiting. As polite and smooth as warm molasses, they had made it quite clear that *Meester Sha-hahn Banneestah* was no longer welcome in the Kingdom of Thailand. If he would just clear the room, they would escort him to the train for Bangkok, where he would be met and escorted to the Don Muang International Airport. They did not care where he went, just so it was outside the borders of the Kingdom of Thailand. Sputtering and fuming, Shawn had collected his suitcase and clothes. His confiscated cameras, tape recorder, and radio had been returned at the air base. In the room had been a slender Thai girl with wary eyes. Shawn had called her Souky. Souky had said nothing, not even as Shawn walked out. Court had had the impression she was there merely as an observer. Shawn's final words to Court had been, "Dad's going to hear about this, you military piece of shit."

Court thought about his dad, who was now a few positions away from the wealthiest Americans list in *Forbes*. Sam had set up trust funds for the two boys to guarantee them at least, under current earnings, five thousand a month for life. Court continually plowed his proceeds into a portfolio his father's investor managed for him. Outside of an occasional splurge, he lived on his Air Force salary of $1,256 per month, before taxes.

It had been tough, getting established, making his own way in the Air Force, fighting both disdain and sycophancy because of his background, but he had succeeded. Now divorced, his mind hadn't been diverted in combat by concerns for wife and children, and the self-preservation feelings that came in combat when you were in rib-aching love, feelings that can distract – and kill.

He stared at the rain. But it was different now. Not that his career was going sour, it surely wasn't. But something was very wrong, and he felt maybe it was in the way the war was being fought. If I'm not allowed to fight, and if my own country doesn't want to win the very war they put us troops into, well . . . why should I lay my ass on the line? He took a pull on his beer. Why should I lay my ass on the line? Why?

He picked up his watch. He was due to be at Trailer 5 in the General Officer's area in forty-five minutes for dinner with Brigadier General Leonard Norman. He barely knew the man, but the dinner invitation from the general who ran the Intelligence Directorate was tantamount to an order. And he followed orders.

He drained the beer, stripped, wrapped a towel around his waist, grabbed his dop kit, and padded down the hall to the communal toilets and showers. He showered carefully, favoring his ribs, toweled down, and returned to the room. The rain was heavier, and alternately drummed and tore at the window as gusts whirled around the corner of the BOQ. From his B-4 bag on the bed, he withdrew a pair of light slacks and a blue singlet. He slipped the pants on and picked up the rib protector. He fingered it for a moment, then threw it in the corner. He finished dressing and left the room. Loud rock music sounded from behind closed doors as he walked down the hallway. He smelled cooking odors from forbidden hot plates. At the end, before the narrow wooden stairs, the doors of two rooms across from each other were open. A party in progress spilled into the hallway. "I'm a Believer" by the Monkees echoed down the drab halls. He excused himself as he passed by, turned down a friendly Mai-Tai, and descended the steps to the door by the street. An airman in a glistening poncho was just entering. He stood and stared at Court for a moment.

"Sir, are you Major Bannister?"

"Yes. What's up?"

"The General's compliments, sir, I'm to drive you to his quarters." He handed Court a poncho. The staff car was a

1964 Ford Fairlane sedan, painted Air Force blue. Court climbed in back. It was stiff vinyl, steamy, and smelled of mildew. Ten minutes later he was deposited at the entrance to the General Officer's area, which was surrounded by a twelve-foot chain-link fence. USAF senior officers were required to live on base. Army officers could and did live in downtown Saigon, some in sumptuous villas. The rain was streaming down. A guard waved him through, he found Trailer 5, and knocked twice on the narrow door.

Brigadier General Leonard Norman let him in. He was tall, slender, and straight as an Irish walking stick, and had a thatch of reddish-brown hair. He was smiling.

"Welcome, Major Bannister. Come in, come in. I trust you did not get too wet." Two men in civilian clothes with drinks in their hands were seated in the small living room of the two-room trailer. With a start, Court recognized both of them.

The taller and older of the two was the four-star general in command of 7th Air Force, the other was a public information officer he had known a few years before at Bien Hoa.

Commander, 7th Air Force, was a man who managed to look both quizzical and wry at the same time. He had good reason. He was responsible for 70,000 airmen and pilots and 1,500 airplanes on twenty bases in South Vietnam and Thailand. He also had operational control over 400 more airplanes based in the Philippines, Okinawa, and Guam. He was an old-head fighter pilot, competent and very much in command. He was the general who two months earlier had pinned Bannister's second Silver Star and other medals on him.

The second man, Major Angelo Correlli, was Court's age, medium height, and weight. He had dark hair to match his dark and brooding eyes, and a handsome pockmarked face. Not a pilot, he held the unenviable position as one of the PIOs (Public Information Officers) for 7th Air Force under the office symbol DXI.

Commander, 7th, extended his hand. "Good to see you

again, Bannister. Correlli here says you were stationed together at Bien Hoa." They shook hands.

"Yes, sir, we were." Court and Correlli shook.

"What are you drinking?" General Norman said.

"Beer, sir." He thought about lighting a cigarette and decided against it. Norman handed him a beer and pointed to an open spot on the rattan sofa next to Correlli.

"How are you? Feeling better?" Commander, 7th, asked.

"Yes, sir. Just fine." Now what in hell is this all about? he wondered. Four-star generals didn't call in majors to inquire after their health. If they must know, there are any numbers of staff members who could procure the information at a twist of a telephone dial.

"I understand you have some convalescence leave coming? What do you intend to do?"

"Off to Singapore for ten days, sir," Court said, surprised at such intimate questioning and wondering when the boom would fall. This was a strange way to set up an ass-chewing.

"I didn't want the DO, General Berzin, to receive you in his office because – for the moment – I want what we talk about to be off the record. And if I had seen you, my exec would have had to log you in along with the topic of our conversation." Commander, 7th, sighed. "That's how it goes once you get some horsepower. You're not really your own man anymore." He smiled and handed Court a packet of photos. "Take a look at these. You might just find them of interest."

Court thumbed through the pictures. They were grainy and obviously from a gun camera. Then he recognized them for what they were: single-frame blowups of his dogfight with the MiG-19s last week. MiGs in two photos were circled with red grease pencil. One, at a 30-degree angle off, showed Court's gunsight pipper placed squarely behind the cockpit of the MiG he could not shoot at. The numbers 2010 on the nose of the enemy fighter were circled. The second shot clearly showed 2010 over Kep Air Base with its gear and flaps down. Hostettler had done a good job breaking out the pertinent photos. Court looked up at the general.

"You're off the hook, Court," Commander, 7th, said. "Those MiGs were attacking the strike force, you were there to defend the strike force, so you went in hot pursuit of the attackers. At least," he said dryly, "that is how I choose to interpret the battle. From further interpretation of the photos and from the debrief of your flight members, you have been given credit for two possibles and one probable from that mission. And, in case you are having trouble adding them up, you now have four MiG kills confirmed, three possibles, and two probables. And I know about those Thuds in your flight path on your first missile attack, the kill you gave your wingman. That's a classic example of mature judgment, for which we thank you. Sorry it blew your fifth kill. Nonetheless, congratulations." He stuck his hand out. "You are the leading MiG killer in the whole of Southeast Asia." They shook.

"But there is a kicker," the general continued. "Unfortunately there will be no fifth MiG for you. No more Rolling Thunder missions, no more flying north into the Route Package system under any circumstances." That meant Court's chances of getting his fifth MiG were nonexistent, because beyond one or two rare cases, North Vietnamese MiGs never flew over Laos, the DMZ, or South Vietnam, only North Vietnam.

There was silence in the trailer. Court's lips involuntarily compressed. One does not ask a superior officer why he chooses to put a certain order into effect. One does hope, however, the superior explains a controversial order, or an order that causes hardship, or – in Court's case – great unhappiness and bitter disappointment. He was destined to remain the Ivory Ace, Court thought. And Commander, 7th, had chosen not to divulge his reasoning for why he could not go north. Hell, this just proves I'm better off out of the service, he reasoned.

Leonard Norman refilled the drinks.

"Now for the next subject," Commander, 7th, said. He motioned to Correlli. "While not painful, it isn't exactly one of great joy."

Correlli opened a briefcase he had at his feet. He extracted copies of the tabloids that were sensationalizing the two sons of Sam Bannister. They were much the same as Court had in his room.

Commander, 7th, cleared his throat. "This is the off-the-record part of our little chat," he said.

"Do you know where your brother – excuse me, *half*-brother – is right now?" Brigadier General Leonard Norman asked.

"Here in Saigon, I believe, sir. I had seen some of his articles datelined Saigon. He usually stays at the Caravel Hotel."

"He has a room there," Norman said, "but he hasn't occupied it for several weeks now. We are, if not concerned, at least curious as to his whereabouts, and we know where he is."

Court looked up. "Can you be legally tailing him, sir?"

"No," Norman said. "We in the military can not. But the FBI can – and are, or were. He gave them the slip here, then surfaced in San Francisco. Based on that big article he wrote last fall about his interview with the VC colonel, and his broad hints in that article about a big drive or VC push coming, we are naturally curious about what he knows. We have many indicators something is about to pop. As to where he is in San Francisco, he's running with some left-wing politicos."

Court took a long haul from his beer. He leaned back and shook his head. Shawn had been a problem since childhood.

"You know more about his activities than I do," he said.

"Did you know about this?" Brigadier General Leonard Norman asked. He handed Court a page from a copy of the *Nhan Dan*, a newspaper from Hanoi. With it was a translation of an article with Shawn's by-line. The article gave detailed information about F-4 bomb loads and takeoffs from Ubon, along with a diatribe on how the Western giant was attacking a defenseless people who wanted merely to unify their country against foreign imperialists. It had been written two months before, when Shawn had been at Ubon.

"Yes, I did," Court said, anger tightening his lips. "Shawn used it in his defense when the OSI picked him up. It's not illegal, is it?"

"No, actually it is not," Leonard said. "In the last war, though, we would call it giving aid and comfort to the enemy." He sighed. "But then, this isn't a war, and there is no press censorship."

"About these tabloids," Correlli said, indicating the papers. "I've been getting a big ration of shit from SAFOI in the Pentagon."

Commander, 7th, rolled his eyes. Junior officers weren't supposed to say "shit" around senior officers. But Correlli was, well, Correlli. SAFOI was the office of information of the Secretary of the Air Force.

Correlli continued. "I hate to ask this of you, but for the record, have you given any interviews or are you going to give any interviews? SAFOI really wants to know. Supposedly everything has to be cleared through them, in addition to a PIO officer being present at any interview."

"Interviews about Shawn or about the MiGs?" Court asked.

Correlli grinned. "About Shawn. SAFOI thinks an interview with a reputable publication about your MiG kills would be just fine."

Court frowned. "I haven't given any interviews and I'm not going to give any interviews . . . on anything, Shawn, MiGs, my dad. Nothing. In fact I'm thinking of resigning my commission."

Commander, 7th, nodded, unperturbed. "Leonard," he said, "better break out some scotch." Brigadier General Leonard Norman did as requested and poured scotch all around, except for Court, who took another beer.

"I'll just let that resignation statement be for the moment, if you will keep your mind open," Commander, 7th, said. "It's not that I've been testing you, Court, it's just that a rather interesting project has come up that might interest you." He held up his hand. "It will not begin until some time after you return from Singapore. You'll have plenty of time to make up your mind, but I want to talk about it this evening. Granted, you've just given me new information, but supposing you do remain on active duty, I just want to make sure you are, ah, free of any other problems – like making Ace, or a half-brother that bothers you."

Court hesitated, then nodded. "I have no problems, General." I'm lying, he thought. I've got problems with the way this stupid war is being run. I've got problems because I can't seem to get interested in much of anything anymore. I've got problems . . .

"Good. Hand me the maps, Leonard." The intelligence officer gave him a folded 1:250,000 map of the Laotian panhandle, that part of Laos that runs between Cambodia and North and South Vietnam. Commander, 7th, pointed to the hydra-headed black traces coming from North Vietnam through the mountain passes of Mu Gia and Ban Karai into Laos, then south in Laos to re-emerge into South Vietnam. The areas the hydra – the Ho Chi Minh Trail – transited in Laos were code-named Steel Tiger and Tiger Hound.

"In a nutshell, we are stepping up our interdiction efforts in Steel Tiger and Tiger Hound. We've got them pretty well bottled up now in the daytime. But now I want to stop them at night. I think a night fast FAC program using F-4s could do it. They could sniff out the trucks, then call in air strikes to destroy them."

"*Night* FAC?" Brigadier General Leonard Norman echoed. "Night reconnaissance? Strike planes dive-bombing at night in the karst? That's rough stuff. It's never been done before."

Commander, 7th, gave him a withering look. "To continue," he rasped. "Bannister, you had Commando Sabre experience, helping to set up the first program to use airborne forward air controllers in jets. That led to the Misty FACS in F-100s. From that came other fast FAC programs in F-4s. They are doing a good job of bottling up the Trail, but only in daylight. So I want you to establish a night schedule to cover Steel Tiger and Tiger Hound with F-4s from Ubon. The mission would be to find and destroy trucks, truck parks, maintenance and supply depots, fuel pipelines, and the guns that protect them. Upon activation we will frag Air Force and Navy fighters to your group. Do you follow me so far?"

"Yes, sir."

"This would be a dedicated night mission." He glanced at General Norman. "And it's never been done before." He looked back at Court. "Isn't that correct?"

"Yes, sir."

"It would take an exceptional man to set up and run the program, right?"

"Yes, sir."

"Yes indeed, an exceptional man. Tell me," Commander, 7th, ordered, "why are you considering getting out?"

Court shrugged. He decided to tell the general exactly how he felt. "Sir, if Washington doesn't want to win this war, and I'm not allowed to fight in all aspects of it – "

"You mean continue to go after MiGs up north, don't you?"

Court hesitated a moment. "Yes, sir, I suppose I do."

"Well, Bannister, this new position would give you all the fight you could handle, even if you can no longer go to Hanoi. But I'd like to add something. This war isn't being run for the convenience of the participants. A military man goes where he is sent, does what he is told to do, and does it as well as he possibly can." He took a sip of scotch. He decided not to push that aspect any further. For some time he had been not only displeased but dismayed at the attitude emanating from Washington – both the Pentagon and the White House. It was an attitude both cowardly and ambivalent, and he weighed telling the young major from just how high up the order had come that forbade him to fly in North Vietnam. He decided not to, reasoning that if Bannister was upset about what Washington was doing or not doing right now, it was best he not learn it was also meddling – meddling even down to individual troop level such as Bannister. He had no idea why such an idiotic order had come – and from the President himself. He pictured the message that had been delivered to him a few days earlier by his SSO, the Special Security Officer that handled encrypted messages.

====================================
IVY TREE MESSAGE FOLLOWS: SECRET, EYES ONLY
TO: CO/7TH AF
FROM: MG A.G. WHISENAND/WHNSC
DATE: 25 JAN 68
SUBJ: POTUS RESTRICTION
1. (S) POTUS DESIRES USAF MAJOR COURTLAND EDM.
    BANNISTER, FV3021953, 8TH TFW, UBON RTAFB,
    THAILAND BE FORBIDDEN TO FLY NORTH OF DMZ
    UNTIL FURTHER NOTICE.
    IVY TREE ENDS.
====================================

POTUS meant President of the United States. Any message from him as Commander in Chief of the Armed Forces was transmitted with the Ivy Tree label to ensure prompt and restricted handling by SSOs.

Commander, 7th, knew he had to play Bannister easy, like a flycaster with a wary trout. He needed this man to take this particular job, and not just because of his talent.

He wasn't quite alone in pushing this hazardous night-FAC idea. He and one other general in Washington, Whitey Whisenand, had been the only two general officers to take seriously a staff study by a former student at the Air Command and Staff College.

A Major Harry "Skip" Rington had postulated that since the Rules of Engagement prohibited sealing the North Vietnamese war-supply route at the source, and since the day FACs were becoming more and more successful in throttling day traffic on the Ho Chi Minh Trail, it was obvious that a night FAC program was the next logical step.

Rington himself, now a lieutenant colonel in the Pentagon tactics shop, had been instrumental in setting up the

90

Wolf FAC program at Ubon, but hadn't been able to get the support he'd needed from the 7th Air Force for the night mission before he'd rotated back to his current Stateside desk job.

USAF Major General Albert G. "Whitey" Whisenand had seen Rington's study because he had a good friend at the Air University who flagged things like that for Whitey to review. In the late nineteen-fifties, when he had been assigned to Maxwell Air Force Base, home of the Air University complex, Whitey had noted that some extraordinary good ideas thought up by students in the various schools and seminars didn't make it past the confines of the AU library. Usually the ideas were, as the faculty would say, ". . . not in consonance with current USAF thinking." These ideas weren't necessarily scuttled, just filed in dusty racks in the back storeroom of the library. They were there because nonconformists simply weren't chosen as faculty members. And that was ironic, Whitey Whisenand knew, because one of the best at nonconformist tactics had gotten the whole concept started. Claire Chennault had begun an air tactics school back in the thirties, then gone on to set up and command the AVG – the American Volunteer Group – better known as the Flying Tigers. They'd flown P-40s, defending China before the Japanese even attacked Pearl Harbor. Chennault's Air Tactics School at Langley AFB in Virginia had evolved into the Air University at Maxwell AFB, at Montgomery, Alabama.

Whitey Whisenand had picked up on these studies. One, from a captain in the early sixties, he had passed to the proper place at Wright-Patterson. It had involved side-firing guns from transports and had been based on how missionaries let buckets of trinkets down a rope from a Piper Cub making pylon turns over South American tribesmen. Because of that, Commander, 7th, now had AC-47 gunships on hand, with AC-130 gunships due over in a few weeks.

Commander, 7th, smiled wryly to himself. How could he tell all this to such a young man as Court Bannister? How could he tell him that deft politics mixed with amiable subterfuge could often get a mission accomplished, whereas strict conformance to the regulations might bog results forever? How the higher in rank a person goes, the more strings he must have available to pull at just the correct time. Now, in Vietnam, there was added complexity. God knew that what he was sometimes a party to in bending the Rules of Engagement could get him cashiered from the Air Force. He was not at all comfortable running a war when he had to resort to trickery to get the job done. How dare the politicians send their military out to accomplish a mission, then restrict their means to do so? How dare they place their best men in a position where they had to cheat to win?

Not only that, he sighed, there were a few tactical things the current regime at the Department of the Air Force did not like: the fast FAC program was one of them. For the Commander of the 7th Air Force to start up a night fast FAC organization, in addition to the day program, was pushing the tolerance envelope. And this is precisely where and why Bannister came in. Commander, 7th, reasoned that besides his obvious talent to do the task, whatever operation the well-known Court Bannister ran for the Air Force was sure to receive favorable publicity. The news clips from his grand appearance at Tan Son Nhut last November after downing his fourth MiG had been spectacular. The coverage, mostly favorable, for one of Sam Bannister's sons as a hero in the Vietnam war had made the international press. His reticence to disembark from an airplane at his awards ceremony had been likened to the boyish shyness of the Lone Eagle, Charles Lindbergh. The Chief of Staff had been pleased, SAFOI had been ecstatic. So, if Bannister successfully organized and ran this night program and actually stopped the enemy traffic, that, plus his public relations value, should be enough weight to ensure the longevity of the night FAC operation. A tough way to circumvent Washington, but a method that might help win the war. At least it would save GI lives by destroying enemy equipment before it got to the battlefield. If we can't turn off the tap, Commander, 7th, thought, we can try to chop up all those hoses snaking through the grass.

Commander, 7th, looked at Angelo Correlli, one of his best public information officers. Correlli was to see to it that some USAF operations didn't make the news. Correlli's job was vital in these tricky times, when the American government had not quite acknowledged that U.S. forces were doing anything in or over Laos or even flying missions from Thailand. There had been enough bad publicity. Just recently a disheveled man in the front ranks of the war protesters had said he was a former F-105 pilot who had hideous nightmares due to his indiscriminate bombing of civilians. His picture and the words made all the nightly news channels, none of which bothered to verify his background. When the Pentagon released the fact that he had been a malcontent corporal who had never served in SEA and had been discharged "at the convenience of the government," none of the channels were interested. The *New York Times*, however, had carried a small article in the bottom left-hand corner on Page 35 citing the Pentagon release about the corporal.

What a war, the general mused, and returned his thoughts to the task at hand. He gave Court Bannister a thin smile.

"Of course you need both night combat-flying experience and day fast FAC experience. If you decide to take the job, my DO will arrange for both. So make up your mind in Singapore. You have ten days. When you decide to take the job – and you will – submit your plan to me. It must include number of aircraft and aircrew to provide full night-time coverage and how you will accomplish maintenance for the planes and personal equipment for the aircrew. State your intelligence-processing method. And, lastly, how you will handle the administrative details such as Officer Efficiency Reports, Form 5 flying-time records, and related items."

"Where would I get the pilots and the backseaters, sir?"

"Set up some criterion, like so many missions, so much total hours in the front or back seat day and night. Take an equal amount of crew from each squadron or other places if need be. Another thing – each man has to be a volunteer."

"Would this be in writing, sir?"

Commander, 7th, looked perturbed. "If you accept, of course. By TWX." He spread his hands. "Colonel Bryce might be a bit upset about not being allowed to pick his own night FAC leader. On top of that, for training purposes he will be directed to place you in the night squadron for twenty missions, and the day FAC unit for an additional ten. I'll square that away. If you have any problems, talk to Colonel Bryce first. But since this is, initially anyhow, a command-directed mission, I want you to keep my Director of Operations in the know. By the way, the night FAC commander also must be a volunteer. Do you have any questions?"

"No, sir."

"Right, then. With the exception of the night FAC program, everything we have talked about here this evening is off the record." He turned. "Now, Leonard, how about some more of that excellent scotch? Then I've got to go."

Ten minutes later, when the general was in the middle of a humorous P-51 story, there was a knock on the door. Leonard Norman opened it. Major General Milt Berzin, Director of Operations, 7th Air Force, entered. It was still raining. He delivered his message without preamble.

"Sir, the enemy pressure on the Marine base at Khe Sanh up near the DMZ has increased. COMUSMACV has tasked us to double the aerial resupply and to increase tactical and strategic air support. Even use B-52s if we have to. And he is going to appoint you as single air manager over all air assets in South Vietnam, including *Marine* fighters up in the Eye Corps."

Commander, 7th, made a lopsided grin. "So the USAF is finally being allowed to help the mighty Marines of Eye Corps. The very same Marines who scorn single air management." He looked around at them. "This is going to make some Marine generals mighty unhappy."

The gathering broke up. Norman, Berzin, and Commander, 7th, stayed behind to confer. Court and Correlli hurried out into the rain.

5

1845 Hours Local, Monday 29 January 1968
Lang Tri Special Forces Camp
Republic of Vietnam

They made the outer perimeter of the Lang Tri camp just after the heat of noon, gave the proper signal, and entered. Once in the compound, they went immediately to the buried command bunker. Besides being well fortified, it was cool. The bunker was larger than normal. In addition to the standard map and radio room, there was a small storage room with extra food supplies, water, ammunition, and radio batteries.

Along one wall of the large room were three wooden folding cots. Lopez led Toby Parker to one and told him to drink water and lie down. Toby, dizzy from heat and exhaustion, did as he was told. He put away two quarts of tepid but pure water and promptly fell into a deep sleep. Lopez tenderly cut his flight suit and underwear off, wrinkling his nose at the smell. He sponged Parker's body the best he could, replaced the bandages on his feet, and covered him with a poncho liner.

Ryder and Dickson came over. Both were five-nine and wide as barn doors. They almost looked like twins; same build, same brown hair, same large-jawed faces.

"He sure stinks," Ryder said.

"Kind of runty, too," Dickson added.

Lopez bristled. "He saw some tanks, dammit, and got

shot down trying to get pictures. His buddy was killed and he's been a POW for a few days. You'd stink, too." He pulled out his map and pointed to Toby's mark. "Right there. PT-76s."

"Christ," Ryder said, "we're right between them and Khe Sanh."

"We'd better get on the horn and let Fifth Group know what's happening," Lopez said. "But the first thing I've got to do is get out a White Hat report about one recovered USAF POW."

"And the tanks he saw," Ryder added.

Lopez looked strange. "Well, I'll mention he saw tanks."

"Don't you believe him?" Dickson asked.

"Well, hell, now I don't know. You'd think we'd have heard something about tanks anyplace on the Trail, not just down this way. But there has never been a report of any tread activity. No recon team has ever said anything about armor along the Trail or in South Vietnam."

Lopez went to the radio table and wrote up a message and gave it to the commo man for transmission on the ANGRC-109 (called the Angry 9), the long-range Morse code transceiver.

An American Army Special Forces A-team composed of twelve men was stationed at the Lang Tri camp. They were well equipped. Beside the Angry 9, they had a UHF and a VHF, and two FMs on a Mark-28 pallet. A large outside generator and small backup provided power. The antennas sprang up from the top of the bunker. In the fortified compound were a mess hall, two ammo dumps, several mortar pits, and assorted lean-tos and shed-type structures for nearly one hundred Vietnamese soldiers, composed of a civilian defense group and Vietnamese Special Forces commanded by the American A-team.

Lang Tri was located one mile from the Tchepone River, which formed the Laotian border to the west. Five miles to the east was the 6,000-man U.S. Marine Corps garrison at Khe Sanh. The Lang Tri team's mission of border surveillance had become more and more hazardous as they ran into larger and better-equipped hard-core North Vietnamese forces as the weeks passed. No aerial recce had been able to get into the weeds and see what was going on because the valleys to the west into Laos were full of fog and had been since the time Toby Parker crashed. At Khe Sanh itself, the weather opened up only sporadically, allowing limited aerial resupply and air strikes on the attacking hordes. The air strikes, code-named Niagara, used Navy, Marine, and USAF air, including B-52s. A few weeks earlier, during the hill fights, the terrible attacks by the communists on hills 880 and 881 near Khe Sanh, the Marines had used only Marine air support with some Navy fighters. That limited use of air power had changed. Requirements had overcome prejudice and parochial thinking. Everything that could drop or shoot something was welcome now.

Toby slept on and off until late the next afternoon. He had awakened only for soup, bread, and fresh salve and bandages on his feet. The troops had given him a pair of jungle fatigues to wear. Bad weather prevented helicopter resupply for Lang Tri, so Toby had not been able to get med-evacced out. Now he woke up, stiff but refreshed, and asked for a little exercise. Lopez, his AK slung over his shoulder, led him to the mess bunker and gave him a hand as he hobbled along. It was early evening. Toby looked around. "You've got quite a fort here."

"Yeah, we do. Because we're so close to the Laotian border and at the end of the supply string, we've beefed up our defenses with extra Claymores, concertina and tanglefoot wire, and, listen to this – a couple four-point-deuce mortars, two eighty-one-mil mortars, and twenty of those sixty-mil mortars. We've also got nearly a hundred M-72 LAWs. What with the Marines at Khe Sanh ready to help us with bodies and artillery, we are ready for anything." A LAW was a one-time, shoot-and-discard, light antitank weapon fired from the shoulder.

Besides the firepower, Lopez told Toby how the team leader, Captain Michaelis and the men, had scrounged concrete and actual 8-by-8 pieces of lumber to build the roof of their fortresslike command post, which had been sunk deep into the red clay.

Once in the mess hall, Lopez rustled up some soup and lemonade for Toby and a beer for himself. "Tell you what, though," he said. "There's a grunt full bull up there on that Marine hill, and he doesn't like us. Says we are wretches who think we are a law unto ourselves. Hah. Maybe we are. But it doesn't make any difference." He took a long pull at his beer. "We'll be okay."

"What do you mean?" Toby asked.

"Captain Michaelis, our team leader, had their artillery forward observer over here. We worked out a plan to get their support if we need it. They've got a bunch of howitzers that can reinforce us. All we got to do is call 'Jacksonville' on the arty net, and pow, we get all that heavy 105 stuff we want."

"Where is Captain Michaelis now?"

"Stuck at Nha Trang. Been trying to get back for two days now. It's the weather. Our XO is out on patrol with another team member and some local tribesmen."

The gray of the overcast day became darker as the sun set beyond the hills. Fog rose from the streams and valleys. Lopez checked his watch. He motioned to Parker, and they started to walk back to the command post. Lopez wore all his webbed gear and carried a radio and a CAR-15 (a Colt Automatic Rifle).

"Sleep in the CP tonight," Lopez said. "I've got the commo watch. If anything happens, keep out of the way. In fact, stay on your cot and watch the whole thing."

They were halfway across the compound when a series of incoming heavy mortar shells exploded in the northwest corner of the compound and started to march toward them. Men yelled and ran for cover. The camp's hand-powered warning siren wound up from a low moan to a high-pitched scream. More shells fell on the camp. One made a direct hit in a mortar pit, blowing the tube and pieces of men high into the air. The next would land on top of Toby and Lopez.

In the Writer's Bar, Court Bannister stood just inside the
open door that led to the Palm Court and the guest suites.
The cool evening breeze held the scent of the orchids and
the frangipani trees in the two-acre grounds. Both he and
Susan Boyle had arrived the day before; Court from Saigon,
Susan from Tokyo. Tonight Court wore a white linen suit,
high-collar shirt, and pale-blue tie. When he had cabled
and called Susan at her apartment in Los Angeles, they
had eagerly agreed to meet at the old Raffles Hotel in
Singapore. He had ten days, she had eight. Nothing could
be more remote from the sweat and horrors of the Vietnam
war than a former colonial hotel in the newly formed
Republic of Singapore. They had laughingly agreed on a
colonial mode of dress.

Court had cabled Terry Holt, his father's friend and
business manager, to make all the arrangements for two
suites and appropriate clothes for him. When Court arrived,
his suits, shirts, and accompanying socks and shoes were all
laid out and waiting in his suite. The manager gave him a
personal welcome and explained how well they remembered
the days in the thirties when Sam Bannister and Errol Flynn
had stayed there, and the days-long parties they had put
on.

Court and Susan each had a suite, down the open veranda
from each other. The high-ceiling suites contained a sitting
room, bedroom, bath, and walk-in closet, just as the Sarkies
brothers had designed them seventy-five years before. The
furnishings were elegant but understated. Although the
suites – which were named after famous writers who had
once stayed there – were air conditioned, there was a brass-
and-hardwood ceiling fan slowly revolving in each room.

He saw her now, descending the steps from the veranda

into the greenery of the Palm Court. She was tanned and sleek. Her clothes were of the casual and languid colonial style so popular in the late twenties. Her dress was white silk and short-sleeved. It accentuated her bosom and waist, then flared into many pleats that extended down to midcalf. Her pumps were white. She wore a white, wide-brimmed lady's sun hat with a light-blue ribbon down one side. Her long blonde hair fell smooth and tawny past her shoulders; one golden wing brushed her forehead, then swept back under her hat. Her right hand rested on a light-blue over-the-shoulder bag. Her legs flashed tan and lithe, the silk rustling and flowing, as she strode purposefully through the garden of the birds. I have never seen anyone so beautiful, Court thought as he absorbed the sight. At the last moment he stepped to the doorway and spoke to her.

"You are a most gracious and beautiful lady. Might a gentleman inquire if you are free this evening?" Court said in a thick and terrible British accent.

"Why, prithee, kind sir, inquire away." She made a coquettish curtsy. Her quick smile was wide and warm.

Court offered an elbow. "Accompany me, if you will, to yon watering hole for friendly libation, and we will talk of kings and things."

They drank and laughed and joked in the small Writer's Bar, then quieted when a tiny, exquisitely dressed waitress from the outside garden informed them in the Queen's English that their table was ready. They followed her to a table in a far corner of the garden near the veranda of the suites. Candlelight cast a glow on the crystal and china service set impeccably with Georgian silver on white linen. They ate under the stars, while a string quartet played quiet background music. They started with white wine – a 1966 Chablis Grand-Cru – and Escargots Chablisienne. Then soup, lobster, a salad, and another bottle of the Grand-Cru. They dined with the very silver that had been buried in the courtyard to escape theft by the Japanese, when they had occupied the hotel in February 1942 after capturing Singapore. Finally, their waiter presented a cheese plate.

"'Enough, enough,' the fair maiden cried," Susan said, sitting back. Court selected a wedge of Brie and a cracker, then waved the platter away. Susan took some fruit when the waiter returned with a tray.

The candles flickered and danced as they had cognac with their coffee and cigarettes.

Court placed his hand on Susan's. As only lovers can, they looked deep into each other's eyes. "I didn't know it could be so good," he said. "Thank you for taking the time off to come here." He handed her a cognac and wound his arm through hers for a toast, his emotions working. *This is what I want, to be with this woman the rest of my life.* A great exultation filled his chest to bursting. War and airplanes were far away.

"To us," he said in a voice suddenly gone hoarse. "May we go on forever." He held the snifter to her lips.

She was silent for an instant, and her mouth twitched. He saw something come up behind her eyes. She blinked it away and tossed her golden hair back with a quick movement of her head. "Yes," she said, "to us."

"Let this go on forever," he prompted.

She looked down, then up into his eyes. "Forever," she whispered. Still looking into each other's eyes, they drank.

Later, they danced near their table to the music of the forties from the orchestra in the Long Bar. She clung to him as she swayed in his arms, willowy and warm, nuzzling and singing near his ear in a low voice.

"The Rockies may tumble, Gibraltar may fall . . ."

"They're only built for a day . . ." he sang back.

"But oh my dear, our love is here to stay . . ." they harmonized, his voice deep and rumbling, hers husky and warm. They had stopped dancing and were swaying in place, his arms strong around her, her knees bending in slow time to the music. "Our love is here to stay," they sang to each other in whispers as the music ended. Arms about each other, they went to her suite.

2115 Hours Local, Tuesday 30 January 1968
Lang Tri Special Forces Camp
Republic of Vietnam

"Quick, in here." Lopez pulled Parker into a mortar pit already manned by two Vietnamese soldiers. They dove into the hole as a four-pound mortar shell exploded where they had been standing. Dirt and rocks pelted them as they hugged the earth. Explosions thundered about them, then marched past the rim of the pit and across the camp. Lopez shouted orders at the Vietnamese and pointed along the directional markers. They nodded and started returning fire with their big 81mm mortar. In a well disciplined ballet, one man would adjust the aim, then pull back while the second rose to drop a shell down the tube. After the *whumpf* of firing, the ballet would begin again. Toby estimated they were firing a round every five seconds. He heard mortars firing from other pits. More rounds, heavy stuff, began coming in from the big NVA guns at Co Roc. Light rifle fire started from the western perimeter. It was now completely dark. The flashes were pronounced and brilliant, the explosions sharp and loud.

Using a red flashlight to identify the ammunition boxes, Lopez grabbed some illumination rounds and handed them to the Vietnamese. "Fire two high-explosive, then one illume, then white phosphorus. Keep that up. Understand?" They nodded and said they did. The first illumination round burst over the camp and swung in its parachute. The eerie yellow light exaggerated shadows, yet outlined the camp well enough for Toby to make out the buildings and the defensive positions just inside the wire.

Firing picked up all along the western perimeter. The brilliant white light of the exploding white phosphorus strobed the battle.

Lopez grabbed the PRC-25 radio. Nicknamed the Prick-25, the FM radio transceiver was the size of two shoeboxes.

102

"Spunky Seven, this is Spunky Eight," Lopez transmitted into the telephone handset attached to the radio. "We've got heavy inbound from two six zero degrees. Counterfire going outbound, but we're gonna need Jacksonville for illumes and HE."

"Roger Eight. Will call them." Toby thought it was Dickson that answered. Bullets began to zing and crack over the pit.

Lopez made a hurried radio check with the outposts. They were all under heavy fire, and reported masses of troops running at them from the direction of the highway and the area west of the camp. Outside the wire, there were screams and yells as Claymores and grenades exploded. In the heavy fog, the loud bangs were swallowed up, leaving no echoes or reverberations.

Overhead, Toby heard a familiar drone. "Hey," he said to Lopez, "there's a Spooky overhead." Lopez handed him the PRC-25. "See if you can raise him." Spooky was the call sign for an AC-47 gunship that was rigged with three side-firing 7.62mm miniguns that spewed out 18,000 rounds per minute. The pilot flew a left-hand orbit and used a gunsight set up on his left window frame. The firing button was attached to his control column.

In the flickering light Toby dialed in the emergency frequency, 60.75 megacycles, and spoke into the handset. "Spooky over Lang Tri, Spooky over Lang Tri, this is Covey Four One, do you read?" His mouth felt dry and he wished he had water with him.

"Rog-ger, Covey Four One, this is Spooky Two Two. What's your position? Don't want a midair, don'cha know. Weren't told you'd be up here." The voice was deep and measured, with a hint of Oklahoma.

"Spooky, Four One, I'm on the ground at the Lang Tri camp. We got real problems here to the west. We need light and guns, you copy?"

"Rog-ger, Covey. We've got some problems up here. We are at five thousand over an overcast. All we see down there are some glows through the clouds. We can give you light,

103

but we can't shoot till we find a break in the clouds."

"Oh shit, Spooky," Toby said in a rush of remembrance, "we've got crossing incoming arty from Jacksonville and incoming from the bad guys at Co Roc. You better get some altitude."

"Uh oh, make that *seven* thousand feet, Covey. We gonna climb a bit, don'cha know. By the way, old son, would you authenticate Kilo Lima for me."

Toby hesitated. "Oh shit, I don't have my code wheel, lost it in the crash. And we're trapped outside the CP, so can't use one from there."

"Ahh, okay," Spooky answered, then spoke as fast as he could. "Tell me ASAP what's left when you bump two bits from a buck-fifty?"

"Buck and a quarter. Now do you believe?"

The voice slowed down. "Roger, old son. We'll give you some flares."

A new and milky-white glow from the 200,000-candlepower flares illuminated the inside of the clouds over their heads, diffusing light onto their area as if they were under fluorescent tubing.

"Perfect," Lopez shouted above the noise. He threw his CAR15 to Toby and pointed west. "Shoot anything that comes through the wire," he said, and went to help the Vietnamese get the mortar rounds off.

Toby peered over the sandbagged rim of the pit. He estimated the wire to be two hundred feet away. He fired three-round bursts at what looked like shapes wriggling and writhing outside the wire. He stopped firing when he realized they were enemy soldiers that had already been hit and were dangling in the wire. He heard a noise behind him and whirled around in time to spray an NVA soldier as he came over the edge of the pit. At the sound of the shots, Lopez grabbed an M16 propped up by one of the Vietnamese mortarmen and ran to Toby's side. They eased up to look over the rim exactly in time to shoot two more enemy soldiers running toward them. There were no more close by.

"Nice going, Captain. That will get you a Cee Eye Bee," Lopez said in an excited voice, then returned to get the mortar firing.

Toby turned back to his position at the rim, wondering what a CIB was. Then he heard sounds that made his stomach leap.

From beyond the wire came the unmistakable squeak and clank of treads and the loud roar of diesel engines revving up. At the same time he heard a cry from one of the forward posts.

"Tanks in the wire. Tanks in the wire."

"Over there," Toby yelled at Lopez. He pointed to the closest perimeter, where two huge shapes were rumbling over the wire and posts as if they weren't there. Flames from the burning outpost buildings reflected red from their sides.

A man in a tiger suit rose from a fighting pit and fired a recoilless rifle at the tank on the left. When it punched a hole in the hull, two tankers boiled out of the top hatch. The man in the tiger suit grabbed an automatic weapon and blew the two men off the tank. The turret of the second tank swung around, its 76mm gun coughed once, and the man in the tiger suit disappeared in the explosion of the shell.

Lopez wrestled a box out from the side of their pit. "Give me a hand," he said. They ripped it open and took out the containers of six LAWS (light antitank weapons). Lopez showed Toby how to take a LAW from its container, arm it, brace it on his shoulder, flip up the sight, aim, and press the rubber trigger mechanism.

The first one Toby tried did not fire. Lopez grabbed one and the same thing happened. The tank pointed its main gun at them and started firing its coaxial 7.62mm. Both Vietnamese mortar-men fell dead, their chests ripped open by the barrage. Lopez pulled Toby down next to him. "Got to try again," he yelled above the uproar. They set up two more LAWS, Lopez double-checked Toby's. At Lopez's command, they both rose and fired. As before, nothing happened with Toby's. But Lopez's LAW fired.

The rocket left the tube with a whoosh, trailing fire and sparks, and struck the tank squarely on the hull. Instead of penetrating, it rocketed skyward into the night fog.

"Heysus Christos," Lopez breathed. "We gotta get outta here. C'mon." He grabbed the radio, dialed in the CP frequency.

"Dickson, Lopez. We're coming in. It's too hot out here."

They peered over the rim, waiting their chance. "My God, look at that," Toby said. A figure clad in a tiger suit got up from a pit and ran up to the side of a tank and exploded a grenade in its treads, causing it to lurch sideways and stop. A companion tank blew the man to shreds with its co-ax machine gun. Neither tank was concentrating on the pit where Toby and Lopez hid. A second figure, carrying a rifle, got up from the shell hole and ran in a crouch toward the command post. Toby could see it was Ryder.

"Now!" Lopez yelled. He grabbed the radio and bolted for the CP, Toby running behind, pain forgotten. Toby looked back as he ran. In the light of the flames, he saw three tanks at each end of the camp, climbing and churning over the wire, surrounded by infantrymen with assault rifles. All the defensive positions had been overrun, and except for a few scattered pops, the defensive firing had stopped.

Lopez screamed into the handset of the radio he carried, "We're coming in, we're coming in." They tore past the 55-gallon-drum concrete stoppers and down the stairs, around the 90-degree grenade-trap turn, and through the thick door that Dickson held open for them. Ryder slid down the steps behind them. When they were through, Dickson slammed the door shut and slid two thick planks into place like giant barn-door bolts.

Toby stood panting and gulping for air. In the room were Dickson, the radio operator, and three Vietnamese Special Forces men. Toby noticed the main generator must be running, because there was still light from a bare bulb hanging from a crossbeam.

"That was Olson out there," Ryder said, bloody and hollow-eyed. "He just blew that tank. " He shook his head and sank down onto one of the cots. "I thought we were dead. We had just made the rounds. All the posts are overrun."

"Who got the tank with the 106?" Lopez asked about the man with the recoilless rifle.

"One of the Viet SF guys. Then he got blown away," Ryder said. The radioman pointed to his Prick-25s. "There isn't a damn one of them on the air anymore. We've lost contact with everybody," he said.

"The tanks are through the wire in two places," Lopez said. He was the ranking NCO, and now in charge. "Captain Parker, you see what Spooky can do – hook this into an outside antenna." He handed him the Prick-25 and showed him how to screw in the lead wire from the outside antenna. "And you," he said to the radioman, "contact Jacksonville. Find out why they haven't been shooting. Tell them to put the arty on Position Niner."

"Niner? That's us. You want it on top of us?" the radioman said, eyes wide.

"You got a better idea?" Lopez said. "This is a strong, deep bunker. We can take a direct hit from anything except a five-hundred-pound bomb. Get talking." The man bent to his task.

Before Toby could call Spooky, the lights went out. In seconds the men had flashlights on and lit a Coleman lantern. Toby picked the handset.

"Spooky, Covey Four One. How do you read?" he transmitted.

"About Three By, Covey. There is a solid undercast now, can't see a thing down there. Not even sure we're kicking the flares out over the right spot. Understand, we can't see, so we can't shoot. In about thirty minutes we got to RTB for fuel. We can get a standby up here, but the weather's bad-bad and forecast to remain that way for a couple days. You copy?"

"Roger, Spooky, copy."

"Sorry 'bout that, old son. But them's the cards tonight. We'll stick around long as we can so at least you'll have someone to talk to. Spooky listening out." Toby put the handset down.

The radioman reached Jacksonville, the Marine artillery unit at Khe Sanh.

"Spunky, Jacksonville. We got problems here. We're under heavy attack. We're taking rounds from a couple of NVA 152s on Co Roc."

Lopez grabbed the microphone. "Listen," he said. "We've got tanks on top of us RIGHT NOW. We need fire support. Put it on Position Nine."

There was a pause while the man at Jacksonville looked up from his code table. "Spunky, you must be in big trouble. Position niner is right on your location."

Twelve long minutes later the big shells from the Marine artillery at Khe Sanh screamed into the overrun Lang Tri compound. There were three barrages, each two minutes long, then silence. The men inside the bunker listened. There was no activity outside.

Lopez spoke on the radio. "Okay, Jacksonville, it's quiet. We're going out for a look-see."

"Come on," he said to Dickson, "take the three Viets and cover me outside the door. Ryder, you take care of Captain Parker here." Dickson spoke a few words to the Vietnamese Special Forces men. They followed him out the door with Lopez, who still carried the radio. In seconds Lopez was transmitting back.

"It's a shambles out here. Nothing left standing. I'm checking the forward positions." There was silence for five minutes, then a boom followed by heavy rifle fire.

"I'm hauling ass. Everything's occupied by the NVA. Get that door ready. They're coming out of the ground, and the tanks are moving again." Lopez was breathing hard and speaking as he ran.

"We're in deep shit," Lopez yelled when he came in the door. Dickson fired a long burst and came in behind him with the two of the Vietnamese supporting the third. They slammed and bolted the door. The Vietnamese lowered their wounded man to a cot and tended to a fragment wound in his left thigh.

Lopez got on the radio to Jacksonville. "We can maybe hold out until morning, but once it's daylight and those guys see where the entrance to this bunker is, they'll just keep blasting and open us up like a sardine can. We got to have a relief force in here by first light or we're dead meat."

"Spunky, Jacksonville. You bet, partner. We got a bunch of Marines here that are ready to whip some NVA ass."

"Hey, great, Jack," Lopez said. "Spunky listening out." He motioned the men around the map table.

"Here's the way it is," he said, pointing to an overlay of the camp. "The wire is down on the north and west walls, all the buildings are blown away, and the NVA are in just about every pit out there. Their tanks have withdrawn to God knows where, but you know they'll be back. The way I see it, we have two choices. We can chance an ex-fil out of here tonight and try to make it up to the Khe Sanh camp, or we can wait for the Marine reinforcements tomorrow and fight our way out."

"What's our chances of making it out tonight?" Dickson asked.

"Dog shit," Ryder said. "We'd have to slip out through the east wire, then through the fucking jungle and through the NVA lines at night, then hope the jarhead listening posts don't blow us away."

"Well said," Lopez said. "Now let's see if we can get through to Nha Trang and give 'em a sitrep."

He tried the HF on batteries without luck. "I think the antenna is down." He looked at Toby. "How about you raise Spooky and have them relay a message to Green House Six at Nha Trang?"

"Who is Green House Six?" Toby asked.

"Colonel Bull Dall," Lopez said. "He's the commander of the Fifth Special Forces Group."

Toby tried the Prick-25 wired into the external antenna.

There was no answer. He screwed the regular blade-antenna back on and stuck it up an airshaft. This time he got an answer.

"Roger, Covey Four One. Spooky Two Seven here. Read you three by three. We replaced Two Two. We still can't see to shoot, but we've got enough gas to orbit your location until daylight."

"Spooky, we need you to contact Green House Six at Nha Trang and relay the Spunky sitrep. Our HF is out," Toby said.

"Can do, Covey. Stand by." After five minutes Spooky called back. "Covey, Spooky. We've patched you direct to Green House. Begin your transmission."

Lopez took the handset and gave the details to Green House, and added that the Marine relief would be in at first light. "You're covered, Spunky," Green House Six replied. "Just hold out until morning. You copy?"

"Roger Green House, nice to know the wheels are concerned," Lopez said.

"Nothing's too good for our boys in the field. Green House listening out."

An hour later the explosion knocked down every man in the bunker and blew Toby off the cot. The overpressure snuffed out the Coleman lantern. Acrid smoke and dust stung their nostrils. Toby felt as if he had been hit on both ears with cupped hands.

"What in hell was that?" someone moaned.

"Light the fucking lantern," Lopez commanded. There was a sput of matches. The lantern revealed the Vietnamese and American men in various stages of shock and disarray, getting up from the ground and brushing themselves off, their eyes vacant and shocked. Dirt streamed from the roof, then stopped.

"That was no ordinary blast," Ryder said. "That was a highpower job put together with a dud Mark Eighty-One and C-4 as the detonator." The Mark 81 was an American 250lb bomb that had failed to explode when it was dropped from an airplane. As with all the duds, the NVA had sawed out the explosives and wired a detonator into it.

"How the hell do you know that?" Dickson asked.

"Because, dickhead, I smell the C-4 and I know 250 pounds of shit going off when I hear and feel it." Ryder, cross-trained into demolitions, examined the door to the bunker. "It's holding, but maybe one more of those and it might let go." He took the lantern to look overhead and check the beams. "We've got eight feet of concrete and dirt up there. Willoughby built a helluva CP, we're in good shape. For a while anyhow." Willoughby was the former team commander. Ryder crossed to check the ventilation shafts. They went out at angles with two U-traps in each to keep out rainwater and, most important, grenades.

They involuntarily flinched as two smaller explosions sounded outside the door. Dirt trickled down from the ceiling. "Grenades," Ryder said. "They're too small to do any damage to us."

Lopez took a long pull of water from a canteen. "Drink up, guys, it's going to be a long night."

"Or a short one if they work up another Mark Eighty-One," Dickson said. The three Vietnamese sat quietly in the corner, eyes flashing, clutching their rifles. They had bandaged the wounded man's leg.

Two loud bangs sounded from the ventilator shafts. The concussion caused Toby to clasp his hands to his ears. Acrid smoke poured into the room. Then two pops came from each shaft, followed by a hissing noise.

"GAS, GAS," Ryder screamed. "*Hoi, hoi,*" he yelled to the Vietnamese, and pinched his nose in pantomime.

A thick white smoke began to flow from the shaft vents. Dickson and Lopez ran to the supply room, ripped open a carton, and threw gas masks out into the main room. Coughing, eyes streaming, Toby held one to his face, but it was too late for him, and for the Vietnamese. All four started vomiting into whatever rags and containers were handy. Toby used the poncho liner thrown over his cot. They couldn't help themselves. The more they vomited and

111

gasped, the more tear gas with vomit kicker they inhaled. Toby felt convulsed and helpless. The spasms were like bands of fire across his stomach, and his throat felt like he had drunk lye.

Dickson and Ryder frantically picked up every bit of cloth they could find and stuffed it into the vents, stopping the gas flow. Toby and the Vietnamese rinsed out cloths with canteen water and bathed their eyes and mouths, then they flapped wet towels in the air to absorb the remaining gas.

Lopez looked at his watch. "With those vents closed, we haven't much air in here. Maybe only ten, twelve hours."

"Maybe we'd better call in those Marines from Khe Sanh. Their CO said he'd send two rifle companies," Dickson suggested.

Ryder snorted. "We'd never hear the last of it. Since when do we need the Marines to save our asses?"

"We don't need them yet. If we can't get Spooky to shoot by daylight, then I'll call," Lopez said.

There were two more grenade explosions at the door, then silence.

"Let's fix things up," Lopez said. "Get every weapon, clean 'em, check the ammo, police up this place so there's no paper scraps to catch on fire, see what else we have to barricade the door in case they do have that second Mark Eighty-one. Inventory the supply room."

The men busied themselves at the tasks. They cleaned up the paper, inventoried the guns and grenades, and set about cleaning their weapons and the ammunition. Toby took several boxes of 5.62 cartridges and started filling M16 20-round magazines. He had filled four when Ryder noticed what he was doing.

"How many rounds did you put in each magazine, Captain?" he asked.

"Twenty. Why?"

"These magazines have weak springs. Any more than eighteen and they jam. Would you mind taking two out of each one?"

112

Toby did as he was told until the magazines were heavy and oiled with cartridges. In the supply room, the Vietnamese started scraping dirt from the bare wall with their trenching tools and filling sandbags and empty ammo boxes, which they passed to the others, who placed them against the main door.

Toby eyed the cavity in the dirt wall as the men scraped. "How about an escape tunnel?" he asked. No one answered. The men filled every sack they could find and sat back. The air was heavy and damp. Dickson pulled out a pack of Camels and offered them around. "No smoking," Lopez said. He picked up the radio handset.

"Spooky, Spunky here."

"Hi, down there. This is Spooky, on station for the nation."

"Yeah. Can you shoot yet?"

"Negative, Spunky. Solid undercast. We don't even see a glow anymore. Sorry, guys."

Lopez signed off.

Suddenly the whole bunker vibrated and groaned. Streamers of fine dirt gushed from the ceiling.

"What in hell is that?" Dickson yelled, springing to his feet.

"Oh Christ," Ryder said, looking up, his lips drawn back. "They got the tanks up there on top of us."

"Now will you call the goddamn Marines?" Dickson cried.

"You bet your ass," Lopez said. "Now you guys start that tunnel." As Ryder scrambled to organize diggers and packers among the Americans and Vietnamese, Lopez picked up the microphone.

"Jacksonville, Jacksonville, this is Spunky. We got bad problems, you copy?"

"Spunky, Jack here. Go."

"We're trapped in the bunker and they've got tanks making like can openers. We only have ten, twelve hours of air. We need your troops, man. Fast. You copy?"

"Spunky, Jack. Good copy. We got some boys ready

113

right now. Stand by one while I get the details. Jack out."

Lopez looked at his new tunnel rats, frantically digging at the wall, grinned, and made an okay sign with his thumb and forefinger.

In five minutes Jacksonville called back, his voice hollow and slow.

"Go ahead," Lopez told him.

"Cougar says negative relief. Copy?"

"Negative relief!" Lopez exploded. "What the fuck do you mean, negative relief?" He clutched the handset. "Who the hell is Cougar?" he muttered as he fumbled through a three-ring binder. He found the communication section of the emergency ops plan worked out with Colonel Lownds, the commander of the 26th Marine Regiment at Khe Sanh. The diggers and packers stopped and listened, sweat gleaming on their bodies in the lantern light. Lopez read where Cougar was the commander of III MAF, the Marine Amphibious Force at Da Nang. He was a lieutenant general.

There was a long pause. An anguished voice came over the loudspeaker. "Aw Gawd, like I said, negative relief. We . . . we aren't allowed to launch. Cougar says we can't go." He stopped transmitting. He clicked on his transmitter, started to say something, then clicked off.

Lopez switched to the Spooky gunship frequency.

"Spooky, I need a patch to Green House Six," he said.

"Coming up, Spunky."

After a moment Green House was on the line.

"Roger, Green House," Lopez said, "we got a real problem here." He outlined their air and tank situation. "If we're not out of here by ten tomorrow, we're dead meat."

"Spunky, Green House Six. Here is the situation. The weather is full down and forecast to remain so for twenty-four hours. Further, we have been denied air assets. Cougar assets are to handle the situation. Right now this is his show." Bull Dall's voice was heavy.

"His show!" Lopez shouted into the microphone. "God almighty, we've got Americans dying here. Does COMUSMACV know about this?"

114

"Affirmative. I've been on the horn to him all day and half the night." The voice of Green House vibrated with anger. "Hang on, I'm going down . . ." The bunker quivered under a muffled explosion and the radio went dead. Lopez tried another radio. No answer.

"They got the antenna," he said. There was momentary silence in the bunker, then, with muffled curses the diggers went back to work. Toby helped pass the dirt out to the Vietnamese, who packed it by the door. Lopez drummed his fingers on the radio table, then started passing sandbags.

Overhead, two tanks crisscrossed the bunker, working on the corners, stopping and spinning on a tread, diesels roaring, slowly grinding the bunker down.

6

1430 Hours Local, Tuesday 30 January 1968
Aboard Air Force One En Route to
Bergstrom AFB Austin, Texas

"How many times do I have to tell you that I want diet root beer on this fucking aircraft at all times?" The big man's voice boomed across the table at the man in the blue uniform standing at rigid attention. "You hear me, Sergeant? I want an order sent out to all Air Force Bases: *Stock root beer*."

"Yes, sir," the staff sergeant said to Lyndon Baines Johnson, the thirty-sixth President of the United States. He took the President's empty root beer bottle and turned for the galley.

As soon as he was gone, the President pressed a buzzer and leaned over to speak into an intercom. "Since the Air Force doesn't see fit to keep its Commander in Chief in root beer, bring me scotch and fresh soda."

The President sat at a kidney-shaped desk aboard Air Force One. The plane was at 40,000 feet en route from Andrews AFB outside of Washington, D.C., to Bergstrom AFB, Austin, Texas. The call sign, Air Force One, was used for any USAF aircraft the President happened to be aboard. Today he was aboard a USAF C-137, a VIP version of the Boeing 707, operated by the Military Airlift Command's 89th Military Airlift Wing at Andrews. His big desk fronted a large table surrounded by airliner seats. Below the phone

116

bank that put the President instantly in touch with the WHCA (White House Communications Agency) was a switch that could raise or lower the desk, not the chair, to suit the President's whims. The chair he sat on behind the desk was as big as a throne.

Across from the President sat his press secretary, four reporters from the press pool, and USAF Major General Albert G. "Whitey" Whisenand. It was supposed to be an informal get-together initiated by the President. Each man had a drink in front of him or in his hand.

General Whitey Whisenand was in his mid-fifties, slightly portly, and had graying, almost white hair. He had a cherubic face that looked as if he had just removed his jet pilot's oxygen mask. That appearance was due to burn scars he had received from an F-80 crash in the Korean war in the early nineteen-fifties.

A male steward entered and poured the President a scotch, then refreshed the other drinks. The Press Secretary declined with a wave. Whitey Whisenand quietly held a hand over his glass.

Whitey currently held a position on the National Security Council as special assistant to the President for Air Power. While the title specifically meant air power in SEA (Southeast Asia, the term used to denote Thailand, Cambodia, Laos, and North and South Vietnam), the job description of the position was not so specific. The duties were vague and unspecified in writing by LBJ. Yet there had been some activity. Several times the President had dispatched General Whisenand to MACV in Saigon to get answers to questions such as "Why is the U.S. suffering so many airplane losses over Hanoi?" and "Is the U.S. winning or losing the war?" Beyond the two trips there had been little else for General Whisenand to do, outside of some studies and his daily monitoring and reporting the aircraft and pilot losses in the skies over Hanoi. Unfortunately the only input from Whisenand to the President as a result of his trips to Vietnam had been what the President had not wanted to hear.

After his first trip, Whisenand had said, "Sir, our extraordinary losses over Hanoi are because the civilians, led by you and Secretary of Defense McNamara – civilians who revile the military, I might add – are picking inconsequential targets and forcing bad tactics, while constraining the airmen to outrageous rules of engagement."

After his second trip Whisenand had said, "We are not winning the war simply because we have not declared war and we have no declared goals. As a result the American people do not know why we are there. They, not to mention your political opponents, do not back you. Meanwhile the members of the American press are capitalizing on the situation and are selling stories and TV time at an unprecedented rate, thereby compounding the predicament. What it adds up to is, without clear-cut goals, our military is – although it doesn't know it – at a loss as to how to proceed."

LBJ had reacted to Whisenand's straightforwardness by once calling him an old fart; another time by yelling he was a pissant that he kept around just to see how long he could keep from stepping on him. But for some capricious reason of his own, LBJ had indeed kept Whitey Whisenand around, while others, including his Secretary of Defense, Robert Strange McNamara, were being let go. Or quitting because of the President's apparent unwinnable approach to the war in Vietnam.

Whitey had spent long hours talking to his wife, Sal, about whether or not he should resign from the Air Force he had served so long. He had felt for some time that he was more a token military representative to LBJ's staff than a fully participating NSC member whose words had weight when it came to decisions regarding the prosecution of the Vietnam war.

"Maybe he's just using me," Whitey had said to her. "Lord knows he doesn't ask the Joint Chiefs or the Chairman for advice. Maybe he keeps me merely to show he does have a military advisor actually positioned within the White House."

"My dear, if you resign," Sal had said, "it will just give the critics and the press more grist. If you stay, you are the buffer between the White House and the Department of Defense. You have some influence on the man. Look at the trip he made to Vietnam last December. It was at your urging he do it to buck up sagging morale. To let the troops know that Washington really cared." After careful thought, Whitey had stayed on.

He was on this trip because the President had asked him to come with him to the LBJ ranch outside of Austin, Texas. Lady Bird was already there preparing a big Texas feast for local politicians and heavy campaign contributors.

Now Major General Albert G. "Whitey" Whisenand listened to the President of the United States hold forth to the members of the press pool.

"Look around the world," he was saying. "Khrushchev's gone. Macmillan's gone. Adenauer's gone. Segni's gone. Nehru's gone. Who's left – de Gaulle?" Johnson sneered when he said the French president's name.

LBJ picked up his glass, drained half, and held it aloft. "Hah," he bellowed, "I am the king." He lowered the glass and looked around with slitted eyes at the reporters. "Remember this, anything I say with a drink in my hand or after nine at night is not to be repeated."

Later, before landing at Austin, the press secretary spoke to the reporters. "Gentlemen, this was a social gathering, you were not on board as news reporters. You are not to quote the President of the United States today."

When Air Force One bobbed to a stop exactly on time at Bergstrom, an entourage of automobiles swept up to the air stairs. Sandwiched in the middle between Secret Service station wagons was Johnson's favorite, a white Cadillac convertible. Hard-eyed Secret Servicemen scanned all directions.

"See you at the ranch," LBJ breezily said to Whitey, and swept off the flight line, frantically followed by his protection and the military officer with the "football," the briefcase containing the atomic-weapons release codes.

The USAF flight crew buttoned up the big jet. Three Andrews air policemen and their dogs stepped from the airplane to join the Bergstrom SPs to set up the guard exactly in accordance with AF Reg 207-13.

A tall USAF colonel stepped up to Whitey and saluted. "General Whisenand, I'm on my way to the ranch, may I offer you a ride?" Whitey recognized him as Ralph Albertazzie, the pilot of Air Force One. He accepted, and twenty minutes later they were on the road. Albertazzie drove an Air Force staff car from the Bergstrom motor pool.

"I'm invited," the colonel was saying, "but I don't know why. The President has his ways."

On the way out, Albertazzie told the story of an Air Force colonel named Jim Cross who had once run the Military Office in the White House. The duties of the office ran from arranging covert Presidential trips, to international security arrangements; from scheduling military medical facilities and doctors to the maintenance of Camp David, and of course the operation of the air fleet based at Andrews Air Force Base.

"The President is big on showers," Albertazzie said, "and the one at his ranch didn't have enough pressure. LBJ badgered the Military Office to put in new water lines and a pump – charged to DoD, of course. When the day came to use it, he stripped, got in, but jumped right out and began hollering for Jim, who was there in full uniform as his aide. 'Cross, you son of a bitch,' he hollered out the window. 'Get up here.' Cross walked in and LBJ said, 'You lying bastard, you said it was all set. It doesn't work.' So Cross went into the shower and turned the handle, only to be hit with heavy spray from all sides. He turned it off and stood there in full uniform, soaking wet. LBJ, stark naked, snarled, 'Well, the son of a bitch didn't work for *me*.'"

That night a Texas cowboy band played Western toe-tappers, while expensively garbed men and women in hand-tooled boots and form-fitting cowboy regalia ate from paper plates and drank from plastic cups under a huge

Texas moon. Whitey estimated over 200 people were present. The noise was absorbed by the vast expanse of the ranch. Outside the perimeter he noticed guards and patrol cars. In the sky, helicopters with searchlights discreetly bobbed along the horizon. LBJ had spoken to Whitey only once, when he had detached himself from a crowd of admirers. "Come see me in the fireplace room around midnight," LBJ had said in a surly voice.

At midnight Whitey met with the President in front of a huge stone fireplace. Flames leaped from six-foot logs, yet the room was cooled by air conditioning. Outside of a small lamp by liquor bottles on a credenza, the fireplace provided the only light in the room.

"Come in, come in," LBJ bellowed from the sofa. On the table was a drink and a half-eaten bag of potato chips. He was watching a late news broadcast. On the screen was Democratic Senator J. William Fulbright from Arkansas, Chairman of the Senate Foreign Relations Committee. "These men," Johnson said in disgust as he got up and snapped the sound off, "these knee-jerk liberal crackpots." He faced Whitey and shook a finger at him. "The Russians play a big role in this, you know. They're in constant touch with these antiwar Senators. They eat lunch together and go to parties at the Russian Embassy."

Whitey wondered whether LBJ really meant this absurdity, or if he was saying it just to ventilate, or maybe for some ambiguous reason to shock him. The President continued.

"The Russians think up things for the Senators to say. I often know before they do what their speeches are going to say."

Embarrassed, Whitey stared at the fire. This wasn't for shock or humor, this was raw paranoia. The President was wound up, wound up much too tightly.

"Here is what I believe," the big man continued. "I honestly and truly believe that if we don't assert ourselves, and if the Chinese communists and the Soviet Union take Laos, Vietnam, Cambodia, it seriously endangers India,

121

Pakistan, and the whole Pacific world. Then we – the whole United States – will really be up for grabs. We're the richest nation in the world, and everybody wants what we've got. And the minute we look soft, the would-be aggressors will go wild. We'll lose all of Asia, then Europe, and then we'll be a rich little island all by ourselves. That means World War Three." He shook his head, a lion bothered by gnats. "And when that comes to pass I'd sure hate to depend on the Galbraiths and that Harvard crowd to protect my property."

He walked to the credenza and poured another scotch. Whitey accepted a red wine that LBJ carefully poured for him. It was dry and velvety. The bottle had not been open more than a few hours, he decided.

"Well, what do you think?" LBJ said in a loud voice.

"Excellent wine, sir."

"Goddammit, that's not what I meant. What do you think of my theory?

Whitey looked thoughtful. "I'm not as certain as you are that our congressmen are controlled by anything other than a desire to do what they think is best." He stopped short of saying what he thought a congressman thought best – which was, he was sure, re-election and whatever it took to garner votes.

"That's not saying anything at all," LBJ scoffed. "Now, here, I want you to read something that came in tonight." He pressed a button and his Marine military aide entered with a briefcase. LBJ took it and waved him away. The man saluted, did a clicking about-face on the inlaid stone, and departed. The president took a sheaf of papers from a red notebook in the case and handed several to Whitey. "Read these," he said. "What do they mean? Here I am, trying to set up peace talks with Ho, and I get messages like these."

Whitey read the top sheet.

```
= = = = = = = = = = = = = = = = = = = = = = = = = = = =
```
FROM: COMUSMACV
TO: ALL COMMANDERS
QQQQ
SECRET NOFORN
SUBJ: OPERATION HOBBY HORSE (U)

1. (S/NF) GOV'T SOUTH VIETNAM HAS ANNOUNCED THAT
   A 36 HOUR TET CEASEFIRE WILL BE
   OBSERVED DURING THE PERIOD MONDAY 291800H TO
   WEDNESDAY 310600H JAN. THE US POSITION FOR TET
   HAS NOT BEEN FORMALLY DECLARED AT THIS TIME.

2. (S/NF) OPERATION HOBBY HORSE, OUTLINED HEREIN,
   WILL BE IMPLEMENTED ON RECEIPT OF THIS MESSAGE
   TO MAXIMIZE OUR TACTICAL POTENTIAL. HOBBY HORSE
   WILL BE EXECUTED IN TWO PHASES:

A. (S/NF) PHASE ONE. EFFECTIVE IMMEDIATELY,
   COMMANDERS WILL INITIATE A COMPREHENSIVE AND
   INTENSIVE INTELLIGENCE COLLECTION EFFORT TO
   IDENTIFY AND PINPOINT ENEMY TROOP LOCATIONS,
   BASES, FACILITIES, AND LINES OF
   COMMUNICATIONS. THIS INTELLIGENCE COLLECTION
   EFFORT IS STRESSED DURING THE TET CEASEFIRE.
   THIS HQ WILL PROVIDE, BY SEPARATE MESSAGE,
   SPECIFIC INSTRUCTIONS TASKING AIR AND GROUND
   RECONNAISSANCE. ALL COMMANDERS WILL PREPARE
   DETAILED ATTACK AND FIRE PLANS FOR ALL WEAPONS
   SYSTEMS INCLUDING ARTY, NGF, TACAIR, AND B-52
   ARC LIGHT WHICH WILL BE EXECUTED DURING PHASE
   TWO, HOBBY HORSE.

B. (S/NF) PHASE TWO. IT IS ANTICIPATED ENEMY
   ALERTNESS WILL REACH A PEAK IMMEDIATELY
   FOLLOWING CEASEFIRE PERIOD. COMMANDERS
   WILL DETERMINE THE MOST ADVANTAGEOUS TIME
   SUBSEQUENT TO CEASEFIRE TO STRIKE THE ENEMY
   WHEN HE IS MOST VULNERABLE AND LEAST EXPECTING
   AN ATTACK. IT IS ASSUMED THESE OPPORTUNITIES
   WILL VARY BY AREA AND TARGET. THE DISCRETION
   AND JUDGMENT OF THE RESPONSIBLE COMMANDER WILL
   PREVAIL IN ALL INSTANCES.

3. (S/NF) IN THE PAST, FREE WORLD FORCES HAVE
   DERIVED NO DISCERNIBLE MILITARY ADVANTAGES

FROM HOLIDAY CEASEFIRES. IT IS ESSENTIAL,
THEREFORE, THAT OUR INTELLIGENCE CAPABILITIES
BE EMPLOYED TO THE LIMIT OF THE IMPOSED
CEASEFIRE CONSTRAINTS DURING THE TRUCE PERIOD;
AND THAT THE FULL WEIGHT OF OUR FIREPOWER AND
MANEUVER MOBILITY BE APPLIED WITH PRECISION,
MASS, AND PREEMPTIVE SUDDENNESS FOLLOWING
THE CEASEFIRE.

4. (S)TO BE FULLY EFFECTIVE, HOBBY HORSE PLANNING
    MUST BE CLOSELY COORDINATED WITH FRIENDLY
    FORCES.

5. (U) ACTION ADDRESSEES ACKNOWLEDGE BY MSG OR
    TELEPHONE MACV 2927 OR EAC 381.

= =

The second sheet was a summary of Disums (Daily Intelligence Summaries) with pertinent points extracted.

On 5 Jan 68 troops of the US 4th Infantry
Division captured a detailed plan titled "Urgent
Combat Order Number One" for an attack on Pleiku
province to begin before the Tet holidays. On
10 Jan, Commander II Field Force, General Fred
Weyand, put together pieces of intelligence
to conclude the VC in the III Corps Tactical
Zone were moving from border sanctuaries toward
population centers including Saigon. On 15 Jan
men of the 4th Division detected movement from
beyond the Cambodian border of two NVA regiments
toward the Vietnamese border. On 18 Jan ARVN
security troops in Qui Nhon captured eleven VC, a
tape recorder, and two tapes exhorting the people
and armed forces to go over to the side of the
attacking Viet Cong. The VC admitted they were
to be played during the attack on Qui Nhon and
other cities during the Tet holidays.

The next sheet contained two classified messages from
General Westmoreland, COMUSMACV, to the U.S. Army
Chief of Staff:

124

```
= = = = = = = = = = = = = = = = = = = = = = = = = = = = = = =
```
20 JAN 68

SECRET, NO FORN

TO: CHIEF OF STAFF, US ARMY

1. (S/NF) THE ENEMY IS PRESENTLY DEVELOPING A
    THREATENING POSTURE IN SEVERAL AREAS IN ORDER
    TO SEEK VICTORIES ESSENTIAL TO ACHIEVING
    PRESTIGE AND BARGAINING POWER. HE MAY EXERCISE
    HIS INITIATIVES PRIOR TO, DURING, OR AFTER TET.

2. (S/NF) ACCORDINGLY, UPON MY REQUEST PRESIDENT
    THIEU HAS REDUCED TET CEASEFIRE FROM
    FORTY-EIGHT TO THIRTY-SIX HOURS, AND WILL
    MAINTAIN FIFTY PERCENT OF ARVN TROOPS ON
    ALERT.

SIGNED WESTMORELAND/COMUSMACV
```
= = = = = = = = = = = = = = = = = = = = = = = = = = = = = = =
```
22 JAN 68

SECRET

TO: CHIEF OF STAFF, US ARMY

1. (S) I THINK THE ENEMY'S PLANS CONCERN A MAJOR
    EFFORT TO WIN A SPECTACULAR
    BATTLEFIELD SUCCESS ON THE EVE OF THE TET
    FESTIVAL NEXT MONDAY.

SIGNED WESTMORELAND/COMUSMACV
```
= = = = = = = = = = = = = = = = = = = = = = = = = = = = = = =
```

Tet was the Vietnamese name for the traditional holiday
to celebrate the lunar new year. It was like combining
Christmas and New Year's into one big celebration.

Whitey looked up. He knew all about these messages.
He was one of the few who had insisted they be in the
President's hands.

"Remember last year," Whitey said. "During the truce
Ho increased supplies down the Trail to an unprecedented
level. And when the Pope urged Thieu to grant a thirty-
six-hour extension of the Tet holiday truce, Thieu did,
and the Viet Cong attacked the 25th Division in force."
He stood up. "I think what these mean is that our
commanders are concerned that a major attack by VC
and NVA troops is imminent. But this time I don't

think we have any Battle-of-the-Bulge or Red-Chinese-attack-from-Manchuria syndrome, as we did in World War Two and Korea. Both attacks were a surprise and initially successful because both were clear intelligence failures on our part; no one predicted or foresaw those events, based on clear and current intelligence at the time. Now we have reasonable intelligence that suggests a major attack during the Tet truce period. I wish General Westmoreland had been able to get President Thieu's permission to cancel the entire truce period and put all his troops on alert."

"Well, now, which is it?" the President said. "Do they just want to take and hold land in preparation for the Paris peace talks that are due entirely to my initiative? Or is it a prelude to a sneak attack?" He looked at the fire for a few moments, then spoke again. "No, they wouldn't make any sneak attack. Ho knows I'm trying to talk to him. He wouldn't do that. He's a reasonable man, a right-thinking man. He wants the same thing for his people I do – peace and prosperity."

Although LBJ hoped the contacts from North Vietnam were real, an NSC report said there was very little of substance from the Swiss intermediaries who had suggested that Ho Chi Minh might want to send representatives to Paris to meet with the Americans. Backroom opinion had it that LBJ wanted a dialogue with the North Vietnamese communist leader so much that he was making reality out of his hopes. Ho Chi Minh, whose other names were Nguyen Ai Quoc and Nguyen Tat Thanh, had been a founding member of the French communist party in 1920. He had been out of Vietnam for decades working as a Soviet-trained Comintern agent in China, Hong Kong, and Indonesia. Emulating Stalin to gain power in Vietnam, he had murdered thousands of *kulaks* – land-lords – in 1955. When a revolt over the murders had broken out in his own province, he had had 6,000 peasants killed or imprisoned. Currently, he had over 4,000 government officials and local village authorities in the South assassinated each year. His goal was an Indochina communist party wherein he ruled North and South Vietnam, Cambodia, and Laos.

"Mister President, Ho is capable of anything. He may well attack during Tet."

"Goddammit, why do you say that? There you go, all doom and gloom. You and those other generals have got to see the bright side of life someday."

"Sir, all those messages in your file point to such an attack. May I?" He pointed to the red notebook. When LBJ nodded, he picked it up, thumbed through, and handed the book to the President, opened to the excerpted TWX. "This one proves," Whitey said, "that even Thieu is now convinced of such an attack."

= =
SECRET 30 JAN 68
1. (C/NF) THE GOV'T OF VIETNAM HAS CANCELED THE
    36 HOUR CEASEFIRE FOR TET.
    ACCORDINGLY, THE TET CEASEFIRE FOR US FORCES
    IS HEREBY CANCELED.
2. (C) EFFECTIVE IMMEDIATELY ALL FORCES WILL
    RESUME INTENSIFIED OPERATIONS, AND TROOPS
    WILL BE PLACED ON MAXIMUM ALERT WITH
    PARTICULAR ATTENTION TO THE DEFENSE OF
    HEADQUARTERS COMPLEXES, LOGISTICAL
    INSTALLATIONS, AIRFIELDS, POPULATION
    CENTERS, AND BILLETS. ALL UNITS WILL BE
    PARTICULARLY ALERT TO DECEPTION MEASURES BY
    THE ENEMY AND BE POISED TO AGGRESSIVELY PURSUE
    AND DESTROY ANY ENEMY FORCE WHICH ATTACKS.
3. (U) ACTION ADDRESSEES ACKNOWLEDGE BY MSG OR
    TELEPHONE MACV 2927 OREAC 381.
= =

"Yes, yes, I saw that. I think maybe it's foolish."

"Sir, just last month the Agency reported there would be an all-out attack on or before Tet." By the Agency, Whitey meant the Central Intelligence Agency.

"Yes, yes, I know that too. But one of their own men said the report was a lot of bullshit."

The problem was, Whitey knew exactly about that dichotomy. In December a group of CIA operatives in a small office in downtown Saigon had turned in a field report stating that the war had reached a turning point and that under Giap there would be a major offensive on or before Tet. It even went on to say that, over his objections, Giap had to be ordered by Ho Chi Minh to commence planning and to implement the attack. The report had gone up the chain to the DCI, Director Richard Helms, who had turned it over to his Vietnam-watcher, a specialist named George Carver. Carver's memo saying the report wasn't accurate had permeated the White House staff. End result, there could be no Tet attack, even the CIA said so.

"You must not be so pessimistic," the President said. "Ho is a reasonable man. He would not attack during a religious holiday. Too much to lose. I think he wants to negotiate."

"Sir, with all respect, I do not believe he is seriously considering any negotiations with the United States until he sees the results of the presidential election this fall."

The President's face tightened, his eyes took on a wounded look. He fell into a chair and stared into the fire.

"Don't you ever let go? One of these days . . ." He took a deep swallow of his drink. "How many Americans do we have in that Godforsaken country now?" He turned the glass of scotch in his hands. The flames made dancing shadows on the stone floor. The possibility of a Tet attack was forgotten.

Whitey Whisenand knew the figures. "We have 485,000 in-country, sir. And 17,600 combat deaths." As he spoke, Whitey reached into his briefcase and extracted a small poster board with a black border and grease-pencil figures. He read the headings and figures for aircrews, that he updated daily, to the Commander in Chief of the United States Armed Forces.

Aircrew			
	MIA/KIA	POW	Aircraft
USAF	387	199	855
USN	221	127	363
USMC	71	14	201
USA	156	56	444 (Helios)
TOTAL	835	396	1863

"You and your damned blackboard," the President said. His eyes flashed. "I thought you said we were winning the war. You said that after your last trip."

General Whisenand stood next to the mantel. "I said we *could* win, sir," he said gently.

The President straightened up and looked at him from under furled brows. "Didn't you set up some operations in Laos to stop supplies coming down that goddamn Trail? Didn't I say go ahead on that a few months back? What came of that? What are the figures?"

"Sir, Air Force and Navy planes have stopped about eighty percent of the daylight traffic coming through the passes."

"What about traffic at night?" the President asked.

"Sir, in a short time we will be implementing increased night strikes on the Trail, and soon after we will have a night fast-FAC program using F-4 fighters that will use strike planes on the supply trucks."

"What's a FACK?"

"FAC is the term we use for a Forward Air Controller, a man airborne in an airplane who searches for targets, then calls in strike aircraft to destroy them. They fly slow or fast planes. We want to use FACs to stop the traffic at night."

Commander, 7th Air Force, had sent Whitey a coded backchannel TWX outlining the progress of the night FAC program they both thought necessary. To his surprise he

129

read that a Major Courtland EdM. Bannister was to head the unit. Court Bannister, and his half-brother, Shawn, were like nephews to him because Sam Bannister was his cousin.

"Night strikes will be tricky," Whitey continued, "but I think we can do it." He didn't think it wise to tell the President that the Chief of Staff of the Air Force was less than enthusiastic about the fast FAC program in the daytime, much less at night.

"Plug that Trail and I'll win the war," the President said.

"Sir, allow us to take out all the supplies and supply ships and trucks and railroads before they hit the Trail and you'll *maybe* win the war."

"Goddammit, Whisenand, how many times do I have to tell you? I don't want to start World War Three. I just want to keep those commie bastards out of South Vietnam. You and those generals over in that five-sided craphouse are all alike. You don't do what I want you to do. You never listen to me, so I have to put the screws to you." He waved his drink, animated once more with a tangible enemy at hand. "That Kennedy general," LBJ said, "that Max Taylor. He had it right. You read his book? That *Trumpet* book? He had it right. He said the Joint Chiefs of Staff belong to the Administration in power and are expected to be the spokesmen for the President's policies. That's what I want. I want you generals to *support* my policies."

"Mister President, General Taylor, as Chairman of the JCS, refused in July 1963 to let John Paul Vann brief the JCS on how bad the situation was in South Vietnam."

"Well, maybe Taylor was right. We don't need any negative people now, do we? Just who the hell is John Paul Vann?"

"Sir, John Paul Vann is a former infantry officer who served in Vietnam as an advisor, then got out of the Army. He became a civilian advisor to serve better, he believed, the Vietnamese people who sincerely wanted to fight a communist takeover."

"Well, I just don't want any negative reporting." The President stared into the flames.

Negative reporting, Whitey mused. No, he doesn't want any negative reporting. He really can't accept that we are having trouble over there because of the restrictions. And he thinks the subtlest of nuances from Ho Chi Minh mean peace negotiations are close at hand.

Whitey returned his thoughts to the fireplace room. POTUS, President of the United States, didn't seem interested in following up on who John Paul Vann was, so Whitey didn't continue.

There was a knock on the door. After the President barked an enter command, his senior military aide, an Army Brigadier, walked in. He held a teletype message and looked ashen.

"What is it now? What does that say?" the President asked irritably.

"Sir," the brigadier began. He was nervous and shaking. "The Viet Cong have attacked in force all over Vietnam. The air base at Tan Son Nhut, MACV Headquarters, and the city of Cholon are taking heavy fire. Hue City is invaded. And the wall of the United States Embassy in Saigon has been breached."

7

1145 Hours Local, Wednesday 31 January 1968
Quang Tri Army Air Field, Northern I Corps
Republic of Vietnam

The late-morning rainsquall pelted the Quang Tri runway and the tin roof of the Operations shack next to it with such ferocity that the two men inside had to stop talking rather than shout to make each other heard. An overhead light bulb shone on a wall map of the entire I Corps area. A major, a tall, well-built man wearing a two-piece Army Nomex flight suit, traced the flight path from where they were at Quang Tri to the Special Forces camp at Lang Tri, 35 miles to the west. Black thread outlined Army aviator wings and a parachutist's badge on the major's left breast, and his name, Doug Clifton, on the right. He was the commanding officer of C Troop (Armored) in one of the Air Cavalry units at Quang Tri. They flew the UH-1C helicopter gunships. These particular ships, called the Huey Hog, mounted a variety of weaponry ranging from two 7.62mm M60 door guns to a chin turret firing 40mm grenades. Pilots loved the XM-5 system using the M75 grenade launcher that chunked 240 grenades a minute out as far as 1,500 meters. Birds with these chin turrets were called chunkers or thumpers because of the sound the launch charge made as it propelled the grenade from the stubby barrel. The same device, the M79 grenade launcher used by ground troops, was called the blooper for the same reason. Other versions of the Hog carried, in addition to the chin turret, combinations of 2.75-inch rocket launchers, four 7.62mm M60 machine guns, and/or two 5.62mm miniguns that fired 4,000 rounds per minute. A ship with just the 2.75-inch rockets and two miniguns was called a Frog. A Slick was the larger UH-IH that carried up to fourteen troops. The only protection for a Slick was two door gunners firing mounted M60 7.62mm machine guns. When the rain noise subsided, the major continued.

"Cougar is responsible for all ground and air assets in the Khe Sanh-Lang Tri area. His message says he backs his colonel at Khe Sanh who won't risk the two Marine rifle companies set up to relieve Lang Tri. He says there is a hundred-percent chance of an ambush on the road to Lang Tri. And he will not risk Marine helicopters because, he says, all the LZs at Lang Tri are surrounded by NVA. Understand, Colonel Lochert, we don't have command authority to launch you and your troops in Army helicopters. In other words I'm not allowed to fly you to Lang Tri."

The man listening was Wolf Lochert. His jaw was clenched, bushy black eyebrows knotted in concentration.

"I know all that," he growled. "And I know Westmoreland so far, note I say 'so far,' agrees with Cougar."

Cougar was Lieutenant General Robert Cushman, the commander of the III MAF (Marine Amphibious Force). There had been some problems between Cushman and his theater boss, General Westmoreland. Westmoreland felt Cushman was reluctant to use the forces he had placed at his disposal, particularly the Army forces. Westmoreland also didn't like the way Cushman was employing air power, particularly USAF air support. He simply was not using it. General Cushman had been fighting the concept that COMUSMACV wanted, in which Commander, 7th Air Force, would be the single manager for the use of air power in South Vietnam. Under that method Cushman would no longer have exclusive control over his Marine fighter aircraft. If Cushman had used USAF air better, and given Marine air support to the Army's 1st Cavalry

Division, the problem probably would not have arisen.

Lochert continued. "Bull Dall has been to MACV and later called Westmoreland three times with no results."

Lochert remembered his conversation as he flew to Nha Trang earlier with Colonel Bull Dall. Wolf had told him about the attack by Buey Dan and the TV film of his killing the Vietnamese. Dall had nodded and said that war manifested itself in ways both strange and hellish, that Wolf wasn't to worry, the Army would take care of him.

Then Dall had briefed Wolf on the situation in I Corps between the Marines and the Special Forces. Dall had become almost incoherent with anger. "Wolf," he had said, "we are going to send help, I don't care what the Marines say. Get some troops and work something out at Quang Tri for transportation." Wolf was now at Quang Tri trying to work something out.

"How about you fly us to Lang Tri or I'll break your legs," Lieutenant Colonel Wolf Lochert said to Major Doug Clifton in a menacing voice. He was deadly serious.

"I get your point, Colonel. You're trying to protect my ass if I'm hauled up on charges when we get back. All I do is plead coercion and I get off." Clifton smiled at the fiercely scowling Wolf Lochert. "Look, I've never met you before, but I've heard a lot about you."

Lochert's scowl deepened. He wasn't used to being smiled at when he threatened to break someone's legs. He didn't like being figured out at all, much less so fast. And by a junior major who by the looks of him was a fast burner, a man on his way up. Something Wolf Lochert was not. His scowl deepened further. Clifton grinned back.

"You know the official word. We can't go," he said.

"Listen, *Scheisskopf* – " Wolf rumbled, but Clifton cut him off.

"Hold on, Colonel Lochert. Hear me out. My buddy and I are supposed to make test hops today on two Hueys, a gunship and a troopship. The weather is so bad, all combat operations are on hold. But we just might go ahead with our test hops. You understand?"

134

Wolf Lochert was surprised. This was not the way fast burners got ahead. A fast burner got promoted early – below the zone, it was called – by making decisions based on what was best for his career, not what was best for the mission. He looked at Clifton's left hand. He was married. Then he looked at his right hand. Clifton noticed, and held it up so he could see the ring.

"Woo Poo," he said, "Class of '59." Woo Poo was the not-so-favored nickname for West Point.

Lochert's scowl disappeared as he raised an eyebrow. "You feeling all right, son?" he asked in a normal voice. He could tell there would be no trouble with this man.

Clifton laughed. "Just fine, Colonel. When do you want to take off?"

"Whenever you're ready."

"Put your men under the group of palms at the east end of the taxiway. Keep them out of sight. The first time the rain eases even slightly and the ceiling is above a few hundred feet, we'll swing by and pick you folks up. My ship has 'Strange Striker' painted on the nose. Put your antitank team with the RPG in there. The rest of the guys in the number-two bird."

"Strange Striker?" Wolf said, a frown on his face. "Odd name. A guy in your outfit?"

Clifton laughed. "No. It refers to our illustrious Secretary of Defense, Robert Strange McNamara."

"Who'd want to name a gunship after *him*?" Wolf rasped.

"In a very unusual way, without him there would be no Air Cavalry. In sixty-two he wrote a directive to the Secretary of the Army telling him to get off his ass on tactical air mobility. At the same time he appointed General Hamilton Howze – a real air buff, I might add – and a bunch of other guys to set it up. McNamara told George Decker, who was Secretary of the Army, to get with it or else. But on Christmas eve 1964 he told Creighton Abrams to cancel all Army aviation, said it wasn't justified. Then he reversed himself again. In July '65 he visited Vietnam and sent message after message back to DoD saying to get the lead out and produce helicopters once again. Problem was, we didn't have enough pilots. That's why some of our guys are back on their second and third tours." Clifton spread his hands. "So I fly Strange Striker. I just wish he'd have let it go at production of our ships. Now he's trying to tell us when and where to fly."

Wolf Lochert looked thoughtful. Another rainsquall drifted over the field.

"You're a good man, Clifton," Wolf said, slamming him on the back.

"Yeah, I know. My wife says that all the time," Clifton said as drumming rain engulfed the shack.

Twenty minutes later, as low clouds boated across the field, releasing a light drizzle, two helicopters eased off the asphalt, one behind the other. They flew nose-down four feet off the taxiway to the east end of runway 22. After they settled on their skids, blades turning over, fourteen men carrying weapons and wearing light rucksacks ran from the cover of the palm trees and boarded; two into the gunship and twelve men, including Wolf Lochert, into the Huey troop ship. The two helicopters pulled pitch and disappeared off the west side of the field. They made no calls to Quang Tri tower.

"I thought this was a test flight. How come you didn't call the tower?" Wolf Lochert in the number-two helicopter asked the pilot, a warrant officer, in the right seat. He used the intercom in the flight helmet he had put on.

"Ahh, sir, the weather is a little below test-flight minimums," the pilot answered, concentrating on following his leader. "Way below, in fact. We had a little chat with the boys in the tower. They agreed to be looking in the other direction for a few minutes." He flew twenty feet above the ground, twisting and turning in trail behind the troop ship as he followed his leader to the west.

Major Doug Clifton flew the lead helicopter, the gunship. The plan was for him to follow Route 9 to the Lang Tri camp, prep with gunfire the best area near the besieged bunker to land, and fly cover while the troopship disembarked Wolf Lochert and his troops. Wolf had told him his team would use the call sign Dakota. Clifton carried two SF men on board for some special action and as a small reserve for the twelve on the ground. He would put them down for diversion, counterattack, flanking fire, or whatever function they might perform to make the rescue a success. In addition to their M16s and grenades, the two men carried an RPG-7, a Soviet Rocket Propelled Grenade launcher, and ten High Explosive Anti Tank (HEAT) rounds. Time was short. Darkness would soon blanket the area.

Clifton could not check the map in his lap, he was too busy flying his helicopter around the twists and bends of Route 9. His copilot in the left seat followed the road with his finger on his map. The hills on both sides of the road rose into the low clouds.

"Uh oh," Clifton said. Ahead was a rainsquall completely obscuring the road and the surrounding hills. "Pull it up, pull it up, Sabre Two," he transmitted to the second helicopter. He grunted as he pulled his ship up into the clouds. "Steer two four zero, Sabre Two. I'll steer two five zero. Go back to two four five in five minutes. Meet you on top." They could not fly formation in the clouds, so Clifton gave a divergent heading to Sabre Two to prevent a collision. After five minutes they could resume parallel courses and hope to find each other.

"If there is a top," Sabre Two said as he pulled up. On this mission proper radio procedure was of no importance.

At 4,000 feet Clifton was in relatively clear air in a deep chasm between towering clouds.

"I'm in the clear, Sabre Two," he transmitted. "I'll orbit right at four thousand two hundred."

Wolf Lochert stood behind the warrant officer's seat in Sabre Two. They popped through the clouds into the chasm. "Over there," the copilot said, pointing his finger to the right. They could see the ghostly form of a circling helicopter in the murk.

"Gotcha, Sabre Lead," the warrant said. "Roll out heading west. I'll be on your left."

"Roger, roger," Clifton transmitted and rolled out. He looked ahead. "The low stuff is thinning out," he transmitted. "We're about ten minutes out, I'm going to VHF Guard channel."

He switched to 121.5 megacycles, a frequency reserved exclusively for emergencies. All aircraft of all services monitored Guard channel at all times. On UHF it was 243.0 megacycles. Clifton wanted to see if there was anyone else in the Lang Tri area.

"Any aircraft in the Lang Tri area, this is Sabre One on Victor Guard. Give me a call." Because some aircraft monitored many radios, Clifton had identified which Guard channel he was on. Victor stood for VHF, Uniform for UHF.

A voice from a strong transmitter replied. "Sabre One, this is Khe Sanh Control. Who are you and what is your mission? We do not have you scheduled into Khe Sanh. Get off Guard channel. Come up 127.1 and explain."

"Uh oh," the warrant officer said to Wolf Lochert.

"Ah, just passing by, Khe Sanh," Clifton said on the new frequency of 127.1.

A new voice came on the air. "Sabre, this is Covey One Zero. Go Covey common on Fox Mike." Covey common, 50.4 megacycles, was known to most of the Special Forces as the discreet frequency the Coveys used to talk among themselves. The numbers were taken from the 504th Tactical Air Support Squadron. They called it the bullshit freq. Clifton gambled Khe Sanh Control did not know what it was.

Both Sabres switched to 50.4 and checked in with Covey One Zero.

"Roger, Sabres, what's your position?"

"About ten miles east of Lang Tri. What's the weather there? Do you have contact with the camp?"

"The weather, comrades, is delta sierra, but usable if you're a duck. Many buildups in the local area extend

138

up to thirty grand or better. The low stuff is thin for the moment. Rainsqualls passing through. Altimeter twenty-nine thirty-two. I do have occasional contact with the camp on their survival radio, but their battery is low. Are you gentlemen here for an exfil?"

"That's affirm, Covey. Sabre One is a gunship, Sabre Two a troopship. What's the situation on the ground?"

"Grimsville. I just put in a B-57 and some Navy A-1s. They got one tank and a bunch of gomers. But there are maybe two other tanks grinding around. Lots of bad guys, heavy groundfire. What are your intentions?"

"We want to get those guys out of there. What frequency are they on?" Clifton asked.

"Uniform two four two point five."

"Sabre go two four two point five." When Sabre Two and Covey checked in, Clifford tried Lang Tri.

"Spunky, this is Sabre, do you read?" There was no answer. He tried twice more with no results. He called the Covey FAC.

"Look, Covey, we got to get on the ground. I'm going to be over the camp in about two minutes. I'll find what I think is the best LZ, prep it, then my number-two man will land and offload troops and take off. I'll gun around as required, two will orbit off to the side. Can you get any air in the next ten minutes?"

"Sabre, I've had a standing request for the last hour. It all depends on the weather. I'll have to say right now it ain't gonna improve."

Clifton motioned to the SF man with the RPG. "Load that thing," he said, "hang out the right door. Point the tube forward parallel to the fuselage. Get your buddy to hold you. If I see a tank, I'll aim at it and tell the door gunner to point it out to you. Get ready."

The man checked the five-pound projectile mounted in the mouth of the three-foot weapon and positioned himself outside on the skids. His assistant held him by the back of his collar and his belt.

Clifton suddenly was over the camp at fifty-feet altitude.

For a few precious seconds he had the element of surprise. The camp looked like a burnt-out junkyard on the moon. Craters, ashes, hulks of jeeps and three tanks, and burned-down structures littered the area. Smoke rose from half a dozen smoldering fires.

"Over there," Clifton shouted to his copilot and door gunner. He spun the Huey toward a lone tank crouched under a tree clump outside the camp where it had hidden from the air strikes. The man holding the RPG-7 on his shoulder hung out the right door, left leg kneeling inside the helicopter, right leg extended to the skid. The door gunner slapped his shoulder and pointed at the tank. The man shifted the tube slightly and squeezed the trigger. There was a tremendous backblast and the rocket sped on its way. In a fountain of red fire and black smoke, it impacted just under the turret. Immediately, flames poured from vents. The hatch slowly opened, an arm appeared, then fell back in the tank as fire shot into the air.

As soon as he had fired, Clifton swung his Huey back and forth, spraying an area next to the command bunker. There was very little return fire. No fighting positions or mortar pits in the open parts of the camp were occupied by the NVA soldiers, probably, he reasoned, because of the air strike.

"Land your people, Two," he ordered the warrant officer, who immediately started down. The Special Forces men began spilling out even as it flared to a moving hover five feet off the ground. In less than ten seconds all twelve men were out and deployed in a tiny perimeter around the helicopter. As the last man leaped out, the warrant officer lowered the nose of his craft and sped off across the camp and pulled up sharply to clear the trees.

In the silence after the helicopter disappeared over the treeline, Wolf made arm signals to deploy his men in a wider perimeter around the bunker. From Wolf's pre-brief, each three-man team knew in which direction to extend. They quickly flopped into craters and the old fighting positions. They carried a mixed bag of weapons: M79 grenade launchers, heavy slings of grenades and ammunition for their M16s and CAR-15s, every third man carried a SOG-60, a cut-down version of the M60 machine gun. One team stayed next to Wolf.

"Okay, George," Lochert said to the leader, George Heaps, "let's crack that bunker." Bent over, they ran to the bunker. Lochert carried a PRC-25 radio and his M16. Next to the bunker was a burned-out tank hull and two dozen or more green-clad NVA bodies testifying to the immediateness and accuracy of the B-57 and Navy A-1 strikes. With Heaps and his two men, Wolf Lochert ran to the steps leading down into the bunker. Bodies and pieces of bodies littered the way. The dirt walls, even though shored up by PSP (Pierced Steel Planking, used to make runways), had collapsed on the bottom of steps covering the door to the command post. One man on each team had a folding shovel. "Start digging," Wolf said. He positioned himself on the lip of the steps and took the handset of his Prick-25. Rifle fire started to pop and rattle. He heard his people returning fire with their M16s and M60 machine guns. He spoke into the handset.

"Sabre One, this is Dakota Six. The bunker is partially collapsed. We've got to do some digging. Might take a few minutes. Starting to take some fire. Not heavy yet." Sabre acknowledged the call. "Hurry up, guys. Gonna get mighty black here toot sweet."

Wolf looked back down the steps. All three men were digging, one with the shovel, the other two with torn pieces of the pierced steel planking used to build the bunker. They had the top five inches of the door exposed.

"Start knocking," he commanded. "See if anybody's alive in there." The fire picked up. He heard the bloop of the M79 and the bang of exploding grenades. His men beat on the door with the shovel. There was no answer. They continued their frenzied digging. The fire outside was rapidly increasing in intensity.

Major Doug Clifton banked his gunship sharply around

the perimeter, keeping low over the trees so the NVA could not get a clear tracking shot on him. Searching green-and-red tracers crisscrossed the sky directly over the camp and disappeared into the overcast. Sabre Two orbited to the east. He checked his fuel.

"Time, gentlemen, time," he transmitted to the men on the ground.

Wolf Lochert heard the caution on his radio. He was shooting from the bunker stairwell at the heads that would pop up from a gun pit to fire at his troops. He shifted as the fire picked up to his left. Nearly a full squad of NVA was attacking one of his teams. Through the smoke he could see the enemy figures dodging around wreckage, hopping from hole to hole, making a probing thrust from the south side of the camp.

"From the south, they're coming from the south," he warned over the FM.

"I got 'em," a team member radioed back.

"Rolling in," Doug Clifton said from his helicopter. He turned sharply from his position over the trees and swept the south compound with his four forward-firing guns. Both door gunners and SF men were shooting out the side, sweeping the ground with their fire. The helicopter took several hits in the tail section and one through the front windscreen. The attack subsided.

"You got anybody out yet?" Clifton asked.

Lochert's men had just cleaned the dirt from the scarred and battered door, but couldn't open it.

"Hey, in there," they shouted, and beat on the door. "Anybody alive? We're Americans."

"New attack," Clifton suddenly transmitted, "from the west and north. Looks bad." He looked down and saw dozens of the NVA soldiers massed in the treeline, some already running at the smashed perimeter wire, then the rest followed in a stream. He positioned himself for a re-attack and rolled in.

"We can't hold them," Team Two radioed to Wolf. Three teams had the NVA in a crossfire, but despite many going

142

down, the communist soldiers kept coming. Doug Clifford's UH-1C clattered across the clearing, firing furiously.

"We need some help," Wolf hollered behind him to the men in the stairwell. "Two of you get up here."

Two men flopped into position next to Wolf and began shooting in careful two- and three-round bursts.

"What's going on down there?" Wolf asked.

"We heard someone rap on the door from the inside," one of the men said between volleys. Wolf looked down the well. The door was opening and the remaining man, George Heaps, was sliding through.

"Two minutes, Sabre," Wolf radioed to Clifton. "We'll be ready for pickup in two minutes." He returned to his shooting.

"Sabre Two," Clifton called, "get ready for extraction on my count."

"They're on us," Team One cried out on the radio.

Wolf looked over to their position. It was closest to the north wall where the NVA were pouring in. "Get that north wall," he radioed to Clifton, who rolled in immediately, door guns spraying hundreds of 7.62mm bullets, chin turret lobbing grenades into the green hordes.

"Let's go down there, George," Wolf yelled down the stairwell.

Sergeant First Class George Heaps helped a man in a torn and bloody tiger suit out the bunker door. He trailed an AK-47 behind him. "Five more inside," he gasped. "Some dead, some alive. I'll help . . ." He collapsed on the red dirt piled by the door, barely conscious. Heaps saw the name Lopez on his torn and filthy shirt.

"Stay here in the well," Heaps said and disappeared in the door. Inside, the air was full of dust and the stench of wounded men and full cans of human waste. He began to make out forms and shapes as his eyes became adjusted to the dim light from the open door. "Over here," a man waved from a corner. Heaps found two men, an American and a Vietnamese, lying crumpled against the wall, holding M16s pointed toward the door. The torn body of another

American lay against the intersecting wall. Heaps briefly touched them, then searched through the small door to the supply room. Inside he saw the legs of two men protruding from a mound of dirt that had broken away and avalanched down from a large section of the wall. He fumbled under their pant legs to feel their ankles. Both were cold and rigid. He crawled back out to the two men against the wall.

"Anyone else?" he asked. "Yeah, the cot," the American mumbled. "An Air Force guy. Under the cot."

"I'll get him," Heaps said. "You guys get out of here. Stay just outside the door. Don't poke your heads over the stairwell." The two men helped each other up and hobbled to the door. Each clutched his rifle. Heaps heard a hissing sound. Looking down, he saw two green oxygen cylinders for an acetylene torch lying in the debris. Someone had opened the valves, releasing life-giving pure oxygen into the dank air of the bunker.

Heaps tipped the broken cot back, revealing a figure lying in a tangle of poncho liners and bloody bandages. He found a strong pulse, then started to look for wounds. The man stirred, then jerked in a convulsive motion and tried to bring a .45-caliber pistol to bear on Heaps.

"Hey, it's okay," he said, pushing the big automatic away. "I'm an American. Can you move?"

Toby Parker focused his eyes in the gloom on the big man kneeling over him. "You bet your sweet ass I can," he said.

1200 Hours Local, Wednesday 31 January 1968
Raffles Hotel, Singapore City
Republic of Singapore

The noon sun bore down on the city of Singapore with

144

crushing intensity. Court and Susan sat in rattan chairs in the shade of the Long Bar, sipping iced tea. They had slept late, and were still groggy with lovemaking and wine.

Each day had been the same. For sightseeing Susan wore sundresses and sandals, Court wore light slacks and occasionally short pants. Once he wore a light-blue scarf knotted at his throat. They both wore Raffles pith helmets and laughed at each other. In the evenings they dressed and dined formally. Always they would return to her room.

In the morning, at dawn, when the birds in the Palm Court were chatting themselves awake, Court would walk down the open veranda to his room. He would shower, then drink coffee in the courtyard while thinking of his future. He decided they would marry very soon, and he would get out of the Air Force. Maybe go airlines while looking for good movie scripts he could produce. Certainly no acting, he chuckled to himself. And Susan could fly or not for American Airlines as she saw fit. Soon he would call the General's office at 7th Air Force and tell them of his decision to get out of the Air Force. Soon. Maybe next week.

They took the ferry to Sentosa Island. The boat heaved and splashed through heavy chop as it made its way between ponderous oil freighters and rust-bucket cargo ships. After the twenty-minute ride they disembarked and walked away from the construction sites of the new park to the new beaches of the small island. They wore shorts and sandals. Susan had her hair in a ponytail. Court carried a bagful of iced Tiger beer slung over his shoulder.

When they rounded the tip of the island to see the South China Sea, Susan spoke up. "My God, Court, you're striding along these beaches like MacArthur's return to the Philippines. Give me a break, O mighty warrior."

They sat barefoot under a palm tree and drank the cool beer. The sea breeze made the heat endurable. At first they spoke of the trips Susan now took – she was back on MAC contract. That meant she flew the flights chartered by the USAF's Military Airlift Command to ferry GIs to and from Vietnam. MAC simply wasn't geared to shuttle tens of thousands of GIs between the U.S. and Vietnam every week. American Airlines was just one of the many civilian carriers MAC had chartered to do that job. She said how young the GIs looked going over, and how old on the return trip. "Enough of that subject," she said. She leaned over and gave him a big kiss and snuggled in his arms. "What are your plans when your tour is up?" she asked.

"Well, funny you should mention that. I've been giving it a lot of thought lately. In fact, I've been thinking a lot about us, and maybe getting out of the Air Force. You see, I'd kind of like you and me – "

"Get out of the Air Force?" she interrupted. "What do you mean? You told me you were a career fighter pilot."

"I know I did. But there just doesn't seem to be a big demand for career anything these days, much less a career fighter pilot."

"Hmm. I seem to remember you once said you owed your government and the Air Force something for all those great years of flying."

"I did, and I've paid them back. I'm in the top ten percent in total fighter combat time. I've got more MiG credits than anybody else in this war. So I think maybe it's time to pursue other things."

"You once told me that another reason you went back to Vietnam was because your buddies were all there."

He was silent for a moment, thinking of Wolf and Toby. "I know," he said. "It's still true. But now so many are dead . . . or captured." He thought of Flak Apple. He had been with him when he had been shot down, and his own backseater, Ev Stern, had been captured on the same mission.

She leaned back in his arms to look up into his face. "Court, I want to ask you a kind of funny question, do you mind?"

"Go ahead." He stroked her cheek.

"I once thought you, well, *liked* combat. That you thrived on it. Don't you feel that way any longer?"

He put his hand down and looked out to sea. "Christ, you're tough. You just won't let this go, will you?" He looked at her with a wry expression. "Maybe you have a point. I do sort of *enjoy* what I do. I'd be lying if I said I didn't. And that's one of the things that scares me. That's maybe another reason why I should quit it now before it's all I *want* to do – or worse yet, is all I *can* do." He took a long pull of Tiger beer.

Concern knotted her brows. "You sound confused. You don't sound like the firm, dedicated man who used to lecture me on God, country, and being the world's greatest fighter pilot."

He looked out over the water. "I don't know if I can explain this or not." He took another long pull. "I feel as if a lot of things are closing in on me."

"What is the main thing that seems to bother you?"

He made a snorting sound. "You sound like a jolly shrink, or Doc Russell. He's always asking questions. Seems to me you were on my case in LA one fine morning. You didn't like the answers you got, so you took off. It was raining."

She stroked his arm. "I . . . shouldn't have done that. I had asked for it, and you were telling me exactly what you thought. I am sorry about that. But this is different. You weren't so . . . so morose then. You were all jolly and eager to tell me what you thought. Now you are doing a lot of heaving great sighs and staring out to sea. Tell me about it. Is it because you can't go after MiGs anymore?"

"I thought that was it, but no, it isn't really. At least not by itself. There are other things. One is the feeling that no matter how hard we – me and my buddies – try to win this damn war, or even just fight it properly, we're held back. Or we're on the edge of a court-martial for treading too close to the edge of the rule book. That makes us feel kind of abandoned, like our own government doesn't support us, maybe even doesn't like us very much. By 'us' I mean all the GIs over here, not just aircrew." He rose to his feet, face flushing with anger. "We're not just fighting a half-assed war, we're fighting a bunch of politicians back home who think they know more about war than we do."

"Hey now, take it easy," Susan said, and opened another Tiger beer. She got to her feet and handed it to him. "Cool off. I'm sorry I got this started."

He took the beer and sat down. "Oh hell, Susan, don't be sorry. I get this way every so often. Maybe there is more to how I feel, maybe there isn't. Let's drop it for now."

They strolled the beach in silence for a while, then sat under a palm. "So, what are your plans? What are you going to do if you get out?"

He shifted to face her. "Do?" He looked at her for a second, his eyes became firm. He put his arms around her. "What I'd like to do is quit now, and then I'd kind of like you and I to spend our lives – "

She put a finger to his lips. "Oh Court, wait a minute. I didn't mean any . . . I mean, I don't expect you to . . ." She untangled from his arms and stood up. "No," she said, "I just don't want to talk about this."

"Hey, wait a minute yourself. You're the one who brought up the subject about what I was going to do."

"I know." She turned to look out to sea. "I just want to hear about you." Small waves slapped the shore.

"So you've been hearing about me. More than I intended. And hearing about me brings me around to us."

"It doesn't have to."

He stood behind her and put his arms around her waist. "You're trembling," he said. "Did I say something wrong?"

She took a deep breath, then turned to face him. She had a too-brilliant smile on her face. "Look, flyboy, I'm your personal bunny for this whole R-and-R of yours. Take it, take *me*, for what I'm worth . . . which is a hell of a lot, I might add. Don't let's get involved in any long-range stuff. Let's take the here-and-now and . . ." She broke from his arms and pirouetted on the sand. She grasped corners of her shorts and flashed her legs like a Spanish hat dancer. "Party," she sang out. "More beer. Let's party, señor."

✳

The message was with Court's key when they returned to the Raffles. He was to report back to the Director of Operations, 7th Air Force, Tan Son Nhut, RVN, ASAP. Court had the concierge book him on the next plane to Saigon. He said it was in the early morning and a taxi would be waiting for him at 0600.

Susan stood by the gift shop, worry lines creasing her face. "What do you think it's all about?" she asked when Court returned.

Court flicked a copy of the *Straits Times*. "That," he said, and pointed to the headline: MASSIVE COMMUNIST ATTACKS BREAK TET TRUCE.

"What will you have to do?" she asked.

"Join my squadron, I expect. Fly air support for the troops." He wasn't aware he had a faint smile on his face and a look of expectation in his eyes.

That night, both in white, they dined again at a corner table in the Palm Court. They ate a light Sole aux Crevettes with a young white Macon, skipped dessert, and lingered over their coffee.

"Considering it's our last night, you seem awfully happy," Susan said.

Court gave her an evasive smile and stroked her hand. "I'm not. Believe me, I'm not. I'm going to miss you something bad. Let's dance."

"Methinks he doth protest too much," she said lightly and accompanied him to the dance floor.

They danced in silence, holding each other. Moonlight complemented the soft glow of the ground lights set among the flower beds.

"Court, about today. About marriage, I mean. Not now. It wouldn't work. And you belong in the Air Force. You know that."

"I guess I do," he said slowly.

She leaned back and traced his lips. "I love you."

"And I love you."

"This is not a good way to part."

"No, it isn't."

149

"I'll come to Bangkok. That's close to your base, isn't it?"

"Yes."

"Do you want me to come?"

"Yes, of course."

She looked at him and smiled. "You're a surprise. Here you've been talking about resigning from the Air Force and our getting married. Now I don't think you feel that way anymore. Funny what a little war can do. You probably think the MiGs will fly south any moment."

He looked anguished. That was exactly what he had been thinking. "Susan, I – "

She put her fingers to his lips. "Shh. Don't say anything. I understand." She felt a relief and a loss. I love this man, she told herself. But we simply cannot get married. Not now, maybe not ever. He is already married to his airplanes. And I . . . I have a little problem of my own. They danced close to some slow swing.

"I want us to sleep in your room tonight," she said a few minutes later. "I want us to go there, now."

He signed the check and they walked across the grass of the Palm Court to the wide stairs leading up to the veranda. After he unlocked the door to his suite, he swept her up in his arms and carried her across the threshold into the sitting room and on into the bedroom where they laughed, and danced a few steps. He lit a candle, poured white wine from the bar, and found some low piano music on the radio. They undressed each other, with slow and sensuous delight. They snuggled and danced, their bare skin warm in the darkness. They clung to each other. Finally, quite late, they went to the big four-poster. In the night, he half-awakened and thought she was weeping.

He awoke to soft rain and gray dawn, dressed and packed quietly. Finally he knelt by the bed and slipped his arms around her. She was warm and smelled of girl. He nuzzled the hair over her cheek. She moaned softly and put her arms around his neck.

"Time," he said.

150

"I know." She looked up at him. "I want to stay right here." She drew his pillow into her arms. "I want to pretend for a little while longer. I want to go back to sleep and wake up in Bangkok. I love you."

After he had gone, she buried her face in her pillow. Oh God, Court. I love you so much, so much, she cried in a husky voice, her body shaking. I want to marry you, but I can't, I just can't. It wouldn't be fair to you.

The tires of his taxi carrying him threw up sheets of silver water as it pulled out of the Raffles driveway toward the Singapore airport. He sat back and lit a cigarette, his mind already in the cockpit.

8

1545 Hours Local, Wednesday 31 January 1968
Lang Tri Special Forces Camp
Republic of Vietnam

Outside the ruined bunker, Wolf held the radio. "Sabre One," he transmitted, "drop those two guys of mine in the pit in the northeast corner. Tell 'em I want flanking fire from there on the north wall."

Clifton acknowledged, swept the area in front of him with gunfire, and swooped low over the pit into a slow-moving hover. The two SF men leaped from the helicopter into the pit, with their weapons, ammo, and the RPG-7.

As Clifton started to climb away, two streams of tracers converged on the cockpit and engine bay of his helicopter. Smoke spurted and began to trail from the exhaust stack of the turbine engine. His copilot stiffened, then fell over sideways in his harness. The right door-gunner went down, cut nearly in half, intestines spilling from his belly like entwined yellow snakes from a ghastly red nest. Clifford felt a hand lightly slapping his helmet and shoulder from behind. Fighting the controls, he barely cleared the trees. Leveling for a moment over the jungle top, he looked over his shoulder. His right door-gunner stood, behind him, arms dangling, helmet and safety harness shot off, shocked eyes staring directly at Clifton from the bloody mask of his face. Then the man slowly toppled out the open door into the mass of trees below.

Clifton eased his crippled helicopter into a slow climb away from the battle zone. "I'm hit bad," he radioed Wolf. "Real bad." He checked the controls and the gages. He had warning lights and gages running into the red, and his controls felt like they were being pulled out of his hands. Then he felt the throb in his left leg. He looked down and focused on a fountain of bright-red arterial blood shooting up from his thigh. Ahhh, shit, he said to himself. He saw Barbara's face. He pressed his transmit button.

"Bob, you gotta get those guys out. I got to get on the ground. We're all dead in here." He pulled his helicopter back toward Route 9, the only clear spot to land outside the overrun compound. He saw his wife's face again, clearer this time.

"Sabre Two, roger," Warrant Officer Bob Berry radioed, holding his voice as level as he could. He turned away from his safe orbit and headed toward the Lang Tri camp. "Give me smoke, Dakota," he transmitted to the men on the ground.

Wolf Lochert couldn't acknowledge any of the radio traffic. He was fighting hand-to-hand with two NVA soldiers who had broken through the protective cordon around the bunker. Wolf held a K-Bar knife in his left hand and a .45 automatic in his right. He knelt in the stairwell and shot the lead attacker twice in the head. The momentum carried his body down the steps to flop on top of Lochert. The second man jumped into the well and started to kick the body away to get a shot at Wolf, who feinted right, then thrust his knife straight up into the man's groin. The soldier screamed and dropped his rifle, Wolf shot him twice in the face. Brain matter and white bone splinters sprayed from the back of his head.

Lopez flopped down next to Wolf and started shooting at the attacking figures.

" 'Bout time you got to work, Paco," Wolf said, busy inserting his last magazine into his M16.

"By God, Wolf," Lopez gasped, "if I'd have known it was you, I'd of stayed asleep." The two men squeezed off three-round bursts at the scurrying soldiers.

Heaps crawled up behind them. "I've got three more ready to go," he said.

"Yeah? Go where?" Wolf rumbled. "Look there." He pointed to an open area to the west. A single tank was rumbling directly toward the camp. Its main gun fired three rounds in rapid succession. The three explosions bracketed their position in the stairwell, showering dirt and debris on them.

"Team Four, get that tank," Wolf radioed to the two SF men in the pit with the RPG. "Get him." There was no answer or movement from the pit. The remnants of the other three teams were firing at the NVA infantry, holding them at bay for a brief moment.

"Anybody got anything to use against that tank?" Wolf asked his teams.

"Two, negative."

"Three, negative." Their voices were laconic and strained. Team Four did not answer.

"We gotta get out of here. And I don't know if we can make it by helo. Sabre Two, do you read?" Wolf said.

"Dakota, this is Sabre Two, I read you."

"You can't land here. We got a tank almost on top of us, he'd run right over you. We're going to E and E east, maybe to Kilo Sierra. You copy?" E and E meant escape and evade.

Before Sabre Two could answer, Doug Clifton's burning helicopter zoomed across the clearing and flew directly into the tank. A tremendous explosion shot a fireball a hundred feet into the air, stunning the guns of both sides into silence for an instant.

"My God," somebody transmitted on the FM.

"Okay, Dakota. Sabre Two coming in," Bob Berry transmitted, calm as if on a practice pickup. "Cover me." He brought his big UH-1 over the treeline and began to flare for the landing, both door gunners blazing at the many targets available. The firing in the compound picked up, heavier than before.

154

The teams emerged from their pits and shell holes, ducking and running, stopping to fire back, and zigzagging their way to the helicopter. Heaps helped Lopez and his men from the stairwell. Toby Parker ran behind them. They were fifty feet from the waiting Huey when Heaps went down and Lopez slowed to help him. Wolf stopped and turned back to cover them. "Go on, go on," he yelled above the noise to the others.

The left door-gunner of the big Huey was shooting to each flank and almost directly over their heads as Parker and the other team members approached his ship in a straight line, giving the gunner open fire-lanes to either side of them. Some of the men were crawling, some carrying others, wounded and dead, several were shooting back, trying to delay the final attack. Wolf Lochert was still forty feet from the helicopter when a half-dozen NVA broke through the south wall and attacked from the left. Wolf whirled and pulled the trigger. In four rounds the gun quit firing, it was empty. The NVA ran at an angle to cut them off from the helicopter before coming in for the kill. Two of the NVA went down, but the remainder cut the three men off from the helicopter. They raced toward them, shooting from the hip and running. In another ten feet they would flop down and accurately spray Wolf and his defenseless men. Lopez and Heaps drew their knives. Wolf, lying prone next to them, leveled his .45. "Hell of a note," he growled.

Just as the NVA soldiers went to the ground and started to open fire, five screaming men darted into the camp, each holding and firing a big M60 7.62mm machine gun, and charged the NVA from the side. Two others knelt on each side of the charge, firing M79 beehive rounds. Hundreds of tiny nails called flechettes scythed large gaps in the charging enemy. The NVA attack wavered and broke as scores of their men went down under the withering fire.

Wolf stared as three of the men ran up to him. "Move it, move it! " they yelled as if Wolf and his men were rookies on an obstacle course. "Get to that chopper. We'll be right behind you."

Gritting his teeth at the commands but thankful all the same, Wolf helped his men to the helicopter and boosted them inside. Except for a few rounds the firing had stopped. Wolf took a good look at his rescuers. It was as he had thought when he first saw the camouflaged uniforms they wore: they were Marines. He wondered why there were so few, or where their officer was, but didn't have time to ask.

Warrant Officer Bob Berry looked out from his seat on the right side of the cockpit and beckoned Wolf to him. Wolf climbed in and bent his head next to the pilot.

"You got to dump all your weapons or I can't take off with these extra guys," Berry yelled. Wolf relayed the message but couldn't bring himself to part with his own .45. He had to roar at the Marines before they would part with their big guns. Ten seconds later Berry lifted off the overloaded Huey slick and headed for Khe Sanh.

He flew under the weather down Route 9 toward the Marine base. The sky was overcast and dark. After a moment Berry yelled back over his shoulder, "Is Covey Four One in here?"

"Yeah," Toby Parker said. He was sandwiched in with all the other men and bodies and couldn't move.

Berry said something into his boom mike, listened for a moment, then called back to Toby. "Covey One Zero says well done and he'll see you back at Da Nang." Toby nodded at this message from his boss, Colonel Charles Annillo.

Berry snaked his heavy helicopter up the road, then climbed the ridge to the Khe Sanh plateau. He radioed the Marine operations people that he was en route and just needed a little gas. He decided not to mention his Marine passengers. Wolf Lochert wormed his way around inside, talked to his men, and checked their condition, congratulating them for a job well done.

He slammed each Marine on the shoulder. "I owe you guys," he said.

"We may just need a job," the smallest one, a gunnery sergeant, said.

"Talk to you on the ground," Wolf said, puzzled. He turned to Lopez, who had finished tending a wound in Heaps' leg.

"Let's see that Air Force guy," he said. Toby Parker sat next to Lopez on the floor, jammed up against a bulkhead.

"Hey, Wolf," he said wearily. "You sure get around."

"Got to keep you Air Force pukes out of trouble," Wolf said, a huge grin splitting his grimy face. The two men clasped hands briefly.

Five minutes later Berry put the Huey down on the ramp near the heavily sandbagged operations center at Khe Sanh and stopcocked the big Lycoming turbine engine. In the distance the burned and twisted hulk of an Air Force C-130 lay blackened and bare. Wolf Lochert jumped down.

A lance corporal ran up to him. He looked dirty and harassed. "You guys have about two minutes to get the hell out of here. We're under constant mortar and rocket attack. Your chopper is a magnet." He skidded to a stop and saluted when he saw he was talking to an officer and not a warrant officer. Wolf returned the salute, surprised the man was saluting in a combat zone. The corporal pointed to the north. Fog rolled just to the edge of the east-west runway.

"Sir, the NVA has heavy guns and the biggest mortars in the world looking at us. The minute that fog burns off and he sees your bird, he'll shoot. Probably already trying to zero in on the sound."

"All we need is a little fuel and some oil, Corporal," Bob Berry said as he climbed down. One by one, most of the men untangled themselves and stiffly climbed out. They walked around and stared at the holes in the machine. Three stayed inside tending the wounded. Four dead lay under the rear canvas pull-down seats. Wolf began checking the Marines. Two were lightly wounded.

"Nobody stays on the ground long enough to refuel anymore," the corporal said. "Our fuel facilities are all blown to hell anyhow."

"Where is your operations officer?" Wolf asked the gunnery sergeant.

"Actually, sir, we didn't have one right now. You see, he was hit . . ."

A Marine major in battle gear leading four Marines with rifles walked up. The major nodded at Lochert, and, with the help of the riflemen, began to round up the seven Marines next to Wolf.

"Wait a minute, Major. What's going on here?" Wolf asked.

"Sir, these men are under arrest for desertion in the face of the enemy."

"THEY ARE WHAT?" Wolf Lochert thundered.

"Sir, they're – " the major began. Lochert cut him off. "WHERE IS YOUR COLONEL, YOU BLITHERING SHITHEAD?"

"Sir, the Colonel is the one who sent me to arrest these men."

"Do you know where they went or what they did?" Wolf rasped. Without waiting for an answer, he called the gunnery sergeant to him. "Tell me, why did you come to Lang Tri?"

The man, whipcord muscled and thin, looked embarrassed. He licked his lips and glanced at the major. "Ah . . . well, you see, sir, we, ah, were part of the original team, and when we heard you were in deep shit, but we couldn't go, weren't permitted, you know, so, ah, a few of us decided to, ah, you know, sort of mount a patrol . . ."

"Were you or your men on any assigned duty at the time?" Wolf asked.

"No, sir."

"Did you desert any post or miss any duty because of the patrol."

"No, sir, we did not."

Wolf Lochert turned and leaned toward the major, fists on hips. "Then why is the charge desertion in the face of the enemy?"

The major licked his lips. "Because we could have been

158

attacked at any time, and they would have failed to meet an all-hands muster."

"Were you attacked?" Wolf asked.

"No, sir."

"Then how do you know they would have failed to make the muster?"

"Sir, they were absent without leave."

"WHAAAT?"

The major was flustered. "Sir, I'm only doing what my colonel told me to do."

"I want to see this colonel." Wolf knew he was violating all protocol by subjecting a fellow officer to abuse in front of junior officers and enlisted men. Yet he felt it only right. Americans had rescued Americans, by God, and no one was going to get in trouble over that. A mortar crumped on the runway, then another.

Warrant Officer Bob Berry stepped forward. "Sir, we've just enough fuel to make Quang Tri. The oil we can do without. We are ready to launch. In fact, we've got to launch if you want to get the WIAs to Quang Tri today. There are no hospital facilities here."

The gunnery sergeant from the rescue team stepped forward. The name sewn on his blouse was Woods. "Sir, we'll be okay."

Wolf clasped the man's hand. "You're right, you'll be okay. I'll be on the horn to COMUSMACV tonight." He turned to the major. "These men just saved our lives. I'm putting each one in for a Distinguished Service Cross, and it will be approved – *outside of Marine channels*. Tell that to your colonel." He spun toward Berry. "Okay, let's get out of here."

For the first part of the forty-minute run to Quang Tri, Major Wolf Lochert talked to his men and wrote into a green field notebook. Then he sat next to Toby Parker and gave him a bear hug that bulged Parker's eyes.

"You dummy air jockey, you stupid zoomie. Don't you ever learn? You're supposed to run around the *sky*, not the *ground*. See, look at your feet. Just look at them." Wolf's

159

simian face looked concerned. He and Toby Parker had become close two years previously during Toby's time at Bien Hoa. Lochert and a few members of the III Corps Mike Force had been cut off and trapped. Toby had been overhead in the backseat of a tiny O-1 with a pilot who found the team. Then the pilot had been killed, and Toby, who had been an administrative courier, not a pilot, at the time, had kept the plane aloft long enough to call in a rescue team. Then the plane had crashed. Toby had been extracted with Lochert and his men.

Toby pounded Wolf's knee. "Wolf, these guys rescued me. I was captured and they rescued me."

"Of course they did, young mister captain. That's what they get paid to do. Lopez said you've earned the CIB."

"What's the CIB?" Toby asked.

"The Combat Infantryman's Badge. Now shut up and sleep." He punched Parker lightly on the arm. Toby blinked once, unfocused, and went out.

Berry eased the helicopter to the ground on the Quang Tri dispensary pad twenty minutes later. Though there was a light drizzle, the ceiling had lifted to 300 feet. Medics with stretchers ran to the craft even before Berry shut off the engine fuel. He had radioed ahead he was coming in with two KIAs and three WIAs. In minutes the helicopter was empty. A crowd of helicopter crews gathered. Wolf, Lopez, Toby, Berry, and his copilot stood by the tail boom of the UH-1D, counting holes, when an Army jeep driven by a major pulled up.

A colonel – Wolf recognized him as the G-3 – climbed out and walked over to them. He was a flinty-looking man, erect and sparse. The black name tag on his jungle fatigues said Rennagel. Wolf and the others saluted. While they remained at attention, the colonel inspected the shot-up Huey helicopter. He fingered the bullet holes and looked at the blood on the cargo deck. He walked back to face Wolf. Although his mouth was compressed to a thin line, there was respect in his eyes. He spoke in a crisp voice.

"Lochert, I could charge you for conspiracy to steal

helicopters. Additionally, I was just a moment ago advised by landline from Khe Sanh to charge you with unauthorized landings at a Marine base and insulting a fellow officer while there."

The others glanced out of the corners of their eyes at Wolf, who stood rigidly at attention, his dark eyes focused on a far-away spot.

"But," Colonel Rennagel said, "I am not pursuing any of those options until I hear your side of the story. I want you to come and brief me." He motioned to the major. "Take care of these men. See they have quarters, showers, food, and sleep. They've been through a lot." The major saluted. Rennagel took Wolf into his jeep and drove off.

An hour later Colonel Harry Rennagel heard the last of Wolf's story. He stood up and looked out the window at the low clouds and shadows of the approaching night. He clasped his hands behind his back.

"I hate to hear that about Clifton and his crew. He was as brilliant a man as they make them. A genuine leader. General officer material. I'll put him in for the Medal of Honor, of course. Small consolation for his widow and children. But I know he earned it. He could have saved himself." Rennagel was silent for a moment. "He didn't have to go on that mission," he said with a trace of bitterness in his voice. "He really didn't have to go." He turned to Wolf and regarded his red-rimmed eyes, his filthy and bloody fatigues, his mud-caked boots. "How do you get people to forget all their training and do things like that for you?"

Wolf remained impassive. He had never considered the question before. It had never been put to him, and it never occurred to him to wonder why men did what he wanted them to do when he wanted them to do it.

"No," Rennagel said, "don't try to answer. Not that you would," he added dryly. "Well, I'm not putting you in for anything. Consider yourself fortunate to come out of this without at least a reprimand, if not an Article Fifteen." He escorted Wolf to his office door. "But Lopez and the

161

other men – I'll put them in for something. Give me your supporting statements by tomorrow."

"Yes, sir. I will also have the writeups for those Marines who came down to rescue us. Each man deserves the DSC. Will you endorse my recommendations?"

"Most likely, Lochert, most likely. But right now you look beat. Come see me in the morning and we'll make arrangements for you and your people to get out of here." He clasped Wolf on his shoulder. "Don't worry about anything. I'll call Bull Dall and tell him you're alive and well."

After he showered and ate, Wolf found Toby in a tent for transient company-grade officers. There were ten GI metal cots with thin mattresses. Three were occupied by sleeping lieutenants from the field, their gear shoved underneath their cots.

A drowsy Toby Parker came fully awake when Wolf sat on the edge of his bed.

"Wolf, what happened? Are you in trouble?"

"Not at all," he said in a low voice. "Just want to tell you we'll get out of here in the morning. See you in the mess tent at six sharp." He slapped Toby's foot and silently walked out.

It was past midnight before Lochert finished the awards writeups for the Marines and Army men who had performed so well at Lang Tri.

9

By six-thirty that morning Toby and Wolf had finished a
breakfast of reconstituted eggs and B-ration ham. They
went out and stood in the cool dawn air with Lopez and
the others of Wolf's Dakota team, by a helicopter that
would take then to Da Nang, if it was still open to landings. They spoke of the battle and the mounting frenzy of
the Tet offensive. Colonel Harry Rennagel drove up in a
jeep and skidded to a stop. He motioned impatiently for
Wolf to come over. At the same time a warrant officer
leaped out and ran to the operations shack. Wolf walked
over and saluted the colonel.

"Lochert," he said without preamble, "I knew you were
good, but I didn't know you were that good. Some State
Department people are trapped at a house or a villa in the
old city in Hue, and somebody at MACV thinks you are the
only one who can save them. Or at least you are the closest
person to give them a hand. Bull Dall agrees." He nodded
at the operations shack. "Mister McClanahan will get you
down there. He's in getting the weather and local battle
information in the Hue area." He handed Wolf a brown
envelope. "Here is what I have from MACV to pass on to
you."

Lopez heard the exchange. He called the men and they

163

started assembling and checking their gear and put together a kit for Wolf. In short minutes they had a clean M16, ammo, grenades, knife, and canteens on a harness to present to him.

"Get a kit for yourself, Lopez. You're coming with me," Wolf said.

"Thank you, sir," Lopez said. "I didn't think you could do it alone."

"I can. I just want someone to talk to. Get a move on."

Toby Parker grabbed Wolf's shoulder. He struggled to put his thoughts together. "You saved my ass, Wolf," was the best he could manage. Wolf banged him on the arm.

"Parker, you *Scheisskopf*, you look terrible. Tell your boss I told you to take a week off. Then get yourself an airplane and I'll see you over the Trail someday." They shook hands.

The door of the ops shack slammed open. McClanahan gave a thumbs-up to Colonel Rennagel, then he and his copilot and two gunners dashed to a gunship.

"That's it, Lochert," Rennagel said. "Good luck. God, how you snake-eaters get around." He reached in back of the jeep and brought forward an old parachute bag that was lumpy and full of things that rolled and knocked together with heavy sounds. "Take this. Claymores and a few other items you might need in there."

After takeoff Lochert looked down and saw Rennagel and Toby Parker rendering perfect hand salutes at them. He and Joe Lopez returned the professional courtesy.

1015 Hours Local, Thursday 1 February 1968
Headquarters, Military Assistance Command,
Vietnam (MACV)
Tan Son Nhut Air Base
Republic of Vietnam

COMUSMACV, General William Childs Westmoreland,
sat in an aisle chair, front row, and listened as his staff
briefed him on the chronology of the events of what was
now being called the Tet offensive. His thick white hair was
brushed back, his square face smooth, his fatigues spotless.
He watched a staff brigadier from G-2 Intelligence brief
from a posterboard chart. He was finishing his review
of the attacks throughout South Vietnam. Waiting to
brief next was the Director of Operations, 7th Air Force,
Major General Milton Berzin. Next to COMUSMACV
sat Commander, 7th Air Force.

"In summary, sir," the brigadier said, "some eighty
thousand VC and NVA troops have attacked thirty-six
of the forty-four provincial capitals, five of the six major
cities, sixty-four of the two hundred forty-two district
capitals, and fifty hamlets. With the exception of elements
in Cholon and Hue, they are being repulsed. It certainly
helped when six units attacked twenty-four hours too
early at Nha Trang, Qui Nhon, Ban Me Thuot, Kontum,
Pleiku, and near Da Nang." He flipped to a chart depicting the action in the Hue area.

Hue, with a population of 140,000, was the third-largest
city in South Vietnam. The big city was split into north and
south sectors by the Song Huong, the River of Perfumes,
that flowed east to the South China Sea five miles away.
North of the Perfume River lay the Citadel, the fortified
city built 150 years earlier by emperor Gia Long. The
Citadel was surrounded by high walls with ramparts and
turrets, and water-filled moats. The walls ranged from
60 to 200 feet thick. Inside the Imperial City was the

Imperial Palace, with its ornate throne room and grounds of oriental gardens, temples, and pagodas. Next to the Palace was the Lycee Quoc Hoc, where Vo Nguyen Giap, the general commanding the North Vietnamese Army, had attended school. Also within the Citadel was the small Tay Loc airfield, located near the headquarters of the 1st ARVN Infantry Division.

South of the Perfume lay the new city, in which was located the stadium, the university, the Cercle Sportif, a Department of State and an AID (Aid for International Development) enclave, and a small MACV compound. The 1st ARVN Army had responsibility for overall Hue City and local area protection. Some U.S. Marines were stationed eight miles to the southwest at Phu Bai. Although in a state of flux as they re-enforced Khe Sanh, the Marines still managed to field some troops.

"Hue is the cultural center of Vietnam," the G-2 brigadier said. "It would be of great psychological importance to the communists to capture and hold the city. Of military importance, it sits on the railroad and the main highway between Da Nang and the DMZ. One of our radio intercept stations at Phu Bai has picked up enemy transmissions indicating two Viet Cong regiments, the Fifth and Sixth, comprising seventy-five hundred VC and hardcore NVA, have gained control of most of the old city, including the Citadel, and an area south of the Perfume River. Our MACV advisory compound in the southeast section was surprised and is under siege – "

"Didn't they get a copy of my message last week?" Westmoreland interrupted. He was referring to his message of 22 January to the Army Chief of Staff in the Pentagon stating he expected a multibattalion attack on Hue before or during Tet.

"Apparently not, I'm sorry to say," the brigadier said. "It, ah, went to the Headquarters of the Third Marine Division, but, ah, neither they nor our headquarters passed it on to the men in the MACV compound."

"What's the latest situation there now?"

"Sir, elements of the First Marines from Phu Bai have reached the compound to assist the men."

"Assist," Westmoreland said. "Rescue is more like it."

"Yes, sir," the brigadier said.

The Marines had taken heavy losses getting to the MACV compound and were really pissed when at first the Army colonel in command of the compound would not share ammo and weapons. In fact they had found him a pompous staff type who had been there only one week and had no idea of what to do. Fortunately his junior officers had disregarded his commands to hoard ammunition and stay in the compound. They had consolidated fighting positions within the compound and charged out with the Marines to rescue buddies that were pinned down. They were Army fighting men and no paper-shuffling REMF (Rear-Echelon Mother Fucker) ass-kisser was going to keep them from doing what was right and proper.

The brigadier continued. "Then the Marines were ordered by their headquarters to assault the Citadel. In concert with Vietnamese paratroopers and armored units, they crossed the Perfume River and were repulsed." The brigadier spoke in a monotone, his voice flat.

"What is it you're not telling me, Phil?" Westmoreland asked.

The brigadier swallowed, then set his jaw. "Sir, the Marines have a shit sandwich up there. Third MAF at Da Nang has ordered them across the Perfume River and into the old city without any arty prep, aerial recce, or intelligence of any sort. They don't know the enemy strength or disposition. I think Third MAF believes Hue is a palm-frond-and-straw-hut kind of village. In reality it's steel and concrete and narrow passageways. A terrible place for street fighting. Further, unofficial reports have it that the ARVN armored troops are not helpful. In fact they are not engaging when ordered."

"Get somebody up there to Da Nang and straighten this mess out. Better yet, I'll go. Check my schedule. I have a lot of people up there I want to talk to." COMUSMACV

167

looked grim. "Right now I have some tough news. All the Corps areas are under operational control of the South Vietnamese. The entire Eye Corps area of operations is under control of Lieutenant General Hoang Xuan Lam in Da Nang. Here is the really tough part. He has ordered us not to use artillery, bombs, or napalm in Hue. For the moment, anyhow, I agree. I don't want the old city destroyed. No air strikes into the Citadel, no artillery into the Citadel, no offshore naval bombardment. Make sure all responsible commands understand that."

The liaison officer from the Marine Corps started to say something and decided against it. Ever since a newsman made up the quote (some said it was some guy named Dan Rather) from a Marine about a village, "We had to destroy it to save it," the Marines had been very touchy. Besides, he mused, Marines could fight house-to-house. Marines are **Tough** and like to do things **The Hard Way**.

The USAF segment kept their mouths shut. They had been avoiding city strikes, and when they had to, they used soft munitions. But if ordered to do so they could level Hue or any other city with conventional bombs. Few civilians knew it, but the American military had stopped city bombing in World War Two. The Allies had bombed Dresden and Hamburg in retaliation for Hitler's bombing of London and other cities. In neither case had the tactic worked. They were not city-bombing in Vietnam. Not Hanoi, not anyplace.

"Now, what about the American civilians in the city?" Westmoreland asked.

"Sir, the Marines rescued several from the CORDS building south of the river. That's all they could find. Then they ran across twenty nuns and forty children and brought them into the MACV compound also. Early this morning we received a message through the Agency's net that several civilians were trapped in a villa north of the river in the old city." The brigadier looked slightly uncomfortable.

"Well, the Marines can't make that run from where they are," Westmoreland said. "Who can we send in? Who is available?"

"Ah, sir, just a few hours ago I took the liberty of already sending a team in."

"You look strange, Phil. What's going on?"

"Sir, I sent Wolf Lochert. He, ah, was closest."

Westmoreland sighed. He and his G-2 brigadier, Phil Davis, had just the day before pondered over a classified backchannel from the Secretary of the Army concerning LTC Wolfgang X. Lochert. He was in trouble, big trouble. He nodded to the brigadier.

"Continue," he said.

The brigadier flipped to a new chart. "Sir, in the Saigon area the Viet Cong attacks on the American Embassy, the Presidential Palace, the Vietnamese Naval Headquarters, Radio Saigon, and National Police Stations have all been repulsed. There is, however, heavy fighting in the Cholon and Phu Tho area." He checked his notes. "The final Embassy report states that nineteen guerrillas of the C-10 Battalion of the South Vietnam People's Liberation Army, the Viet Cong, had attacked the U.S. Embassy complex on Thong Nhut Street in Saigon by blowing a hole in the surrounding wall at 0245 hours local, 31 January. After a six-hour battle the nineteen attackers had been killed." He put up another chart.

"Here at Tan Son Nhut the men of the 377th Security Police Squadron did the best they could." He tilted his head in appreciation to Commander, 7th Air Force. "They had their bunkers manned. They had rigged up two M-54C armored vehicles, with four .50-caliber machine guns each, to use as a mobile reaction force. Still, they took some heavy hits. Just before the attack a number of Vietnamese from the ARVN 2nd Service Battalion assigned to base defense had abandoned their posts." He used a long pointer to tap a chart. "All in all, the VC and NVA threw four infantry battalions and one sapper battalion at us yesterday morning. The main assault was against the southwest perimeter between Gate 51 and Bunker 51, manned by USAF Security Policemen. The sappers approached the perimeter fence along National Highway 1 in a Lambretta taxi – a taxi, for God's sake." The brigadier was losing his briefer's cool. He started telling of the attack as if it were a story to friends at the bar and not in the formal briefing room of a four-star general. General Westmoreland leaned forward, entranced. The brigadier continued.

"The VC leaped out of the taxi and blasted through the fence with a bangalore torpedo. The Air Force men in the bunker attacked, but there were too many VC. The last radio transmission from the SPs came an hour later. The Viet Cong had overrun the bunker. By noon USAF Security Policemen and members of the 25th Division from Chu Chi had closed the hole in the fence and taken back the bunker." He inhaled deeply. "The attack had been a complete failure for the VC and NVA. Although by last count we lost four SPs killed, and nineteen Army troopers dead, we counted over nine hundred VC bodies. We captured nine of the bastards. That's how we got their order-of-battle information. We were lucky. Only thirteen airplanes on the base were damaged, and lightly at that."

The brigadier stopped. He realized where he was and looked painfully flustered. "Ah, sir – " he began.

General Westmoreland cut him off with a wave of the hand. "You tell a great story, Phil. Maybe you should do it more often." He chuckled. "Sometimes your briefings are a bit dry."

"Yes, sir. Thank you, sir." The brigadier was clearly relieved. He glanced at his notes and continued.

"President Thieu has declared martial law and press censorship throughout all of South Vietnam, and a twenty-four-hour curfew in Saigon. Late yesterday the Viet Cong consolidated positions in the Cholon area, the An Quang Pagoda, and near the U.S. PX. VC members slipped through portions of the Fifth and Sixth districts of Saigon, distributing propaganda leaflets urging civilians to join them and rise up against the government. We have reports of this in other communities as well. So far it doesn't seem to have worked. There is no popular uprising taking place."

"Is the TV coverage still the same?" Westmoreland asked.

"Yes, sir. They do not have the whole picture. And of course they slant it their way. Your conference yesterday, and pictures at the Embassy, did not come out well."

After a six-hour battle, the VC who had blasted through the wall surrounding the American Embassy in Saigon had been killed. Westmoreland had toured the Embassy and the compound shortly after the battle, pronounced it secure, and had gone on to say that by coming out in the open as they had during the Tet offensive, the VC were exposing themselves to tremendous casualties and inviting defeat. As luck and American newsmen serendipity would have it, the newsies and their cameramen lived in the plush, tree-lined area close to the Embassy, so that during and after the attack they swarmed over the grounds.

"They were repeating Westmoreland's words while showing scenes of the fighting and the destruction – but they did not always have their facts straight." The brigadier flipped over another chart. "In summary, the attacks in the Saigon-Cholon-Tan Son Nhut area are under control. In Saigon the twelve-man team attacking the Viet Navy HQ was wiped out, the battalion sent to raid the Saigon jail got lost and wound up being decimated in a cemetery. The VC do, however, have full control at the moment of the Phu Tho racetrack outside of Cholon. Meanwhile, here within the confines of Tan Son Nhut, while we have over three hundred enemy dead, we lost nearly twenty Military Policemen defending BOQ Three, which houses many of our senior officers."

"What is surprising," Westmoreland said, "is that so few American officers' quarters were struck. Either Giap didn't think of it or he was afraid it would inflame public opinion." He turned to Commander, 7th Air Force. "You did well in that respect." He was referring to the fact that Commander, 7th Air Force, would not allow his men to live off the air base. As a result, when the attack came they were not cut off from their place of duty by the street fighting. As it was, most senior Army officers were very fortunate. They lived by twos and threes in villas throughout Saigon that were not attacked by Viet Cong squads. Their protection varied from eight-man American MP squads to Vietnamese watchmen, who disappeared the night of the attack. Some were protected by Nung guards, who would fight to the death. VC units never tried to kill or capture these officers, which would have nearly paralyzed MACV's response to the offensive.

Westmoreland thanked the brigadier and signaled for Major General Milton Berzin to begin. Westy appreciated what air power could do ever since it had broken the siege of two hardcore NVA battalions on the Marines at Con Thien near the DMZ in October 1967. Even before they had started the shrill defeatist headlines with Khe Sanh, the newsies had been calling Con Thien another Dien Bien Phu. True, Con Thien was a dismal place. But under a concept called SLAM, put together by USAF General Spike Momyer, the NVA had suffered defeat, with over 2,000 dead. Momyer's SLAM – seek, locate, annihilate, monitor – had coordinated B-52s with tactical air, naval guns, and Army artillery to destroy the NVA battalions. It had been a clear victory of air power and artillery. As Westy had written in a message, "Massed firepower was in itself sufficient to force a besieging enemy to desist." For this reason Westmoreland was happy and relieved to use all the air he could for the defense of Khe Sanh. Now he wanted to know how it was functioning during the Tet offensive.

"The Tet offensive is a battle tailor-made for FACs and gunships," Berzin began. "The reason is because all the fighting is between troops – troops in contact or massed enemy troops in the wire. With the FACs and the USAF AC-47 gunships and the Army helicopter gunships, we have the precision of the surgeon's knife to help friendly forces cut these enemy forces down."

The AC-47 gunship, call sign Spooky, was a pre-World War Two DC-3 aircraft outfitted with three side-firing 7.62mm Gatling-style miniguns. Each gun shot 6,000 rounds per minute. Because each fifth round was a tracer, the bullet stream looked like a curving tongue coming down to lick the earth. The moaning roar of the three guns spooked the VC, who first thought it a fire-breathing dragon. Spooky was also referred to as Puff the Magic Dragon, or just plain Puff. Spooky carried 24,000 rounds of 7.62mm (.30 cal) ammunition, forty-five aerial flares of 200,000 candlepower that floated down in parachutes, and enough fuel to shoot and illuminate for hours. No SF camp or hamlet protected by Spooky all night had ever been overrun.

Berzin tapped the weather map pinned next to his chart. "We are, however, hampered by two factors: bad weather and city fighting. The ceiling and visibility in Hue has been miserable. Even the helicopters are having trouble getting in and out. Unlike Khe Sanh, where we use radar to put in B-52 and A-6 strikes on top of VC and NVA units in the jungle, we cannot do the same in Hue because we don't want to destroy the city. Hue is like the house-to-house fighting of World War Two. Here in Saigon and Cholon it is the same thing. We are using fighters to strafe at the Pho Tho racetrack because it is open terrain, but that's about it so far. The USAF has been called in on very few city targets. Each request, unless it is a tactical emergency, must be cleared through Seventh Air Force right here at Tan Son Nhut. Meanwhile, on the airlift side of operations, we have over two hundred eighty airlift aircraft moving reinforcement troops to the required locations." Berzin pointed to the map.

"As to air-base status," he said, "all the Air Force bases are open for business with the exception of Bien Hoa. The fighting is still too close to the runway to permit our planes to take off or land. Armored Cavalry from the 9th Infantry Division have just secured the area. Right now the 101st Airborne and Huey Cobras are mopping up. The base should be open by tomorrow. Elsewhere, we are launching over six hundred Tet-related sorties per day in support of U.S., ARVN, Australian, and Korean troops. We have the planes, the pilots, the weapons. On the fighters, we are using almost exclusively the close-air-support weaponry such as 20mm strafe, Mk-82 high drags, napalm, and CBU

One and Two. The only holding factor is the weather. We use the MSQ, the radar bombing method, as much as we can. But when the troops are in contact and the weather is down around their ankles, they are on their own. However, we can use B-52 air strikes within three kilometers of the friendlies through radar bombing." He turned from the chart to face the audience.

COMUSMACV turned to Commander, 7th Air Force. "We need to get those bombs closer to our lines. How are the close-in tests progressing?"

"Almost completed. Once our beacons are in and triangulated, we will make the first runs."

The SAC B-52 commanders were testing a procedure involving radar beacons that would allow them to bomb within one kilometer of friendly troops. A few months back a B-52 had accidentally dropped a load of bombs one kilometer from the Marines at Con Thien. The troops had suffered no harm, but numerous secondary explosions from enemy supplies had boomed for hours after the drop. Learning from that incident that the VC had been benefiting from the restriction, General Westmoreland had asked the Air Force to develop a method to place bombs closer than three thousand meters to friendly troops.

"But on the subject of air support in Eye Corps," Commander, 7th, said, "we still need more control over which aircraft will be allotted where and when – "

"And by whom," Westmoreland said.

"Yes," Commander, 7th Air Force, agreed.

All the Marine aircraft in I Corps were under the control of the 1st Marine Air Wing at Da Nang. The Marines felt the air belonged to them. After all, Marine fighter tactics were developed and organized, and their pilots trained and equipped, to support Marine ground units. They were Marines and they didn't *need* anybody else. Hi diddle-diddle, right up the middle. We don't need anybody else's air (we'll take Navy but not USAF) and we sure don't need anybody else's ground troops. (Westmoreland had placed many American troops from the Americal Division and the 1st Cav, plus the Korean Marine Brigade, at Marine disposal in I Corps. So far the Marines had not used them.)

Now the situation was getting terse. The Marines needed more than Marine air at Khe Sanh – and they were getting it. But it wasn't being used well. Control was a tangle. USAF and some Navy fighters were stacked up to 35,000 feet, waiting to be controlled in on targets. Frequently they ran low on fuel and had to jettison their loads and return to base or ship.

Only ten days ago, on 22 January, COMUSMACV had told Third MAF (Marine Amphibious Force) at Da Nang that he wanted him to link his air-support center with that of the USAF for use in the Khe Sanh Operation Niagara.

Nothing doing, Third MAF had said. We don't *need* and we don't *want* a single non-Marine person managing *our* air assets.

No, COMUSMACV had said, I'm not placing Commander, 7th, as a single air manager. (At least not yet, he had said to himself. Just four days before, on 18 January, he had approached CINCPAC with that very idea. So far CINCPAC hadn't agreed.) For now, he said, I want improved coordination. COMUSMACV was still pissed because the Marine air had not even made contact with the 1st Cav at Quang Tri to see if they needed any air support. (They didn't. Their own troops were doing quite well, thank you.) It was a mess. Third MAF wouldn't *use* non-Marine air, and Third MAF wouldn't readily *give* air to non-Marine requesters.

Commander, 7th, had said an airborne command post linking the Marine and USAF control centers was just the ticket, and the USAF had just the right bird to do the job – a C-130. Third MAF had reluctantly agreed. *Oh, and by the way,* Commander, 7th, had said, *best we also control or at least coordinate artillery strikes in the area so we don't fly fighters through a barrage.*

Now just hold on there, Third MAF had said. *We don't want any blue-suited zoomie telling us leathernecks where and when to put* our *airplanes and* our *artillery in support of* our *troops. Like I said before, no single air manager for us.*

Just get the coordination going like I'm telling you, COMUSMACV had insisted. And COMUSMACV had gotten things done.

The USAF provided an ABCCC (Airborne Command and Control Center) C-130 to fly over the battle area. The C-130 carried an air-conditioned capsule in its innards with computers, secure radios, and fourteen control consoles and a standup plotting board. The whole arrangement was like a ground or shipborne air-defense command post. It functioned as a forward extension of the command section of 7th Air Force exclusively for Operation Niagara over Khe Sanh. Although there were two permanently established ABCCC orbits for operations in Laos and North Vietnam, this was the only one of a one-time nature.

"Very soon," General Westmoreland said to Commander, 7th, "I am going to have one man managing all the in-country air assets." He looked at the four-star USAF general. "And that man will be my Deputy Commander for Air Operations." Commander, 7th, nodded. As the commander of the Seventh Air Force, he *was* COMUSMACV's DCAO.

Westmoreland swung back to his briefer, Major General Berzin. "What about Khe Sanh? What's happening right now?" he asked.

Berzin flipped up a chart titled "Operation Niagara." In the center was an aerial map of the Khe Sanh plateau. Listed on one side was the tonnage and sortie count of tactical air and B-52s, on the other was the command and control linkage for the air strikes.

"As of 31 January, B-52s had flown 463 sorties against sixty-five targets in direct support of the Khe Sanh battle," Berzin said. "Each day we are supplying up to 350 Tacair sorties. They are, however, not all being used." Berzin kept a straight face and a normal voice. "Some days, up to twenty percent are kept holding so long they get low on fuel and have to depart."

COMUSMACV gritted his teeth. That cinched it, he had

176

to have a single manager for all the in-country air and soon, very soon. This meant he would have to come down hard on the Marine command structure in I Corps.

"All right, gentlemen. That's it for the moment. I want hourly updates." He checked his notes. "I will be going to Da Nang within the next two days." He looked at Commander, 7th Air Force. "Give me your exact control plans and how they will integrate with the Marine Fire Support Coordination Center. They are, after all, on the ground and must have final say as to what is placed where." The Marine FSCC had control over all the ordnance that impacted the Khe Sanh plateau, whether from Marine mortars, from Army 175mm tubes from Camp Carrol to the east, or from any aircraft from any service overhead.

Commander, 7th, said, "Yes, sir," and departed with his DO. COMUSMACV looked at his brigadier from G-2.

"What are we going to do about that Lochert message?"

The brigadier knew better than to answer. The Lochert message referred to was an order to arrest Wolfgang X. Lochert. Westmoreland sighed heavily. He had to comply, he knew, but was loath to implement the order. Wolf Lochert was . . . well, Wolf Lochert. A warrior of long standing.

COMUSMACV stared without focus at the American flag mounted next to the briefing platform. His thoughts narrowed to one man. *Although I am that warrior's commander, I obey orders from my commander.*

"Have him brought in," he told the brigadier. He rapped the table. "Here," he said. "Not to Long Binh. Don't let him be put in the Long Binh jail. Confine him to the MACSOG compound."

10

1030 Hours Local, Thursday 1 February 1968
Tan Son Nhut Airport
Republic of Vietnam

The big Thai Airways Boeing 707 began its descent to land at Tan Son Nhut Air Base outside of Saigon. The airliner had flown through the rain clouds over the Malay Peninsula into the sunlight an hour before. Court Bannister sat in First Class Seat 2A and stared out the window at the thin layer of white stratus clouds four miles below. They were brushstrokes of white paint on the slate blue of the South China Sea. The face of Susan Boyle kept appearing just behind his eyes. His senses still savored her smell and touch from a few hours earlier in his suite at the Raffles.

He felt vague and unfulfilled, and guilty. Bannister, you don't know what the hell you want, he admonished himself. One minute you're all hot to leave Vietnam behind and get out of the Air Force, marry the nicest girl in the world, and maybe go fly airlines. The next minute you can't get back to the war fast enough. Is that all you can do, fly airplanes? Fight wars? He fought with only limited success to dismiss the deep cynical laugh he heard in the back of his mind.

He fixed his eyes on the water below. The 707 was banking and beginning its approach up the Saigon River. He watched the wakes of the river traffic. Then he saw the smoke rising from areas in Saigon, and a heavy pall over Cholon. He could see the VNAF helicopters and A-1s

178

diving and swarming over the tops of buildings. Once over the air base, Court could see the watch-towers and fighting bunkers protecting all of the base except the southern and eastern perimeters that abutted metropolitan Saigon.

"You're in luck, folks," the pilot announced over the PA system. "The tower says it's safe to land. Yesterday we couldn't get in."

Court scanned the area below. Numerous small villages in the opposite direction from Saigon made Tan Son Nhut International Airport awash in a sea of humanity. The base itself was huge and overflowing with workers. In addition to 230 aircraft belonging to the VNAF, the USAF, and the Army, TSN housed the headquarters of the MACV (Military Assistance Command, Vietnam), 7th Air Force, the South Vietnamese Joint General Staff compound, the headquarters of the VNAF including its induction center, and of course TSN was the hub airport for international and domestic civilian airlines. Some 25,000 military people lived and worked on the base, another 30,000 military and civilians reported in each day from quarters located off-base. Dispersal of parked aircraft to protect them from mortar and rocket fire was impossible. Further, some aviation fuel tanks and bladders were within fifty feet of the base perimeter. Munitions storage was not much farther off. It was an easy base to attack.

The 707 straightened out and the landing gear came down, then a few degrees of flaps. The pilot made a turn into a steep approach and banged the big ship on the end of the runway.

As they taxied in, Court noted the increased activity. Helicopter gunships were on patrol around the base perimeters, Security Policemen on foot and in vehicles patrolled the flight line, barricades were at the end of each row of revetments. Camouflaged F-100s waddling under the load of bombs moved down taxiways, RF-101 reconnaissance jets vied with them for space. Tiny 0-1 and 0-2 FAC propeller planes with both USAF and VNAF markings mixed with C-123s and AC-47 gunships – big

179

multi-engined propeller aircraft – headed to and from the active runways.

In one revetment Court saw an F-4 with WP, the Ubon tail code, painted on its vertical stabilizer. Court felt his pulse increase. Hell, I guess I *am* glad to be back, he admitted to himself. A lot more than I thought.

An hour later he checked into the BOQ, changed into his khaki 1505 uniform, and caught a ride to 7th Air Force Headquarters. Tan Son Nhut was covered with armed men standing grimly behind barriers, and armored personnel carriers (APCs) grinding around corners and along ditches. The linoleum-covered halls of 7th Air Force Headquarters were alive with people scurrying back and forth with papers and briefcases in their hands. They all wore fatigues. Stacked along the hall and in the offices he passed were steel helmets sitting on top of olive-drab flak jackets. He found Major General Milton Berzin's office.

"You're who?" the thin captain in fatigues said as he hung up one of the three phones on his desk outside the general's office. He stared at Court through red-rimmed eyes. His fatigues were rumpled, a stubble of beard was on his chin. "Just a minute." He picked up a ringing phone, identified himself, listened, and said the general was in the commander's office. He hung up and thumbed through a worn stenopad. "Oh yeah, Bannister. Here you are. Christ, it's a madhouse around here." He studied his notes. "Look, Major, the general isn't here, he's in with the big boss. But, ah," he thumbed through his notes again, "you're supposed to give him some decision – I don't know what it is, maybe you do, and, let's see, oh yeah, you're supposed to fly some airplanes or something." He looked past Court, jumped up, and dashed over to a colonel who was rapidly disappearing past the door. "Colonel Mayberry," he called. "Colonel Mayberry. That Ubon pilot is here." He turned to Court. "Go with Colonel Mayberry," he said and returned to his cluttered desk.

Colonel Tom Mayberry, assistant to the DO, took Court to his office one door down the hall. He was a stocky man with black hair. Command pilot wings were stitched in white thread over his left pocket, big white colonel's eagles on his collar tips. He had a wide and pleasant face and heavy wrinkles around his eyes.

"Heard a lot about you," Mayberry said as they shook hands. "We're up to our ass around here. Hope you're not too hung over from your R-and-R. Gonna fly you right away. The VC have broken the Tet truce in a big way all over South Vietnam. Cities, villages, camps, bridges, air bases, all under attack. The Army is crying for air in Three and Four Corps and we can't even get an airplane off the runway at Bien Hoa. For the moment VC groundfire has four squadrons padlocked to their revetments up there. We're putting everything in the air we can from here and using everything from Phan Rang and the other air bases up the coast." He offered Court a cigarette. They both lit up from Court's Zippo. Mayberry rubbed the stubble of his beard. "I haven't hit the sack in the last forty-eight hours. Right now VNAF A-1s and helicopter gunships are strafing and bombing within the city of Cholon and the outskirts of Saigon. We don't want to risk USAF or Navy fighters on those close-in attacks. There are hundreds of cameramen and newsmen in Saigon. Once they leave the bars, they act like ambulance-chasing accident lawyers. They damn near create traffic jams trying to get to the latest fire or explosion. I could just see the pictures of an F-100 or Army Huey gunship rolling in on some building in downtown Cholon. And I already know the caption: 'They Had to Destroy It to Save It.' Hell of a war when you have to arrange your battles and weaponry in accordance with what will play in Peoria. I wish to Christ these guys were in Hanoi. We'd win the war by noon on their first day up there." Mayberry took a drag on his cigarette. "I've got to get off that subject. Gets me too riled up." He stood up and stubbed out his cigarette.

"Okay, Bannister, here's the deal. The pilot of one of your Ubon F-4s delivered some classified papers two days ago and is now in the hospital with some mortar fragments in his legs. So is his backseater. We are fresh out of current operational F-4 jocks here, and the general thought of you and your local area experience in F-100s out of Bien Hoa. Knew you were just a few hours away in Singapore. Told me to chase you down. We need to get every airplane we've got in the air for the next couple of days." He took a short puff. "So go on down to the 416th, draw some gear, get ready to fly. We found you a backseater. He's a pilot that was en route to Ubon via a MAC flight that put in here. They had a delay taking off so we shanghaied him for you. Seems like a sharp kid. He's already at the squadron learning local area procedures." Mayberry walked him to the door of his small office and back to the captain's desk. "See that Bannister is signed in from leave," he told him. "Notify Colonel Bryce at Ubon where he is and get him some wheels to the 416th."

"Oh God, it's Bannister, Court, one each," Major Mac Dieter shouted across the operations room of the 416th Tactical Fighter Squadron. He stood by the scheduling board, where all the combat flights were posted. "We wanted a real fighter pilot, not a two-holer bus driver. What's the Air Force coming to, anyhow?" Dieter, a rail-thin, balding man who wore a size "38 Small" flight suit, threw up his hands in mock despair. He commanded the eighteen-plane F-100 squadron.

"Get off it, Dieter," Court said as he walked up, "I have my own airplane and it's got twice as many engines as yours do."

"Yeah, and twice as many assholes on board, too." The two men met at the operations counter and grasped each other's shoulders. They had been Section Commanders in A Wing at Squadron Officers School in the early sixties. They had enjoyed great rivalry in the soccer and flickerball games, but Court used to wipe him out spiking in volleyball.

"You're getting uglier by the day, Bannister."

"You should talk, chrome dome."

"I'm not bald. All the rest of you guys are hairy. When God made heads, he covered up the ones he didn't like." He laughed and motioned to Court. "Good to see you. It's been a few years since we wore the red pants at Maxwell." Only faculty members at SOS wore red pants on the athletic fields. "Come on back with me, we'll get you rigged up."

He led Court past the ops counter to a room down the hall that had the sign "Personal Equipment" over the door. Inside, a staff sergeant found Court a flight suit, boots, heavy socks, helmet, gloves, and a kneeboard. All but the helmet were new and stiff. The K-2B green flight suit was baggy and creased with lines from the clear plastic bag in which it had been packed. The staff sergeant produced a brand new G-suit. Court opened the package and worked the zippers a few times to loosen them up. The staff had Court put on the helmet. He produced a new oxygen mask, fitted and tightened it, then plugged the hose and the radio connector into a large test set. He moved the switches and lever supplying oxygen under pressure. Satisfied there were no leaks, he tested the microphone in Court's mask and the headsets in his helmet. From a refrigerator he took two baby bottles full of frozen water for Court to fit into his harness. After a functioning parachute, water and a survival radio were the two most important items a pilot needed if shot down.

"Okay, Major, if you'll just sign here, you're ready to go." Court signed AF Form 538, Personal Equipment and Clothing Record.

Dieter took Court to the flight-planning room. It was dominated by a large Ping-Pong-sized table covered by a heavy sheet of clear plastic that overlay a 1:250,000 aeronautical chart of South Vietnam, Cambodia, and Laos. Pictures and charts of F-100 weapons and delivery data lined the walls. Two pilots were leaning over the table, plotting flight routes on hand-held cockpit maps. Dieter led Court over to a third man, a thin captain whose wings on his name tag showed he was a pilot.

"You know this guy?" Dieter said. "He has some F-4 time."

"Hi. Court Bannister," Court said and stuck out his hand.

"Dick Connert." The pilot shook Court's hand and gave him a broad smile. "I'm very glad to meet you. I just finished the F-4 upgrade course at George. Although I'm a pilot, I guess I don't mind flying in the backseat of the Air Force's leading MiG killer."

Court studied him. His face was youthful and clear of lines or wrinkles. He had sand-colored hair, neatly cut and combed. His flight suit was form-fitted and clean. His black boots were polished to a high gloss. He carried a flight bag with patches from all of the training squadrons at George Air Force Base.

Dieter then introduced them to the two captains, Jim Morelli, the flight lead, and Joe Jensen, his wingman for the flight.

"Since we schedule flights composed of three F-100s for each mission, you will be flying with these two guys," Dieter said. "I think it best always to fly with the same two while you are here, so you all can learn how to adapt to each other's procedures and airspeeds." Court's F-4 was several tons heavier than the F-100, had twice the thrust from its two engines, and could carry nearly three times as much ordnance. Flying dissimilar airplanes in the same pattern would require some adjustments.

"Everything we are doing these days is close air support for American and ARVN troops here in South Vietnam." The Army of the Republic of Vietnam was referred to by pronouncing its acronym, ARVN. "As always, Court, everything is under the control of an airborne forward air controller, the FAC. He uses his FM radio to talk to the ground troops who need help. He establishes their exact location, the position of the enemy, and what kind of ordnance is best for the target. When you check in with your lineup and mission number, he'll give you all the target information, the terrain altitude, wind direction, altimeter setting, and the heading to a safe bailout area if you get hit and can still control your airplane. He will clear you in on every pass." Dieter turned to Dick Connert.

"I don't know if you ever worked with a FAC before,

but no pilot drops anything or fires a single round from his cannon without clearance from the FAC on every single pass. When he clears you, he'll say 'hot' if you're cleared in to drop, or 'dry' if you are not. If you have radio failure, you orbit high and dry until the flight finishes the mission, then joins up on you to take you home." Connert nodded, an eager smile on his face. "Yes, I know all about that," he said. Dieter continued.

"The call sign of the FACs here in the Saigon and Bien Hoa area of Three Corps is Copperhead. Those in Four Corps down around Can Tho are Beaver. They'll be flying 0-1s or 0-2s."

The 0-1, smaller than the 0-2, was a single-engined, high-wing two-seater Cessna. The 0-2s were replacing the 0-1s. So far over 100 O-1s had been shot down.

Court briefly thought of Toby Parker. He had won his Air Force Cross as a nonpilot flying an 0-1 from the backseat when his pilot had been killed trying to rescue a Special Forces unit near Loc Ninh. His pilot, Phil Travers, Copperhead 03, had flown from Bien Hoa that day.

Dieter excused himself, saying he had to get back to his real job as an airplane dispatcher, and turned the briefing over to Jim Morelli.

"Things haven't changed much since you flew Huns up at Bien Hoa, Major Bannister. Still no formation takeoffs. You will be Silver Three Three, the number-three man in Silver flight. Joe and I will make single-ship takeoffs at fifteen-second intervals. Since the F-4 accelerates so much faster than the F-100, you'd better use twenty or even more if it looks like you'd run over him. I'll come out of burner and hold three eighty knots indicated airspeed until you and Joe join up. Usually I'd hold three-fifty, but I don't want you waddling around out there."

"You're right on that," Court said. "The F-4 really isn't worth much under four-fifty. At that speed and above, she really handles nicely."

"That's right," Connert said. "I always flew above that speed at George." He flashed a wide smile.

Morelli regarded him steadily for a moment, then continued. "After takeoff I'll have us switch from Saigon Departure Control to Paris Control, the local radar site that will clear us out of the Saigon area. He will turn us over to Paddy, the radar site at Can Tho, who will direct us to our FAC." He took a large file card clipped to his kneeboard and pushed it over where Court and Dick Connert could see it. "Here's the lineup. We still don't know about your ordnance. The weapons people haven't had that much experience loading F-4s."

He handed blank forms to Court and Dick Connert to fill out. When they were done, he took them to the map cases and helped them select the appropriate maps for III and IV Corps in South Vietnam.

"You can see" – Morelli pointed to an area on the map – "we are going down in the Delta to the Whiskey Romeo grid."

Although the USAF navigated from aeronautical charts using latitudes and longitudes and distance and bearings from radio sites, on strike missions they used Army maps that were oriented to the UTM, the Universal Transverse Mercator, a system that blocked most of the earth's surface into squares one hundred kilometers on a side. Each square had a two-letter designator. Silver 33 flight was heading southwest of Saigon to the 218-degree radial for twenty-three nautical miles from Channel 41, the Can Tho Tacan station. That point of aerial navigation coincided with WR 5181 UTM coordinates (slanged to *cords*; kilometers to *klicks*) near the village of Vi Thanh. The Army UTM maps were read "right up." That meant to find the WR 5181 grid point, start from the bottom left corner of the WR grid, read 5,100 meters to the right and 8,100 meters up. At this point was, if not the target, at least the point to rendezvous with today's FAC, call sign Beaver 24.

"Right here," Morelli said, "Vi Thanh is at the intersection of two canals and a road. It's all flat delta down there, barely above sea level. The village itself has been under severe attack since the Tet truce was broken. The

186

Intell people tell me two American advisors are with a company of Vietnamese local defenders who stand between the VC and the village. The terrain is flat, so our weaponry for this mission will be a few Mark Eighty-Two Snakeye high-drag bombs – "

"Good stuff," Connert interrupted.

"Ah, yeah," Morelli said, eyeing him. "Anyway, the Snakes are to open things up, then napalm, CBU, and strafe for close-in work. Of course it depends on the FAC. Whatever he says, whatever order of delivery he wants, that's what we'll do. Usually he wants bombs first, and we like to get 'em off so we can maneuver better for the next deliveries."

Dive-bombing is as complex a maneuver as a fighter pilot can perform. It is part art, part science. Art, in that the pilot must have absolute mastery over both his tradecraft and his aircraft; science, in that the inexorable laws of gravity and aerodynamics rule with constant results. The art, then, is the variable. The pilot must be able to calculate mentally the exact release point in the air where he mashes down on the red button – called the pickle button – on top of his B-8 control stick to release a bomb from an ejector rack under his wing. The rack uses a cartridge the size of a shotgun shell to push the bomb from the plane.

Using figures from a chart, the pilot dials in a set number of mils to depress his gunsight below his flight path. Then he must position himself at a point two miles above the earth (if the groundfire is minimal) and roll in on a heading, dive angle, and engine power setting such that he will arrive at the altitude of the invisible release point at exactly the correct angle and airspeed with the pipper of his gunsight centered on the target. Too fast, too high, or too steep and the bomb will hit long. Too slow, too low, too shallow and it will hit short. Further, if the pilot does not compensate for wind drift as well as hold his airplane aerodynamically stable with no skid or slip, the bomb will impact off to one side.

The release altitude must be high enough for the bomb

to arm – dud bombs provide the Viet Cong with free, air-delivered explosives – yet not so high that accuracy is affected. But release should not be so low the pilot will be hit by his own fragments or be exposed to heavy groundfire for a long time. The anti-aircraft threat in South Vietnam was not nearly as lethal as in North Vietnam. Thus pilots in the south could release much lower.

However, because bomb fragments travel at 1,300 feet per second, the pilot must release several thousand feet in the air. Added to that release altitude must be the altitude consumed in the 4- or 5-G pullout. Since a high release altitude reduced accuracy, a mechanical compromise had been invented to create drag. Attached to some 500lb Mark-82 bombs were the Mk15 retarding devices that were big steel umbrellas fixed to the rear of the bomb that opened up after release to slow the bomb. This device gave the pilot the option to release the bomb at a lower altitude and a shallower dive angle than a "slick" low-drag bomb. Accuracy improved dramatically. With a delivery speed of 450 knots (515 mph), a dive angle of 15 degrees, and a release altitude of 500 feet, the pilot could put the bomb through the front door of an enemy bunker. The same bomb, dropped from 5,000 feet in a 45-degree dive without the high-drag device, could easily miss by 30 or 40 feet.

Today, Silver flight was using slick Mk-82 bombs with the M904 fuze that could be set to detonate the bomb on contact or up to several seconds delay, allowing it to penetrate earth or concrete bunkers or bridges. Their fuzes were set on contact.

The napalm Silver flight carried consisted of 750-gallon tanks holding a jellied gasoline that splashed and burned in the direction of flight at several thousands of degrees Fahrenheit. Since there were no fragments or arming requirements (they were armed as soon as they left the airplane), napalm could be released as low as the pilot felt prudent. Normally, pilots dropped napalm from 100 feet altitude in straight and level flight, or shallow dives indicating 450 knots.

Their CBU (cluster bomb units) were bomb-shaped tanks that held several tubes open to the rear. Packed into the tubes were hundreds of softball-sized bomblets that dribbled out of the tubes, opened little winglike vanes, and floated down like so many tiny, softball-sized helicopters. They contained either explosive or white phosphorus. Pilots dispensed CBU from straight and level flight, indicating 450 at exactly 300 feet AGL (above ground level). Too high and they would drift away from the target, too low and they would not arm.

Each F-100 carried four 20mm cannons that could fire 200 rounds each. F-4Ds, like the one for Court from Ubon, did not have a built-in gun (the E-model in production would have one). The USAF had designed a Gatling-style gun that could fire 6,000 rounds per minute to be slung underneath the F-4. The F-4 assigned to Court did not have one, nor were any on the base. The 20mm cannons could be fired at any range; ball ammunition didn't need to arm, and high explosive or incendiary rounds armed within a few feet of leaving the barrel.

All these weapons were designed for use against enemy troops in the open or under thin shelter. The accuracy of the F-100 pilots flying close air support was legendary. "FAC, TAC, and napalm" the Special Forces men would say while making the sign of the cross. However, except for the bombs dropped slick with a delayed fuze, all these weapons were useless if the enemy was under triple or even double canopy jungle. The napalm would splash in the trees, the CBU would detonate up in the treetops, and the branches and trunks would absorb the cannon shells.

"Court," Morelli said, "you're an old head around here. You remember the wheel?"

"Sure. You want us to fly a circle around the target area and roll in in sequence from random headings." The wheel was more safe than a box pattern because in the box the base and final leg of the run was always the same, making it easy for gunners to zero in on the diving planes.

"You got it. That's what we'll use." Morelli tapped

the map. "The weather is reported at fifteen thousand overcast and six miles visibility in the target area and forecast to remain that way. Locally, we've got twenty-five hundred overcast with occasional thunder bumpers. If it looks bad landing back here, normally we go to Bien Hoa, but the bad guys still are too close to the runway. So plan for Phan Rang. It's zero eight zero degrees for one forty-five nautical." Court jotted the information down and noticed Connert did not.

They went to the pilots' locker room, suited up, and walked out into the overcast day to the flightline van. Morelli and Jensen both wore parachutes on their back because the ejection seat in the F-100 did not have a built-in parachute like the F-4. On board the blue van that carried them to their airplanes, Morelli briefed Court on the airplane signals for the flight members to keep the radio chatter down. When the flight leader fishtailed, the flight would spread out; nose bobbing up and down meant slide back into the trail position – one behind the other; wing rock meant close it up; a sharp dip of the wing one way or the other meant for the flight to echelon on that side. Then he covered the hand signals used for radio-out procedures. Finally Morelli gave Court the radio frequencies he wanted to use, starting with the squadron check-in channel.

Court and Dick Connert got out of the van in front of the Ubon F-4. In the distance they heard the crump of artillery.

Their Phantom was parked in an Armco revetment made of earth-filled corrugated steel bins 12 feet high and 5.5 feet wide. The revetments stood side by side in rows, each containing two F-100s or one larger aircraft such as a C-130 or C-47.

A weapons and a maintenance officer, both lieutenants, came up to Court and saluted. The maintenance officer was the first to speak.

"Normally, a transient alert airman would handle your aircraft, sir, to get it cranked up so you can fly home to Ubon. But since you're going to be flying combat out of here, I'll handle it myself. I used to be an F-4 crew chief at George before I went to OCS." He grinned shyly. "And I'm really proud to be crewing your aircraft, sir. Sorry we didn't have time to paint a cowboy hat on the tail. Maybe this will do." He pointed to a chalked outline of a cowboy hat on the nose.

Court was both touched and embarrassed. The F-4 with which he had shot down his MiGs had had a cowboy hat painted on each side of its nose.

"Thanks," he said.

"We did the best we could, sir," the weapons man spoke up. He pointed at the airplane. "We got you your bombs and napalm, but we couldn't get a compatibility check with the CBUs. Something in the wiring to the pylons. We're kind of new to these Phantoms. Had to get all our books out to figure what went where."

Court looked at the F-4. It had a 600-gallon drop tank under the fuselage in the centerline position, three Snakeyes on each inboard pylon, and one napalm can on each outboard pylon.

"We don't have the right Mers and Ters to hang any more bombs, sir. Sorry 'bout that," the weapons officer said. Mers and Ters were multiple and triple ejection racks that could increase the bombload of the F-4 up to sixteen Mk82 500lb bombs; 8,000 pounds of bombs.

Court looked at the AIM-7 radar-guided air-to-air missiles in each of the four missile wells in the fuselage.

"Didn't know whether to down-load the missiles or not, sir," the weapons officer said.

Connert spoke up before Court could answer. "Yeah, take them off. We don't need missiles down here in South Vietnam."

"Hold one," Court said, trying not to frown at Connert in front of the others. "Leave them on. Bad enough not having a gun, I'd feel naked without a missile. Besides, you never know where we might get diverted." Although he certainly didn't expect to see MiGs in the south of South Vietnam, he wanted the twelve-foot Sparrow missiles left in their bays. In these hectic days anything could happen.

He turned to the maintenance man. "Is the fuel tank full?"

"Yes, sir."

"Could be," Court said, "we have enough internal fuel to keep up with the F-100s even if they do have drops. I'll let you know when we come back. We may demount the centerline tank and hang some more bombs."

He walked to the ladders for the front and rear cockpits. The maintenance lieutenant handed him the AF Form One booklet, the maintenance record of the airplane. There were no major discrepancies, and he signed for the aircraft. Then he led Connert around to preflight the aircraft, checking its general condition, the hanging and fusing of the weapons, the tires, hydraulic leaks. A big auxiliary power unit stood by to supply electrical power and air under pressure to start the engines. The lieutenant crew chief took their helmets and kneeboards to the cockpit and returned with the parachute harness.

Connert spoke up as they were strapping their harnesses on. "I think you'll see that I'm a good pilot." He gave Court a brilliant smile and slapped him on the shoulder.

Court looked at him through narrowed eyes. "Listen, Connert, I'll tell you how great you are after I see you fly. How much time you got in this airplane?"

"Ah, almost one hundred hours. I was in the F-4 course at George Air Force Base."

"GIB or AC?" Guy In Back or Aircraft Commander?

"Aircraft Commander of course."

Court nodded. "Okay, now pay attention to what I'm saying. If we take a hit and have to get out, I'll try to give you a warning. If the intercom is out, I'll punch the EJECT light on. Don't ask questions, just go. If we do lose comm, but there is no reason to eject, just tap the stick lightly if there is some direction you want me to look, or even dip the wing toward an immediate threat. Only in case of absolute emergency do you take the controls. Before we taxi, do your normal backseat checks, get the INS aligned, and read off the checklist to me. I'll also expect you to read me the checklist before takeoff and before landing. Any questions?"

"When do I get to fly?" Connert had a bright quizzical look on his face. "I am a pilot, you know."

"You prove to me you can handle the duties of a backseater first, then we'll talk about when you fly." Connert's cheeky attitude was beginning to wear on Court's nerves. "Let's get going."

The two men mounted the ladders and settled into their cockpits. ACs and GIBs in F-4s were attached to their Phantom by four belts, two garters, a high-pressure air hose to inflate their G-suits, an oxygen hose for their mask, and a thick wire connector for the microphone built into the oxygen mask and the headsets built into the helmet. The crew chief hopped back and forth between each cockpit, helping the men find and adjust their straps and hoses. Court picked up his helmet from the front canopy bow and put it on.

"How do you read?" he asked Connert when he had signaled for power and placed the master electrical switches on.

"Loud and clear. Do you want me to start the INS alignment?"

"Of course." Court was surprised. It was automatic for a backseater to start aligning the heading of the Inertial Navigation System from the rear cockpit. In fact it couldn't be done from the front seat on this model F-4.

While preflighting, the crew chief wore a headset and large microphone mask to communicate with the pilot. He plugged into the intercom system and asked Court how he read him.

"Loud and clear, chief." Court started the engines, then began the litany of the fifteen Before-Taxi checks he had to make. When he was ready to taxi, he performed his cockpit check and noticed neither the radar nor the INS was operating.

"Hey, Dick, you having trouble getting the radar and INS on line?"

"Yeah. They don't seem to respond."

"Chief," Court said, "put your ladder back and see if you can find the problem."

The crew chief ran up the ladder and bent into the cockpit. In seconds Court's radar screen and INS readouts came on.

"She's okay now, sir," the chief said over the intercom. "Just a little switch problem was all." Even though the roar of the engines reverberated in the revetment, Court could tell the chief was working hard at making his voice remain neutral.

"Thanks, chief. Ladders away and we'll be off."

He checked in with Silver flight.

"Roger, Three Three," Morelli said. "We were wondering when you'd be up." Court was chagrined to see the two F-100s already out of their revetments and waiting for him by the taxiway like two giant birds of prey with spread wings. He added power, returned the lieutenant's departing salute, and taxied out of the revetment. He followed the two F-100s to the armament area by the edge of the runway. All three pilots placed their hands and arms on their canopy bows to show the armament crews they weren't touching any switches. The lead armorer came to Court's F-4, looked up at him, and shook his head no, and pointed to the backseat. Court understood.

"You got your hands out of the cockpit, Connert?"

"Oh yeah, right away," Connert said in a startled voice. The armament man nodded and waved his crew under the wings to check the pylons, to insert the bomb-rack ejection cartridges, and to make the final electrical continuity check, and finally to pull the pins that secured the bombs to the racks and the racks to the pylons. He held the pins aloft and waved Court on his way.

When the three fighters were cleared on the runway, Morelli lined up on the left side – the downwind side – of the runway. Jensen lined up in echelon formation on his right wing, Court lined up in echelon to Jensen. That way any crosswind would blow the jet exhaust of the lead plane away from the one behind it. Morelli gave the windup signal by twirling his forefinger next to the canopy on Jensen's side. Jensen repeated the signal to Court. The two F-100s ran their engines up to 100 percent, performed their checks, then throttled back. Court could not run his engines up to full military power (as 100 percent RPM without afterburner is called) because the tremendous thrust would skid the F-4 along on its locked brakes. When he finished his checks, he signaled he was ready. Morelli released his brakes, kicked in his afterburner, and was off, followed by Jensen fifteen seconds later. Court saw the slow acceleration of the F-100s and realized he would have to delay thirty seconds or run over Jensen. Without the full bombload on his F-4, it was lighter and more responsive to the thrust of the engines.

"All set back there?" he asked Connert.

"Yes, sir. Let's get this show on the road."

Court released the brakes, ran the throttles all the way up, then outboard to the afterburner position. In seconds the airplane was at nosewheel rotation speed, then they were off the ground at 175 knots (200mph) barely 3,500 feet down the 10,000-foot runway. Court saw Silver Lead come out of afterburner and turn right so he and Jenson could cut him off and join up in formation. Court kept his burners in until 420 indicated to use the extra speed to catch up faster, then throttle back and slide into position. A fighter pilot always wants to make the cutoff turn and be in formation on his leader's wing faster than anybody else has ever done. It's an automatic reflex. He doesn't even think about it.

"HEY," Connert shouted from the backseat. "We're too fast. We're gonna hit him." Court felt the throttles pulled back. When he shoved them back into position, he felt the pressure of Connert's hand.

"You're crazy," Court yelled. "Get your goddamn hands off the throttle. Put 'em in your lap and don't touch anything. I'm flying this airplane."

"Well, *all right*, Major. If that's the way you want it. I was just trying to be helpful."

Court had rammed the throttles up and now was slowly dragging them back as he slid into position on Morelli's right wing. Jensen had taken the left. The three airplanes entered the overcast in a tight Vee formation.

Morelli was smooth and the clouds were not turbulent. The climb-out was smooth as Court gently fingered the controls to hold position. He thought about Connert. "Who'd you fly with at George?" he asked.

"One of the squadrons," Connert answered in a low voice.

"Which one?"

"What is this? The Inquisition? What difference does it make what squadron I flew with? Don't you think I can fly?"

Something wrong with this guy, Court thought. "Take it easy, Dick. We'll talk about it on the ground. Tune in the Can Tho Tacan, will you?"

Court concentrated on flying formation and following Morelli's signals when they climbed through the overcast and leveled at 16,000 feet in clear air. Morelli fishtailed them out into spread formation.

Court checked his Tacan and found it still reading from Channel 38 at Tan Son Nhut. He took command of the set and flipped it to 41 for Can Tho.

"How come you didn't change to the Can Tho frequency?" he asked Connert.

"Well, I didn't think you needed it yet."

"Connert," Court snapped, "when I say I want you to do something, that's an order. An order I want carried out immediately. It is not subject to your interpretation. You understand?"

"Well, sure, Court. I understand."

"That's Major to you, Captain." Court's voice was edged with steel. Connert didn't answer.

Morelli, Silver 31, first made radio contact with Paddy, the Can Tho radar site; then with Beaver 24, who instructed him to give his lineup.

"Roger, Two Four," Morelli said. "Silver has mission

number eleven dash six eight two. We are two Fox One Hundreds and one Fox Four." He unkeyed for a second, as all good radio users did, so as to not tie up the frequency too long in case of an emergency.

"Fox Four?" Beaver Two Four repeated. "What's up?"

"Those Phantom drivers get lost, so we got to drive 'em around. We have Mark Eighty-twos, CBUs, Nape, and twenty mike-mike."

"Roger on your lineup. I'm in an Oscar One holding a left-hand orbit at fifteen hundred at the canal intersection just north of Vi Thanh. As soon as you have a tally, I'll mark the target. You copy?" Beaver Two Four's voice was cheerful yet businesslike. As with all FACs, he knew the local area like the palm of his hand. He flew from a small dirt strip next to an American unit where he received his daily frag orders. He had a crew chief who handled maintenance, weapons, and radios for him,

"Silver copies."

"Your target today is a company or more of VC troops trying to take the town. A local ARVN platoon and two American advisors are trapped up against the canal east of town. They are not well dug in. The bad guys are in the treeline running north and south. Copy?"

"Silver copies." The undercast broke up into scattered layers as Morelli approached the rendezvous point. Haze and smoke from burning rice fields covered the ground up to several thousand feet like layers of gauze. The rice farmers burned the harvested stubble in their dry paddies for fertilizer before planting the next crop.

"Target elevation is seventy feet, altimeter is twenty-nine sixty-two, surface winds from the west at ten. Visibility maybe only five miles. Scattered to broken clouds around ten grand, but you can see that better than I can. So far there has been no groundfire. Best bailout is zero four zero for twenty at Can Tho. You could even put your bird on the runway if you had to, but it's only six thousand feet long. Copy?"

"Copy. I have you in sight." Morelli pumped the control stick of his F-100, signaling Jensen and Court to drop back into loose trail, where they flew about 500 feet behind each other. This gave them space to check their switches inside the cockpit and the target area outside without having to concentrate on close-formation flying. Once in the bombing pattern, the space would increase until they were at even intervals flying around the target in the wheel pattern. Court put his Master Arm switch on and moved his armament selector to Bombs Single. On the dial he had the choice of Pairs, Ripple, or Single.

"FAC is in to mark," Beaver Two Four said. His tiny Cessna rolled into a bank and dived earthward. Seconds later Court saw a billowing splash of brilliant white smoke as the phosphorus head of the rocket exploded against the base of a treeline.

"Tally on your smoke," Silver Lead said.

"Two tallies."

"Three tally."

"Okay, guys, hit along the treeline from a hundred meters south of my smoke to a hundred meters north. You can run in from the north or the south, but break east when you come off. We'll start with the bombs." It was a required procedure for attacking aircraft always to fly parallel to friendly troops and never attack from over them or break away from the target over them. An early release or a hung piece of ordnance falling off could impact on the friendly position. Such an event was called a short round.

"Lead's in, south to north, FAC in sight." Pilots were equally divided whether or not to use simple codes such as Miami to New York for south to north to foil possible radio interception. Some said with a twinkle that they had flunked geography, others said the VC had eyes, they could see where the attackers were coming from. The main reasoning against the code use was that interception of the UHF (Ultra High Frequency) radio the pilots used required receiving equipment too expensive and too sophisticated for everyday use around every hamlet and town, not to mention instant translation from English to Vietnamese and relay to the gunners. In North Vietnam such radio interception

198

effort was real and feasible. Not so in South Vietnam.

Morelli rolled his F-100 into a 45-degree dive from 12,000 feet. Court followed Jensen, who rolled in as Morelli was pulling off. The idea was to try to have one set of guns on the target at all times to pinpoint and take out a gunner who suddenly decided to shoot. Good gunners liked to shoot as the attacker pulled off so that neither the pilot going away nor the pilot rolling in could see the muzzle flashes.

"Three's in, FAC in sight." Court started to roll in as Jensen pulled off a mile and a half below him.

"Roger, Three, you're cleared. Put your bombs just beyond Lead and Two's."

"I'll pickle at fifty-five," Court said on the intercom to Connert. He concentrated on lining up his aircraft and his gunsight on the treeline. Unlike the single-seat F-100, F-4 pilots had a backseater to read off altitude, airspeed, and dive angle as they positioned their aircraft toward the target. Court had given Connert his release altitude so that he would know what to expect as he read off the figures.

With a practiced eye, Court plunged his aircraft down the chute at exactly 45 degrees. His airspeed built such that he knew he would have 450 at one mile above the ground. From force of habit from his single-engine days, he glanced quickly into the cockpit from time to time to cross-check his speed, altitude, and angle. He became aware that Connert's altimeter calls were 500 feet too early. At 6,000 he called 55, which, if Court had not been looking, would have caused an early release, making the bomb fall short of Court's aim point.

"Watch your altitude calls," he growled at Connert.

As he flashed through 55, Court pressed the red bomb-release button on his stick twice, releasing a bomb from each inboard rack. Had he selected Ripple, all six would have dropped, alternating from side to side. One did that in high-threat areas where multiple passes were sure death.

He grunted against the G-force as he pulled up and rapidly turned left, then right to the east, in an automatic jink reflex. Neither Morelli nor Jensen had jinked, he noted.

Too complacent, maybe. Then he realized that with a full load and without the afterburner on, the F-100 just didn't have the thrust to make twisting pullouts. Using the afterburner would burn too much fuel. Court had had to make his pattern wider and slower than normal to accommodate the F-100 pilots who, with less thrust, couldn't blast their way around as easily as the big Phantom.

He was cleared for his next pass and rolled in. Again Connert called the altitudes 500 feet before they were actually reached.

"You're calling out the altitudes too soon," Court said on the intercom.

"I thought you wanted it that way. For me to lead your altitudes, I mean."

"No, I don't want you to lead the altitudes. I want to know exactly when I pass through them, not before, certainly not after." Court bit his words off. There were usually some adjustments to be made when flying with a new GIB, but this man would vex the Sphinx, he fumed.

On the next pass Court dodged a cloud and rolled in late and not quite at 45 degrees. He knew he would release 500 feet lower at 5,000 feet to make up for the shallow angle.

"Silver Three Three in, FAC in sight," he called.

"Roger, Three Three, you're cleared. Put your bombs fifty meters after those of number Two." Court acknowledged.

As he flashed down the chute, Court didn't hear Connert make *any* altitude or airspeed calls. This guy is one weird fellow, he thought. But I'd better let him know what I am doing. Regardless of problems, a good frontseater always kept his backseater informed.

"I'll be releasing at five thousand," he said. Connert didn't reply. At 6,000 feet Court had things under control and was ready to press the pickle button at 5,000. At 5,500 he was startled to hear the chung of an ejector cartridge and feel the release of one bomb. With a start he realized that Connert had hit the red release button on top of his stick in the backseat. That bomb would be short. He felt back pressure on the stick to pull out.

"Get your goddamn hands off the stick," he snapped. He held his dive and pickled the second bomb at 5,000 and junked off-target.

"Your first was a little short, Three, but your second was right on," Beaver Two Four transmitted.

"Roger," Court replied in as level a voice as he could summon. Then he spoke to Connert on the intercom.

"What in hell you doing back there? You hit the pickle button, then tried to pull back on the stick."

"Well, I thought you forgot or were hit or something, so I thought I should do it for you." Connert's voice was breezy and seemingly unconcerned.

"Christ Almighty!" Court exploded. "You thought . . . Look, from now on put your hands in your lap and shut up. I'm going cold mike. I don't want to hear from you unless it's Mayday." He snapped off the intercom switch that cut out their open microphones. Now if either one wanted to talk, he had to press a button on the throttle. He made the next pass without hearing from Connert.

"Nice bombs, Silver," Beaver Two Four said. He led the three airplanes through two more bomb passes, then started them in on the low-level CBU and napalm runs. Connert had made no comments from the backseat and Court certainly hadn't asked for any. When Silver flight had exhausted its supply of napalm and CBU, Beaver Two Four had Silver Three One and Three Two make two strafing runs each. Court orbited high and dry, wishing he had a gun.

Beaver Two Four was ecstatic as Silver flight checked out.

"Great job, guys," he said, ignoring proper radio procedure. "The guys on the ground have broken out and are back at the village perimeter. They thank you much. Right now I have no BDA for you due to smoke and haze. But I'll give you one-hundred-percent ordnance within fifty meters of the target area. Good job. You're cleared off-target. Beaver Two Four out."

Morelli led the flight to Tan Son Nhut, where they split

up and made single-ship GCAs in the worsening weather. After Court taxied in and shut down the engines of the big fighter, he hurriedly unstrapped and, without waiting for the crew chief to put up the ladder, crawled along the canopy rail to the backseat. Connert sat there, helmet on, still strapped in. Court grabbed his chest strap and shook him.

"Listen, you son of a bitch," he grated, "you don't ever release a bomb or take control of an aircraft without instructions from the AC. You get the hell out of this cockpit and never climb in it again. I will never fly with you again."

The crew chief lieutenant moved the ladders in place and Court climbed down. Connert hadn't moved. He stared down at Court with wide and guileless eyes and a half-smile on his lips.

Court grabbed his gear and stomped over to the crew van that was waiting with Morelli and Jensen. They had seen the action and heard Court's words. He climbed in.

"Let's go," he snarled.

"What about Connert?" Morelli asked.

"Let the son of a bitch walk." The driver let the clutch out and the van moved down the flightline toward the operations building. A light rain dotted the windscreen. Court savagely pulled out his crumpled pack of Luckies and lit one.

"Why crawl to the back cockpit?" Jensen asked. "Why not wait until he had climbed down?"

"Because I'd have broken his jaw," Court snapped. "With his helmet still on, I knew I couldn't hit him."

After the three pilots hung up their gear and debriefed, Dieter called Court into his office. Connert hadn't shown up yet.

"I'd like to turn you guys around right away, but it's too late to get some more F-100s down there. Things are popping at the Tacan station at Can Tho. The station just went off the air and the bad guys are attacking the radar site on the Army side of the base. Spooky will be on station

202

all night, and we'll launch Skyspot from the alert pad when they can work them in. Between the fighting at Can Tho and Bien Hoa, we will be launching just about everything we have at first light tomorrow morning."

Dieter glanced at the scheduling board and the big clock mounted over it. It was almost six o'clock. "Court, get a good night's sleep and I'll launch you first thing in the morning."

"Mac, I got a problem. I need a new backseater. There's something wrong with that Connert guy." His face was hard. "I absolutely refuse to fly with him. Furthermore, I don't think he should fly with anybody."

"How did he get through the upgrade course?" Dieter asked.

"They must be damn hard-up for F-4 frontseaters. He's so bad in the back, I'd hate to see what he is like up front. Look, just give me one of your Hun jocks. I can check him out in the backseat in half an hour. All he needs is to handle the INS and the radar. I'll do all the rest."

"How about me?" Dieter said as they walked out of the office into the ops room.

"Sure," Court said. "I think it would be great to fly with you."

Dick Connert walked in the door to the ops room, a hurt look on his face. "Why don't you want to fly with me, Major Bannister?"

Court glanced around the operations section. The clerk and several other pilots had stopped what they were doing to watch what was happening. It wouldn't do to embarrass a fellow officer in front of the troops.

"Let's just say I want to give Major Dieter the experience of flying in an F-4 backseat."

"Don't you think I'm good enough? Don't you think I can hack it?" Connert's voice became shrill. "Just give me another flight, will you? I'll prove to you how good I am. Just give me another chance. I'll show you what I can do."

"Connert, come here," Court said, and walked back into

Dieter's office. Connert followed him in. Dieter winked, stayed outside, and shut the door.

"Connert, I don't know where you came from and I don't care. You have no business being in an airplane . . . in any capacity, front or back seat. The minute you get to a squadron, someone will give you a check ride and you'll be out on your ass. I really don't know how you got this far." He studied Connert's face. It was smooth and bland, his blue eyes as guileless as a baby's. There was something odd, then Court realized what it was. Connert had no lines around his eyes, under his eyes, around his mouth or on his cheeks. It was the face of a baby or a young priest. There were no sins or mistakes behind that face to give the evidence of experience so obvious in the faces of military pilots and racecar drivers.

"Why don't you like me, Major Bannister? What have I ever done to you?"

Court felt uneasy. He wasn't getting through to this man. There was something about his attitude and his rigid calmness.

"What class were you in?" he asked on a hunch.

"What do you mean?"

"What pilot-training class?" Court asked. Most pilots knew exactly what the question meant, unless it was in another context from a military-academy graduate.

Connert hesitated briefly. "Ah, sixty-four."

"Sixty-four what?" Court knew he was on to something. That answer would have been appropriate for an academy man who had graduated in 1964, but not for a pilot-training class. Several pilot-training classes graduated each year. They were identified by the year and a following letter or number to show when, within the twelve months of the year, they had graduated.

"Where did you graduate from?"

Connert raised his chin. "What's the purpose of all these questions? You want to see my orders? I've got orders proving who I am. I don't need to answer all these questions."

204

"Let me see your ID card and your orders." Court's voice was hard as cold-rolled steel.

"What do you mean? Why should I show you that stuff?" Connert's voice rose again.

Court strode to the door and threw it open. "Mac, get the OSI on this. We've got an imposter on our hands." Court and Dieter had kept Connert in Dieter's office.

In twenty minutes two agents from the Office of Special Investigation arrived, read Connert his rights, and searched him.

"All he has is this, sir," an agent said, and handed Dieter a DD2AF ID card and a folded copy of some mimeographed orders. The card appeared legitimate. Court and Dieter examined the papers. They showed Richard Connert, AFSC 6244, was an F-4 pilot en route from George Air Force Base to Ubon Air Force Base. The two men looked at each other.

"This is not a pilot's AFSC," Court said. "I don't know what it is, but it sure isn't for a pilot or a navigator." AFSC meant Air Force Specialty Code. It was the number identifier for all jobs in the USAF. A fighter pilot was an 1115, a navigator in fighters was a 1555.

One of the agents spoke to Connert. He was very formal. "Sir, please take us to your BOQ room. We would like to examine your belongings."

Connert's eyes grew round. He nodded his head. "Okay, okay. So I'm not a pilot." His face looked sincere and quite young. "Hey, I never meant to hurt anybody." He looked at Court. "Okay, so I'm not a pilot. But I could have been." His eyes grew narrow. "I certainly could have been a pilot." He looked around at the men watching him, his face wrinkling like a small child about to cry. "You pilots think you're so damn good." His voice rose. "You think you're so much better than me. You're just shit, that's what you are. You're just shit."

"Okay, let's go," an agent said and put his hand on Connert's arm. Connert shook it loose and lunged for Court. Court stepped back. The two agents grabbed Connert and

205

bent his arms behind his back. "I'll get you for this, Bannister!" he screamed over his shoulder as they pushed him out. "You'll see. I'll get you for this. You and all the other bastard pilots. You're arrogant assholes, that's what you are. ASSHOLES." The whites of his eyes shone.

The men watching were silent as Connert was led away. "That's almost more than I care to watch," Dieter said finally. He looked at Court. "While you were talking in here, I got on the horn to Personnel. You're right, Connert is no pilot. He is a nonrated lieutenant who ran the F-4 simulator at George. He was on his way through here to set up a simulator at Ubon." He tapped Connert's mimeographed orders. "Easy enough to phony these up. Probably had a mimeograph in his office. Just forgot to enter a pilot's AFSC in place of his own. Otherwise we'd probably still think he was a pilot, albeit a piss-poor one." He shook his head. "That guy really has problems. He'll be mustered out damn quick, probably under a Section Eight."

Court laughed. "Dunno, Mac. Looks to me like he's a natural for your squadron."

He slipped the punch Dieter threw at his shoulder.

11

1045 Hours Local, Thursday 1 February 1968
The Imperial City of Hue
Republic of Vietnam

The imperial city of Hue lay 70 nautical miles to the southeast of Quang Tri – normally 45 minutes flying time for
the Huey piloted by Warrant Officer McClanahan. Bad
weather, the white mist the French call *crachin*, spit mist,
had forced them down at a friendly firebase for over two
hours. Wolf Lochert used the time to study the contents of
the large envelope handed him by Colonel Rennagel before
takeoff. In clipped handwriting it stated:

= =
LOCHERT TO HUE ASAP. PROTECT U.S. NATIONALS.
CONTACT NOMAD NEAR TAY LOC AIRFIELD ON FOX MIKE
48.32 OR 45.52 FOR FURTHER INSTRUCTIONS.
= =

With the notes were a 1:50,000 map of Hue city and the
surrounding area, and a small area-study booklet outlining
the past history and current inhabitants of Hue. He read
of its cultural and religious heritage, its great walls, lush
gardens, flowing moats, tree-lined streets. In the Buddhist
myth, Hue was the lotus flower growing from the mud. Hue
represented serenity and peace in the middle of a terrible
war.

Wolf tucked the notes and map inside a cargo pocket of

his fatigues and opened the parachute bag at his feet. Inside were three Cláymore mines, their convex face reading "This Side Toward The Enemy," a half-dozen M26 fragmentation and thermite grenades, several day-night smoke flares, and an Air Force survival radio. A roll of black electrician's tape brought a thin smile to Wolfs lips. Considerate man, that Colonel Rennagel, he thought. He knows about taping thermite to Claymores. Didn't even ask for a receipt.

He zipped the bag shut and looked over at Lopez, who was asleep, his brown face slack in repose. Wolf saw his fingers twitch and his body jerk slightly as he fought the Viet Cong of his dream. You should be on extended R-and-R, Wolf thought, not off to more combat. He turned away and stared out the open door of the helicopter. He wondered who Nomad was. And who were the U.S. nationals – the term for American civilians. Obviously civilians, not military, they could be Federal employees, newsmen, workers at a charitable organization. Anything but tourists.

Lang Tri had been rough. Wolf felt grimy, bone-weary, and a little sick in his heart. He was all too familiar with this afteraction state of mind. The coming-down from an adrenaline high, the need for sleep, the need for time to himself in a quiet area to reset his mind and body, to recharge his mind and spirits away from killing, away from the ability to assess a threat and kill it in a heartbeat. To kill with no crippling regrets or remorse. To kill without wondering what the man he had just killed was like as a child of ten. Such thoughts had to be dealt with later, after the fight. Thoughts that if allowed to surface on the battlefield brought inattention and sure death.

Yet later, in a secure area after the battle, when it was physically safe to ponder, it was not mentally safe. If it had been a particularly bad time, the thoughts that came sometimes required alcohol to handle. Wolf fought within himself not to drink. It was something he could not handle. Years earlier as a second lieutenant in Korea, after his first battle when he had killed, after he was in a rear area at a makeshift company beer bar, he had let his thoughts wander. He hadn't known any better. It had led to disaster. A monstrous drunk: raging, throwing, punching, finally subdued by anxious friends who had had to put him in chains and hide him from the Military Police. He had had another incident in Germany as a captain. From those incidents he had learned he had to reset and recharge without alcohol that inner part of himself that was the engine of his very being before it spun in furious rage faster and faster until it flew apart in bellowing disintegration.

And now, here in Vietnam, it was different, worse. Now it was a two-part fury that went beyond the killing sickness. The fury was aimed at those in suits who squandered the lives of American men without a plan. Men who wore exquisite ties and spoke in precise terms of expendables, and in vague terms of goals. And his fury was aimed at those who went barefoot and wore beads, those who trivialized and scorned the efforts of men far better than they. Men who through centuries of conflict had always answered the call of their leaders. Rightly or wrongly, Wolf and those like him believed, and, as young men, had gone to do battle with the enemies of their country. So it had always been. Men of the Roman legions, Confucian foot soldiers, Rommel's tankers, in the Pacific Iowa boys not old enough to vote manning their pompoms against other young men hurling themselves at the ships in kamikaze trances. Noble young men, losing blood and ideals while gaining bravery and cynicism in battle.

Wolfgang Xavier Lochert loved these men. As much as he despised those who sent them to war, he loved them. Even the young black-haired soldiers from North Vietnam who gave their all to save their country from what their leaders told them was imperialistic slavery.

But now was not the time for any of this. He was a fighting machine. Later, later. Now he must rest. There was nothing he could do, he reasoned, until he talked to Nomad.

Wolf told McClanahan to wake him in ten minutes, leaned his head back against the seat sling, and tried to

209

doze. The second he closed his eyes, explosions and fireballs from Lang Tri, the cries of the wounded, and the whop of chopper blades roared across his mind. Wolf knew how to quiet himself, how to leave one action behind and how to prepare for the next. He had learned to do it in minutes. He put his mind back in the chapel of the seminary where he had studied as a youth. It was cool there, and held the tranquillity of the heavens.

"Heavenly Father," he began, "here I am once again, prostrate before You. I beg You for strength, humility, understanding." Peace came behind his eyes as he began, "Our Father, who art in heaven, hallowed be Thy name . . ."

Twenty minutes later, when Warrant Officer McClanahan told the door gunner to awaken Wolf carefully, he was amazed at how relaxed and refreshed the burly man looked compared to the devastation on his face an hour earlier. Wolf became instantly alert. He tapped Lopez awake. The weather had lifted enough to resume the flight to Hue. McClanahan started the Huey and pulled it into the air. The gunner handed Wolf a spare helmet with boom microphone and plugged it into the intercom.

"We're ten minutes out, Colonel," McClanahan said a few minutes later. "I've dialed in Nomad's freq. Press the button on the cord and you're transmitting." Wolf nodded. As he was about to press the button, he realized he hadn't been assigned a call sign. He grinned and pressed the button.

"Nomad, Nomad, this is Wolf. Do you copy?" He had to call three times before Nomad came up on the radio.

"Wolf, this is Nomad. I read you loud and clear. How me?" Wolf could hear the sounds of shots and explosions in the background.

"Loud and clear, Nomad. Sounds like you're in it. Can you give me your position?" Normally, position coordinates were transmitted in code. In terse situations there wasn't time enough to code and decode.

"Wolf, Nomad, roger. Everybody else knows where I am,

and they're shooting at me. Not much time left. We gotta get out of here. Can you get to Tay Loc? I'll direct you from there."

Lochert looked at McClanahan, who peered forward through the gloom and smoke searching for the Tay Loc runway. He shrugged.

"Nomad, this is Wolf. We'll try, over."

"When you're at the south end of the runway, I'll pop smoke. We'll talk about what I need once you have an exact fix on my location." Although the enemy knew where Nomad was located, Wolf could tell he didn't want to discuss any rescue plans until the last minute.

Suddenly the left door-gunner opened up with the nasal hammering of his M60, followed quickly by the right gunner. The nose dipped and the helicopter started a rapid descent, blades biting the air. Below, red muzzle blasts shredded and tore the morning mist. Wolf opened his lap belt, checked his harness, and crouched next to the left gunner, Lopez behind him. Both had their equipment strapped on, Rennagel's bag at their feet. The copilot handed Wolf a portable telephone version of the PRC-25 FM radio. Wolf gave back the helmet and boom mike and picked up the handset.

McClanahan spiraled down, leveled at 200 feet, tipped, flew one way then the next, then zoomed for the side of the runway, blades slap-slapping. Wolf saw green tracers reaching for them. Then purple smoke billowed from the flat roof of a two-storey French-style villa 200 meters to the south of the airfield.

"Nomad, I got purple," Wolf barked into the handset.

"Purple it is, Wolf. Put her down on the roof, stay light on the skids. There's three of us and we got to vamoose." His voice was strained.

Wolf looked over his shoulder at McClanahan. The pilot nodded, his hands busy on the controls. The door gunners yammered as McClanahan pulled his craft over to the besieged building. They could see huge pockmarks in the concrete, a collapsed wall at ground level, blown-out windows, and smoke curling from a burned-out vehicle in the yard. He noted the yard was surrounded by a high concrete wall, with a gate that was as yet still intact. Outside the gate on the street, he saw several crumpled bodies clad in the olive-drab fatigues worn by ARVN infantrymen. He saw furtive movement along the trees farther up the street to the north. McClanahan pulled over a stand of tall palms, then mushed in toward the roof.

Wolf saw two people in civilian clothing, a man and a woman, crouched next to a third along the low concrete barrier at the western edge of the roof. Dirt and leaves blew up, nearly obscuring the landing zone as McClanahan eased his Huey to the rooftop. The door gunners ceased firing as their line of vision was obscured by the concrete retaining walls lining the edge of the roof. McClanahan held his ship such that the skids were barely touching the surface of the roof.

The third person, a man, was flat on his back, wedged in the corner formed by the wall and the roof. His shirt was ripped away and his upper body was lacerated and bloody. Heavily stained strips of what looked like bedsheets were wrapped around his chest and arms. His eyes were closed and his face was blue and sunken. Wolf knew at a glance he was dying. The woman, with long blonde hair hastily tied in a knot behind her head, crouched over him. She held his hand and shielded his face from the blowing dirt. Her face was twisted and lined with tension. Next to her was a thin man with dark hair, holding an M16. Several magazines and frag grenades were in a box at his feet. Nearby lay a PRC-25 radio. Both the woman and the man were dotted with blood specks and had rips in their clothing.

Wolf slipped from the doorway, holding his M16 like a pistol in his right hand, and ran crouched to the civilians. Lopez flung himself down behind a wall, rolled onto his stomach, and poked his rifle over the wall. The door gunner unhooked, grabbed an M16, and dashed behind him.

"Get in the chopper," Wolf yelled above the din of the rotors to the civilians. The retaining walls bounced the

212

sound and the downwash back in his face. Smoke from the yard swirled and spun. "We'll get him." He pointed to the dying man. The girl scrambled to one side. Wolf slung his rifle over his shoulder and reached for the man's shoulders. The gunner bent over his legs. Before Wolf could move, a motion in the air caught his eye. He saw a mortar shell starting to arc down from the apex of the high lob. The finned shell appeared to be headed straight down on them.

"Incoming," he yelled, and ducked low over the man's body. The shell flashed over the far side of the roof and exploded in the courtyard.

"Stay down," he pantomimed above the roar of the helicopter to the civilians. He pointed at Lopez and the gunner, then over the wall. "We gotta get that mortar or we're not gonna get outta here," he yelled in his ear. He looked up, the others following his motion. Another high wobbling lob was now at the apex over their heads, the fins and curvature of the shell perfectly clear in stop motion in Wolf's eyes. As it started down, Wolf knew beyond doubt it would land on the roof. He had to restrain himself from emptying his M16 at it. The insane thought of shooting down mortar shells like skeet with a shotgun crossed his mind.

The shell impacted on the flat roof on the far side of the helicopter next to the pilot's compartment. The explosion, confined by the retaining wall, blew hundreds of fragments up and into the cockpit. McClanahan absorbed most of the blast and died instantly in a welter of gore and shredded flight suit. His copilot lost his helmet and his right arm. With his left arm he made dazed and feeble movements at the collector. The right door-gunner was thrown from the helicopter over the wall to the courtyard below. The helicopter settled heavily on its skids and began to scream and rock from side to side as the mangled controls sent impossible commands. Soon it would tip over and flail the entire rooftop with the blades as they broke up. The gunner kneeling next to Wolf threw down his weapon, scuttled in a scrambling crouch to the left cockpit door, flung it open, reached inside, and shut the turbine off.

As the hissing and whopping of the blades wound down, Wolf looked up and saw another mortar round approaching the apex. He felt a slight breeze from behind, and knew it was enough to make the shell fall short. He sighted along the azimuth from which the shell came, and estimated the range from which a shell that size could be lobbed to its altitude. That threat had to be eliminated before any other decision or action could take place. He unslung his rifle, rose on his knees, quickly poked his rifle over the wall, and opened fire in the general area he had fixed in his mind. He hated shooting without a definite target, but had to come up firing to keep the enemy's heads down. He triggered two- and three-round bursts as he looked for the mortar crew. He spotted a thin wisp of smoke, looked upwind from it, and saw a natural depression behind a wrought-iron fence in a villa across the street. He could just make out the top of a tube and two crouched figures through the fence grille.

"Over there," he yelled at Lopez, who was still shooting from his position at the edge of the roof. Then he fired two quick bursts to keep them from dropping another round down the open mouth. When Lopez picked up the fire with his weapon, Wolf ducked down and grabbed several egg-shaped hand grenades. As he knelt and pulled a pin, he saw the gunner trying to help the badly wounded copilot from the helicopter.

"Get over here and shoot where I tell you," he commanded. "We'll take care of him later." He turned and flung the first grenade, then a second and a third as fast as he could. The girl crawled to the copilot's door. The gunner flopped down next to him and kept up a steady stream of fire into the dirt and dust blown up by the explosions. A second gun started yammering to his left. He looked over and saw the civilian coolly sighting and placing his bullets with great care. He looked back at the mortar position. As the smoke cleared, he could see part of the fence was blown across the mortar position. The mortar tube protruded through the grillwork.

"Okay," he said to the gunner and Lopez, "we got him.

214

Crawl around each wall. See what's out there, how close they are. Fire a round or two each time you poke your heads up. Make 'em think we have plenty of people up here." Lopez and the gunner nodded and crawled away. Wolf rolled back to face the civilian.

"Let's go get the copilot," he said.

They crawled to the cockpit and crouched next to the woman, who knelt there holding the pilot's left hand. Inside, they could see the blanched face of a young man shrunken inside his flight suit. He had bled to death.

Wolf looked at the woman. "Better get over to the side," he said gently. She looked up at him with a face smeared with dirt and gray eyes that seemed strangely calm. She nodded and crawled back to the dying man at the wall.

"You know how to fly a helicopter?" Wolf asked the civilian. He shook his head. "Well then, let's get what we can use out of this machine," Wolf said. They pulled a door gun with ammunition, the private weapons of the two dead men, canteens, and several boxes of food and emergency medical supplies. Wolf reached into the gore of the pilot compartment and pulled out the pilot maps and flight cards. He looked for a code wheel but couldn't find one. He stuffed the papers in the parachute bag. They crawled back to the shelter of the wall.

"You handle a weapon pretty well," Wolf said, eyeing the man. He was slender, with short-cropped dark hair and a strong face.

"I should. Infantry, early sixties."

"Who you with now?" Wolf began checking their weapons and inventorying the supplies. Lopez and the gunner had almost completed a circuit of the roof. They snapped off rounds every few seconds.

"Aye Eye Dee," the man said. "Police activities." Wolf took a closer look at him. Some Agency for International Development (AID) people with strong military backgrounds were hired to teach police techniques to the appropriate Vietnamese departments.

Wolf held out his hand. "Lochert," he said.

215

"Jim Polter." They shook. The girl crawled over.

"He's gone," she said in an accent that Wolf recognized as southern German.

"This is Greta Sturm," Polter said.

Wolf nodded. "What happened here?" he asked. Lopez was firing short bursts now. The gunner was busy replacing a magazine.

"The attack started late last night. By two this morning it was a full-scale operation," Polter began. "We were having a social function. Some of the people from State, AID, and from the German Maltese Aid Society, sort of a Red Cross mission – that's where Greta is from, she's a nurse. It was downstairs in this house." He tilted his chin at the dead man. "His house. Then all of a sudden the whole city was under attack. Rockets, mortars, heavy machine guns. There had to be infiltrators to open the gates, because right away the city was swarming with NVA troops. Most of the ARVN First Division is off on Tet holiday. Their headquarters and part of the city and airfield is defended by the Hac Bao, the Black Panther company from the First. We're looking down the muzzles of a whole damn NVA regiment, the Sixth, I think. This place is going to go. We've got to get out of here."

"Who is that?" Wolf pointed to the body.

"Chuck Felton. He is, he was," he corrected himself, "the Agency man here in Hue. He had quite an arsenal." Wolf noticed Polter said "agency" of the CIA and not "company," as many of those who were not fully informed said.

"Was he Nomad?" Wolf had been wondering why he had been singled out for the rescue attempt of some low-key employees. It became clear. Although he didn't know Nomad, most of the Agency people knew him. Through the years he had performed mány almost impossible tasks for them, and was, he knew, highly regarded as one of the few Army men that didn't let the whole thing go to his head.

"Yeah."

"Where is everybody else?"

216

"Downstairs," Polter said. "Blown away. When it got rough, Felton called Saigon for help on the Agency HF net. I heard him mention your name but had no idea they could track you down. Later he was hit bad, so it was me on the horn when you checked in."

"How come the activity is slow right now?" Wolf asked.

"At dawn the Panthers sent some troops out. Best I can tell, they flanked the NVA, fired a few bloopers to take the pressure off us, then fell back to their CP when the NVA started to rush them. They're taking the city house by house. They have plenty of time, so I expect they have been firing just enough to keep us pinned down. Things changed when the chopper came in. Now they know somebody big is here, they might get serious again."

"Are you two okay? Think you can run for a bit?" Polter nodded. Wolf looked at Greta Sturm. She seemed sturdy and capable.

"Yes," she said, "I am all right." She was well-featured and athletic-looking.

"Can you shoot?" Wolf asked.

She pursed her lips. "No," she said. "I cannot shoot."

Something about the way she said it made Wolf ask, "Can not, or will not?"

Her chin rose. "*Will* not." Her wide-set gray eyes held Wolf with a measure of defiance. "I am, after all, a nurse."

"Sir," Lopez called, "I need some help." Wolf and Polter crawled to his spot on the west wall. The street below ran north and south. He pointed to the north. "Up there. Looks like a lot of bad guys coming together in one location."

Wolf saw an armored vehicle and a dozen or so green-clad infantrymen ducking behind it. "Looks like they've captured an APC and are about to head our way." He looked to the south. What appeared to be a squad of the enemy had formed a blocking group. Wolf quickly crawled around and peered over the remaining three walls, looking for a way to escape the trap. The only open direction seemed to be to the east toward the rear of the villa. Wolf looked down into the yard. Well-kept shrubbery and low trees surrounded a pool and a tennis court with a high chain-link fence. Beyond the tennis court were one-story concrete servant quarters set against the rear concrete wall of the grounds. Over the wall was a dirt road, then an open field next to the Tay Loc runway. He saw a South Vietnamese battle flag flying over a sandbagged complex near the control tower.

Wolf crawled back to the others. He pointed to the far edge and described what he saw. "That's where we have to go. I want us to link up with the Viets." A mortar sailed over the roof and crashed in the south courtyard.

"We go *now*," Wolf said. "Polter, get us to the back door."

"What about them?" Greta Sturm asked, pointing at Felton's body and the ruined men in the helicopter.

Wolf looked at her anxious eyes, and shook his head. "Move it," he said in a brusque voice.

Laden with their equipment, they crawled across the roof behind Polter to an open hatch over a ladder down to a storeroom. In the room, Wolf took a quick look around. Empty mover's crates and cardboard boxes marked with Felton's name were stacked along one wall next to an old chair with a broken leg. The far wall had a metal rack filled with boxes of whiskey, beer, and soda water. Two military boxes of ammunition on the bottom shelf caught Wolf's eye. Next to them was a Soviet Rocket Propelled Grenade RPG-7 launcher and a canvas sling holding five shells. He quickly knelt by the boxes. "Take as much ammo as you can," he said. Polter carried an M16, a radio, and had stuffed his pockets full of grenades. Lopez did the same. The door gunner carried his big M60 and had slung several bandoliers of ammunition around his neck. Wolf motioned to Greta Sturm. "You carry these," he said, and handed her the RPG and the sling with the shells.

"*Nein*," she said. "No. I will not shoot, I tell you."

Wolf shook her by the shoulders. "*Du brauchst sie nicht abzuschiessen, sondern nur zu tragen.* You don't have to *shoot* them, you have to *carry* them." In shocked silence she shouldered the sling and picked up the heavy RPG.

They went quickly out of the room, Polter in front. He led them down a wide marble hall past several doors and past stairs leading to the front of the villa. In the rear, he opened a door to a narrow set of servant stairs that descended into a large room used as a kitchen and pantry. Bullets splatted against the marble and concrete of the front of the villa. A mortar exploded on the roof, jarring their ears with concussion. They hurried down the steps to the rear door. Greta Sturm carried the RPG awkwardly. "Carry it like a *Besen*, a broom," Wolf said. He opened the door and studied the grounds for a moment.

"We're going to go over the rear wall and try for the airfield," Wolf said. "I'll take the lead. Polter, you take the girl. Don't move until I signal you each time I stop. You . . ." He looked at the name tag of the gunner. "Rizzo, you be tail end Charlie. Joe," he said to Lopez, "pick a spot just outside the door and cover us. I'll holler when I want you to catch up."

They all nodded, the girl's eyes big and white now as if she finally realized she had a good chance of being killed. Wolf bolted out the door in a running crouch, crossed several meters of patio, and dove to the protection of low brick wall by the pool. He flattened as he heard the chugging of an AK-47 and several bullets threw up spray in the pool behind, then spanged the concrete by his face. He flipped over the wall, crawled along it for ten feet, rose quickly, looked back in the direction from which he thought the rounds were coming, and shot instantly at movement he saw on the wall of the north courtyard. A lone man toppled to the ground. Wolf heard several shots from where Lopez was holding. He waited a few seconds, saw no more activity, and waved to the group in the doorway.

They ran, crouching, to the safety of the wall. "That was the advance man, the scout. They don't know on the other side of the wall where the shot came from that killed him. With luck they'll think we're still in the house. They know we're armed, so they'll be careful. We've got a few minutes before they rush the place. I'll have to get Lopez out of there now." He looked over his shoulder, down the length of the pool to the tennis court. He pointed to the bushes lining the pool. "We'll use them for cover." He crawled away until he was concealed behind the trim bushes. They smelled sweet and earthy. He waved for the others to come. When they were next to him he called Lopez to join them. There was no answer. He called again.

"Lopez, move up, move up. Fire two rounds if you hear me."

There was no response. Wolf bit his lip for a second, then crawled around the base of the bushes to look at the back door of the villa. He saw three NVA dragging a slumped and inert Lopez around the corner of the villa away from him. He sighted for an instant and realized he couldn't shoot for fear of hitting Lopez. "Damn, damn, damn," he said and pounded the earth. Then he pushed himself back to his group.

"Let's move it," he said in a gruff voice.

It was easier running the length of the pool behind the bushes. At the end they came to the tall chain-link fence around the tennis court. "This way," Wolf said. He led them just short of the path he had seen from the roof that led to the servants' quarters. It paralleled one end of the court and the north wall. "Wait until I signal," he said. Crouching once again, he peered up and down the path. Nothing moved. He pulled a Claymore from the parachute bag and rigged it among branches on one side to point up the path. He taped a thermite grenade to the face and put a coil of detonating wire next to it. He pointed at Rizzo. "Bring that with you," he whispered. He checked the path again and, holding his M16 at port arms, dashed toward the small servants' house. Halfway there he rolled to one side and rigged another Claymore.

Ten feet short of the small open porch he threw himself at the base of a tree and aimed his rifle at the door. He listened, heard nothing, sprang to his feet and crashed the door, finger on the trigger, ready to spray anything that moved. The empty main room was furnished with a thin table, cheap rattan chairs, and a wicker sofa. He crashed each door of the other three small rooms in the same way. There was no one in the two bedrooms that contained several sleeping pallets and small dressers topped with thin cloth and female toiletries. The third room, the cooking area, was bare except for a heavy table, a large, tiled sink, and a four-foot-high clay pot full of water. Out the window Wolf saw a small structure that contained the opening to a septic tank. He eased back to the front door and waved for Polter and the others to advance. Rizzo covered Polter and the girl as they ran down the path, then he backed down after them, holding the big M60 with one hand, unwinding the wire with the other.

When he was inside, Wolf fixed the wire to a detonator he took from the bag. "Here." He handed it to Rizzo. "Take this and set up your gun in the doorway. Cover the path."

Polter and the girl sat on the floor, backs against the wall. Calmer now, after the run, in charge of herself once again, Greta Sturm glared at Wolf. She unslung the shells and pushed away the RPG she had been carrying. Wolf ignored her and flipped his hand at Polter. "Let's look around."

The small house was made of the Asian equivalent of cinder block. The rear wall of the villa grounds also served as the rear wall of the house. Like the villa, the structure was flat-roofed. In each room Wolf looked at the ceiling. There were no openings to the roof.

"We've got to get to the roof and see about getting over the wall," he said.

"Or blast through from down here," Polter said.

"I don't think a Claymore or an RPG round would do it, the wall's too thick. Besides, the noise would give us away, and the backblast would blow us away." He moved to the kitchen, shoved the table against the back wall, and climbed up. He tapped the white plaster ceiling with his rifle butt a few times. "Sounds like wood," he said. "Get the girl in here and we'll start taking it apart." He stepped to the floor, propped his gun in the closest corner, removed his harness, and eased it to the floor. He

221

bent over, pulled his K-Bar knife from the webbing, and climbed back on the table. He inserted the tip of the knife in a small crack and pried. A few chunks of white plaster fell to the floor. He scraped and bared a small section of wood lath. He poked his knife between two slats and stood to one side as a few inches of mortar crumbled and fell out. He began pushing and moving his knife, forcing out more and more of the crumbling mortar that streamed down on the table and the floor. When he had several feet cleared between laths, he began sawing on a lath at one end. After a moment Polter and Greta Sturm entered the room. His face was flushed and angry.

"She wants to go talk to them," he said angrily.

Wolf stepped down and handed the knife to Polter. He pulled the girl down to sit against the back wall. He took out a faded blue bandanna and wiped the sweat and mortar dust from his face.

"What do you want to talk to them about?" he asked quietly.

"About letting us go," she said.

"You mean letting *you* go, don't you?"

"No. I mean us. We are civilians. They – "

"Fräulein Sturm, *we* are not civilians. I am in the military and I have just killed some of their men. Rizzo and Polter will do the same thing before we are out of here. What makes you think they will have anything to do with us besides a bullet in the back of the head?"

"I have tended their men. They know me. We can go out under a white flag. They would not shoot. I will go in front and explain." She put her hand on Wolf's arm. He shook it off.

"That's sure death. Just relax. We'll be out of here soon as we get over that wall and make contact with the Black Panthers."

"I do not want to go with you." She sat back and folded her arms over her breasts. Her hands and forearms were dirty and scraped. Her forehead was smudged and damp. Wolf handed her his bandanna.

222

"Here, wipe some of the dirt off."

She flicked it back at him. "That has more dirt than I do."

"Why don't you want to go with us?"

"I am a nurse. You do not need me. They do." She nodded in the direction of the NVA. "I go where the wounded are."

Wolf stared at her. "How old are you? How long have you been here?"

She calculated the English words. "I have twenty-six years. I have here at the Hue Mission six months time. We have taken in the wounded Viet Cong. They have gratitude."

"Sure they have gratitude. You give them better medicine and treatment than their own side can give. They get a chance to study the layout of the city and its defenses. You bet they have gratitude."

"I do not know such things. I am not on any side."

"You don't have to be. But if you go out there they will at best kill you, at worst capture you."

"I do not believe you. You are like all the Americans. You think you are better than these people. You think only you have the right to tell people what to do. Why are you here?" Her gray eyes were filled with contempt.

"We're here," Wolf snarled, "because we didn't stop *your* great leader Adolf Hitler at Munich or at the Saar – "

She jumped to her feet. "You are a terrible man. I am leaving."

Wolf reached up and caught her wrist. "I won't let you go out there." She twisted with surprising strength. Wolf bent her arm behind her back and forced her to her knees by the sink. He wrenched her arms around an iron support and tied her hands palms together with his bandanna. She had to lie flat on her stomach. Polter, scraping and sawing, had witnessed the scene. He grinned and winked at Wolf, who glared.

"Just keep sawing," he snapped and went to check on Rizzo. He crawled next to the gunner and looked up the pathway.

"See anything?"

"No, sir. Haven't heard any firing either." His voice was terse, almost hostile. Wolf turned his head to look at the young man.

"Where you from, Rizzo?"

"What difference does it make?" He clenched his jaw.

"Look, Rizzo," Wolf said softly. "I'll overlook your insolence if you'll tell me what's eating at you. We're in a tight spot here and we need everybody backing everybody else. Now what is your problem?"

Rizzo tightened his jaw. "You shouldn't have made me leave Mister Craig. He was a good man."

Wolf thought for a moment. He remembered yelling at Rizzo, right after the mortar exploded by the helicopter, to get away from the wounded copilot and help him and Lopez destroy the mortar.

"On the roof, when you came to where I was and started shooting, did you see anything below? This time say sir."

"Yes, sir," Rizzo answered reluctantly.

"Did you shoot?"

"Yes, sir."

"Many times, right?"

"Yes, sir."

"Don't you think that saved our lives? We took out the very mortar pit that had our range. We would have all died if they had kept on firing." Rizzo didn't answer. "The nurse went to Mister Craig," Wolf continued. "His arm was gone. No tourniquet in the world would have stopped the massive bleeding. And he was in full shock. He was as good as dead the instant he was hit."

"You have an answer for everything, don't you, Colonel?" Wolf looked closer at Rizzo. He was in his early twenties, stocky and muscular, had clear brown eyes, an intelligent face, and full lips formed into a sneer.

"Yeah, Rizzo, I do." Wolf's voice was full military now, not loud but authoritative and crisp. "And I'll tell you why I do. I have all the answers because I've seen more men wounded in combat than you had in your basic training unit. You've been flying over the jungle of Vietnam while I've led men far younger than you into those jungles and into tunnels and caves you couldn't imagine in your worst dreams. Men with pride and grit who knew the chances they were taking. Men like Mister Craig. Men who know the success of the mission depends on each person believing in the other. Men like Joe Lopez who held the rear guard so we could get away. You start letting this thing fester in you and you'll be worse than useless to us. You shape up or so help me, I'll tie a white flag to you and the girl and boot both your butts out on the street. You do your job now, and I'll give you a chance to punch me out when we get back. You slack on your job now and I'll wrap this M60 around your head." He stuck his face up next to Rizzo. "*Capice*? Say sir."

Rizzo glowered. He looked determined. "I understand. I'll be glad to punch you out when we get back . . . sir," he added with scorn.

Wolf slammed him on the back. "Good man. I knew I could count on you." He crawled back to the kitchen.

12

0515 Hours Local, Friday 2 February 1968
416th Tactical Fighter Squadron
Tan Son Nhut Air Base
Republic of Vietnam

The squadron was alive with noise and activity. The pilots
were busy checking the flight schedule, their equipment,
making maps, discussing tactics. Their blood was racing.
All night while in the BOQ they had heard the sounds of
fighting coming from Cholon and the Phu Tho racetrack
area. Some had slept in the squadron building. They were
ready to go dish it out. The Skyspot alert crews staggered
in, fuzzy-eyed and haggard. Each flight had been launched
three times to beleaguered friendly outposts.

Court and Mac Dieter brought their coffee into Dieter's
office. Court pulled deeply on a Lucky.

"Still into those, are you? Thought you quit at SOS,"
Dieter said.

"I did. Got divorced, got to combat, got back on 'em,"
Court answered.

"They'll kill you, you know."

Court pulled out his pack from his sleeve pocket and
shook one out. He offered it to Dieter.

"Don't mind if I do. Thanks." Court lit Dieter's cigarette
with his Zippo.

Dieter saw the rubber band wound around the lighter.
"Why the rubber band?"

"Provides friction. Keeps the lighter from slipping out

226

of my pocket. Learned it out on patrol with the Special Forces. Lots of ways to get killed. One of them is to have a shiny lighter slip out of your pocket and make a noise as it falls." He took another deep inhale.

"What happened with Connert?" Court had left the squadron after the OSI agents had taken Connert away.

"Wow," Dieter said. "There's a nut case. You're lucky to be alive, having him in the backseat. Nothing really to hang on him, though. Impersonating a pilot isn't all that heavy compared to impersonating an officer. He'll be outprocessed right away, I expect."

"I hope so." Court grinned. "Although I've maybe flown with worse backseaters."

"And maybe one today, is that what you're trying to say?"

"Listen, Mac, don't worry about it. I'll check you out in ten minutes. All you do is turn on a few switches and I'll do all the rest. Then you just sit there with your hands in your lap."

Dieter's eyebrows shot up. "Hands in my lap? Bullshit, hands in my lap. I at least get a takeoff and a couple patterns or you ain't got no backseater and cain't fly. So there. I am the boss around here, you know."

"Okay, all right." Court laughed. "Your logic is compelling. Since you said fly, let's go do it."

"I set us up with Morelli and Jensen. No sense changing a good thing, and you guys are getting used to each other's airplane. Let's go brief."

They took their coffees and met Morelli and Jensen in the map table room.

"Hi, guys," Morelli said. "Same place, same station." He nodded to Dieter. "New backseater."

Dieter spoke up. "The weather is really bad down there," he said. "I've had the armament people load us up with wall-to-wall nape and CBU. Court, I gave you six high-drag Mark eighty-twos. Morelli, you got the nape, Jensen you got the CBU." A pilot cannot visually dive-bomb in bad weather, but he can do shallow-angle dive – under fifteen

227

degrees – and straight and level flight under the clouds if the threat isn't too high and the ceiling isn't too low."

They all made notes on their kneeboards, then Morelli kicked off his briefing with a joke about a one-eyed prostitute. No one even cracked a smile.

"Hey, you guys are a tough audience," he said.

"Morelli," Dieter said, "for your information, it is not even six A.M. yet and here you are trying to gross us out.

"It was funny last night."

"Shut up and brief."

When Morelli finished the briefing, the four men got their equipment, refilled their water bottles, and climbed into the blue van. At his F-4, Court helped Mac Dieter strap in, explained the ejection sequence, then showed him how to align the INS, how to set up the radar, and how to do the BIT (Built-In Test) check.

Ten minutes later Morelli called on the radio.

"Silver Flight check in."

"Lead, this is Three Two. You've got to scratch me. I've got hydraulic problems and there is no spare." Joe Jensen sounded let down.

"Roger, copy. There goes our CBU," Morelli said. "Silver Three Three, you are now Three Two," he transmitted to Court.

After flying south for forty minutes, Paris Control handed the two planes off to their FAC, Beaver Two Two, who was flying an 0-1. Morelli checked in with the lineup. He orbited over their rendezvous point, using the Tan Son Nhut Tacan. Channel 41, the Can Tho Tacan, was still off the air. A solid overcast blocked any view of the ground.

"Roger, Silver," Beaver Two Two said. "Glad to see a Phantom down this far south. Here's the situation. The Can Tho runway runs east and west. The bad guys are spread out parallel to the south side of the runway. The operations building and the radar site are on the north side." He unkeyed, then keyed again. "The good guys are in bunkers and trenches along the north side. They say the VC have heavy mortars and recoilless rifles that are hammering them pretty bad. They've repelled one charge but don't think they can hack another." He unkeyed.

"What's the weather down there?" Morelli asked.

"Double delta sierra. The cloud bases run from five hundred to fifteen hundred above the ground. There's a strong surface wind from the west that's really moving this stuff around. By the regs, I'm afraid I can't bring you guys down."

Although the terrain in this part of South Vietnam called the Delta was flat and near sea level, F-100s had no radar to guide them on a letdown. Nor could they use the ground facility, the Can Tho Tacan, to make a weather penetration. Beaver Two Two had said the weather was delta sierra. That meant it was dog shit, double dog shit.

Court spoke up. "How bad is it down there?"

"Stand by, stand by. They're talking to me now."

All FAC aircraft had several radios: FM to talk to ground troops, UHF and VHF to talk to fighters and helicopters. The FAC monitored all radios at all times via a jack box that fed whatever he wanted into his headset. Neither the ground troops nor the pilots could hear the other. Many times the FAC heard multiple transmissions. A good one never had any trouble sorting out who was who. After a few minutes Beaver Two Two came on the air.

"Looks bad. The mortars and shells are rolling in. They think a charge is due any second. They've had it. I'm orbiting north at eight hundred. I can barely see the runway. Rainstorms all over the place. Shit. They've had it."

"I've got radar in this beast, I can get us down there," Court transmitted. "If you will clear us, Two Two, I'll put lead on my wing and come on down."

"They're dead men without you. You're clear," Beaver Two Two said.

"How about it, Silver lead?" Court asked Morelli.

"Just tell me what wing you want me on," he said.

"God, Court," Dieter said from the backseat. "I haven't a clue how to handle the radar."

229

"Just put the switches where I tell you and we'll be fine. I have a scope up here." Court told him where to put each switch, signaled Morelli onto his left wing, and told Beaver Two Two he was coming down.

"Roger, Silver. I'm still north at eight hundred. No bad guys up here so there's no groundfire. Come in from the northeast quadrant and you'll be okay. Highest terrain around is only eighty feet."

"Copy, Beaver. I'm going over to Paris for one." Court switched frequencies. Paris Control answered his call and identified him on the scope. Court explained what they were going to do, then asked if there was any traffic in the air flying in the clouds.

"Silver, Paris. Negative traffic. We can paint you down pretty low. Maybe down to fifteen hundred. We'll keep an eye on you and give you a growl on Guard if anything enters your area." Court thanked him and switched back to the strike frequency.

"Silver is on the way down to the northeast," he told the Beaver FAC, throttled back, and started down. Morelli hung in close formation on his left. Court gave Dieter one more switch instruction, then monitored his own radar as he let down into the clouds.

Four minutes later he was level at 1,500 and had the outline of the runway and its radar reflectors on his scope. They were still in the clouds.

"Okay," he said to Morelli, "I don't think we'll break out. I'm going to ease on down until I see the ground."

"Press on."

At 900 feet, Court saw tantalizing glimpses of the ground directly below.

"We're four miles out," he transmitted to Beaver and Morelli. "I'm going to dogleg it south, then run in east to west parallel and south of the runway. Stay tucked in and be ready to drop when I tell you, Morelli."

"Roger."

Court eased the stick forward just enough to start a 400-feet-per-minute rate of descent. He held 400 knots indicated rather than the usual 450. He adjusted his gunsight depression to account for the speed differential.

"I'll hold four hundred," Court said to Morelli. "I'll set 'em up ripple. One pass, haul ass. In this weather they won't see us coming." Court could feel his pulse rate increase.

"Or going," Dieter responded.

Suddenly they were under the ragged clouds. House-sized wisps of dirty white flashed past the canopy.

"There it is," he said. Below and ahead he saw the strip of concrete and tiny holes and lines that could only be fighting positions. The hexagonal-sided low building that housed the Tacan was on the enemy side of the runway.

Court held a 5-degree dive parallel to the south side of the runway. No chance of a short round. He had a fleeting glimpse of figures running north toward the concrete strip. He rechecked his switches, then he was on the targets.

"Ready, ready, PICKLE," he said. All six of his Mk-82 high drags and both cans of Morelli's napalm slammed into the ground among the enemy troops. Six huge geysers of dirt erupted from the curling red-and-yellow flames of the napalm. Court pulled his flight up into the clouds.

"Hey, wow, shit hot," Beaver Two Two erupted. "You got most of them. You should hear the ground troops."

"I thought you were orbiting north," Court said as they climbed up through the clouds, Morelli tucked in as tight as a wingtip.

"Had to sort of slip down this way to see what was happening. Got to earn my pay, you know. Let you guys run strikes by yourself and I'm out of a job – oh oh." Beaver Two Two unkeyed. "Oh shit, I'm hit, I'm hit . . . engine burning . . . going down right in the middle of them. Make a pass, make a pass. I'll run – "

"Okay, Morelli, break it off. Climb out on your own. I'm going back down."

"Roger," Morelli said as he continued his climb-out. He didn't need radar for that. "But you don't have any bombs left."

"Or a gun," Dieter said from the backseat.

"I got four missiles," Court answered. He turned his plane back to Can Tho and set up his gun switch to missile. He told Dieter how to free up the firing circuit from the back so he could fire a missile "interlocks out" every time he pressed the pickle button. The missiles didn't need to lock on to anything, but wouldn't guide either. Firing them was nothing more than firing huge 12-foot unguided rockets.

"How big are those warheads?" Dieter asked as Court slid back around in the same pattern he had just flown to the Can Tho runway.

"Not much, eighty-eight pounds. Better than nothing." He concentrated on his scope and his instruments and lined up for another approach.

"Two Two, do you read?" he called. For a few seconds there was no answer. Then Court heard a tiny voice in his headset.

"Silver, this is Two Two on Guard . . . survival radio, in ditch next to runway . . . bad guys moving in . . ."

Court didn't have time to reach down and switch his radio to Guard channel to tell Beaver Two Two he had heard his call. He concentrated on his instruments. Then, as before, the runway came in view when he was down to 500 feet. In a split second he located the crashed 0-1. It lay south of the runway with a wing torn off. Court could barely make out figures running toward the plane and a figure in a ditch near the runway. The image froze in his mind as he slammed the stick forward to zoom down the remaining few hundred feet and ran the pipper of his gunsight down and into the running figures. He pressed the firing button four times, then slammed the throttles forward and hauled back on the stick. They were very close to the ground.

"COURT," Dieter yelled from the backseat, "we're not going to make it. I'm getting out."

"NO, NO," Court commanded. He held in just enough back pressure to keep them from hitting the ground, but not so much as to cause a high-speed stall. The big Phantom cleared the ground with twenty feet to spare. Green tracers split the fog and damp like ghostly fingers trying to bat

232

them from the sky. In seconds they were in the safety of the low clouds.

"Bannister," Dieter said, "no wonder you have back-seaters who can't keep their hands off the controls. My God." Court climbed out on an easterly heading, then doubled back to the Can Tho area. Even though he could not see the ground below, the latitude and longitude co-ordinates of Can Tho that he had helped Dieter set in the INS before takeoff gave him bearing and distance to the runway. He cross-checked the TSN Tacan, then had Dieter switch the radar to air-to-air. He found a solo blip.

"Silver lead, Three Two has contact." Morelli didn't answer. They were in the clear now, at 18,000 feet.

"There he is, eleven high," Court said to Dieter. He joined up on Morelli's left-hand-orbiting F-100.

"How do you read?" Court asked when he joined up on his left wing.

"Boy, am I glad to see you. My antenna has vibrated loose," he said. It was a common occurrence in an F-100 for the antenna connection for the UHF radio to come unplugged. It was in the nose and unreachable by the pilot. "I can only transmit and receive to someone who is within a couple hundred feet. Was afraid you forgot about me. I don't have much fuel left, about to thrash home alone. You got the lead." He pointed his index finger at Court, then motioned him forward.

"Let's do a damage check," Court said. He slowly slid his airplane around Morelli's F-100, looking for holes. "You're clean," he said. Morelli in turn checked Court out and pronounced him clean of any holes, then slid into position off his right wing.

Court set a course for the Tan Son Nhut Tacan and contacted Paris Control.

"Squawk five three and Indent, Silver Three Two."

Court put a dial on his IFF (Identification Friend or Foe) to 53, and triggered another switch that sent a burst of energy to the screen of the Paris controller that showed up unmistakably as the coded blip for 53 on the controller's radarscope.

"I have positive contact, Silver Three Two. Be advised, the Tan Son Nhut weather has gone below minimums in heavy rain and thunderstorms. Bien Hoa is still closed. Advise you divert to Phan Rang. Steer zero six five degrees."

"Stand by, Paris. Silver lead, you copy Paris?"

"Negative."

"Tan Son Nhut and Bien Hoa are closed. They want us to go to Phan Rang. That's thirty minutes more. Can you hack it?"

"Negative," Morelli said. "I've got about ten more minutes of fuel, then it's nylon letdown time."

"I'll bring you down if you want to try it," Court said.

"Press on."

"Paris, Silver. My number-two man has no radio and a fuel emergency. Bring us down and turn us over to GCA. I'll keep him on my wing down to touchdown."

"Roger, copy Silver. Be advised, the active runway is two five, altimeter is two niner eight eight, ceiling is one hundred feet, visibility quarter of a mile to zero in heavy rain, wind from three zero zero at twenty-five gusting forty."

"Copy," Court said. He repeated the information for Morelli. The controller then said, "Silver, steer zero two zero, you are cleared to descend to two thousand feet."

Court eased his throttles back to 80 percent, held his altitude until the airspeed bled off to 280 knots, then gently lowered the nose of his Phantom until he had a 4,000-feet-per-minute rate of descent. Just before they entered the clouds below, he looked over at Morelli, who gave him a thumbs-up.

"Glad you got a Hun driver in your backseat in case you don't remember the airspeeds," he transmitted to Court.

"Never fear," Dieter replied from the rear cockpit.

After the penetration down through the clouds, Paris turned Court over to Tan Son Nhut Ground Controlled Approach.

"Silver, this is Tan Son Nhut GCA. How do you read?"

"Loud and clear." They were at 2,000 feet and the turbulence had increased. The clouds were dark and angry.

Court turned up his cockpit lights and put his external lights on bright-steady for Morelli.

In the clouds, the bright flashing lights of the leader would blind and confuse the wingman trying desperately to stay in close formation using only visible indicators; the wingman visually aligns his leader's wing light under the star on the fuselage. These two tiny visual cues give the wingman proper positioning in the fore-and-aft and up-and-down planes. Only experience can tell him how close to be. In clear weather the planes can spread out in the night sky and both turn their lights to Bright Flash. In bad weather, such as Silver was experiencing, the number-two man tucks in as close as he can and hopes he can hang on through turbulence that causes him to push and pull the pole all over the cockpit while cursing and shoving rudder and throttle scant inches to stay in position and not get slung off. An inexperienced or rough leader can sling off a wingman in a heartbeat. A highly experienced pilot flying wing, however, will sit in his own airspace on the wing, monitor his own gages with quick sidelong glances, and let the leader thrash himself to death in his airspace – even if it is only three feet away.

"Silver, you're fifteen miles out. Slow down to approach speed. Be ready to lower gear and flaps. Be advised, there is a thunderstorm directly over the field. Steer two four five degrees."

"Silver, two four five."

"Lower gear and flaps now, Silver flight."

Court motioned to Morelli with a closed fist and thumb pointed down. "Gear down, now," he said, and reached to his instrument panel and placed the landing gear handle down. He felt his gear doors open and the heavy landing gear swing down and lock in place. His swift glance at Morelli showed his gear down. He was bouncing up and down in the increasing turbulence. Past him, Court saw a giant streak of lightning illuminate the black clouds. Court put his windscreen blower on maximum, which supplied air from the engine so hot and fast that if there was no rain, the windshield would shatter. He hunkered down in front of his gages and slowed the Phantom to the final approach speed for an F-100.

Although the Phantom was bigger and heavier than the F-100, it had a different flap layout and a system that blew hot air over the wing and trailing edge flaps that cut turbulence and drag. It could fly an approach to landing several knots slower than the F-100. But to safely bring in the F-100, it had to fly faster on the final approach to landing.

"About one seventy-five should do it, Court. That should handle the gusts as well," Dieter said.

"Got it," Court said.

The GCA Controller gave more instructions. "Check gear and flaps down, Silver flight. Start normal rate of descent . . . now."

"Silver, gear checked, starting down," Court said. Suddenly he was in heavy rain and crushing vertical winds that one second wanted to fling the two jets up and out and the next minute smash them to the ground.

All he had was a voice in his ear telling him to fly left or right a few degrees, to increase or decrease his rate of descent a few feet per minute.

The voice belonged to a sergeant sitting in a small darkened room, intently watching an electronic bug crawl down his radar screen toward two converging lines. The sergeant could tell the bug in terse words to fly left or right, increase or decrease descent, and if the bug obeyed promptly and smoothly, the bug would drift down the lines until – out in the real world of rain and slashing winds – an airplane would flash over the end of the runway. The two planes were one thousand feet above the ground, cocked 7 degrees into the wind by the sergeant to hold a ground track leading to the runway. They were descending at 400 feet per minute.

In his cockpit Court had a few gages to tell him how high he was, how fast his airplane was traveling in the air mass, his attitude referenced to a horizon he could not see, what

236

direction he was heading, at what rate he was climbing or descending.

The gages weren't that precise. They had lag due to friction, wobble due to long use, and inexact readings due to minor installation errors. It was up to the sergeant in the GCA shack to correct for all of those errors. He had to keep feeding corrections to the pilot until he saw the bug on the heading and in the descent pattern his brain told him was correct.

But the sergeant had never had to bring a plane through heavy rain. Rain so heavy, the water was returning his radar signals before they could ping off the airplanes hidden within. Heavy rain that splashed and tumbled on the runway so fast and so hard it created a six-inch river the drainage system could not handle. The two planes were at 400 feet above the ground. Because of the terrible gusts, Court held the airspeed at 180 knots, 207 miles per hour. They were approaching the end of the runway over 300 feet per second while settling toward the earth at six feet every second.

It was tricky, at over 200 miles an hour, as the gusts buffeted and tossed the planes flying barely five feet from each other. There were additional complications. With the gear and flaps down and at the slow landing speeds, the planes were not half as responsive to the control inputs as when flying fast and clean. With everything hanging, they wallowed in exaggerated motions.

"Silver flight," the sergeant said in a calm voice, "I've lost you in the rain. Maintain present heading and rate of descent. If you have not broken out by two hundred thirty-seven feet on your altimeter you are cleared for a missed approach."

"Negative missed approach," Morelli said. His voice was as quiet as the sergeant's. "No gas."

The two airplanes descended through 300 feet. Court held what he had. Even though he had his Tacan on and had been monitoring the whole letdown and approach with the instrument, it could not give him the precision of radar

237

necessary to get him the few final feet to the end of the runway at the proper heading and altitude.

The jets dropped ever lower through the thick clouds, black and swollen with rain. The changes in wind direction and velocity at the lower altitudes underneath the thunderstorm were abrupt and substantial. As smooth as Court was on the controls, and as hard as he tried, the big F-4 wallowed and pitched as he continued down the glide scope.

"Sorry," he shot to Morelli. "Below four-fifty, this thing's a pig."

"Yeah, I noticed," Morelli said, voice tight.

Court had to keep his eyes constantly in the cockpit on his instruments. He noticed the last heading from GCA had been 7 degrees to the right of the runway heading. That would be to counteract the stiff crosswind from the right. He didn't dare raise his eyes to look directly forward out the windscreen until his peripheral vision told him there was something to see. Even minute mistakes at that point could result in catastrophe. Though he had enough fuel to make a missed approach, Jim Morelli did not. Court's altimeter was now unwinding through 250 feet above the ground, then 200. He was below legal landing minimums and, by the book, quite illegal to continue the approach.

Then the clouds shredded to wisps, then a flash of green, then a flash of brown, then cloud wisps, then green again directly below. Court risked a quick glance forward. The dim outline of the runway appeared to his left a few degrees. The silver bouncing rain on the concrete looked like a canal of boiling quicksilver. Court sliced his plane to the left and added power.

"Set it down, NOW," he transmitted to Morelli. There wasn't enough room for the two of them to land at the same time. Court's violent maneuver meant that Morelli needed all the runway he could find to straighten out and touch down with some semblance of control. "I hope to hell he can see the runway," Court said to Dieter as he wrestled his wallowing Phantom away from the ground on the far side of

238

the runway. He retracted the speed brakes as he spoke and pushed the throttles forward. He started to ease the nose up in a climb. He was aware of black shadows of buildings beneath him as he clawed for altitude and turned his plane back to the right to parallel the runway heading.

"Silver Three Two missed approach," he told the GCA controller.

"What's your fuel status, Silver?"

Court checked his gage. "Not enough for Phan Rang," he said. "I've got enough for one more pattern, then I've got to land." Dieter hadn't said a word from the backseat.

"Silver, maintain present heading and climb to one thousand five hundred. The rainstorm is shifting and I have you on my radar."

"Did Three One make it okay?" Court asked.

"Roger, Silver. He flamed out on the runway and coasted into a turnoff. Soon as maintenance can find him, they'll tow him in." Court's pulse returned to normal. He flew the rest of the pattern and landed under the precise control of the GCA sergeant.

"So that's how you Phantom flyers gin around," Dieter said to Court as he and Morelli shared coffee and cigarettes in Dieter's small office. Dim light through the small window confirmed the rain had let up, yet the morning sky was still dark and low with overcast.

"All fun and games, Mac," he said.

"Maybe so up front, but I couldn't see squat from that pit back there."

"Well, he got me down," Morelli said. "But I don't want to go through that again. That sucker hydroplaned and weathervaned and turkeyed all over the damn runway. Hell, I didn't taxi off, I flamed out and slid off. Just lucky that wide turnoff was there."

"Look at it this way, gentlemen," Dieter said. "Beaver Two Two is alive and well and Can Tho is back on the air. We broke up the attack and the local friendly ARVN troops moved in. They seem to think we did good works.

239

A guy from Blue Chip called and said they'll probably put us in for the Vietnamese Cross of Gallantry." He turned to Court. "How about a cigarette?" Court gave him one. "Damn," Dieter said, "now you've got me hooked."

The armament lieutenant stood in the open doorway. Dieter waved him in. The young lieutenant looked mortified.

"Major Bannister, I don't know how to say this, but I need a report of survey on your expenditure of those AIM-7 missiles."

"Report of survey?" Court echoed. "That means I might have to pay for them. What is this all about?"

"Sir, they weren't expended in combat, so according to Air Force Reg 67-1, I – "

"Weren't expended in combat? They certainly were."

"Sir, the armament regs say they are for air-to-air use and you –

Court could see the lieutenant was trapped in the paperwork jungle and didn't know how to get out.

"Didn't you know? I jettisoned the things for safety-of-flight purposes. That's why I didn't bring them back."

The lieutenant looked relieved. "Sir, will you sign that off in the log book?"

"You bet I will. I'll catch it the next time I preflight."

The phone rang. Dieter said his name and listened. "Got it," he said and hung up. "You might be preflighting sooner than you think," he told Court.

"How's that?"

"We've got two more flights for you today, then alert for single-ship Skyspot missions tonight. And, since you need an experienced backseater, I have the dubious honor of being the man to accompany you. After we fly at noon and fifteen hundred, we must report to the alert trailer by eight tonight." Dieter pursed his lips. "Think you can hack it?"

"Why don't you give me something really tough?" Court said.

13

The hole Jim Polter had made in the kitchen ceiling opened into a dark area containing the trusses and crosspieces of wood that held up the corrugated tin roof. Wolf climbed on the table and helped pull down and break the remaining slats. Large chunks of plaster and a stream of mortar bits crashed to the floor.

"Give me a boost," Wolf said. Polter made a cup with his hands and boosted him into the opening. Wolf rested his elbows at the edges and looked around in the stifling crawlspace. The tin roof rose from the front of the house up to a height of five feet, where it was attached to the back wall of the villa grounds. The air was hot and fetid and it smelled of small furry things that had crawled in and died. He tested the rafters. They would hold, but the plaster between would not. He envisioned the four of them climbing from the table top through the hole, across boards laid on the rafters to where the tin met the top of the wall. There he would pry up a corner, check in the direction of the villa, then see about getting everyone over the wall and en route to the Black Panthers' compound. He climbed back down.

Greta Sturm's gray eyes blazed at him. She was covered with mortar dust. Wolf could see where she had tried to get

241

her head under the sink and around the post to gnaw at the bandanna. It hadn't worked.

"Go to the bedrooms," he told Polter. "Get the boards from the beds. Lay them across the rafters." He picked up the PRC-25. "I want to see who I can talk to. See if we can patch into the Panthers." Polter nodded and went out.

Wolf switched to the emergency frequency of 60.75 on the PRC-25.

"Anybody read Wolf on sixty seventy-five, give me a call." He waited and repeated the call three more times. There was no answer. He turned the frequency-control knobs down to their lowest point, 25 megacycles, and started clicking them up the band. He was listening for radio traffic. At 42.4 he heard faint voices but couldn't even tell what language they spoke. Higher up, he heard Vietnamese, but it was so rapid and faint that all he made out was some numbers. He couldn't tell if it was a friendly or enemy voice. At 51.10 he heard an American voice loud and clear.

". . . don't care what your problem is. Keep that track in line or I'll put a round through you afore Charlie does."

Wolf broke in. "American unit on Fox Mike, this is Wolf, how do you read?" After a short silence Wolf repeated the call and got an answer.

"Lookee here, you Wolf, what you doing on our net? Who you? What you want?" The thin voice was right from the Appalachian mountains.

"This is Wolf. Our helicopter got shot down and we've got some problems."

"*You* got problems," the thin voice snorted. "I'm suppose to move these h'yer . . ." He paused. "Never mind. How do I know you are who you say you are?" he asked in a voice suddenly grown wary.

Wolf took a deep breath. "Because, you simple cracker bastard, if you don't do what I tell you. I'll come over there and rip your gizzard out through your nose."

"Whooee, you show talk rough. I guess you ain't no Charlie."

"Put your six on," Wolf demanded. "Six" was the term

used for the commander of an Army unit.

"I cain't. What you want? We got man's work to do here, an' yur hoggin' the freq."

"Put your NCO on," Wolf said.

"I am the NCO, friend."

Wolf had a thought. "Are you out of Papa Bravo?" Papa Bravo was local slang for Phu Bai, where a Marine unit was stationed.

"Maybe, jus' maybe."

"I need some freqs to contact the local friendlies, you copy?"

"Maybe. What's your location?"

"We're in the gook Disneyland north of the big smelly, you copy?" Wolf hoped the man would connect the big smelly with the Perfume River.

"Ha – yeah, I copy that one good. Stand by." After a pause the thin voice came back up. "Okay, friend. All I know is, ah, fifty-one sixty-five and fifty-three eighty-five. But I'll tell you somethin'. You gotta knock two bits off one, and four bits off t'other. Now git off'n my freq."

Wolf made a grim smile. The cracker was shrewd. Just in case they were being monitored by the VC or the NVA, he had told him to drop 25 numbers from the first frequency and 50 from the other. He dialed in 51.40

Chao, ong, he said in Vietnamese. *"Here is an American unit calling the Hac Bao. Answer, please."* He tried for several more minutes with no response. Polter came through with an armload of slats from the beds. He gave them to Wolf, then climbed up into the rafters. Wolf handed the boards up to him, then tried the PRC on 53.35.

"Chao, ong," he said. *"Here is an American unit calling the Hac Bao. Answer, please."* A very clear voice came over the handset.

"American unit, this is Panther. Who are you and what do you want?" The voice was of a young man who spoke clear and only slightly accented English.

"Panther, this is Wolf. I am near your location and require assistance. Do you copy, over?"

243

"Wolf, this is Panther. Roger, I have a good copy. Please to authenticate Golf Kilo."

"Panther, Wolf is unable. We are from a crashed helicopter." He pulled out the maps from the parachute bag, made some rapid calculations, and told Panther the azimuth and range to where they were.

"Wolf, this is Panther. Stand by." After a few moments the voice spoke again.

"Wolf, this is Panther. We have seen the helicopter. What can we do for you? Over."

Rizzo's M60 suddenly started booming from the front room. The hammering sound blowing back in the tiny marble house was deafening. Cartridge smoke filled the kitchen. Greta Sturm kicked and pulled, a look between fear and anger on her face.

"Stand by, Panther," Wolf said into the handset. "We've got problems." He knelt, cut Greta loose, then rapid-crawled into the main room next to Rizzo, whose cartridge belt was just running out. Wolf picked up a fresh belt he had laid out and helped feed it into the machine. Something lobbed down the path and rolled to within ten feet of the door.

"Grenade," Rizzo yelled. Both men rolled behind the wall as a thunderous explosion blew dirt and debris through the open door and window. Bullets spattered the outside of the house and zinged through the door into the kitchen and the far wall. Greta screamed from the kitchen.

"Keep her down," Wolf yelled to Polter.

"Right," Polter yelled back.

Wolf rolled away from the door to the window, lay on his back, and held the M16 over his head upside down and fired at knee level down the path. He pulled the gun down to his stomach and inched back to Rizzo's side. Rizzo was firing madly down the path, spraying both sides. Wolf slapped his shoulder. "Go easy, you don't have all the sixty ammo you carry on a chopper. Don't fire until you see something. And when they're close, use this." He pushed the Claymore detonator to his side. The path disappeared into heavy leaves and bushes as it turned past the tennis court. The Claymore was hidden at the turn.

He crawled back into the kitchen. Greta was huddled in a corner, the whites of her eyes showing. Wolf grabbed the RPG and the canvas sling of projectiles and crawled back to Rizzo. As he settled down, he saw figures up the path. No time to fit a round into the big RPG. He squeezed the plunger on the Claymore detonator.

A great light blossomed and flared and a tremendous roar sounded. Leaves and pieces of trees and men flew down the path, propelled by hurricane force. After a shocked silence, screams and moans echoed down the path.

"Gawd," Rizzo said in awe. "I've never been down on the ground before when one of them things went off."

Wolf fitted a rocket to the RPG. "Get away from the door," he yelled to Greta in the kitchen. He rested the big tube on his shoulder and fired straight down the path at an old palm tree. Greta shrieked as the backblast whooshed into the kitchen. Wolf hoped the explosive head would spew splinters at the men crouched around its base. The older, hard-core NVA would be hiding in the bamboo, for they knew the tough, stringy bamboo absorbed explosions and metal fragments without shattering or splintering. The palm exploded with a roar, shooting shards of wood scything into the surrounding bushes. The tree shrieked and toppled across the high fence surrounding the tennis court and the firing stopped.

Wolf crawled back into the kitchen. "In about two minutes," he told Polter, "they're gonna get smart and get up on the roof of the villa and lob grenades at us. Get out there and use your M16 low on the path and high on the roof. Make them keep their heads down. Squeeze 'em off, we don't have much ammo." Polter crawled out. Wolf looked at Greta Sturm.

"You still want to walk down the road with a white flag?" She made a sour face and looked away. When he picked up the radio handset, it came off in his hand. The radio had been shattered by one of the many bullets that had been fired through the door.

He pawed through the parachute bag and pulled out the RT-10 Air Force survival radio Rennagel had included. He turned it on and transmitted on the 243.0 megacycles, the UHF Guard channel monitored by all aircraft for emergency transmissions. He hoped Tay Loc control tower was on the air.

"Tay Loc Tower, this is Wolf on Guard channel. How do you read?" He called twice more with no response. Then he made another call. The range of the tiny survival radio was limited. A receiving aircraft had to be directly overhead or within a few miles to adequately communicate.

"Any aircraft reading Wolf on Guard, give me a call, please."

A faint voice answered. "Wolf, this is an American MAC Flight. If you do not have an emergency, get off Guard channel."

"Yeah, we got an emergency. I need you to pass a message through whatever radar has you under control to Green House at Nha Trang. You copy?" Wolf figured he could get Nha Trang to relay to the Black Panthers what was happening, and to give them covering fire so they could get over the back wall. The firing still had not picked up outside toward the villa. He knew that respite wouldn't last.

"Ah, Wolf . . . cannot . . ." The voice faded and was lost.

Wolf tried a general call again and received nothing.

The girl stirred. "I knew I should have gone out to them. Now what's going to happen to us? You are a shameful man." The anger on her face had a tinge of fear.

Wolf gave her an exasperated look and took advantage of the lull in the firing to stand on the table and inspect the entryway to the rafters. By now bullets had punctured the tin in so many places that daylight came through like tiny stars into the dark crawlspace. When the firefight started again, the rafters would not be a healthy place.

"Oh my God," somebody cried from the front room. "Wolf, come look at this. Jesus."

Wolf leaped down and crawled to join the others.

Crouched by the window, Polter pointed at the upper storey of the villa. His face was a mask of outrage and horror. The bile rose in Wolf's throat when he saw what was dangling from the villa roof.

Suspended from the roof on ropes tied around their necks were the naked bodies of the two helicopter pilots and the CIA man. Their arms and legs and genitals had been cut off. Their bodies left red smears where they had scraped the villa wall as they had been released to swing down as ghastly pendulums. Their ears had been cut off, and their eyes had been gouged out. Something bloody and bunched protruded from their mouths.

Wolf groaned and made the sign of the cross, thankful that Lopez was not hanging there. Maybe he was still alive. Behind him he heard the girl gasp and choke as she crawled up and saw the shocking sight. The splatter and stench of her vomit overpowered the smell of gunpowder. Tears started down her face, which was twisted in horror and revulsion. Wolf gave her his bandanna to wipe herself.

A stream of fire commenced from the roof of the villa. The bullets spanged and ricocheted from the walls and the porch floor and punched holes in the tin roof of the servants' quarters.

Inside, Wolf looked around. He lay near one side of the door with his M16. At his feet was the RPG. Rizzo lay on the other side of the door with his big M60, Polter crouched at the window with his M16.

"Okay," Wolf yelled, "this is it. Space your shots, shoot only when you have a target." He distributed the grenades and magazines equally between himself and Polter. Rizzo had over a hundred rounds remaining. The loud, nasal *chukka-chukka* of the M60 alternated with the crisp *blam-blams* of Polter's MI6. The air filled with billows of gunsmoke, and the sharp coppery smell of gunpowder filled their nostrils. Wolf readied the RPG.

"Please to tell me," Greta Sturm asked from the corner behind Wolf, "please, what did you mean 'this is it'?" She frowned with concern.

"Look out for the backblast," Wolf said, ignoring her question. He sighted the weapon at the section of the retaining wall on the roof where dots of heads and streams of smoke from the snouts of weapons protruded.

With a terrific *whoosh-whoom,* the projectile launched and a split second later blew a great gouge of concrete from under the NVA firing position. The bodies of the three mutilated Americans fell to the ground and the shooting stopped.

"Helluva shot, Wolf," Polter said in the sudden lull.

Greta Sturm tugged at his pant leg. "Please," she said, "what will happen here?"

Wolf didn't answer as he fixed the wiring into the last Claymore and poked it through the door to rest against the outside wall facing the path. He placed the detonator next to his elbow.

"Please," Greta Sturm said again. Wolf began fitting another round to the RPG. "What will happen here?"

Wolf slammed the projectile home. "What will happen here," he said, "is that they will keep shooting at us and finally make a rush on our position."

"A rush?"

"They will charge."

"Why cannot we go out the roof and over the wall?"

"We would be in plain sight of them. We'd be cut in two."

"They will come in here?"

"Not if we keep shooting at them."

She looked at the remaining half-dozen magazines and grenades. She saw the three remaining shells for the RPG. "We do not have many bullets, do we?"

"No."

"What will happen when they make a rush?"

"We have knives."

"Knives. *Mein Gott.* " She put her hand to her throat. Wolf took a good look at her. She looked vulnerable and exhausted. He resisted the temptation to tell her to go take a hike up the path, carrying a white flag.

"Will they come soon?" she asked. She seemed nervous and wanted to talk. Wolf could see the effort she made to keep her eyes away from the door.

"As soon as they get some reinforcements they'll come, but we have a good defensive position. They can't flank us or attack from the rear. They have to take us head-on. Or use something like this." He patted the RPG.

"I'm sorry for what I said to you. I . . . I see them differently now. I did not believe they did such things. I do not want to go out there. They are barbarians, what they did to those men."

"Those men were lucky," Wolf said.

"Lucky. How could they be lucky?" She drew her head back. "They were dead when they were cut up." He remembered an Air Force FAC pilot who had parachuted from his burning aircraft into VC hands. They had cut him into five pieces and used his survival radio in an attempt to lure in a rescue helicopter. Many times VC had disemboweled live GIs, then pulled their entrails out and laid them on a path to be walked on by unsuspecting American patrols. Americans had been found with their genitals crudely sewn into their mouths.

She looked at Wolf for the first time with compassion in her eyes. She made a visible effort to calm herself. "You have seen much of this, haven't you?" she asked in a quiet voice.

"Too much." He didn't like questions like these, but this girl seemed genuinely interested, and furthermore, it was a way to keep her mind off what was about to come.

"Do you not become afraid?"

"Yes," Wolf said. "I become afraid."

"Do you believe in God?"

"Yes."

"Do you pray to God when you are afraid?"

"No."

"What *do* you do when you are afraid?"

"Charge."

She smiled. "Like rush. You make a rush?"

249

Wolf's voice was soft. "Yes, that's it. I rush."

"When do you pray to God?"

"Afterwards."

"What do you say?"

Immediately Wolf's face lit up. "I thank Him. I thank Him for allowing me to survive . . . and to win."

She thought for a moment. "Do you like to kill?"

Wolf looked away. "No. I do not like to kill."

She saw Wolf's eyes flicker, and touched his arm. "I am sorry. I should not have asked that question." She was silent for a moment. "You said your last name was Lochert. It is very German. I don't know your name, your first name."

"Wolfgang."

"That is even more German."

"I'm German, all right. Minnesota German. South Minneapolis Powderhorn Park German."

"Are you married?"

"No."

"Do you have a *Freundin*, a girlfriend?"

Wolf thought of the worn picture in his wallet of the green-eyed Charmaine, the Hollywood dancer with long legs and lush mahogany hair. *Just for you, Wolf. Just for you,* she had inscribed. They had met at Bien Hoa, where she had visited her ex-husband, Court Bannister. Charmaine was the only girl Wolf had ever truly become interested in. His Catholic background and years in the Maryknoll Seminary had prepared him for a life of celibacy and prayer. Now he devoted himself to the Special Forces and warfare with the same intensity. He had left the seminary not because he did not choose to remain celibate, but because he could not remain impassive to the vicissitudes of life. He was driven by an inner compulsion to always step in and make the situation conform to his idea of right or wrong. Unless his athletic coaches, military commanders, peers, or subordinates were doing what Wolfgang Xavier Lochert thought was right and correct, they heard from the Wolf, promptly and loudly. He had found nothing wrong with Charmaine. As a result, he had been, he was sure, a simpering fool around her. He just knew women like Charmaine had no time for simpering fools.

He looked at the girl and tried to smile. She looked afraid again. "No," he said, "I don't have a girlfriend." He reached over and patted her arm in a fatherly way. *"Moechtest Du nicht meine Freundin sein?"* Will you be my girlfriend?

She tried to smile, and failed. Her eyes filled. *"Ich fuerchte mich."* I'm so afraid. "It is not like I thought it would be. They are so brutal." He patted her arm again, not quite sure of what to do. She reached and took his hand in both of hers, then pulled herself against him. She crossed her arms over her bosom and huddled against his chest like a little girl against her father. Wolf stroked her hair and shoulders, and rocked back and forth. "There, there," he said. She settled down.

"Am I going to die?" she asked in a muffled voice.

Wolf held her arms and pushed her upright. He figured that she was the reason the NVA had not brought their big mortar into play, or their RPGs. They knew a girl was in the house and wanted her alive.

"That, young lady," he said in a loud, authoritative voice, "is what's known as a dumb question. Now, do you want to sit there and let things happen to you? Or do you want to take control of yourself and be a part of what is happening?"

She straightened up and seemed to be responding, but before she could answer, a roaring cascade of sound erupted from the villa and a fusillade of bullets smashed into the front of the little house and tore through the door. Concrete and marble chips and dust flew about. Wolf hastily thrust Greta to the safety of the wall, telling her to stay down and out of the backblast, and crawled back to his fighting position. Rizzo and Polter were returning the fire, carefully squeezing off their shots. Wolf grabbed the RPG, quickly aimed and fired a round at the top of the roof wall. The blast took a chunk out of the wall and hurled cartwheeling bodies through the air.

"On the path," Rizzo yelled. He lowered his big machine

251

gun to hammer at the bases of the palm trees. Wolf quickly placed another round into the RPG. Furtive movement at the end of the path caught his eye. Suddenly more than twenty NVA emerged to run along the sides of the path, dodging and ducking, the lead men firing their AKs from the hip. They didn't throw grenades because the unreliable fusing could cause them to explode as they ran over them. They would wait until they were in position outside the house, then lob them in.

Wolf waited a second, until they were lined up, and fired the RPG round. It didn't have time to arm and passed through the first man's stomach, hydraulically disintegrating him, and exploded against the hip of the next man in line. Eight men behind them went down with fragments in their bodies. The wave of men behind screamed and yelled and ran over the bodies, continuing the attack. Several went down as Rizzo yammered the big gun, and Polter's M16 blammed and sent the tiny 5.56 rounds like supersonic bees into the enemy soldiers. The path became littered with downed soldiers, but the remaining dozen continued the charge. Wolf loaded the last RPG round and placed the weapon next to him. When the charging men were twenty feet from the door, he pushed the detonator, exploding the second Claymore into an ear-shattering roar. The blast pistoned pellets and thermite down the path, ripping and dropping all but two men, whom Rizzo tore in half with his 60. Wolf and Polter shot several wounded who were trying to bring their weapons to bear on them. Silence settled over the smoke-filled air. It was broken when Polter snapped off one last round into a feebly moving body.

At first the men didn't react to what carnage they had done. Then Rizzo let out a whoop, and Polter joined him. The two men screamed and yelled victory cries and breathed deep of the gunsmoke. Wolf looked back at the girl through eyes wide with bloodlust, breathing hard, nostrils dilated, lips pulled back over his teeth. She met his eyes and stared back with a newfound awareness. Gone was the lost-little-girl look. Her mouth was slightly open and she was panting.

252

Her hair had come loose and hung over her shoulders in blonde twists, damp with sweat and humidity. She blinked rapidly, and seemed to be trying to hide an emotion. She looked almost eager. She wet her lips.

"Are there more?"

Wolf nodded.

"Will they charge again, after . . . what happened there?" She nodded at the carnage on the path.

Wolf nodded.

"They do not use that, what? . . . that *mortar* to destroy us." She looked at the villa, then back at Wolf. "They want me, is that it? They want me?"

Wolf shrugged. "Maybe."

She sat up straight and wiped her mouth. She looked distraught.

"Something has . . . happened to me," she said, slowly. "I am not sure I like it, but something has happened. I feel very . . ." She searched for the word. "Angry. Yes, that is it. I am angry." She looked at the dwindling ammunition supply. "There must be a way I can help you."

Wolf pushed the detonator of the last Claymore toward her. "Push this lever when I tell you."

"They would be very close then, would they not?"

"Yes, they would be very close."

She licked her lips. "Do you . . . do you have a gun for me?" Wolf pulled the 7.63 Mauser from his ankle holster and handed it to her. She took it and fitted her hand around the gun. She stared at the weapon for a long moment, as if seeing someone she didn't like. She pushed the button to drop the magazine from the gun, caught it in her hand, then worked the slide and dry-fired a few times. Satisfied, she popped the magazine into the grip and jacked a round into the chamber. Wolf raised a bushy black eyebrow.

"You seem very familiar with weapons, like you've handled guns before."

She caught his expression. She had a new set to her face; a grim and determined expression had taken over. The little girl had been blown into oblivion.

253

"I am far more reliable and tough than you think. I have made up my mind. I *can* shoot, I *will* shoot." She waved the pistol. Wolf caught her hand and smiled.

"Just be careful *who* you shoot."

She put her hand on his and squeezed. "Wolfgang, I will help you."

She jerked as a flat crack echoed from the roof. Rizzo cried out and slumped over his M60 machine gun. Immediately a fusillade worse than before opened up from the villa, engulfing the little house in a torrent of lead.

Greta curled up and covered her head, and Wolf's heart leaped as he heard her moan. But he had to prepare. He checked that the last round was loaded into the RPG. He laid the weapon next to him, then checked his M16 and laid that next to the RPG. Then he picked up the M79 grenade launcher and fitted a grenade in place. There were five rounds remaining. Wolf silently blessed the prescient Colonel Harry Rennagel, who had supplied such a variety of weapons.

Greta peeked from between her fingers and saw the wounded Rizzo. Then she felt the warmth between her legs and realized she had lost control of her bladder. *"Mein Gott,"* she spit out in disgust. She pulled her hands away, and with a look of determination on her face, swiftly scuttled across the open doorway to Rizzo's side.

Wolf caught the move. When he saw she was safe, he turned back to the fighting and, peering around the base of the doorway, saw a row of marksmen shooting from behind the roof wall. He quickly blooped three grenades in their midst as fast as he could load and pull the trigger. One exploded by the helicopter and started a fire. He risked a quick glance at Rizzo and Greta. She had opened his shirt and was pounding his chest.

"He's hit bad," Polter yelled over his shoulder as he squeezed off rounds. "Push his gun over here," he said to the German girl.

"I cannot," she yelled. "He is dying." She bent to give him mouth-to-mouth.

"If he's dying you can't help him. Give me the gun or

254

we'll all die." With reluctance she left the side of the dying door-gunner and awkwardly pushed and slid the heavy M60 over to Polter. He turned and handed her his M16. "Here, use this." He seized the machine gun and rested its barrel on the windowsill. He checked the cartridge belt, then opened fire. The gun bucked and yammered, and cut down the first two NVA soldiers trying to creep down the path. "Here they come again," he yelled.

Wolf waited until he had a clear target, then dropped two soldiers with his M16. When the firing commenced anew from the top of the villa, he blooped another grenade onto the roof, silencing them.

Greta took the M16 and went back to Rizzo. She pounded his heart, cupped his mouth, and blew into his lungs, then put her ear to his chest. She sat back slowly and arranged his shirt. She buttoned the buttons and straightened the collar. Seemingly oblivious to the racket going on about her, she made the sign of the cross and bowed her head for a moment, lips moving. Then she tugged and pulled the body from its firing position. She took the same prone position that Rizzo had, poked the snout of the M16 out the door, and fired at a movement down the path.

Wolf was busy shooting and only half aware of what she was doing. When she fired again, he glanced over in surprise. She was all business. She held the rifle correctly and had positioned her body to take the most advantage of the cover the doorframe and wall provided. Her blonde hair had fallen over the right side of the stock as she sighted down the barrel. Her gun bucked slightly as she squeezed off two shots on semiauto. Wolf Lochert had never seen a more attractive picture.

"You said you didn't shoot," he called over.

"No. I before said I *will* not shoot. I did not say I *could* not shoot." She expertly fired two more rounds toward the villa and looked across the doorway at him. Her eyes were bright with defiance, her jaw set. "My father is a major in the Landwehr. He insisted I learn."

"Well then, get shooting," Polter said in the lull, "they're going to try us again." He opened up with the last belt of ammunition for his machine gun.

A storm of bullets flew through the open doorway and window. Polter gave a cry and fell back, a look of shock in his eyes for an instant. The M60 clattered to the floor. He shook his head, picked up his gun and resumed his firing position. A narrow stream of blood ran from his left bicep down his arm.

Screams and yells echoed from the base of the villa as a mass of the green-clad NVA soldiers charged down the path. At the same time, many heads appeared on the villa roof, shooting from over the wall and from the jagged edges where chunks had been ripped out by Wolf's RPG.

Wolf blew out another piece of the wall with his last RPG round, then picked up the grenade launcher. He exploded a grenade at the feet of the closest NVA soldiers. They went down, but more hurtled through the smoke past their bodies, screaming and shooting.

Greta triggered shot after shot. "Easy," Wolf yelled across the open door to her. "Make each one count." She put her head down for a moment and drew a deep breath. When she resumed firing, her shots were better paced and aimed. She was killing people.

Polter hammered out his last rounds. "I'm out of ammo," he yelled.

"Here," Wolf said, and threw him his M16 holding the last magazine. He turned and fired a grenade that stunned the charge but did not stop it. He fired his last grenade, then began throwing the remaining frag grenades.

The smoke from the weapons obscured the path. Three soldiers broke into view and ran screaming toward the door. Two had grenades in their hands ready to throw. Wolf slammed his hand down and detonated the last Claymore and thermite grenade into their faces. The explosion from the four-pound device was deafening. Smoke billowed back into the room, causing all three to cough and choke. The attacking soldiers were shredded, their grenades were blown back into the next rank, where they exploded killing two and wounding three. Still the others came.

"That's it," Polter yelled above the din. "I'm out." He grabbed the M16 by the muzzle like a baseball bat. His eyes were wide and wild, blood traces ran down his left arm like open veins.

"Me too," Greta Sturm said, her voice almost lost in the roar of the battle. "I have no more to shoot in this gun." She picked up the Mauser and looked across at Wolf. Her face was strangely calm. "The last bullet is for me," he heard her say.

Wolf pitched his last grenade, then pulled out his K-Bar knife. He crouched and gathered his body beneath himself.

"*Prepare to charge,*" he bellowed. "I'm with you," Polter yelled back, and stood to one side of the window, ready to leap out and start swinging his rifle. Greta Sturm's face was contorted now. She pulled behind the wall and rose to her feet, the Mauser clutched in her hand. She looked wild-eyed and disheveled. "Yes," she sang out. "We will charge."

They were ready, waiting only Wolf's final word. Suddenly a hail of fire ripped down the path from behind them. Then so many mortar shells exploded on the roof of the villa that it began to collapse, and a big explosion from inside the small house blew the kitchen wall in. Greta screamed. Concrete dust and smoke billowed from the kitchen, mingling with the battle smoke in the front room.

"Get down, get down. Don't move," Wolf commanded Polter and Greta.

Several figures wearing American-style combat fatigues scrambled through the hole in the villa wall that opened into the kitchen. Then they dashed into firing positions in the door and windows of the main room and sent volumes of M16 fire sweeping along the path and the sides of the path, and up toward the ruined villa.

The leader turned to Wolf and gave him a broad smile. "Hi," he said in perfect Fort Benning English. "I am Captain Tran Ngoc, commander of the Black Panthers. Sorry it took so long to get here."

14

0215 Hours Local, Saturday 3 February 1968
Tan Son Nhut Airport
Republic of Vietnam

The alarm bell inside the alert trailer went off with a reverberating clang that snapped Court's head up from the dirty pillow before he was entirely awake. Fully garbed in flight clothes, including G-suit and survival vest, he swung his boot-clad feet to the floor and stood up. The sudden movement made him slightly dizzy, causing bits of a sour dream to fade quickly. Across from him, his newly created backseater, Mac Dieter, jumped up from the GI cot where he had sprawled with his back against the wall, reading the latest issue of *Stars and Stripes*. The overhead fluorescent pulsed merciless light evenly throughout the trailer. The other two cots were empty. None had bedding. The blue-and-white-striped pillows and thin mattresses were soiled and worn from the heavy use made of them by combat-clad fighter pilots on alert duty. Although sleeping was allowed on alert, the conditions did not encourage it. The alarm ended abruptly as Court plucked up the red phone from its cradle on the wooden desk.

"Alert trailer," he croaked, voice muzzy and raw from too many late-night cigarettes. He had flown three times the day before and felt like he had been in an automobile wreck. He blinked his eyes and listened intently and scribbled vector and radio-frequency information on his mission card. Dieter, a dutiful GIB, copied what Court wrote on his own card.

Seconds later the two men were running through the rain to the F-4, black and looming in the night, a scant fifty feet from the trailer. The armament officer had done better this time finding the proper racks. Sixteen 500-pound bombs under the wings glistened blunt and lethal. Ponchoed ground crews were already responding to the outside repeater alarm. The assistant crew chiefs raced into the revetment to uncover and flip switches on the big yellow APUs (Auxiliary Power Units) cart, causing it to whine into life.

The crew chief punched the canopy-open switch on the fuselage of the plane, then hung a ladder just in time for the two men to climb up. Court seated himself and flicked on the battery power switch, bathing the cockpit in red light. Each chief scrambled up behind Court and Dieter and helped him fasten his harness and leg-restraining garters. Their helmets were already plugged into the oxygen hoses and radio systems. Rain splashed on each cockpit side rail and slid into the cockpit with deceptive and unnoticed ease onto the electrical side panels. A final slam on the shoulder by his chief and each pilot hit the switch to lower his canopy after the chief scrambled down and removed the ladder.

From below, Court's crew chief watched him move, outlined in red, in the cockpit as he positioned switches. Court checked in with Dieter and the crew chief, who had plugged into the intercom from outside. He told the chief to give him power. The chief opened the air valve, causing the umbilical hose to jump and whip once like an alive thing as it stiffened. Inside, Court punched the start button on the left panel, watched the engine revolutions climb on the RPM gage, punched the ignition button at 10 percent, and slid the throttle forward to idle. He completed the start on the right engine and turned on the UHF radio to the ground-control channel and was cleared to taxi to the arming area near the active runway. "Altimeter twenty-nine seventy-eight, winds two niner zero at twelve, gusting twenty, ceiling broken at five hundred feet, overcast at eight hundred, tops reported at twenty-two thousand,"

Ground Control reported. Dieter called that all the checks were complete in the backseat. After getting his bombs checked, Court called the tower.

"Tan Son Nhut, Skyspot Tango number one for the active."

"Skyspot Tango, you are cleared on and off runway Two Seven. Contact Tan Son Nhut Departure Control on 245.5 after takeoff. Skyspot read back."

Court repeated the clearance and taxied onto the runway.

"Roger, Skyspot Tango," the Tower said, "there is no reported traffic. You are cleared for takeoff, and you may go to Departure Control at this time. Have a good flight, sir." During the daytime high-traffic volume, such courteous and comradely frivolities were not in order. Night in Vietnam changes a lot of things.

The men in Tan Son Nhut tower watched the Phantom blast off the rain-slick runway, afterburner flames streaming and vaporizing rain, until they winked out in the low black scud. The ripping sound of the burners softly vibrated the front pane of glass. The tower man who was at the Departure Control position held his microphone, ready for Skyspot Tango to check in.

"Tan Son Nhut Departure, Skyspot Tango."

"Skyspot Tango, Tan Son Nhut Departure has you loud and clear. Vector zero four five degrees. Climb to and maintain flight level two seven zero. Contact Paris on 254.6."

"Roger, zero four five to two seven zero. Paris on 254.6."

"Skyspot, that's roger," he transmitted, then turned to the man next to him. "There goes Sam Bannister's kid," he said.

"Go on, you're kidding. The guy with all the MiGs? What's he doing down here? Thought he was in Thailand someplace."

"No lie, GI. My buddy in Transient Alert told me. Their officer is crewing him personally. Said he's a nice guy but doesn't tip much."

Court switched his radio to Paris Control and checked in. Paris, a radar Control and Reporting Center, confirmed the vector and altitude.

Court settled back in his cockpit. The glow of the backlight from his gages was comforting, almost cozy. His altitude, heading, and flight attitude were precisely pegged as he climbed. From time to time Paris vectored him around thunderstorms building in the early-morning air. He countered the moderate turbulence with control movements that were smooth and all but imperceptible. As they cruised through the black clouds, Court reviewed the Skyspot procedures in his mind. Soon he would be in contact with a disembodied voice that would give him a precise altitude, heading, and airspeed to fly. Then the voice would count down to give a release signal to the receiving pilot exactly when to drop his bombs.

When firepower was needed in the daylight or at night, but the weather was rotten and down to the deck, properly equipped airplanes could drop bombs by radar vectors from a ground station. Former SAC MSQ-77 radar bomb-scoring units were set up in vans at secure sites to track airplanes containing the special beacons. The Mis-que operator would key into his computer fixed information such as target distance and direction from his site, and height above sea level, along with the bomb types for which the computer already knew the aerodynamics and drop rate. Then the operator would add the weather variables: temperature aloft, air density, high and low winds. The computer would then give out a range of aircraft headings, altitudes, and airspeeds to complete the bombing equation.

The Mis-que operator would have the ground target fixed on his radar screen. He would "paint" the incoming aircraft blip with sharp resolution on his radar screen by receiving a sharp pulse of energy from the beacon mounted in the aircraft. The F-4s had been recently equipped with these beacons and so were able to fly the mission, called Skyspot, as necessary. The missions were always over or in clouds, so the pilots never saw what they were attacking. They were dull and boring. The pilots called the mission Skydump or Skypuke.

"How's it going back there?" he asked Mac Dieter.

"As well as could be expected under the circumstances."

"You mean you don't like the pit?"

"I mean I hate this fucking place. What pilot in his right mind wants to fly back here?"

"Not many. Just good navs."

"How come you're still flying, Court? Back at SOS I thought you were just a short-timer. Thought you'd be out of the Air Force by now."

Court chuckled. "Maybe back at SOS I was a short-timer. Now I've grown to like the job. Short hours, high pay. All that."

"You still married to ... what was her name? I see her on the Bob Hope show."

"Charmaine. No, we were divorced a couple years ago. She wanted a career and so did I."

"Tough about you not getting that fifth MiG."

"Yeah." Court didn't elaborate, and they fell silent as the big plane climbed through the thick night clouds. Each could hear the other breathe over the open microphones in their oxygen masks.

Soon they could see sporadic glows of cloud-to-cloud lightning. The turbulence was increasing. When he reached 27,000 feet, Court eased the throttle back to the cruise RPM of 92 percent. Court radioed Paris he was level. Paris told Court to contact Tepee on 280.1.

"Tepee, Skyspot Tango, how do you read?"

"Loud and clear, Tango. Steer 360."

"Roger. Steering 360. You ready to copy my lineup?"

"Affirmative. Go ahead, Tango."

"Skyspot Tango is one Fox Four, mission number 3-0069. We are carrying sixteen Mark-82 500-pounders with quarter-second fuzes." The Mark-82s were slicks. No point in carrying the highdrag Snakeyes on a high-altitude drop.

"I copy, Tango. Turn left 255. Descent to flight 170. You're eight minutes from drop. Nice to have an airplane that can carry a few bombs."

Inside his cockpit, Court had turned his thunderstorm lights up full to counter the lightning flashes. The turbulence was ragged and jolting.

"Tepee," he said, "make sure you're not vectoring us into a thunderstorm. If this weather gets worse, we'll have to abort the run. What's the target tonight? A suspected VC vegetable garden?" Court knew from the vectors and from where his Tacan needle was pointing he was over the western side of II Corps.

"Negative, Skyspot. Wish it were. An Army firebase, I can't tell you which one in the clear, is in bad trouble. So much so, we've got clearance from double-A GS to Skydump within two klicks." AAGS was the Army Air Ground System.

There would be no weather aborting tonight. The target was critical. Court checked his fuel. No problem there. They had been airborne forty-five minutes and his center tank was just feeding out.

"Skyspot, steer 351, hold her level 170, 310 knots indicated."

Court did as he was told. It was imperative to have everything precise. Variation of one degree in heading, a few feet in altitude, or a couple knots of airspeed could dump the bombs in the laps of the friendlies. Because Skyspot relied so heavily on human skill but without visual contact, it ordinarily was not used for close troop support. Close being anything within ten kilometers.

"Skyspot, steer 350." Just as Court complied, Tepee transmitted again.

"Skyspot, steer 349." He led Court down the centerline with great exactitude and steadiness; he even used half-degree corrections at the end.

"Skyspot, Tepee counting down in five seconds."

"Roger," Court answered.

"Skyspot, counting down now. Five . . . four . . . three . . . two . . . one DROP, DROP, DROP." Court pickled and sixteen bombs carrying four tons of explosives gracefully fell away to begin the three-mile curving arc wherein they would accelerate to over 300 miles per hour and impact in a spread no bigger than a football field.

Twenty-eight seconds later the GIs crouched in rain-filled foxholes at Firebase Sally were jolted and their ears rang in the soggy and oppressive night air as blast and concussion 600 meters down the hill blew thirty-eight hard-core NVA soldiers into shredded statistics. The moans of the wounded were absorbed by the incessant drumming of the rain on the jungle foliage.

"Close," the ground commander, a fuzzy-faced lieutenant barely six months from OCS, said on the Prick-25 to his company commander. "Very close. About six hundred meters to the south. Keep 'em coming."

Court heard and felt through the aluminum and sinew of his airplane the chunking sounds as the ejector cartridges in the pylons rippled the bombs away from under the wings. He gave a little forward stick as his airplane, suddenly released of 8,000 pounds, wanted to spring upwards.

"Turn port one seven zero degrees, Skyspot. Contact Paris Control."

Court began his port turn to head back to III Corps and the base at Tan Son Nhut.

The turbulence had lessened since they turned south. Court wriggled and surged against his harness to relieve the stiffness and the restricted blood flow caused by the straps. He took several deep breaths.

To the east, out over the South China Sea, the sun had risen enough to create dawn for those fortunate to be flying five miles or more above the earth. Court never ceased to marvel at the unblemished view of a sunrise or sunset from altitude. The cloud layer, barely a thousand feet under them, took on definition as the sunlight increased. It became a white field patterned with snow-covered tree undulations broken by billowy mountains honeycombed with smooth halls and giant caverns that soared thousands of feet upward. The scene was hypnotic and irresistible.

"Ready for a little fun and games?" he asked Dieter.

"You bet, as long as you let me fly."

"You got it," Court said, and waggled the stick. Dieter waggled back to prove he had control.

With great ease Dieter soared and rolled into the caverns, arrowed down the long white halls, and eased back on the stick to soar a mile straight up. Then, just short of a stall, he pulled the Phantom over the top of a huge Matterhorn of a birthing thunderstorm. While still inverted, they arced over a dome of a thunderstorm now smooth and round and dying of old age. They flew through adjoining vaulted rooms and billowy corridors. The plane soared with grace like a hawk soaring over and around and through snow-covered mountain caverns, through passes and below precipices of whipped cream. A voice in their headsets broke the reverie.

"Skyspot Tango, Paris. You're seventy-five miles out. You may start your en route descent anytime." They were back to straight and level flight at 270.

"Pull it back to eighty-two, Mac," Court said, meaning he wanted their throttles at 82 percent of maximum power. This RPM would ensure maximum distance attained while burning minimum fuel as they started down, losing altitude at a thousand feet per minute. Immediately as they entered the clouds, the world turned jolting and dark. A few minutes later Paris Control gave some more instructions.

"Skyspot, you are thirty miles out. Contact Tan Son Nhut Approach on 342.9." Court made contact with Tan Son Nhut Approach Control, who responded.

"Skyspot Tango, this is Tan Son Nhut Approach. Squawk 62 for positive radar identification."

"Squawking 62," Court told Tan Son Nhut Approach. He made the radio calls while Dieter flew the airplane.

"Skyspot Tango, I have positive identification. Turn left to heading 155. You are now twenty-five miles north of Tan Son Nhut."

In less than ten minutes they were under GCA control. They were at 1,500 feet and the weather was still as thick as old milk.

"Skyspot Tango, turn starboard now to 270 degrees, descend to 1,000 feet, stand by to lower your landing gear in one mile."

"Okay, Court," Dieter said from the rear cockpit, "you can have it back."

"You can keep flying if you want."

"Nah, you got it. I've flown every damn approach here for months and I want to see someone else sweat one out for a change."

Court waggled the stick. "I've got it."

The GCA controller spoke again. "Skyspot Tango, lower landing gear . . . now. Start normal rate of descent . . . now." Court reached with his left hand to the instrument panel, moved the gear selector handle down, then moved his hand back to the flap lever located outboard of the throttle and pulled the lever back. His gear and flaps lowered at the same time as he made the control and throttle adjustments to compensate for the added drag. Court never took his eyes off his instruments. He made his movements by touch alone.

"You are on glide slope, you are on glide path," GCA said. "Turn right heading 278, maintain rate of descent. You need not acknowledge further transmissions." GCA released his microphone key for an instant in case Court had a transmission, then continued his patter, bringing the Phantom to the threshold of the runway. The plane was crabbed 5 degrees to the right to compensate for the crosswind. Court had to straighten it out and lower his right wing into the wind so as to not drift off the left side of the runway.

Immediately after touchdown Court pulled his drag chute, decelerated rapidly, and abruptly had to fight to keep control as the chute deployed from its storage position in the tail of the airplane. The violent crosswind into the chute pushed it downwind, tugging at the tail of Court's F-4, causing the nose to want to weathervane into the wind and run him off the right side of the runway. Court slammed the stick forward, ensuring solid contact between his nose wheel and the runway, and he pushed the button on the control stick to engage the nose-wheel steering mechanism. He quickly slammed pressure to the left rudder pedal and barely avoided running off the runway into the rainfilled drainage ditch. He pulled up his flaps to put more weight on his

266

wheels at the higher speeds. As he slowed below 100 knots, he began to gradually feel out his brakes. Even though the wheels had antiskid brakes they could still hydroplane over the water, causing him to lose control as much as if he were on a sheet of ice. Holding left rudder while tapping the left brake with his toe, Court held the control stick forward and to the right to counteract the crosswind. In this cross-controlled position he slowed so much he had to add power to get to the end of the runway and turn off into the de-arming area. He thanked GCA for a great job. Under the direction of the de-arming crew, he braked to a stop. His body was tingling from the adrenaline flow brought on by his sudden fight to stay on the runway.

He heard a faint cough from the backseat. Then Dieter spoke. "You don't really believe I'd rather do this with you in an F-4 than fly solo in an F-100, do you?"

0930 Hours Local, Friday 2 February 1968
Office of the Assistant Secretary of the Army
Room 2E594, Pentagon
Washington, D.C.

E. Hayworth Pulmer, the Principal Deputy Assistant Secretary of the Army for Manpower and Reserve Affairs (PDASM&RA), had two men from the Audio-Visual section set up the big 16mm camera and show the copy of the now famous Hemms film in his office. Present at the private viewing was a colonel from the office of Army Public Affairs and a civilian GS-13 from the Office of the Judge Advocate General of the Army.

"It's a clear, open-and-shut case, gentlemen," said E. Hayworth Pulmer, "and we want action." He had the film of Wolf Lochert killing Buey Dan and throwing his body into a tree run three times, twice in slow motion. E. Hayworth Pulmer leaned forward as he watched the film. His eyes glistened, and he slowly ran his tongue over his lips. He was fascinated. He was a man who hadn't quite made it all the way through Yale. He had transferred to Columbia and obtained his business degree after five years of diligent study. He was known as Pinky Pulmer because of his habit of extending his little finger when he raised cup or glass to his lips. He did not enjoy being called Pinky. Nor did he enjoy being called Ed or Eddie, from his first name of Edward. He did enjoy being called Mister Secretary, which he was not entitled to. In his early forties, Pulmer was thin, pale, balding, and convinced he knew what was good for the United States Army. He wore a gray pinstriped three-piece suit with school tie. The only uniform he had ever worn was in the Junior ROTC at the high school he had attended twenty-five years before. He had received his appointed position in the Pentagon from a late-night vote concession between the more moderate Eastern Democrats and the liberal California contingent. The concession involved getting his opposite number (a contractor) on an urban housing committee.

"Report, please, the latest status of the case. Report," Pulmer said. He pointed to the colonel from Public Affairs. "You first." Three days ago Pinky Pulmer had started the action he hoped would lead to the court-martial of Lieutenant Colonel Wolfgang Lochert after Pulmer had received a telephone call from his patron, Congressman Oscar Nebals from California.

The Public Affairs man, a bulky colonel, cleared his throat. "We have been deluged with letters and telegrams about what has come to be known as the Lochert Atrocity. They run about ten to one against him. Several organizations and individuals are collecting signatures to send to their congressmen demanding Lochert be imprisoned."

"What organizations?" Pinky Pulmer demanded.

268

"The Women's Strike for Peace, National Mobilization to End the War in Vietnam, Youth International Program, Students for a Democratic Society, and some individuals. All of these people have been to Hanoi."

"Like who?"

He read from a list. "Mary McCarthy, Cora Weiss, Professor Richard Falk of Princeton University, Reverend William Sloan Coffin, David Dellinger, Thomas Hayden, to name a few."

Pinky Pulmer chewed his lip. "Damn it, none of these are impressive enough. What about Spock and Fulbright? Can't you contact them?"

The bulky colonel from Public Affairs shrugged helplessly. "Mister Pulmer, that's all I have to report. As much as I agree that Lochert's actions may have caused serious damage to the United States Army, there is simply no way I can contact civilians to elicit comments, unfavorable or otherwise, about him."

"Further," the GS-13 from the JAG office said, "the slightest hint of command influence and the case would never make it to trial."

"All right, all right. Just give me your report," Pulmer said to the civilian. "Save your negative attitude for another time."

"The only item I have to report is that the Article 32 investigation is under way."

"What is that and how long does it take?"

"The Article 32 investigation is like a civilian grand jury. In the Army, the Criminal Investigation Unit, the CID, goes into the field and examines the evidence, which it presents to the investigating officer. He in turn makes his recommendation to the highest regional commander with jurisdiction for or against a court-martial. In Vietnam it's the commanding officer, a three-star general, of USARV, United States Army Republic of Vietnam. USARV is located at Long Binh, just north of Saigon."

"What if the CID says there is no case or the investigating officer does not recommend a court-martial?" Pulmer asked.

269

"CID makes no recommendations. They merely present the facts as they find them. However, even if the investigating officer does not recommend a trial, USARV can overrule and order Lochert be tried regardless."

"Who is the commander of USARV and what is his attitude in this case?"

"In actuality, COMUSMACV, General Westmoreland, is the commander of USARV. It is one of his collateral duties. However, one of his deputies, Lieutenant General Elmer Farquell, actually runs it. I don't know what his attitude is."

"Is he a Special Forces man? One of those Green Berets?"

The JAG civilian checked his folder. "I don't believe he is."

"Good, good." Pinky Pulmer sat back in his thick leather chair. Pulmer had correctly interpreted the Army's attitude that Green Berets were snake-eating nonconformists that needed to be disbanded. A general officer with no Special Forces background could be reasonably counted on to harbor those very feelings.

"All right, all right," Pulmer said. "You two go back to your offices and make sure this affair proceeds quickly. I want that man tried and held up as an example that the Army does not tolerate such wanton and depraved behavior. And I want you to set all speed records doing it." He looked at Public Affairs. "Prepare your press releases accordingly."

"Sir, I can't prepare anything. The man hasn't even been tried yet, much less found guilty."

"He will, he will," Pulmer said and waved them away. After they went out, and the men from Audio-Visual had taken the camera and screen, Pulmer leaned forward and dialed a California number. The three-hour time difference made it quite early in San Francisco.

"Hello," a sleepy male voice answered.

"Oscar, it's Hayworth."

"For God's sake, it's six-thirty in the morning. What in hell do you want?" Oscar Nebals was a man who valued his time in bed. Particularly when he had a companion.

"Well, well. I just thought you'd want me to report on the, ah, the Lochert affair."

"All right, report," Oscar Nebals said, and absently fondled his bed partner.

"Well, the Article 32 investigation is under way – "

"What does that mean? Will that man be tried or not? I've got my reputation staked on his being found guilty and put away. Why the hell do you think I want you to push this?"

Pulmer explained the Uniform Code of Military Justice method and the role of General Farquell of USARV. "And I have it on good assurance Lochert will be tried," he added.

"Whose good assurance?"

"Well, ah, my *guess*, my *prognostication* is that he will be tried. Of course we could use more public pressure. Particularly from well-known names. Makes the public at large want to identify by following their views. Gives the views more impact."

"Mmm. I have just the man. He's a well-known writer and about to run for office out here. It would make a good issue for him."

"Who is the man?" Pulmer asked.

"Shawn Bannister."

15

1500 Hours Local, Saturday 3 February 1968
Command Post, Black Panthers Company
(ARVN), Hue
Republic of Vietnam

"We must evacuate you," Captain Tran Ngoc said to the
two Americans and Greta Sturm. They were in his heavily
fortified command post at the edge of the Tay Loc airfield.
"My general has ordered me that the Panthers are to join
with him at his headquarters compound south of the river."
Ngoc was wiry and handsome. His black hair was cut short,
his eyes as black as anthracite.

The fighting had been fierce and constant since Ngoc
had broken through the villa wall and rescued them. He
had heard part of Wolf's radio calls, had seen the helicopter
and heard the fighting. It was enough for him to act. He had
taken them back across the airfield to his enclave, the only
position in Hue still holding out against the NVA attack.
They brought out Rizzo's body. Lopez was still missing.

Others weren't so fortunate, Ngoc said. He told them
of the deaths of a civilian USIA representative, an NBC
official, several U.S. advisors, a German doctor and his
wife, two French priests, and several Filipinos. "And,"
Ngoc added, "we're receiving reports of reprisal murders
of hundreds, maybe thousands, of Vietnamese civilians."

Ngoc and his men were fighting continuously and there
had been little sleep. Captain Ngoc wouldn't allow Greta

Sturm to fire a weapon ("Lovely ladies should not get hands dirty"), but had no problems allowing her to uncrate supplies and load magazines with cartridges (which caused her fingers to get dirty *and* greasy). Rizzo's body was off to one side in a body bag.

He pointed to a map. "Sixth NVA regimental commander has three infantry battalions and a sapper battalion against the Citadel. Fifth NVA is attacking southern part of Hue across the river." He pointed to their attack route from Laos to the west, south of Lang Tri and Khe Sanh. "I have ordered helicopter to pick you for a flight to Quang Tri. To pick you *up* for Quang Tri," he corrected himself. "Although fighting is there, it is not difficult or concentrated as here in old city."

Wolf agreed. Ngoc assigned a squad to escort them to the helicopter pickup point. Wolf and Greta squatted behind a wall. Polter stood with the Vietnamese Army men. Smoke rose from all parts of the city. The sounds of battle grew louder as the NVA made determined attacks against Ngoc's last bastion of the ARVN at Tay Loc.

Wolf looked at his watch. "If we're not out of here in half an hour, we're not going to get out of here." Like Polter, he had his M16 and fresh magazines from Ngoc. All three were dirty and grimy from battle. Wolf in particular. He had had no sleep for three days. He rubbed the thick stubble on his jaw. He glanced around through eyes red-rimmed and sunken. "You did a good job back there at the villa," he said to Greta.

"Thank you." She was just as tired. Her shirt was rumpled and torn.

"Toward the end you didn't seem afraid. You held very good fire discipline. As good as any I've seen. That couldn't have come from your father. How did you stop being afraid so quickly?"

She flashed him a self-deprecating smile. "Because I prayed all the time that I would be killed quickly and cleanly. I wanted to die rather than be captured." She shrugged her shoulders. "So I was not afraid."

Wolf couldn't take his eyes from the flaxen-haired Greta Sturm. "But you said you were going to save the last bullet for yourself. Yet when it was time to make a charge, you were ready to go. Why was that?"

She tilted her head in thought. "Because I had decided it was better one of them should die by my last bullet, not me. I would not give my life over to death without any struggle." She looked into Wolf's eyes. "I think you can understand that?"

Wolf gave a short bark. "Oh yes, I can understand that. Very much can I understand that."

They heard the whopping sound of a helicopter. In minutes a UH-1B with the roundel of South Vietnam on the fuselage had picked up the three of them and Rizzo's body. The Vietnamese pilot cut across the Perfume River to relative safety before turning north to Quang Tri. Door gunners on both sides scanned the earth below and intermittently returned fire at ground positions shooting at them. The groundfire was from automatic weapons and inaccurate. Wolf noted the NVA had no big AAA guns in place within the city. This was an infantryman's battle, and it was being fought under the toughest of conditions – street fighting.

When they were clear, the gunners sat back and the noise abated. Polter grinned and looked away when Greta took Wolf's hand in her own.

"Wolfgang, thank you," she said. She pronounced it Vulfgang.

"What for? Saving your life? I didn't do that, Captain Ngoc and his troops did." It was noisy and windy inside the helicopter. They had to lean over and speak loudly into each other's ear.

"Thank you for stopping me from going to those soldiers. For not letting me carry a white flag. Maybe I have been carrying a white flag too long."

"What do you mean?"

Greta Sturm blushed. "There was a man. Back home. An older man who worked as an administrator at the hospital where I was a nurse. He wanted to marry me. My father, he thought that was a good idea. Always I had done what my father wanted me to do. As a child, I wanted to become a doctor, but father wanted me to become a nurse. 'Girls do not become doctors,' he told me, 'girls become nurses.' So I became a nurse. But when my father wanted me to marry that man I ran away. I joined the Maltese Aid Society. I thought this was a way to get away from him and a way to help the Vietnamese people." She looked out the door at the earth below, then turned and spoke again, her eyes veiled. "So I did get away, and I feel free at last from my father and that man. But now I find that instead of helping Vietnamese people, I have killed some. That is not a good thing."

Wolf clasped her fingers in his powerful hands. He chose his words carefully. Though the thoughts he was about to express were never far from his mind and he had wrestled with them many times, he had never allowed anyone to know how he felt.

"The act of killing is not a good thing. God did not put us on this earth to kill each other," he said slowly as he searched for the words. "But sometimes it has to be done. There are those who put themselves in positions where they have to kill or be killed. I do that as a profession. You put yourself in that position indirectly when you signed on with those people for Vietnam. Maybe you are happy you escaped your father and his plans for marriage, but your ability to shoot, the ability your father taught you – *forced* you to learn, maybe – help save your life and mine, and Polter's. You shot, and you killed." He stopped and took a deep breath. His exhausted face contorted in his effort to define his deepest thoughts. "But once you kill, you are changed forever. If you are of low esteem, it becomes a prideful thing. But if you see yourself as an equal among humans, then it becomes a sacrifice, your sacrifice. You lose a little bit of yourself each time you kill. It is not easy to explain." He looked away for a moment. "When you are a member of a profession that defends a country or a city or a village, you are trained to kill, and kill quickly and well. I say kill, not murder. There is a great difference. You are trained to kill those who are intent upon murdering you and yours for whatever rationale; those who have the means and cannot be reasoned out of that intent. And when reason fails, and there is no other way to stop them, you kill them. And another piece of you dies. Unless you are a demented executioner, you lose something. It is the price we who defend must pay. We just hope that our service is finished before there is nothing left within ourselves, so we may enjoy what time we have left. Those who are called upon to serve too much, or who through circumstances kill more than most, who go beyond what their souls can handle, die early. Alcohol, automobile wrecks, gun accidents, or the body one day just quits. They get the sickness and die. They have lost too much." Wolf's weathered face crinkled when he showed his teeth in what he hoped was a smile. "I'm tired, and I'm talking too much." He shook his head. "It was for you I was talking, trying to explain things. So you can go back to Germany and regain what you might have lost."

"Go back and become a doctor," she said. "I could do that, now. I want to and I will. There will be no difficulty with my father, not anymore." She squeezed his big hands. "But Wolfgang, what about you? What do you have to go back to? Are you sure you haven't gone too far?"

Wolf's lips formed a rueful smile. He took a deep breath of air and released it. He slowly disengaged his hand from hers. "When sometimes I think I have gone as far as I can, I see something like we saw yesterday, when they mutilated the bodies. Then the hate takes over . . . but that too is very dangerous. Hate can destroy its creator. It must be controlled. But I am trained, and I have trained myself, to control and . . . to use my emotions." He stopped. He felt foolish. The words weren't coming right. Wolf looked deep into her gray eyes. The world around them faded. There was just the two of them and he wanted very much for this girl to understand him. With an effort, he continued talking, aware as he did so that he had never talked this much to anyone since the seminary.

"You have to understand about me. I am a soldier. There are perhaps things about myself, some of my likes or dislikes, I can change. But I cannot change the fact that I am a soldier. It is my whole life. I don't have to worry about going back to it because I never left it. There are better things to be perhaps in your eyes, but not for me. There are those who build, those who teach or heal, those who research how to do things better. But I am a soldier. A soldier protects people. A soldier enforces laws. A soldier stands guard over what he believes in, sometimes alone when his only fuel is from his faith in himself. He trusts his judgment that his fellow soldier, his leader, his country and his country's cause is just and fair and deserving of his faith. Once that faith is broken and the man still serves, then he is a kept man, a mercenary who serves only for cash, not a just cause."

Wolf was surprised, shocked really, how he had opened up to this girl. Never outside of the confessional had he revealed so much of himself. Was this how it was just before you burned out? Or had this girl tapped something within him that made him want to tell her things, and teach her the way of things as he saw and practiced them? He wasn't sure. He only knew he was greatly attracted to this resourceful and courageous German girl. And in a more complete way than he was attracted to the dancer Charmaine. He wanted desperately to see her again, this girl who was so much younger than he. But how to say it? He swallowed hard but could not find the words.

"You certainly speak right out," she said as if she knew his thoughts.

"Not always," he said. "There are times when . . . when I cannot." Like now, he thought.

She saw the agony on his face. She knew what it meant and took his big hand. "We will see each other again. Many times."

"Yes," he said simply. His face relaxed and he leaned against the seat back.

The heat of the day was on them. The vibration of

the helicopter was soothing to their worn bodies. They sat, still holding hands, and dozed. They awoke when the blades changed pitch and the helicopter started its descent to the Quang Tri runway.

At the change in pitch, Wolf was instantly alert and sat up straight. He stiffened and slowly disengaged his hands from those of Greta Sturm. She smiled through a huge yawn.

"You are back to the war among your own. You must pick up your quiet thoughts and put them away. Yes?"

He nodded slowly. "You," he began, inarticulate once again, but determined to get one last point across. A very important point. "You . . . *understand*," he said, gratitude obvious in his eyes.

The Vietnamese pilot spiraled down over friendly forces and touched down under the raised-arm direction of an American Army crewman. He shut the engine down and asked for fuel in broken English. Polter helped him interpret and busied himself with the preparations to unload Rizzo's body. "He was a brave man," Wolf said, then helped Greta Sturm from the Huey helicopter. He held her a second longer than necessary.

"I don't know how it will be for a few days or even weeks. But we will see each other," he said.

"In Saigon," she said. "I will wait for you." They turned at the sound of a vehicle.

An Army colonel and two other officers dressed in khakis drew up in a jeep. They climbed out, the colonel leading the way, and approached them. The colonel returned Wolf's salute.

"Lieutenant Colonel Lochert?" he inquired in a conversational voice. He was a man of medium height, thin brown hair, and a pleasant face. "Wolfgang Xavier Lochert?"

"Yes, sir," Wolf said, puzzled.

The colonel examined him with a benign expression on his face. "I am Colonel Robert L. Larkin." He did not offer to shake hands. Instead he pointed to a swarthy major standing next to him. "This is Major Gerald S. Remley, my

Provost Marshal. He has a duty to perform." He nodded to Remley, who stepped forward.

"Lieutenant Colonel Wolfgang Xavier Lochert, you are under arrest."

"What for?" Wolf asked. "Stealing helicopters?" Only slightly amused as he remembered the helicopters he and the others had "borrowed" for the rescue at Lang Tri. "Or is it for disobeying orders?" He remembered ordering the men to jettison their heavy weapons and equipment at Lang Tri so Berry could lift the helicopter off the ground. "How about misuse of government equipment?" he offered.

"No, sir," the Provost Marshal said without humor. "It's none of that."

Greta Sturm drew close to Wolf.

"What is it, then?" Wolf Lochert asked, suddenly wary.

"Sir, the charge is murder. Murder of a Vietnamese citizen."

0015 Hours Local, Monday 5 February 1968
Situation Room, Basement of the White House
Washington, D.C.

Major General Albert "Whitey" Whisenand finished his reports shortly after midnight. Seven days had passed since the North Vietnamese Army, in concert with the Viet Cong, had violated the Tet truce and had begun massive attacks on Vietnamese cities and towns. He had studied the intelligence summations collated from the Provinces, from the military commanders, and from the Central Intelligence Agency. Latest reports listed over 100 cities and villages including Saigon, 39 of 44 provincial capitals, and 71 district capitals had come under assault.

The attacks followed a pattern: mortar and rocket bombardment in the early morning, followed by a troop assault. Once inside the cities and villages, the VC rendezvoused with others who had already infiltrated. Guided by local sympathizers, they attempted to capture key spots – radio stations, jails, police and civil headquarters buildings. Other VC units stayed outside the city to cut roads and paths. Political cadres accompanied the attackers and used loudspeakers to exhort the populace to rise up against the "enemies of the people." They weren't having much success. So far very few of the many regular NVA units available were committed to the battle. General Giap, an intelligence estimate said, appeared to be holding the NVA in reserve, especially in the southern portion of South Vietnam. It was as if he wanted the Viet Cong – all southerners – to face the brunt of the battle.

Although the Viet Cong had been driven from Cholon in Saigon, and the heavy fighting north of Saigon and the western suburbs of the city was over, the fighting over Hue, the old imperial capital of Vietnam, raged on. Intelligence reports indicated the Viet Cong had systematically sought out and murdered several thousand civilians. Scattered incidents of terror and sabotage occurred in other parts of South Vietnam, but nothing on the scale of events in Hue.

Whitey had been tasked by the NSC to go through all the intelligence reports sent to them that might have forecast or at least suggested such widespread attacks might take place. He had found ample evidence, from the CIA all the way down to a report from the 101st Airborne, that they had captured a VC with documents that were copies of public announcements about an historic campaign ahead. They urged "very strong military attacks in coordination with the uprising of the local population to take over towns and cities, soldiers should move to liberate the capital city of Saigon, take power, and try to rally enemy brigades and regiments to the side of the revolution. This will be the greatest battle ever fought throughout the history of our country."

Whitey stood and rubbed his eyes, then put the draft paper in his safe. He left his office and went down the hall to the Situation Room, that nerve center below the White House that received all the processed communications and reports from the Pentagon. He showed his pass to the guard and entered. The Sit Room was actually two rooms; one was long and windowless with a conference table; the other a command post, a hub of incoming military information. In addition to the military input, there was wire service from AP, UPI, and Reuters, and three TV sets. On the wall were four clocks with Washington, Saigon, GMT, and official Presidential time that LBJ kept regardless of where he was. The overhead lights were low; the information screens cast a green tinge over the military and civilian duty officers. Tiny colored action lights were sprinkled over a world map on the far wall. A military teletype finished its muted ratatat of news.

He read the situation reports. Another crisis in Asia was being dealt with. A U.S. ship, the USS *Pueblo*, dubbed a spy ship by the press, had been captured off the coast of North Korea. So far, 15,000 USAF and Navy reservists and 370 airplanes had been activated to augment U.S. forces in Korea because of the Pueblo capture. The captured sailors had been paraded in front of North Korean TV, accused of being spies, and North Korea was demanding an apology. Some Senators, including Democrat Frank Church of Idaho, had said the capture was an act of war in which the honor of the United States was at stake. Whitey gave a low whistle: Frank Church was one of the more outspoken doves on the Vietnam war. The senior member of the House Armed Services Committee had called the capture a "dastardly act of piracy." Strong words. The *Pueblo* was indeed an intelligence-gathering ship – like those of many nations – that for some reason the North Koreans had decided to seize even though it had been in international waters.

Further reports from Vietnam stated that there was still fierce fighting in Hue, and that the VC seemed to be making a concerted attempt to retain the old section of the Imperial Palace but probably would be driven out soon.

Whitey glanced up and saw LBJ, sitting in the director's chair, chin on his closed fist. He was dressed in his pajamas and thickly padded slippers. "He does this frequently," the duty officer whispered to Whitey. "He listens to the Tet reports, the air strike reports, the missing planes, the casualty reports. But he never says anything. After a while he just sighs and walks out. But tonight he seems to be staying for a long time."

The President looked up. He stood up and beckoned Whitey to follow him to the conference room. He carried a manila folder. He was haggard and walked slowly on bent legs, and eased himself into a large leather chair. He rubbed his face and forehead as if to stir his mind into action. He rubbed and rubbed, almost, Whitey thought, like an impersonator preparing his visage for a new part. Finally he looked up, a fierce scowl on his face.

"All right, Whisenand," he thundered, "what in hell is going on?" He jerked his chin toward the manila folder. "You told me we knew well in advance those little fellows were going to attack. So how come our boys are getting the pants beat off them?"

"Mister President, we did have a multitude of pre-attack intelligence. General Westmoreland even asked President Thieu to cancel the Tet truce and put his troops on full alert. Thieu did cancel some of the Tet holiday but didn't put anybody on a country-wide alert until too late. As far as our troops are concerned, they were ready but never expected the grand scale of the attack. Yet, regardless of what you hear and see on TV, this is turning into a grand rout for General Giap."

"Bah. I've heard that stuff before," the President sneered. "You generals are always telling me how very nice our little war is going."

Whitey stifled the impulse to inform the Commander in Chief of the U.S. Armed Forces that he – Major General Albert G. Whisenand – had on the contrary been telling his boss how sorry things were in Vietnam. But every time he opened his mouth, LBJ heaped scorn and said he was a negative thinker.

"One of these days, Whisenand, I'm going to step on

you like a bug." The President slapped his hand on the folder. "Dammit, how could they mount such an attack? Just when I thought that Ho Chi Minh was going to sit down and talk, he does this to me." He opened the folder. "On top of that, I get something like this. Read it," he said, and slid a paper across the table to Whitey.

It was a synopsis of a message from COMUSMACV to the Chairman of the Joint Chiefs of Staff regarding the defense of Khe Sanh.

==

1. I consider this area critical to us from a tactical standpoint. To relinquish the Khe Sanh area would be a major propaganda victory for the enemy. Its loss would seriously affect Vietnamese and U.S. morale.

2. We should be prepared to introduce weapons of greater effectiveness. Under such circumstances as the massed enemy infantry attacks, I visualize that either tactical nuclear weapons or chemical agents would be active candidates for deployment. Because the region is virtually uninhabited, civilian casualties would be minimal. Like Hiroshima and Nagasaki to the Japanese, this action would surely signal Hanoi of our resolve.

==

President Lyndon Baines Johnson shook his finger at Whitey. "This is what I mean about you generals always wanting to bomb, bomb, bomb. I told Chairman Wheeler nothing doing. My Gawd. Eighty-three of our *Pueblo* sailors in a North Korean prison camp, the Veet Cong all over the damn place in South Veet-nam, and he wants to drop a nuclear bomb. My Gawd. If the press ever heard about this . . ." He trailed off.

This wasn't the first time someone in the governmental hierarchy had considered using a nuclear bomb. Whitey remembered a televised press conference with Secretary of Defense Robert McNamara in 1961. President John F. Kennedy and the nation had been in the middle of the Berlin crisis. McNamara had looked sleek and assured as he'd answered the questions. One reporter had asked if he meant to imply he would use nuclear weapons in connection with the Berlin situation.

McNamara had answered, "Yes, I definitely do. We will use nuclear weapons whenever we feel it necessary to protect our vital interest. Our nuclear stockpile is several times that of the Soviet Union and we will use either tactical weapons or strategic weapons in whatever quantities, wherever and whenever it's necessary to protect this nation and its interests."

Whitey spoke to the President. "Sir, I don't think it will make much of an issue, since neither you nor the JCS back such usage. But I do think you should be putting some thought into capitalizing on how Ho Chi Minh broke the Tet truce and how he is being so badly beaten. In fact, Mister President, this is turning into a major defeat for the Viet Cong and the NVA troops. We should be informing the American people of exactly what is going on. The way it is now, they see only the TV clips that show Cholon and the Embassy in Saigon under attack. It makes no difference that the sappers at the Embassy never got into the Chancery and that they were all killed. The public sees lots of ruined buildings and dead soldiers as if we have suffered a defeat. Never on the TV did they hear or see the total repulse of the attack on the Vietnamese Navy Headquarters, or the entire battalion scheduled to free five thousand prisoners from the main Saigon jail that got lost and was annihilated by our forces. Or how three hundred VC were killed in the attack on the Tan Son Nhut Air Base. This is what we should be stressing. Intelligence reports said that Ho was calling this 'The Great Offensive and People's Uprising.' None of that has come to pass. We must impress this upon the public."

"It's no use, it's no use," the President said in a bitter voice. "All they see is the dead American military policemen at the Embassy and the picture of that Vietnamese policeman executing a VC." The picture, recorded by photographer Eddie Adams, had been taken at the exact instant the bullet fired by the Chief of the National Police had entered the head of a Viet Cong who had just killed some civilians. "All they see is the Khe Sanh and Hue attacks," the President added. "Wounded Marines piled on a tank, crashing transports at Khe Sanh. Those are the only pictures those press people show. God in heaven."

He arose and poured himself a shot of bourbon from the serving table. He put it down without drinking.

"The press. Ho Chi Minh gets better treatment from the press than the President of the United States." His voice became strident. "Let me tell you that NBC and the *New York Times* are committed to an editorial policy of making us surrender. Editors just won't use the words 'President Johnson' in anything that is good." He sat back. "I feel like a hound bitch on heat. If you run, they chew your tail off, if you stand still, they slip it to you."

16

0530 Hours Local, Tuesday 6 February 1968
Hoa Lo Prison, Hanoi
Democratic Republic of Vietnam

As always, the pain awakened him. Pain from the iron stocks, pain from his legs pressed on the flat concrete, pain from his arms and legs. He blinked back to consciousness from a dream where he and his mother had been walking the streets of Washington, D.C. Somehow he was a childlike man in the dream. Although it was a pleasant dream, he remembered asking, "Momma, why do my legs always hurt?"

The small door to his cell porthole flipped open. A guard with a look of exaggerated distaste handed Flak a bowl. This particular guard, Flak had noticed, was older than most, appeared imbecilic, and often made weird faces at him, like a small child would at someone he didn't like. Once he had stuck his tongue out at Flak. Flak had resisted the instant urge to do the same thing back. The guard slammed the tiny door.

Flak examined his breakfast bowl. The liquid was a slimy concoction with something solid resting on the bottom of the bowl. He dipped it out with his spoon. It was a piece of animal hoof complete with dirt and hair. His stomach churned. He flipped the piece to the floor and tried to sip the liquid. He sipped, retched, and sipped again, until it was all down. He did his number mantra and took deep breaths through his mouth to fight the nausea. After a few moments he could breathe normally.

He lay back and concentrated on his numbers. On the 26th day, the bad king owed thirty-three million, five hundred fifty-four thousand, four hundred thirty-two dollars. No, that isn't right, he thought. I forgot the decimal point. He's doubling pennies a day, not dollars. He started over. On the 26th day, the bad king owed three hundred thirty-five thousand, five hundred forty-four dollars and thirty-two cents.

My mind is slipping, he said to himself. They are starving me to death and my mind is going. He had tried some calculus and some physics. Although a few formulas came to mind, he had a hard time tracking them and remembering exactly what they were for. There was something about MV squared, Mass times Velocity squared. He knew he had used it at the test pilot school at Edwards, both as a student and as an instructor. But it escaped him exactly what it was for.

He was learning to live in the past or in the future, but never in the present. The present was just too painful to contemplate. The only time he had to deal with the present was when he was undergoing torture. Even then he tried to occupy his mind with his numbers or senseless humming. It rarely worked for long, especially when he was in the ropes.

The ropes. His whole body tensed. Oh God. They were coming for him again. He had another session due, he just knew it. Yesterday they had offered him half an orange and a chance to talk about seeing visitors from the United States. He had eaten the orange, peel and all, then refused to talk. They had hung him up in the knobby room by his ankles in a metal stock and poured water in his nose. His ears still crackled and popped from the introduction of the fluid. Again, blubbering and bellowing, he had refused to meet with anybody.

"You think tonight," Rabbit, his chief torturer, had said. "You think tonight about decision. Tomorrow you will be severely punished unless you agree to see your countrymen." Flak knew "severely punished" meant the ropes. None of the guards or torturers would ever use the word *torture*. Instead, *punishment* was the word. For a POW to complain of being tortured would bring a beating – a punishment for maligning the humane and lenient treatment given to POWs by Ho Chi Minh and the Democratic Republic of Vietnam.

And now tomorrow was here. Flak had to think about what Rabbit proposed, seeing somebody from the United States. He didn't know if his bailout radio call had been heard two and a half months ago when he had ejected from his shot-down F-4. He didn't know if he was carried as killed, missing, or as a prisoner of war. Maybe seeing someone would get the news out that he was a prisoner and still alive. His mother would be so worried. He had to talk to someone about this. He needed to know what the SRO would advise.

He bent his head in a torturous way to look over his shoulder at the flipper hole in the door. The best he could tell, no one was looking in. Keeping his eye on the hole, he reached behind himself and rapped with his sore knuckles "shave and a haircut," the opening call like a telephone ring, to Ted Frederick. Rap, rap. "Two bits," Frederick answered.

HOW U, Flak asked.

COPING.

THEY WANT ME TO SEE PEOPLE FROM STATES. MAYBE THEY GET WORD TO MY MOM I STILL ALIVE. WHAT IS POLICY.

NO STATEMENTS, NO TAPES, NO BROADCASTS, NO VISITORS.

RABBIT SAID ROPES TODAY IF NO SEE.

There was a pause before Frederick answered.

YEAH FLAC. WE DONT GIVE THEM ANYTHING. THEY MUST PULL IT FROM US. THEY MUST FORCE US. EVERY TIME. COPE BEST YOU CAN. IS UR JUDGMENT CALL. DO WHAT YOU CAN LIVE WITH REST OF UR LIFE.

WHAT ABOUT LETTING SOMEONE KNOW I
ALIVE.

POW NAMES GET OUT. WE HAVE A WAY.
METHOD TS. GL N GBU.

GL N GBU, Flak had learned, meant "good luck and.
God bless you." Flak felt better. If Ted Frederick said
the names were getting out, then they were getting out.
Frederick said the method was TS, Top Secret. Maybe if
they could be alone together sometime he would find out
how the information got back to the United States.

They came for him an hour later and took him to the
knobby room. Rabbit sat at a small desk table covered
with a blue cloth that hung down both sides. He motioned
to a small stool in front of the desk. "Sit," he commanded.
Flak Apple lowered himself to the stool, which was only
six inches high.

"What is your decision?" Rabbit asked in an even tone.

"About what?" Flak asked.

Rabbit nodded to someone behind Flak. Flak heard a
swish of wind, then something slammed into his right ear,
knocking him sideways off the stool. He picked himself
up and sat back on the stool.

"What is your decision?" Rabbit's voice was the same.

"I've decided I don't like being hit from behind," Flak
replied. Rabbit rattled off something in Vietnamese. Two
guards pounced on Flak, wrestled him to the floor, and
pulled his arms straight out behind him.

The man who had put Flak in the ropes two days ago
came forward. He had small oval eyes like those of a pig.
He spoke Vietnamese words soothingly and in a comforting
tone to Flak as he approached. He began placing inch-wide
green straps flat and even along his arms. Flak roared in
anger and pain when Pigeye stood on the small of his back,
pulling on the straps to get them tighter on his arms, and
to get his arms parallel with each other all the way to
his shoulders. He felt like his chest would split down the
middle and his shoulders dislocate. Then Pigeye passed
a rope from Flak's bound wrists under his buttocks, up

289

through his crotch and around the back of his neck. From behind, Pigeye jerked and tugged the rope until Flak's face was pressed into his own crotch.

Flak's pain was electric and hot and streaming from every nerve end. What little water his dehydrated body possessed was flowing from his nose and eyes and every pore. There was no counting, no mantra. Nothing but overwhelming, shocking pain and agony. He felt sobs and screams pushing against his larynx from the inside, trying to get out, but unable to because his throat was so constricted from his bent-over and contorted position. He couldn't talk and soon he couldn't breathe. He lunged and bucked against the pressure of Pigeye's body. In seconds he saw red in front of his eyes, then blackness.

Moments later, when he came to, he saw Pigeye standing over him with an empty bucket dripping water. The pain was still there, but the rope pulling his face into his crotch had been loosened. His face was level with his knees.

"Now," he heard Rabbit, or someone, say into his ear, "will you agree to meet with your countrymen?"

"Untie me . . . and I'll . . . talk . . . about it," Flak gasped. There was no answer. Twenty minutes passed. He was not set loose. The pain went on and on. It was excruciating. Flak just knew his chest was splitting down the middle and his arms were slipping from their sockets.

"Yes, YES," Flak screamed. *"YES."*

"Yes, what?" Rabbit asked close to his ear.

"Yes, yes. I'll see them," Flak groaned. In the back of his mind, a little voice said, "*See* them doesn't mean *talk* to them."

Pigeye undid the straps. Flak rolled over and tried to massage his arms. They were at first without feeling, just wooden blocks. Then new pain started as the denied blood circulation began. Pins, needles, fire, vises, boiled alive. But not as bad as the ropes and straps.

They gave him ten minutes to compose himself, then Pigeye brought him to the small table.

"Drink," he said, giving Flak a large thick glass full of water. Flak gulped it down. "More," he croaked.

"Oh, no. First we must talk about what you say, how you perform with your countrymen. They will ask you questions. You will say you are happy and well, and you are being treated well. You will say you are sorry for your crimes against the peace-loving people of the Democratic Republic of Vietnam." Rabbit examined Flak's arms and hands. They were without scars where the ropes had been. Yet his left arm was twisted and bent inward where the bone had been broken and healed without a cast. "We will give you clothes. You will leave your sleeves rolled down," Rabbit said in a voice thick with menace. "You will see them tomorrow."

They took Flak back to his cell. This time no one locked his ankles in the stocks. Before the sun was at its zenith, Crazy Face came in, threw a clean rag at Flak, then prodded him outside to an old shed where there was a shower head. Crazy Face gave him a sliver of soap and pointed at the shower.

Flak didn't need any encouragement. This was his first bath or shower since he had been shot down. Not knowing how much time he had, he did a hasty overall wash. Then he used the rag to scrub and grind away at the accumulated scabs and dried waste between his legs, and his buttocks, and down his legs. The water was cold, and the soap yellow with naphtha and lye. Soon his skin was raw and tingling. He decided not to scrape too hard. It might break the skin and cause a rash that would soon infect. Then he scrubbed his head and the rest of his body once more.

Back in his room, two covered metal dishes rested on folded cloth on his concrete slab. Crazy Face pushed him in and went out without putting him in the stocks. Flak examined the metal dishes. They were full of hot rice and steaming vegetables. A large spoonful of sugar had been spread over one portion. He tried not to wolf it down. He ate slowly, savoring every bite. When he was done, he carefully felt with his tongue around his mouth for the last morsels and grains.

Then he unfolded the treasures awaiting him on the concrete slab. There was a mosquito net, a thin cotton blanket, a woven straw mat filthy with dried effluvia, and a pair of pajama-style shirt and pants made of a rough material with purple and gray stripes. He tapped a call to Ted Frederick but got no reply. Rabbit appeared at his cell in midafternoon. He had with him a man who wielded a pair of scissors and set about to cut Flak's hair. Afterward Rabbit handed Flak a wooden handle with half of a razor blade attached to one end. The barber put a small folding mirror on the slab. Flak examined the razor, then tried it. It was dull.

"I have skin problems," Flak said. "This is a bad razor. I don't want to shave." Like many black men Flak Apple had tender skin on his cheeks that required delicate care.

"You shave face or be severely punished," Rabbit snarled.

Flak wet his face and shaved the best he could. Even though he was extra careful, his face felt like he had rubbed sandpaper on it. Rabbit inspected him and gave him a small towel. "You have cuts," he said. "Put on clothes now. You hurry." Flak put on the striped pajamas.

"We go now," Rabbit said. "Be very careful what you say," he added with steel in his voice. He led Flak out of the compound to a jeep-type vehicle. A driver drove them to an old French colonial residence, faded now and in disrepair. The whole neighborhood was in disrepair, Flak saw. They were in what had been a prestigious area near the Lake of the Restored Sword. Inside, he was led into a room that had several chairs and a sofa covered with plastic placed around a coffee table. The articles on the low table drew Flak's eyes. There were apples, and bananas, oranges, and, miracle of miracles, candy and vanilla wafers. His cheek muscles cramped as if he had just bitten into a lemon. He hoped he wouldn't salivate.

A large black man and black female walked into the room. "Hello," he boomed, sticking his hand out. "I'm

292

Robert Williams." He tilted his head toward the woman. "This is my wife." He did not give her name. Flak begrudgingly shook hands with both of them. The man spoke American English.

"Sit down," Williams said as a command. "Eat up." He watched as Flak warily put a cookie in his mouth and chewed. Who *is* this guy? Flak wondered. The cookie simply melted on his tongue. Nothing had ever tasted as good. What the hell, might as well take advantage of this situation. He began eating ravenously.

Williams stared at him. "What's the matter? Don't you get cookies where you are?" Flak didn't answer.

"Well, no matter. They'll take care of you. I've been assured of that. I'm here in Hanoi with the convention. It's the Peoples of the World against U.S. Imperialist Aggression in Indochina." He eyed Flak. "These people here, they wouldn't hurt anybody. The imperialists who bomb and kill women and children here in Hanoi are the same ones who kill and bomb black babies in Birmingham." Williams watched Flak closely. So far Flak had not looked at him. "I'm from the States," Williams said. "They call it the land of the free, but there ain't no freedom there. That's why I live in Cuba. I have a radio program there called *The Voice of Free Dixie*."

Flak awkwardly peeled an orange. His fingers would not do exactly as he wanted. They felt numb and encased in thick mittens.

"Listen, Brother," Williams said conspiratorially. "Would you like to make a tape for your loved ones? Wouldn't your wife like to hear from you? I can do it, you know. Let's make a tape together and I'll broadcast it on my program. What do you say, Brother?" So far the man's wife had not said a word.

Flak began stuffing apples and oranges into his pockets.

"Well," Williams said, leaning forward. "What do you say?"

Flak looked up at Rabbit. His joints remembered the pain from the ropes. He tilted his head toward Williams.

293

"You're no American," he hissed, "and sure as hell not a Brother." Rabbit bent down to listen to the words.

"I certainly am," Williams insisted. Rabbit turned his head back and forth as the two men spoke.

"You are not an American," Flak repeated. "No *American* would voluntarily live in *Cuba*." He tried to say it in a conventional voice so that Rabbit wouldn't comprehend the insult.

Williams looked at Rabbit. "This man is hopeless," he said to him. "A criminal." Rabbit looked confused. Flak decided not to press his luck. Besides, his stomach and pockets were full. "I'm tired," he said, looking down. "And sick. I want to leave."

As Rabbit led him out, Flak watched Williams' eyes. When he had his attention, he pretended to scratch his jaw and gave him the finger.

Rabbit beat on him for two hours and locked him in the stocks because Williams had said he was a criminal and hopeless.

1745 Hours Local, Tuesday 6 February 1968
Ubon Officer's Club
Ubon Royal Thai Air Force Base
Kingdom of Thailand

Court's Pan Am flight landed at Don Muang International outside of Bangkok at noon. He had flown several missions from Tan Son Nhut. When the Bien Hoa F-100s were clear to fly, he was released to return to Ubon. He hired a taxi – a tiny blue Japanese car – to take him to the other side of the airfield, where the USAF shared a large base as a courtesy of the Royal Thai Air Force. He had taken the civilian flight instead of the scheduled USAF courier from Saigon, a T-39 known by its call sign of Scatback, not only because he had the ticket as the last part of his Singapore leave, but because it would be some time before he would be in a strictly civilian environment on an airplane and he wanted to savor the last minutes. At the MAC passenger terminal he changed into a flight suit, and by three he was airborne in a C-130 Khlong Flight that served as courier between all the USAF bases in Thailand. Khlong, the Thai word for canal, was the word the C-130 crew used for their call sign.

Stupefied by the heat and roar of the four big T56 turboprop engines, Court dozed as he hung forward in the straps that kept him in his webbed nylon pull-down seat. The seats lined the interior walls. In the center, running lengthwise down the cargo deck, were tons of boxes and supplies and engine parts for the bases the Khlong Flights resupplied two and three times a day. Court woke ten minutes after level-off. Cool air flooded the plane. He readjusted the yellow, waxy, noise-suppressing substance he had put in his ear. The loadmaster had passed it out to the passengers as protection against the deafening roar of the big engines. As always happened, one man, new to C-130 flying, ate his, thinking it was toffee or some such to keep his ears open during ascent.

Court yawned and pulled from his leg pocket the rumpled copy of the Pacific edition of the *Stars and Stripes* he had found in the passenger terminal.

A large picture of Wolf Lochert jumped out at him from the front page. Stunned, he read the accompanying article.

SPECIAL FORCES COLONEL UP FOR
TV MURDER

Highly decorated Army Special Forces Lieutenant Colonel Wolfgang X. Lochert was charged under a USARV investigation with murder stemming from a TV news clip showing him knifing a Vietnamese man, then throwing his body against a tree. Mal Hemms, TV broadcaster for ITC, said when Lochert saw him filming the murder he attacked him savagely. The attack, though perhaps not as savage as Hemms claims, is clearly shown in the news clip.

Lochert refused comment when contacted by reporters. His court-appointed lawyer, US Army Major Jay Denroe, said Lochert was acting in self-defense and was innocent of the murder charges.

Unofficial sources say the slain Vietnamese, Buey Dan, was apparently a double agent who had caused the death of many of Lochert's men. It is unknown whether or not Lochert can prove this vital point in his defense.

Court rested the newspaper in his lap and thought of the burly colonel. Their friendship went back to Court's tour as an F-100 pilot at the Bien Hoa Air Base in South Vietnam, when Wolf Lochert had been with the III Corps Mike Force team. They had spent time together with Toby Parker in Vietnam and in Las Vegas at an impressive party his father had thrown for the returning veterans. He knew he had to try to help Lochert.

After he landed at Ubon, Court caught a ride to his BOQ, unloaded his gear, and walked over to the USAF MARS (Military Affiliate Radio System) and placed a call to his father in Las Vegas. An hour later a ham operator in California put him through on a collect call. Due to the eleven-hour time difference, it was five in the morning Las Vegas time. Because the phone patch was on one frequency, the speakers had to say "over" to allow the radio operators to switch their transmit buttons on and off.

"Court, are you all right? Over."

"Dad, I'm fine. Sorry to bother you at such an hour, but I need your help on something. Remember when you threw that party for me in sixty-five after my first tour? I brought Toby Parker and Wolf Lochert with me. Lochert was the Special Forces major, the dark stocky guy. He is in a legal jam with the Army and I want to get a civilian lawyer for him. Will you set it up?

He's a lieutenant colonel now, I don't know his serial number, but he's assigned to the Fifth Special Forces with duty at MACSOG in Saigon. Just charge all the fees to my trust fund. Over."

Sam Bannister laughed. "Yes, I remember your Army friend very well. He was following Charmaine around like a moonstruck teenager. I've certainly been reading about him. Between the TV and the newspapers, he's getting a lot of space. I know just the chap to lend a hand, Archie Gant out in San Francisco. He saw combat in the big one, became a lawyer, went back in for a few years as a JAG. Now he's enormously rich handling criminal cases. You're going to need a lot of money if you want me to engage him, more than the five thousand you draw every month. I can loan you whatever you need. Do you want me to get him? Over."

"Yes, Dad, get him. By the way, I don't draw from the account. I try to live on my Air Force pay. The five grand goes directly into savings at around four percent. I think it's up to a couple hundred thousand now. If that isn't enough, I'll take the loan. One thing, you've got to tell Gant that Wolf is not to know who is paying him. He has got to tell Wolf he's doing it because he's interested in the case and won't take any money. Come to think of it, maybe Gant is against the war and won't take the case. What do you think? Over."

"Against the war? Court, Archie Gant invented Attila the Hun. He should be happy to take the case if he's not all booked up. And if Archie wants the case, don't worry, he'll find Colonel Lochert. I'll get onto it and cable you as soon as I have some news. Speaking of news, Shawn is making some news himself out in California. Seems he's been drafted by the People's Peace and Justice Party to run for a state congressman's slot. You never know where that lad will turn up, do you? What a guy. No more news from here. I'll get right on the Gant thing. I hope your missions are going well. I miss you, son. Take care of yourself. Over."

"Thanks, Dad. Gant it is. As to Shawn, I have no comment. As to me, the missions are fine, all easy ones. That's all I have. I miss you too, Dad. Out."

He hoped that helped Wolf, but that was not all he had to worry about.

That night Court had dinner with Doc Russell. As he walked back to his room afterward through the deepening dusk, he thought about their conversation. He had tried to tell the Doc about his ambivalent feelings regarding Susan Boyle and marriage.

He lit a cigarette, slammed the Zippo shut, and jammed it into his pocket. He felt the stored heat from the road radiating on his body. The first few drops from a passing storm made half-dollar splotches on the asphalt.

Damn, damn, damn, he thought. He didn't really know what he felt about Susan Boyle. He was caught between his own emotions – flying and settling down. One side wanted to forget Susan Boyle and the entanglement such a relation would mean. That side just wanted to fly and fight the war the best way he could, regardless of the circumstances. The other side wanted . . . wanted what? Something more stable, he supposed. Whatever *that* meant. He took a deep drag as he walked in the darkness. Ah, to hell with it. Just concentrate on his job and get the night FAC program running. Just fly combat and not be burdened with emotions. Behind him the noise of the Officer's Club increased as the pilots warmed up in anticipation of a floor show.

It had been a good day for Captain Donny Higgens, the aircraft commander of an F-4 Phantom. He, and his GIB, navigator Lieutenant Horace "Rail" Rhoades, had flown a highly successful five-hour mission (they had refueled three times from the Cherry Anchor KC-135 tanker) on the Ho Chi Minh Trail, during which they had uncovered three truck parks (seven trucks destroyed) and won nose-to-nose duels with two separate 37mm gun sites. Donny was flying as a Wolf FAC, a daytime fast-FAC operation designed to stop traffic on the Ho Chi Minh Trail. He and Rail led the pack in finding and destroying trucks and guns. They seemed to have a sixth sense for where the trucks would hide at sunup and the best place for the guns to be concealed.

Now Donny was ready for dinner and some rest and relaxation at the Ubon Officer's Club. After showering in the BOQ he put on a pair of Levi cutoffs, thongs, the red Wolf shirt, stuffed a hunter's duck call in his back pocket, and, humming the lead bars from "Feelin' Groovy," he walked down the screened hall and banged out the screen door.

It was just after seven, dark, and rather cool. There was a hint of rain. In the distance he saw the one-storey Officer's Club. Tonight was the night the Hawaiian dancers were due. He was ready to see some really groovy chicks do those sexy, butt-wiggling dances at the all-male O'Club.

Formally, USAF officer's clubs were titled Officer's Open Mess, with the name of the base preceding the word "officer's." Sometimes the acronym was pleasant, rolled off the tongue nicely, and formed a recognizable and appropriate word such as the Boom Club, the Bien Hoa Officer's Open Mess, at Bien Hoa in III Corps, South Vietnam. Or the Doom Club at Da Nang. Of course a silly female newsie did pick up on the word "doom" and write of the brave but fatalistic jocks who flew death missions daily. She had written a particularly dramatic piece about a doom pussy scratching on the canopies of F-4s and B-57s flying night missions over the Trail that had caused a lot of laughter. At Ubon the Uoom Club name never made it for obvious reasons.

Donny met Rail at the long teak bar that sported a genuine brass rail. Each man's water table was low. They inhaled three Budweisers as fast as they could. Feeling better, Donny pulled out his duck call and coaxed out the sounds that earned him the nickname Duckcall Donny – a resounding *QUACK, Quack, quack*, and some contented duck murmurs. A couple of cheers and a raspberry or two greeted this effort.

Ready to eat, Donny and Rail went to the half-full dining room. The floor of the large room was of a yellow-and-green linoleum. The chairs and tables were constructed of bamboo. Woven place mats were used rather than table-cloths. The two men deliberated over the menu, which was a waste of time because they had memorized the thirteen items during their first week eating at the club.

Ubon Royal Thai Air Force Base was just that, a Royal Thai Air Force Base, an RTAFB. The Americans were, as were the Australians flying F-86s before them, merely guests on the base. Under the SOFA (Status of Force Agreement), the Americans were authorized to expand the facilities and fly from seven RTAFBs within the country of Thailand. In return, all American facilities (not equipment like airplanes and trucks), whether constructed or flown in from the U.S., belonged to the Thais. This impacted even at Officer and NCO clubs. The Thais ran the kitchens, the bars, and the sales concessions. Naturally, although the club officer, Major Richard Hostettler, was an American, Thai personnel performed all the other duties in the club, from barmaid to kitchen chef and table-waiting.

To preclude translation problems, especially for new waitresses, each menu item had a number to facilitate order-taking. The menu, primarily American with steaks and burgers, did have a few ethnic dishes like Thai fried rice and the spicy hot Thai salad. Rail ordered the number 1, steak. Donny ordered number 6 on the menu, a cheeseburger.

"No hab chee-burge," Chooky the waitress said. She was a cute little Thai girl, slender as a bird, with long dark hair and liquid eyes.

"It's on the menu," Donny retorted.

"No hab," Chooky said and giggled. Like most Asians, Thais didn't like to say no to anybody. It made them nervous, so they giggled.

Donny studied the menu. He pointed to number 7, the hamburger. "Do you have hamburger?"

300

"Hab ham-burge," Chooky said. Donny nodded.

"Do you have the cheese sandwich?" he asked, pointing at number 5.

"Hab cheese sand-wish." Chooky smiled.

"Well, then, I'll have the number six." Donny flashed his most engaging smile at Chooky.

Chooky swallowed. "No hab, no hab, Meestair. No hab chee-burge."

"You have number five, the cheese sandwich."

"Hab five."

"You have number seven, the hamburger."

"Hab seven."

"Chooky," Donny said, peering at her name tag. "If you have cheese and you have hamburgers, why in the" – Donny took a deep breath – "why do you say you have no cheeseburgers? Aren't there any cheeseburgers?"

"Yes. No hab chee-burge. They all gone, Meester Donny," Chooky said with a sunny smile.

Donny gave up. "Bring me the five and the seven," he said.

"Yes, Meester Donny. That good idea. You put them together, you hab chee-burge."

When Donny and Rail finished eating, they tipped Chooky five baht and walked back to the main bar. En route they paused at the bulletin board to look at the flying schedule and reconfirm they were not flying the next day. Even though one might be due to be off for a day, last-minute changes frequently occurred. So prudence dictated that if a crewman was going to hang one on, said crewman double-checked the flying schedule.

The schedule could do strange things to a man's digestion, mood, pulse rate, and eyelids. If he was scheduled for a real up-north bangeroo double-pumper and his experience level was low, he suddenly wasn't as hungry, his mood level depressed somewhat, his heartbeat gave a jump and his eyes narrowed, lest anybody see all of the above.

The two men confirmed they were not due to fly the next day. Time to party.

301

There was also a large multicolored sign on the bulletin board reminding everybody that a USO show, the Funelda Dancers, was due to perform tonight.

"Hah," Rail said. "Girls."

"Yes, indeed," Donny Higgens allowed. Each man immediately fantasized a love-at-first-sight, one-night stand with a lovely long-legged dancer.

The crowd stood two-deep at the bar and most tables were taken. There were no standards or conventions marked in this club – or any other fighter club in a combat zone, for that matter. The club was open twenty-four hours a day, and provided all services twenty-four hours a day, bar and dining included. The night pilots flew at night and relaxed in the daytime, the day pilots flew in the day and relaxed at nighttime like normal folk. Except for the misguided rules of the previous wing commander, Delbert Crepens, who had tried to impose teetotaling on the entire air base, the Ubon Officer's Open Mess and the Non-Commissioned Officer's Open Mess had always operated thus.

Life in a combat zone was different, and that's all there was to it. Peacetime rules and regs were relaxed considerably. And, of course, joy of joys, there was no OWC – Officer's Wives Club. At stateside and overseas military bases where the military men had their families, the NCOs' wives and officers' wives formed clubs that all but dominated the only manifestation of their uniqueness . . . The Club. It satisfied not only the innate urge to meet and greet with one's own, it supplanted the deep-down desire to have something similar to, but unique from, the exclusive civilian tennis and country clubs for the affluent. For monthly dues of seven dollars at an officer's club and four dollars at an NCO club, a wife belonged.

Generally, that's also where things turned to shit two ways. Occasionally wives would assume their husbands' rank and act very officious toward the junior wives, and – in almost all cases – the wives tried to run the damn club and turn it into a la-de-dah prissy social mecca. In the old days (mid-fifties and earlier), when a fighter jock wanted to hit the bar with his buddies after a hard day in the office (the cockpit), they did so in sweaty K-2B cotton flight suits and flight jackets. (No hats. Wear a hat in the bar and you buy the bar.) The pilots sang and they swore and they shot their watches right off their wrists. They got noisy and once in a while they said "fuck" right out loud.

Once the OWC got going, such relaxation methods were out, out, out. To further screw up a good deal for the aircrew (it was, after all, *their club*), a SAC general tried to get everybody to wear formal uniforms after 1800 hours: bow ties and white shirts. Well, Jee-sus Christ. That was going too far. Everybody was really pissed, especially the Irishmen. (The SAC general was supposed to be a true son of the sod. He was definitely considered a son of something, but it was not sod.) Something had to be done. Finally a compromise was reached, and the stag bar was born. Fighter pilots in the cruddiest of clothes and green bags could congregate in the stag bar, drink, throw beer on each other, and say "fuck" until their tongues dried out. But only in the stag bar. So it was at peacetime air bases.

But now, in the combat zone, the whole club was ONE BIG STAG BAR. Shit hot. Yay, ray, *fuck*.

Donny and Rail didn't much know or care about all that past hoohah. They were junior officers who hadn't been around all that long. All they knew was that they were flying combat missions and certain privileges went with that noble status. One was combat pay of sixty-five bucks a month (taxable), another was that the first $6,000 of their meager yearly pay was tax-free. (All of the enlisted men's salary was tax-free.) But what was really nifty was the life in the O'Club. The clubs at the pilot training and F-4 upgrading bases were a bit rigid. But here in the combat zone of Southeast Asia . . . wow. No OWC to muck things up in this exclusive all-male environment.

Of course Donny Higgens knew all about clubs during wartime. He was, after all, on his second combat tour. He had flown F-100s out of Bien Hoa. It was there he had acquired two of his many sobriquets: Higgens the Homeless

303

and Duckcall Donny. The former for being banned from the Bien Hoa O'Club for asking a visiting minister's wife to "show us your tits." The latter for his habit of always carrying a duck call around and blowing flatulent quacks whenever he felt the time was appropriate. Few people, particularly those more mature than Donny, agreed with his definition of what was appropriate. As it was, most people considered themselves more mature than Donny Higgens.

Elbowing their way to the bar, each man ordered a pair of double scotches, took one in each fist, and walked to a corner table to join two other F-4 crews. They spoke of their missions that day. One A/C (aircraft commander, the frontseater) said they spent most of their time patrolling between Delta 32 and Delta 69, trying to pinpoint a zipper that had reportedly come up on a Nail FAC (an airborne forward air controller with the call sign "Nail"). The Delta points were code names for various checkpoints on the Trail. A zipper was a four-barrel ZPU 12.7mm antiaircraft gun that had a horrendous rate of fire and an excellent manual tracking capacity. The pilots told how they had made several passes, each lower than the previous, but couldn't get the gunner to shoot. Most NVA gunners on the Trail had good fire discipline.

Duckcall Donny Higgens spoke up. "I found a 37 gunner with no protection. Had to be a new guy, to shoot at me without any 23 backup."

Even though it could shoot up to 13,000 feet, a 37mm gun was most efficient against aircraft between 5,000 and 10,000. The 12.7 zippers, the 14.5s, and the quad 23s accounted for most of the shootdowns under 8,000 feet. The gunner never should have opened up against a fast, low-level jinking aircraft to begin with. But since it did, it should have had at least a twin-, if not quad-barrel, rapid-firing 23mm gun to back it up. This 37 gun did not.

"What did you put on him?" the A/C asked. He meant what type of strike aircraft had Donny called in on the not-so-bright gunner.

304

"My own twenty mil," Donny said with a smile. This was not what a Wolf FAC was supposed to do. Although they carried the 20mm SUU-16 Gatling gun slung under the centerline, in addition to their marking rockets, it was more for a last-ditch strafe against a fleeting target than the normal use such as a strike plane might make of it.

"It was late in the day. No strikers were handy. What's a poor FAC man to do?" Donny held his hands palm up. He checked his watch. "Hey, the show starts in twenty minutes. Let's get some drinks and a good table."

The bar started emptying as the men picked up some beer and found a good table near the dance floor in what was laughingly called the showroom. It was merely a large room used for Officer's Call, which was nothing more than occasional dull, unclassified briefings for all the officers in the wing, and the less-occasional touring USO show. Tonight, tables and chairs were set up around a raised bandstand and an open area. Donny and Rail sat next to the open space. Forty-some other pilots and GIBs crowded the other tables. On stage, a grossly overweight Caucasian man wearing a flaming purple Hawaiian shirt and dark trousers fiddled with the amplifier and tuned an electric guitar. In front of him was a thin folding stand with a few sheets of music in the narrow tray. At his feet rested a set of bongo drums. The man's face was florid. His long dark hair was plastered to his forehead and neck with sweat. The audience buzzed with conversation as the aircrewmen spoke of the events of the day.

". . . we've had it, I tell you. I just got back from the States. GIs are no longer in radio, TV commercials, or in the Coca-Cola ads in *Life* magazine. They just use long-haired frizzies now. Those people hate the military, I tell you."

". . . then the weather went ape and we couldn't find the damn bridge."

". . . Four got it. That new guy from DM. Went straight in. No chutes, no beeper."

". . . so then I grabbed her by the swanch, and . . ."

305

". . . and I said 'Where's the target?' and he said 'Right under the French toast.' He had just barfed on the scope. Guess I was jinking a tad too much for him."

Desultory applause started as a man walked through a side door and stepped up to a microphone on the stage. He was rail-thin, had mousy brown hair and hard lines on his face. He looked the type who had spent many years as a Bourbon Street barker.

"Hey, hey, hey," he bellowed into the mike, then stepped back as it squealed from feedback. "Well, heeeerrrrre we aaarrrre. What a crowd. Boy, am I glad to be here tonight. Just flew in from Bangkok and boy are – " He leaned forward and motioned to the crowd for the rest of the tag line. "Come on, guys. I just flew in from Bangkok, and, boy, are my – Come on, what's tired? Boy, are my – " He leaned forward. "What's tired?" He motioned with his hands, an eager and expectant look on his face.

"Your balls," someone shouted.

"What balls?" someone else yelled.

"Show us your tits," a voice bellowed from the back of the room.

"Bring on the broads."

"Yeah, where are the dancing girls?"

Raucous laughter and hooting catcalls spun around the room. Things were degenerating fast. The MC, no fool, made a "whaddaya-gonna-do" gesture and a hand signal to the fat guitar player, who immediately swung into a deafening rendition of "I Can't Get No Satisfaction." He drowned out the catcalls.

Several of the younger pilots jumped up and gyrated to the twanging music. There was no one in the room over the rank of lieutenant colonel, and few of them. The air war was primarily fought by the captains and the majors, with a strong backup of lieutenants and a handful of lieutenant colonels. The party grew in noise and exuberance. The men started smashing their hands together, spurring the heavyset guitarist to turn up the amp and really lean on the strings.

Noise rolled over the room at an ever-increasing crescendo as the men wildly sang the words to "Satisfaction." Duckcall Donny was doing his thing. "I Cain't Git No . . . QUACK . . . Satisfaction . . ." This was not how the *Air Officer's Guide* prescribed a gentleman's evening at his club.

After several repetitive chords, the guitarist segued into some Hawaiian war-chant sounds. The MC produced a large drum and beat out a good rhythm. The crowd picked it up right away – the girls were soon to arrive – and clapped to the beat. The MC let the crowd build its anticipation, then eased over to the microphone.

"And now I present, for our first act, Funelda the Fire Eater, Funelda the Famous Hawaiian Fire Dancer. Let's hear it for FUNELDA." Yea, rah, the crowd whistled and cheered. The MC pointed toward the side door. The guitarist twanged a crescendo, the MC beat on the drum. The crowd cheered louder. This was more like it. The door opened, flames were reflected, the MC leaned over the mike: "Let's hear it for the great Prince Funelda." He beat his hands together. The crowd started to follow . . . until it registered.

"Prince?"

"Did he say 'Prince'?"

"What the fuck, over."

"QuuaaACK?

From the doorway emerged an oiled and glistening, almost nude, barefoot young man. He had dark hair and a well-toned slender body. He wore plaited palm fronds around his waist, wrists, ankles, and on his forehead like a crown. He twirled in each hand, with moderate expertise, twin torches that left soft wisps of flame trails as they spun. And he spun, around and around, bending, dipping, twirling the torches, now under his legs, now over his back as he bent, then under and behind his knees. The fat guitarist hooked up a Hawaiian war-chant tape to the amp and beat out a surprisingly good accompanying rhythm on the bongos. He was backed up ably by the MC on the big drum.

A GIB from the 433rd found the light switches and manipulated them to bring the big room to near-darkness. The drumbeat was infectious. The aircrew began clapping again. Several flicked their Zippos, adding extra flame twirls to the room. An AC from the 497th heated a scotch bottle over several lighters from his table, then held his lighter near the mouth. The inside lit up and a ten-inch tongue of flame hooted forth. "Dead jet pilot," he yelled. If an empty beer bottle was a dead soldier, then an empty scotch bottle with an afterburner was obviously a dead jet pilot.

The dancer oiled and coiled his way around the floor, bare feet slapping in time to the big drum. He was supple, and bent his legs and arms and bobbed his head in a proper war dance. He played the fire torches close to his body, very close. The oil reflected the light off his skin. As he rolled the torches down his arm and up his legs, they left soft trails. He moved and danced around the semicircle formed by the tables in front of the foot-high stage. He danced close to the pilots, then back, then close again. He was rolling the torches now in front of his face. Quickly, he inserted one into his mouth, quenching it, then pulled it out and passed it over the other, causing a relight. He did this several times.

He popped one in his mouth and gave a startled leap as a loud QUACK blasted through the drums. He coughed out the torch and glared in Donny's direction and resumed dancing. He oiled and coiled around the semicircle as Donny quacked out a few more at appropriate times. Slowly, the dancer eased over to where Donny sat. He stood in front of him, shaking his shoulders and slowly sinking to his knees in an ever-provocative pose. Lower and lower he sank. The crowd hooted. Donny flamed red, duck call forgotten. Then the male dancer made kissy lips at Donny. The crowd shrieked as Donny recoiled in horror. Rail beat his hand on the table, laughing hard, bent nearly double. The male dancer, clearly the winner, eased away and sinewed back to the center of the open area. Donny muttered something and left the table. He walked around the crowded tables and out of the darkened room.

"What's the matter, Donny," somebody yelled, "yer date too hot for ya?"

He spent a moment at the cash register end of the bar and walked back into the showroom.

No one noticed Donny return to his table. The dancer was so campy, yet seemingly oblivious to the rude catcalls, that he was, many said, actually entertaining. Some of the cruder aircrew mentioned the dancer's bulging crotch.

"Hey, I'll bet he's got a hard-on."

"Nah. It's a toilet paper tube."

"Well, there's a hell of a lot of paper still on it then."

"Hey, look. Higgens is back and that fairy is dancing over toward him."

"Quack him out, Donny."

Like a moth to the flame, Prince Funelda the Great Fire Eater danced and pranced toward Duckcall Donny Higgens, Captain, United States Air Force, aircraft commander of an F-4D Phantom in combat. The Prince should have known better. He waved his torches and approached closer and closer, his limpid dark eyes fixed on Donny, a faint smile on his lips. The MC boomed his drum, the fat guitarist coaxed incredible rhythms from the bongos, the Hawaiian war chant never sounded – if not better, then louder. Donny surreptitiously took a swig from a can of lighter fluid and held it in his mouth.

Prince Funelda went into his spraddle-legged, knee-waggling posture in front of Donny. He was just starting the kissy lips when Donny pulled his Zippo from his shirt pocket, quickly flicked it, and blew a ten-foot tongue of flame that licked the Fire Eater's body from anklet to crown.

Prince Funelda squawked and leaped into the air like a hotfooted ostrich. His dance suddenly became more frenzied as he slapped and ran his hands over the little flames on his crotch and ankles as the imitation palm fronds lit up. He leaped and spun and squeaked. The horrified MC jumped from the stage and chased after his spinning lover. The tape continued the loud war dance. The fat guitarist, delighted at what he saw ("serves that bitch right"), laughed so hard his folding chair folded and he went down like a fat mouse in a trap. The pilots were performing what looked like a dance of their own as they hopped and rolled around in jerks and stomps, some on their feet doubled up in helpless laughter; others lay paralyzed on the floor.

A GIB from the 433rd, struck with a brilliant thought, ran from the room and returned in seconds with a fire hose that had a two-inch nozzle. If nothing else, the USAF Civil Engineers kept their emergency fire equipment in top shape, and backed up with hundreds of pounds of pressure.

"Make way, make way," the GIB shouted, snaking the hose through, around, and over the spastic assemblage.

"To the rescue," a buddy shouted, and grabbed some hose to back up the erstwhile nozzleman. They reached the center of the floor, aimed the nozzle at the leaping Prince of Fire, and rotated the brass handle backward. A jet of water capable of knocking down an elephant at ten feet struck the fire-eater full on his crotch and bowled him into the audience, which quickly split like the Red Sea. The two GIBs ran behind, spraying with the hose, propelling the spitting and screaming Prince along the floor like kids shooting leaves across the yard with a hose. His MC lover ran after the two GIBs, screeching and pulling at their clothes. The Prince rolled to the door, rose to his knees against great pressure, and flung it open.

Standing there, hand outstretched for the doorknob, poised to walk in and see what the commotion was all about, stood the commander of the 8th Tactical Fighter Wing, Colonel of the Air Force Stanley D. Bryce. Before the horrified GIBs could deflect the stream, the hose took him full in the chest and flattened him against the corridor wall.

17

0900 Hours Local, Wednesday 7 February 1968
Liaison Office of the Judge Advocate General,
HQ, MACV
Saigon, Republic of Vietnam

"Tell me the whole story, start to finish," Major Jay Denroe
said to Wolf Lochert. Denroe was from the Judge Advocate
General's office at USARV, the United States Army Republic
of Vietnam, based at Long Binh, twenty kilometers from
Saigon. Although MACV was in charge of the in-country
war, USARV had court-martial authority over United
States Army personnel in Southeast Asia. Based on the
results of an Article 32 investigation, the Commanding
General of USARV could recommend whether or not a
court-martial should be convened.

Denroe wore Army khakis with the JAG insignia. He was
a thin man, sparse, almost skeletal, and stood two inches
under six feet. His uniform could not disguise the sharp
angles of his hips and knees. His dark brown hair was
cut close to his skull. They were in a small briefing room
that held a long metal conference table with a 16mm movie
projector resting on one end. A screen stood on a six-foot
tripod crosswise in a corner farthest from the projector.

"I've told everybody the whole story," Lieutenant Colonel
Wolfgang X. Lochert said. He wore jungle fatigues with
subdued (black thread stitching) rank, CIB, and jump
wings. "You have it right there." He indicated the papers

lying on the lawyer's briefcase. An Army Criminal Investigation Division team had conducted the investigation under the command of the Article 32 investigating officer, a full colonel appointed by USARV. Based on the evidence, the colonel had recommended to USARV that Lochert be court-martialed for murder. USARV had agreed that Wolf be tried for murder under Article 118 in a general court-martial. The investigation had been completed with uncommon speed.

"I know, but I want to hear it from you one more time. There may be something somebody has missed."

Wolf Lochert sighed. He stood up and walked to the window overlooking the MACV compound. Soldiers in neatly starched and pressed khakis and fatigues walked the concrete paths with brisk and deliberate steps. Rays of sunshine shone through breaks in the low clouds as the early-morning showers dissipated.

He related the story of that day in the driving rain when he had killed Buey Dan. He told it quietly and without passion.

"Then," he concluded, "I was arrested when I returned to Quang Tri from an operation."

"On a murder charge."

"Yes. On a murder charge." Lochert flexed his hands and resumed looking out the window.

"Were you read your rights?"

"Yes."

"Were you surprised at being arrested?"

"Of course I was surprised." Wolf Lochert glared. "I acted in self-defense against a North Vietnamese agent who tried to kill *me*. I never gave it another thought. Why wouldn't I be surprised to be up for murder? I have killed other Vietnamese, you know. This is a war. And I had no idea these films would be shown all over the world."

"Or that people would be crying for your head? Colonel Lochert, let's review the film. Do you mind pulling the blind?" Wolf pulled the blind as Jay Denroe turned on the movie projector. The screen started with printed numbers counting down to 1, then the action began.

It picked up where Wolf had pulled Buey Dan onto his stiletto as they'd gone down. It showed clearly the point protruding from his back, Wolf pulling the stiletto out, cleaning it, and tucking it in a sock. The camera steadied as Wolf Lochert stood over the body for a moment, then picked it up and flung it against the tree. Portrayed in awful clarity was Wolf s terrible grimace as the camera zoomed on his face. After that were jumbled pictures, then the scenes of the scuffling between Wolf and Hemms.

"Do you have any idea if Mal Hemms was filming when Buey Dan attacked you?"

"I don't think so. As I told you, I didn't notice any camera until after I – after I threw that bastard into the tree. It was raining. I was . . . angry."

"Did you see anyone else in the area that might have seen what happened?"

"No."

Jay Denroe picked up a thick folder from the table. "Here are copies of the text that accompanied the film on the various TV stations, the headlines in the newspapers the day after it was aired, and a cross-section of the letters written to editors, congressmen, and the Department of the Army about you." He withdrew a sheaf of papers and laid them on the table. Wolf pawed through them. Although the headings and titles varied, the majority indeed called for his head.

"The point is, Colonel Lochert," Denroe continued, "failing to obtain film of Buey Dan's attack on you – and there is no such film – then we need something tying him into the other side. Membership or rank in the Viet Cong or the North Vietnamese Army. Do you have any evidence whatsoever of such an affiliation?"

"No."

"I realize I'm new to the case, and new to Special Forces methodology," Denroe said, "but tell me, at any time before his attack, did you ever suspect Buey Dan of being an agent for the other side?"

"No, not an agent, but I began to have some doubts about his enthusiasm for the job with MACSOG."

"Did you do anything about it?"

"Yes. I told my boss, Al Charles, that I didn't think Buey Dan was working as hard as he used to and that . . . that I no longer trusted him."

"Why not?"

"Nothing I could put my finger on. There were too many strange things happening that prevented us from accomplishing the mission. I usually had far more success with my missions before I took on Buey Dan."

"What took you so long to feel, well, strange about him? Why didn't you suspect him long before he tried to kill you?"

"On our first operation he killed several NVA soldiers to save my life. He could have killed me then. Instead he called in a rescue helicopter. On later operations he could have killed me many times."

"Do you know why he did not?"

"I do now. He wanted to kill me under the same tree, with the same knife that I used to kill the man he said was his son."

"Were you ever apprehended or charged for the death of his son?"

"No."

"Describe the circumstances of the son's death to me, please."

Wolf Lochert pointed to the legal pad. "You're not going to take notes, are you?"

Denroe put his pencil to one side. "No."

"On Sunday, the nineteenth of December, nineteen sixty-five, I attended Mass at the Catholic church in JFK Square. Inside, a bomb went off, killing several people, including some young Vietnamese girls. They were near me. I saw their bodies all torn apart. Outside, I found the man who did it. I killed him." Wolf's face became hard as he spoke.

"Did anybody see you?"

"Apparently just old Bee Dee."

314

"What was the relationship between the two Vietnamese men?"

"According to what Bee Dee said, the young man I killed – the man who bombed the church – was his son. Bee Dee wanted revenge on me."

"Took him over two years," Denroe said, "when he had plenty of chances."

Wolf shrugged. "That's the Asian way. Wait until things are right and meaningful."

"Right and meaningful?" Denroe said.

Wolf walked to the window. "Yes. The time had to be right. As I see it, Bee Dee had to keep sabotaging my missions before exacting revenge for his son. When it became clear he was no longer going to go out with us, he knew the time was right. His keeping my stiletto those two years and waiting until he could get me to that particular tree made it meaningful."

Denroe slapped the table and stood up. "God in heaven," he said. "How can we ever beat these people?"

"Easy," Wolf Lochert said. "Just give them a better belief than the one they have now." He turned from the window to face Jay Denroe, his face expressionless. "What are my chances?"

"The Article 32 findings have been approved by the Commanding General. You are going to be tried by general court-martial. Your odds for conviction are fifty-fifty. They have only your word for why you killed what has been officially regarded as an allied soldier."

"And my word is, Buey Dan was a North Vietnamese spy who tried to kill me. I killed him instead. So I *am* guilty of killing him."

"But you must plead not guilty. You did not murder the man, you killed him in self-defense. You must put the burden on the court to prove you guilty beyond a reasonable doubt." Denroe regarded Wolf carefully. "I heard something. Isn't this your second charge of murder in Saigon?"

Wolf made a wry face. "You *heard* something? Check

my confidential MACSOG records. I was under cover for MACSOG to break up a weapon-smuggling ring run by a rich Chinese and an American Army general. To get into the stockade with a serious enough charge, we set it up that I *killed* a man in a bar fight on To Do Street. The *killing* was all play-acting and never even went into a pre-trial investigation." Wolf curled his lips. "I know I don't want to spend any more time in the LBJ. It is not a good place." The LBJ was the acronym the GIs had put on the Long Binh Jail. No one knew how much of a factor Lyndon Baines Johnson's initials played in the nickname.

"It doesn't matter. As far as this court-martial is concerned, it can't be introduced," Denroe said. "Just so the public doesn't hear of it. Even though it was set up as part of an investigation, the papers would have great sport with it." He drew a folder from his briefcase. "In my investigations I thought maybe the CIA people might have something about Buey Dan's background and his use of the code name 'Lizard' for himself. I called an old law-school chum who works for them as an analyst – at least he says he's an analyst. You never know with those guys. Essentially, what he told me was they never heard of Buey Dan, but if they had, they would have tied him in with a former VC rallier directly from Hanoi who once worked at the Cercle Sportif in Saigon, and who was known by his communist organization as the Lizard from Hanoi Lake."

Wolf stared at him. "That means they know exactly who he is in the NVA lineup but won't reveal it." A muscle jerked in his cheek. "Generally I like those guys. But some get the 'Green Door' syndrome. They could prove Buey Dan is an enemy agent, but what they are implying is that their source is too classified to risk compromising by using its output even to save an American from a false charge. Typical reasoning of a man gone too deep in the intelligence business." He grunted. He rose and started pacing. "You know, when I debriefed Al Charles after that last mission, the one that went so badly, I told him then about my reservations regarding Buey Dan. I remember there was an Agency guy in the room. When I finished, he sorted of nodded at Al, who told me to fire Buey Dan."

"We could subpoena him," Jay Denroe said.

"I don't think so . . . it wouldn't do any good."

"Why not?"

"First off he could prove he worked for any organization except the CIA. Secondly he could say nods mean nothing; my debrief was boring and he was sleepy. Thirdly I don't want to get Al involved, and if we brought in the guy in civvies we'd have to bring in Al."

"Listen, I think it's important we call Colonel Charles as a witness. He can verify you had doubts and misgivings about Buey Dan before the, ah, church incident. After all, he suggested you terminate his contract."

"Nothing doing. I'll take my chances alone. These things have a way of going noplace yet hurting everyone involved, and I don't want Al to get bashed for no purpose." Wolf stopped pacing and faced Jay Denroe. "You copy?"

"Loud and clear," Denroe said, and sighed. "So much for that idea. Okay, is there anything, anything at all that might tie Buey Dan to the other side? Any unusual circumstances or details, regardless of how minor, that maybe I could use?"

"Just that he knew his son bombed the church."

"Any proof?"

"Just Buey Dan's word."

"I might try to get that into evidence as a dying declaration, which is an exception to the hearsay rule. It's vital we do everything we can do to convince the members of the court that Buey Dan was an enemy agent. What else?"

"I think he was some way responsible for the loss of a C-130 after we were dropped into Laos in November last year."

"What makes you think so? Any evidence? Anything from the Air Force's review?"

Wolf shook his head. "Nothing. It's just a hunch I have now. Then there was his disappearance right before a battle late last year. At that time the enemy hit extra hard."

317

"Any proof?"

"No, no proof other than my word." He looked away. "I don't know if you can use this, but he took my stiletto from me when I was unconscious back on our first operation in sixty-six. I didn't know he had it until I saw it that day he attacked me. But an Air Force captain told me something that makes me believe he saw Buey Dan take it from me. There's a connection of sorts."

Denroe nodded. "Well, it's something. Hard to say what it will lead to. Give me his name and I'll think about a subpoena."

Wolf gave Toby Parker's name and Da Nang duty station to Denroe.

"How come you don't have any problems with Parker's being called in?" Denroe asked.

"He's Air Force. This won't touch him professionally. But in the Army, just being in Special Forces sets an officer up for promotion problems. A trial like this would have Al's name mentioned once too often. Plus, he's a black man. There are still some who don't think black men should be officers, much less commanders."

"Well, then, would you give me the names of some people I can call in as character witnesses for you? Fellow soldiers, maybe some high-ranking officers. Better yet, some highly decorated sergeants that would testify to what a good leader and man of character you are. They would go over pretty good, I think."

Wolf Lochert looked at Jay Denroe with disdain. "If I have to call in others to say I'm a good guy, then I belong in jail. Let my record speak for itself."

"Complicated, very complicated," Denroe said, and sighed. "I'll have to tell you, Colonel Lochert, I'm just your basic JAG-appointed defense attorney. You have real problems with all the politicians and the press that are after your ass. There are probably many routes to go, but I don't know if I'm smart enough to figure them out. Any chance you can hire a civilian lawyer?"

"For a military court-martial? Is it legal?"

"Sure."

Wolf stared off in the distance. "No. I can't afford one." He had a monthly pay allotment made out to the Maryknoll Church for four hundred dollars, almost half his base pay.

"No savings?"

"No."

"Rich friends?"

"Hah," Wolf snorted.

"Colonel Lochert, I want you to know I believe you and I will do all I can to get the members of the court to believe you." The look on Denroe's face matched the conviction in his voice. "But it is going to be very, very difficult."

1245 Hours Local, Wednesday 7 February 1968
HQ, MACSOG, Rue Pasteur
Saigon, Republic of Vietnam

"It's always nice to have your lawyer believe you," Lieutenant Colonel Al Charles said to Wolf Lochert, who sat slumped in a chair next to Charles' desk.

"But that doesn't mean he'll be able to convince the members of the court," Wolf said, his face a study in dejection. "I'll tell you, it's one thing to take on an enemy in front of me. For that I'm trained, prepared, certainly experienced. It's the enemy behind me, like that TV guy, that I can't handle. And the reaction to the film."

"You did look like something from a Frankenstein movie when you tossed him into that tree," Charles said.

"Maybe so. But this is a real shooting war, not a movie, and people are going to look terrible and ugly when they do what they do. I think those newsie guys are prying. I feel like someone has been in my mind and taken my private thoughts and put them on a TV screen. They don't make much sense to the viewer and no doubt look ugly as sin."

"Can't rightly say. Meanwhile, old buddy, I have to remind you that under the Court's orders, you may not leave the MACSOG grounds except on official duty."

"Yeah, yeah, I know," Wolf rumbled.

"But that doesn't mean you can't have visitors. There is someone here to see you. When she came to the gate about an hour ago, the Nung guard called me for instructions. Said her name was Greta Sturm. She's waiting in the lounge." Charles lifted an eyebrow when he saw Wolf's face brighten. "You got something going?"

Wolf made a puzzled grin. "Something going? No, just friends." Wolf had tried to forget how much he had revealed to Greta on the helicopter. It was, he had told himself, an after-battle reaction; the usual talky reaction as the mind relaxes from the grim occupation of war and survival. But, he knew, he had never been "talky" before.

"Friends, sure. Just friends," Al Charles said, a wide grin splitting his mahogany face.

In the lounge, they stood for a moment looking at each other. Greta Sturm wore a blue linen skirt that, quite unintentionally, accentuated her ripe hips and long, muscular thighs. An off-white blouse, sternly buttoned almost to her neck, did little to down-play her remarkable bosom. She wore her flaxen hair straight and long, and just enough lipstick to show she had a perfect mouth.

Wolf stood still, suddenly very aware of a remarkable contrast. This was not the battle-stained woman, the female soldier he had been so taken with. This was a cool icemaiden. She sensed his hesitation and took his hand.

"I had to come, I had to see you," she began with only a hint of reticence. "You told me about this unit. It was not difficult to find." Then she looked directly at him, her gray eyes warm yet firm and resolute. "I have thought of you so much, what you did, what you said. How you carried yourself. You saved my life. This is difficult to say, but . . .

you not only saved my life, you have changed my life. I am not the same person." She searched his eyes when he did not answer. "Do you understand? Do you?" A tinge of unsureness had crept into her voice.

Wolf placed his big hands over hers. "Over here," he said, indicating an ancient vinyl sofa in one corner. Two men in tiger suits, laughing over some joke, entered the lounge room, saw the intent look on Wolf's face, and withdrew.

"Yes, I understand," he said to her, his deep voice almost cracking in his effort to speak with unaccustomed softness. "I understand, and I, maybe I feel . . . something, too." He had been so shocked by the charges brought against him that he had been occupied with little else. He forced himself to examine his thoughts. He could not tell her *she* had in no way changed *his* life . . . at least he didn't think so. He knew she had made an impression, but more as a female soldier competent in combat than as a female that appealed to him. Females were, well . . . sort of fluffy and helpless, and full of soft curves and secrets. All that talk on the helicopter, well, maybe she misunderstood him.

"I'm not sure it's a good thing," he started, unsure of where he was going, "that I change your life. Maybe you confuse my *saving* your life with *changing* your life. I'm not sure you and I could . . . I mean, I have nothing to offer you – "

"I do not want anything," she cut in. "I have no right to ask anything of you. I come here only to tell my decision not to return to Germany to become a doctor just yet. I have asked. There are many jobs here for nurses right here in Saigon. This is where I will stay. I said I will wait for you and I will." She crossed her arms. "I do not wish to further work with the Maltese Aid Society. It is not realistic to think one can nurse the soldiers of both sides in a war."

Wolf watched Greta Sturm closely as she talked. Her face was animated, her expressive eyes flashed and widened and narrowed as she spoke. The deep breaths she took as she explained her convictions moved her breasts in a way that suddenly became the most erotic sight of his life. He

321

became aware of a slight film of perspiration on her upper lip. With an almost audible groan he suddenly realized he had to control an impulsive urge to kiss those lips. What had started as a friendly holding of hands became an electric coupling of an intensity he had never encountered or permitted himself to encounter. He realized he was sweating. He tried to withdraw his hands.

She gripped his hands tighter. She saw what was happening to him and gave him a soft smile. "You can have the good affection for me. It is permitted, you know." She gave him a light kiss on the cheek. "I know your thoughts are on your trial, as they must. I do not wish to be a burden. I want you to know I am here in Saigon for you, and . . . I am yours if you want me." She leaned her head over and drew his hands to her mouth and kissed his strong fingers once and released them. She gave him a slip of paper from a pocket in her skirt. "Until I take a flat, this is where I now stay, the Astoria Hotel. Come there when you wish." A final cool kiss on his cheek and she was gone.

0715 Hours Local, Wednesday 7 February 1968
Office of the Wing Commander
Ubon Royal Thai Air Force Base
Kingdom of Thailand

Colonel Stan Bryce stood behind his large wooden desk, slamming a fist into a palm. On a wall shelf to his left was a twelve-pound cast-iron bulldog from his football days at the University of Georgia. In front of him was a hand-carved teak plaque bearing his name, rank, and a large pair of command pilot's wings. Colonel Al Bravord, the Director of Operations for the 8th Tactical Fighter Wing, sat quietly

322

to one side on a red-leather couch, smoking a pipe. Court Bannister stood in front of Bryce's desk in a position best described as a relaxed parade rest. All three men wore flight suits.

Bryce leaned over his desk toward Bannister. There was whiteness around the corners of his mouth. "You're here to brief me on this night FAC business I've had suddenly pushed down my throat, and the first words out of your mouth are that you want Higgens in your so-called unit. You must be crazy. I want Higgens out of the Wing. And that backseater of his. I want them both in a hole at Tan Son Nhut where they'll never see the light of day. Or fly an airplane for the rest of their tour." He shook his finger at Court. "And after the endorsement I put on their efficiency reports, they might as well get out of the Air Force." Bryce sat down abruptly. "Does that answer your question whether or not you can have those two for your new outfit?"

"Sir," Bannister said, "I can understand how you feel. Their actions were inexcusable. But I would like to point out something. Higgens and Rhoades lead all the Wings in SEA for truck and antiaircraft-gun killing on the Trail. Part of the latest Seventh Air Force award to this Wing came from the outstanding results they have been turning in. Further, Higgens and Rhoades have a MiG to their credit. Lastly, this is Higgens' second tour. I believe he has earned the right to blow off a little steam, and he – "

"Blow off a little steam!" Bryce yelped. "Setting a man on fire is hardly considered blowing off a little steam. Turning an officer's club USO show into a free-for-all is hardly considered blowing off a little steam. And that ridiculous duck call of his." He frowned at Court Bannister. "Why would you want such men working for you?"

"Colonel, these are combat men in a combat situation. They are not the least bit concerned with promotion, breadth of experience, managerial techniques, or career-broadening jobs that lead to positions on the air staff. That all sounds good at Squadron Officers School. But this is combat. All they want to do is fight. It's what they were trained for, it's what they do best, it's what Uncle Sam pays them for. When the war is over, they will probably leave active duty and join the National Guard to stay current and to be ready if another war starts. If you put them in a hole at Seventh Air Force, all you'll do is deprive the Eighth Fighter Wing of two very competent Phantom crewmen."

Colonel Bravord untangled himself from the couch. His green flight suit was untailored and hung on him like a collapsed tent on a pole. He trailed a cloud of pipe tobacco as he ambled over to the desk of his wing commander. He had gray, almost white hair that surrounded a shiny bald pate, and was eight years older than his boss. He was an ex-sergeant pilot from early World War Two, where he had become double-Ace, then shot down three MiGs in Korea, yet he had always run a little behind on promotions. His lazy manner belied a smooth and shrewd mind. It was understood this was his terminal assignment. After this tour he would retire; a solid airman who had fought in three wars for his country. He took the pipe from his mouth and spoke.

"Bannister has some valid points, Stan. Plus, after all, there is this TWX from Commander, Seventh Air Force." He tapped the message form on the desk.

Bryce glanced at the forms and frowned. "Why do I feel you two are ganging up on me?"

Bannister grinned. "You mean I can have them, sir?"

Bryce snorted. "I don't know how, I'm not sure I know why, but you have a lot of horsepower behind you, Bannister. Yes, you can have them ... if they volunteer, that is. Now I want to see the requirements you have for this night FAC organization." He turned to Al Bravord. "Get Admin, Intell, and Maintenance in here. I want them to sit in on this."

Court pulled a file from his briefcase. In minutes the required members of the Wing Staff were in place around the conference table in the small briefing room next to Bryce's office.

"So that each of you know what is required across the board, all my requirements are listed on one page," he said. Court gave each man a handout that he had cut on a stencil and run through a mimeograph machine early that morning.

= =

NIGHT FAC OPERATIONS
8TH TACTICAL FIGHTER WING
APO SAN FRANCISCO 96304
UBON RTAFB, THAILAND

TO: Director of Operations, 8th TFW
FROM: Major Court Bannister, Chief, Night FAC Ops
SUBJ: Requirements for Night FAC Ops
DATE: 7 February 1968
UNCLASSIFIED

1. For startup operations to commence this date, I request the following from:
    a.) Civil Engineers: Two rooms in Wing Headquarters for: 1) maps and briefing tables 2) desks and file cabinets. Need ASAP.
    b.) Administration/Supply/Logistics: Four desks, two file cabinets, appropriate aerial navigation charts and 1:50,000 Army topographical maps, and telephone service. Need ASAP.
    c.) Personnel: Seven pilots, eight backseaters pilots or navigators, and one clerk-typist. The names of the aircrew will be forthcoming. You may select a clerk-typist providing he has at least eight months before DEROS. Cut orders on the aircrew assigning them to me as I give you the names.
    d.) Maintenance: Sufficient F-4D aircraft painted black with one 600 gallon centerline fuel tank (also painted

black) to fly six sorties per twelve-hour
night on the following schedule:
          1800-2200 Two aircraft
          2200-0200 Two Aircraft
          0200-0600 Two Aircraft
   e.) Armament: Request the following be on
       hand for six-ship night operations to
       average one sortie each with complete
       weapon expenditure per sortie;
       1.) Two SUU-42 Flare pods with 32 flares
       2.) Two LAU Rocket pods (2.75-inch white
       phosphorus)
       3.) Two CBU canisters
   f.) Intelligence: Full round-the-clock
        support as required to include access to
        gun camera film and projectors.
2.   Before each selected aircrewman commences
     night FAC operations, he must have flown ten
     daytime Wolf FAC missions. This will provide
     daytime FAC ops techniques and procedures,
     as well as familiarize the crewman with the
     Ho Chi Minh Trail route system. Then he must
     fly twenty missions with the 497th Night
     Owl Squadron to gain a feel for night strike
     operations, and to familiarize himself with
     the Trail in darkness.

C. Bannister

Courtland EdM. Bannister, Maj, USAF
Chief, Night FAC Ops
= =

   "You don't have all those Wolf or Night Owl missions,
Bannister. Does that mean you are going to fly that many
before activating your unit?"
   "Yes, sir, I do."
   "How long will it be before your unit will be operational?"
   "I need four weeks, sir."
   Bryce studied the message from 7th Air Force on his desk.

"Can't do it. You've got to be up and running by the first of March. That's three weeks from now. Think you can hack it?"

Court calculated he could double up on missions and paperwork. "Yes, sir. I can."

None of the wing staff said anything. This was, after all, the commander's desires. Each colonel inspected his sheet. "Painted black," said the chief of maintenance.

"Yes, sir," Court said. "Same as the Night Owl birds."

"Gentlemen," Colonel Bryce said, "if you have no questions, please take care of the items in your area per Major Bannister's timetable." The meeting broke up.

"One last thing," Stan Bryce said to Court Bannister as the others left the office. "What are you going to call the unit?"

"Sir, I thought I'd leave it to the troops to come up with a name."

18

1530 Hours Local, Thursday 8 February 1968
Suite A, Mills Building, Montgomery Street
San Francisco, California

Archibald "Archie" Gant stood looking at the San
Francisco Bay from the floor-to-ceiling window of his
20th-floor law office. The office was large and traditional:
dark panels, ceiling-high lawbook cases, long conference
table, large mahogany desk, a 30-by-40 Tabriz on the floor,
concealed liquor cabinet and wet bar. In hidden holders
in his desk were the controls of state-of-the-art electronic
equipment: dictaphone, recorders, voice stress analyzer,
telephone trace counters, camera controls, shielded-wire
intercom, and telephone scrambler. Only the muted hiss
of the central air conditioning penetrated the soundproof
and secure room. The four additional rooms in the Gant &
Associates complex were for his secretary, a 12,000-book
law library, a conference room, and his three associates. On
the roof of the Mills Building was his six-room penthouse.
Archie had once called his firm Gant & Gant, but there
was no second Gant anymore, only Archie.

Archie stood five-two, had dark hair around a balding
crown, a voice like a foghorn, and no time for imbeciles,
charlatans, girls in granny dresses, or sociology teachers
who didn't wear socks in the classroom. He was extremely
proud his IQ was fifteen digits higher than his weight (which
was 130). He religiously drank four ounces of scotch each

328

day, no more, no less. One shot at nine, noon, three, and six. He touched no other hard liquor, but would now and then try a good wine with a meal. He and his younger brother, Virgil, were the only issue of Elder Gant, deceased, former owner/publisher of the now defunct Bay Area Daily, a Republican-supportive newspaper that went under just before the old man died in the spring of 1953.

Archie had been a frogman in the Navy's UDT (Underwater Demolition Team) in World War Two (Virgil had been too young). At age nineteen, Archie had been one of the men who had spent an extra twenty-four hours huddled in the water at Normandy, waiting for the invasion that had been delayed due to bad weather. After the war he'd gone to law school on the GI Bill at Georgetown in Washington, D.C. In those postwar years the GI bill had paid all tuition at any school, plus most books and a weekly stipend. The United States had been proud of its military men and proved it by educating millions. A year behind him, Virgil had entered the same school. Bōth boys had had to do it on their own because Elder Gant had made it quite clear he didn't want any damned lawyers under his roof. The boys had gone as far east as possible to get away from the old man.

"We'll be Gant & Gant, biggest law firm in the District," Archie had prophesied to Virgil. He had held a night job as a bellhop in the Willard Hotel to help pay Virgil's tuition. Virgil had worked as a counterman at the White Tower hamburger stand on M Street in Georgetown to help pay his expenses. Neither had worked in the traditional positions as law clerks because the pay was too low. The millions old man Gant had sequestered were of no value to his two sons. Soon after graduation Gant & Gant had opened on M Street.

One year after the Korean war broke out, and against Archie's loud protestations, Virgil had enlisted in the Army and gone to war as a private in the Infantry. "I need the combat time like you got. It'll make me a better lawyer." Less than a year later Virgil had been killed on a frozen mountaintop.

When the Navy had tried to recall Archie as an enlisted diver a month later for Korean duty, Archie had said he was ready. When BuPers found he was a practicing lawyer, they'd offered him a direct Reserve commission as a lieutenant j.g. and a billet in Seoul with the joint commission on war reparations in the last month of the war. He'd accepted the slot. Anything to get away from the memories of Virgil in Georgetown.

After the Korean war had ended in a stalemate in June 1953, Archie had put in his papers to leave active duty and serve in a Navy Reserve unit. The only openings at the time had been Dubuque or San Francisco. Archie had chosen San Francisco only because he knew more people there and could get his business started quicker. He'd passed the California Bar and opened the West Coast office of Gant & Associates in March 1954. By 1965 he'd been a commander in the USNR, worth two million in tax-free bonds, divorced twice, and on retainer to several banks, construction companies, and commercial-real-estate barons. He had built his reputation and bank account on difficult and highly visible security fraud cases.

He had met Sam Bannister in 1960 on a retreat held by the Bohemian Club at The Groves on the Russian River in California. They had run around a bit and had gotten along well. By 1963 he was managing Sam's West Coast affairs of real estate and occasional minor indiscretions.

Sam had just called him about Lieutenant Colonel Wolfgang Lochert. Said he needed a favor and wanted Archie to defend the Special Forces colonel. Archie had the time to take the case but wasn't sure he wanted it. All he knew was what he saw on the TV screen, and it wasn't good. Maybe killing a double agent in self-defense was justified, but throwing the dead man's body at a tree clearly was not, he told Sam. Further, the camera had caught Lochert's face in a rictus of hate that had burned itself into Archie's memory.

"I think he's a goddamn animal," Archie had told Sam Bannister. "What's he to you?"

"He's not an animal. I know him. He's a real soldier. In fact, he's an ex-seminarian. And a good friend of my son. It's so important to Court that he will pay the fee, but he doesn't want Lochert to know about it. Give him a hand, will you?"

"Ex-seminarian, huh? I'll think about it," Archie had said and hung up. He stood at the window and looked at the horizon. Vietnam. He had seen Europe at war, and he had seen Korea at war. Might as well see Vietnam at war.

He turned from the window. "Diana," he blasted into the air for his secretary. Diana Gear entered, notebook in hand. She was in her forties, thin, dark hair pulled up in a bun.

"You could use the interoffice communicator," she said tartly, as always.

Gant ignored the comment, as always. "Get me a round-trip ticket to Saigon. Depart tomorrow. Open return. Ex-seminarian, huh. Find out who Army Lieutenant Colonel Wolfgang Lochert's defense attorney is, tell him I'm coming over. You know, the Green Beret on TV that threw the body. Tell him there is no charge, that this is an interesting case. That isn't the real reason, but make him think it is. Find me a hotel there. No, tell LaNew to come in here. Ex-seminarian. Kee-rist."

After Diana Gear departed, Michael LaNew, a tall, coffee-colored Puerto Rican in his early thirties walked into Gant's office. "Yes, sir?" he said.

"Dammit, LaNew, quit saying sir all the time. You're not in the Air Force anymore. What's a good hotel in Saigon? You spent some time there."

LaNew had just been hired by Gant as an associate lawyer in January. The first week in February he'd passed the California bar. Years earlier, when LaNew had received his law degree from Georgetown (Gant hired only Georgetown graduates), he had not been interested in returning to Puerto Rico. He had suddenly been broke and couldn't take a bar exam in the U.S. until his paperwork was finished. Fluent in Spanish, French, and English, he'd joined the USAF and been classified as an interpreter for the Air Force

331

Intelligence Service. He could not be a commissioned officer until he was a U.S. citizen. After three years, when he had had his citizenship, he had become a special agent in the Office of Special Investigation. When his four-year hitch had been up in December 1967, he'd taken his discharge in Washington, D.C., and answered Gant's ad in the *Georgetown Law Review*. Intrigued by Gant's international reputation, he'd gone to work for him. After an exhausting interview (in which – among other intimidating questions – Archie had asked LaNew why in hell he thought a black lawyer could make a go in San Francisco), Michael LaNew had become the third associate at Gant & Gant. Archie had started him at $14,500 per annum. LaNew had thought the black question odd. He was Puerto Rican (with a strong Haitian background), not a black man.

Archie enjoyed telling the story at his private club of how LaNew had put him in his place at the interview.

"When I asked him how in hell a black lawyer could make money in San Francisco, he said 'by letting his hair grow, wearing sandals, and working undercover in Haight-Ashbury for white law firms on missing-rich-kid cases.'"

"Mister Gant," LaNew answered, "there are three or four good hotels. The Astoria for privacy, the Caravel for the newsmen, the Continental Palace for the business crowd, and the Catinat for old French-style rooms and courtyards."

"Have Diana cable the Catinat. Have a file on the Colonel Lochert case ready for me when I leave. Get me all the visas I need and arrange immunization shots for me. Get moving."

1630 Hours Local, Saturday 10 February 1968
Pan American Ramp, Tan Son Nhut Air Base
Saigon, Republic of Vietnam

Red-eyed and crazed, Archie Gant sat in the first-class section of the Pan Am 707 as it taxied to a halt at the Pan Am ramp. He wore a rumpled polo shirt and tan slacks. The last sixteen hours had been awful, the service surly, the food abominable. What had truly ruined his trip was his seatmate, a portly diamond salesman who'd gotten on at Guam. Archie had booked, as was his wont, seats 1A and 1B for the entire flight, one seat for him, one for his briefcase. Overbooking by Pan Am at Guam had forced the man into Archie's consciousness. After the first thirty minutes of flight, as the man had wheezed out how lucrative it was to sell Cartier diamonds through the PX system to GIs, Archie had exploded.

"GODDAMMIT, I'M NOT INTERESTED IN YOUR WRETCHED DIAMONDS. AND IF YOU SNEEZE, COUGH, OR FART, DO IT IN THE HEAD. I OWN YOUR GODDAMN SEAT, DO WHAT I SAY OR I'LL BREAK YOUR FUCKING SKULL."

For the rest of the trip the man had sniveled and complained bitterly to the stewardesses. They in turn had glared at and ignored Archie Gant, who had so crudely broken the code of causing no stress for the dainty Pan Am girls who demanded their passengers shut up and sleep. Archie had tried to bury himself in his battered 1951 copy of the Manual for Courts-Martial to refresh his memory of how things were done under military jurisdiction. The MCM contained all the numbered paragraphs telling how to administer military justice. Within the book was the UCMJ – the Uniform Code of Military Justice, for the application of justice for all members of the Armed Forces of the United States.

He studied again the file LaNew had put together on

Lieutenant Colonel Wolfgang Xavier Lochert. In less than twenty-four hours LaNew had done an incredible job. A close OSI friend had dug up what he needed from Army files and dictated the information over the phone. The morgue at the *San Francisco Chronicle Examiner* had provided a copy of the photo taken at the Los Angeles terminal in December 1966. An amateur photographer had caught the exact instant Lochert had been splashed with red dye by hippies. In the photo with him were two Air Force officers and a Special Forces sergeant. Archie studied the picture. The sergeant was identified as James P. Mahoney. The two Air Force men were Courtland Bannister, son of actor Sam Bannister, and Toby Parker. LaNew had located all three in case Mister Gant wanted to contact them. Mahoney was at a Special Forces camp near Pleiku, Bannister was stationed at Ubon, Thailand, and Toby Parker was at Da Nang, South Vietnam. The Air Force men would make good character witnesses, Archie thought. The sergeant probably would also, but that would take some thought. SF sergeants had reputations as being fierce fighters but poor performers in front of the members of the press who would be sure to descend on anyone associated with this case. Archie made a note to talk to Bannister and Parker.

The pilot shut down the engines when the big airliner bobbed to a stop at the ramp. Immediately the air conditioning went off. Five minutes passed as the temperature and humidity climbed in the long aluminum tube. When the front door was opened, an interminable time passed as two Vietnamese in white shirts and black baggy pants slowly walked through the cabin from one end to the other, pushing desultory poofs from spray cans of a foul-smelling insect killer in compliance with Vietnamese law that all incoming aircraft be decontaminated. Dripping and muttering, the passengers jammed the aisle. Finally they were given permission to disembark and form up: military to the left, Vietnamese in the middle, all others to the right.

The two-storey Tan Son Nhut Terminal was a crowded arena of sweating, shoving, Asian and American humanity.

Long queues surged into Immigration. Archie's visa was accepted, stamped, and his name entered laboriously into a general ledger. Next was Customs. New to Vietnam but remembering Seoul, Archie used a folded ten-dollar bill to clear his bulging suitcase. He hired a porter to shoulder it to the area where throngs waited to greet arriving passengers.

Archie spotted a tall Vietnamese holding up a sign with the word GANT printed on it. He made sure the porter was following and went up to him. The man had a badly scarred left arm.

"I'm Gant. You from the Catinat or MACV? Let's get going. What's your name? What happened to your arm?" The man only nodded to Archie's machine-gun questions. He led him to a black Citröen sedan parked at the curb outside one of the terminal doors.

Archie sat in back, the Vietnamese man in front. The driver honked and wedged his car through the crowds of vendors, taxis, pedicabs, and motor scooters. Clouds of blue exhaust smoke rose to eye level in the streets of Saigon. The smoke smelled of the castor oil used in the two-stroke scooter engines. The Vietnamese finally spoke.

"Yes, sir, Mister," he said in good English. "I am from the Catinat. My arm was burned in kitchen-oil fire. I am Nguyen Tach. I and this car are hired for your movements."

"Movements? What is this, a rolling crapper?" Archie smiled to himself, and decided Diana was on the ball to have arranged a car on such short notice.

The driver expertly wheeled the long car down Le Loi, turned right at Nguyen Hue, and nosed two pedicabs out of the way in front of the Catinat. Archie told Tach to pick him up at seven the next morning.

The lobby was past a courtyard full of flowers, tall palms in huge planters, and white muslin shade awnings. He checked in and was assigned a suite at the top, on the fourth floor. Water in the large tiled bathroom was brown and tepid. He mixed his six P.M. scotch with water from a carafe and walked out on the veranda that looked over the Saigon River. Sampans, small boats, and rusty cargo vessels churned the muddy water. Archie breathed deep. The street sounds and smells were not as bad as Seoul, he thought. He looked down and saw the street vendors with rows and rows of flowers to sell, revealing why Nguyen Hue was called the Street of the Flowers. Looking up, he saw airplanes to the northwest, circling to land at Tan Son Nhut. Around him, the crowded profusion of roofs and chimneys shimmered in the late-afternoon heat.

Archie was going to beat the jet lag and torpor caused by the long flight. He took a shower, padded around naked to dry, downed a second scotch, made sure his mosquito netting was in place in the non-air-conditioned room, turned the cover back, and lay down on the double bed. He bounced up immediately and pulled the mattress from the sagging springs, threw it on the floor, rigged the net over two chairs, and fell asleep.

Twenty minutes later he was awakened by a discreet knock on the door. A smiling and bowing Vietnamese boy handed him a cable from Diana Gear. Archie tipped him with a dollar bill while reminding himself to buy some piasters in the morning. Use of American green was illegal in South Vietnam.

The cable said Colonel Lochert's trial would start tomorrow the eleventh at 1000 hours at MACV Headquarters. Defense counsel Major Jay Denroe would meet with him there, 0800 hours in the JAG liaison officer's conference room. A pass would be waiting for him at the gate. Tomorrow? Jee-sus. Still naked, Archie fished the MCM from his briefcase, flopped onto the mattress, and began studying. An hour later he fell asleep with the book propped on his naked chest.

"What do you mean, the trial is today?" Archie foghorned at Major Jay Denroe when he was shown into the MACV conference room the next day. "Jesus Christ, you can't DO THAT."

"Well, I'm glad to meet you, Mister Gant. I'm Jay – "

Archie thrust some notes at him. "I want these motions filed right away."

"You can't do that, Mister – "

"The first one is to quash the indictment on all appropriate grounds." Archie pulled out a fat cigar and lit it.

"Sir, we don't have appropriate grounds – "

"Don't interrupt. Listen up. I learned a long time ago that litigation is a war, and I don't fight wars unless I can win. And when I fight a war to win I throw every book I have at them, including all 101 volumes of CJS." CJS was the Corpus Juris Secundum, the Body of the Law, Second: a lawyer's encyclopedia.

"Look at the notes, goddammit!" Archie barked. "Lochert was placed in confinement on the third of February, served with his charges on the ninth, and is due to be tried today, the eleventh. This is in direct violation of Article 33 of the UCMJ, which clearly states the commanding officer shall within eight days after the accused is ordered into arrest or confinement forward the charges to the officer exercising general court-martial jurisdiction. It took them nine days." He waved his cigar. "Secondly, they violated Article 35, which just as clearly states that no person against his objection be brought to trial before a general court-martial within a period of five days subsequent to the service of the charges upon him." Archie took a deep pull at his cigar. "ARE YOU LISTENING?" Denroe's eyes snapped up from the papers in his hands.

"Yuh . . . yes . . ."

"SHUDDUP. Thirdly, read the interview printed on page one in the Feb. ten *Stars and Stripes*. An Army public affairs officer said to members of the press that the result of the trial of Lieutenant Colonel Wolfgang X. Lochert was a foregone conclusion because the TV film so explicitly proved his guilt. That was an officer from USARV, which is the command under which Lochert is being prosecuted. The PAO speaks for the commanding general, therefore the commanding general is promulgating Lochert's guilt without due process of law."

"But, sir – "

"SHUDDUP. Fourthly, the law officer for the case was present and nodded assent at the words of the PAO. That clearly was in violation of Paragraph 42b of the MCM, which states that publication in the public press, radio, or television of the circumstances of a pending case may interfere with a fair trial and otherwise prejudice the due administration of justice." Archie drew on his cigar and grinned. "But mainly there is failure of the charges to allege an offense."

"Failure to allege an offense – "

Archie looked at his watch. "It's nine. The trial begins in an hour. You Army guys know how to make coffee?"

A bewildered and somewhat overwhelmed Jay Denroe led Gant to the tiny snack bar on the first floor of the MACV building. It was nearly bare. There were no tables, only elbow-high stands and shelves along the wall to rest one's elbows or coffee. One did not dawdle at MACV. They drew their coffee from an urn, paid the Vietnamese woman at the register. At a shelf, Archie pulled a silver flask from his briefcase, poured the cap full, and tossed it down.

"Want some?" he inquired politely.

Denroe shook his head, eyes rolling, looking for MPs. He took a deep breath to calm himself. "Sir, Colonel Lochert will be upstairs soon. I'm sure you want to meet him."

Gant lit another cigar. "In a minute," he said. He blew a stream of smoke in the air.

"Where'd you get your law degree, Denroe? How many times you served as defense counsel? You think Lochert's guilty, don't you? Maybe you don't, but you act like you do. I trust you won't mind if I take over as chief counsel for the defense. Hurry up and drink your coffee so we can get back to work. I'm ready to meet Lochert."

Wolf Lochert's paw engulfed Archie Gant's small hand as he studied the man who stood a foot shorter and weighed fifty pounds less. Wolf had long ago learned from combat that size meant nothing.

"Say again why you are here, Gant." Though most Americans had read of the flamboyant trial lawyer from San Francisco in Sunday supplements or had seen shots of him on TV accompanying well-known personages, Wolf had never heard of him.

"Your case interests me. Vietnam interests me. I'm between major cases." The picture of Wolf's hate-filled face as shown on television unrolled in Archie's mind. He blinked it away and studied Wolf in return; noted the burly figure, craggy brows, the combat-worn face, the deep-set eyes. He studied Wolf's eyes. This was not a man who spent his life hating. He silently cursed himself for being taken in by one unfortunate clip of television news. "And, by Christ, *you* interest me."

Wolf flared. "Don't swear in front of me, *Scheisskopf*" he growled.

"*SCHEISSKOPF*," Gant bugled, his eyes wide in mock surprise. He barked a laugh. "Oh yeah, that's right. You're an ex-seminarian." He shook his head. "*Scheisskopf*: Jees . . ." He barked another laugh. "That's great. Let's not waste time. Let's get to work. I have only one question." He fixed Wolf with a beady eye. "Was whatzisname a double agent?" He looked like a terrier barking up to a grizzled bulldog.

"I still don't know why you're here – "

"Goddammit, I just TOLD you."

"You swear again, I'll bust your skull."

"BUST MY SKULL. Oh, God, that's rich . . ." He ducked and dodged when Wolf Lochert made a grab for him. Wolf tried again and Archie Gant moved out of his reach in a flash. He was thoroughly enjoying himself.

"LOCHERT," Archie trumpeted, "knock it off or I'll run through your legs and BITE YOUR BALLS off."

Wolf stopped in midstride. His face started to break up. "Bite my . . . What are you, some kind of a PRE-vert? Bite my BALLS off." RAHTAHA, RAHTAHA, RAHTAHA. Wolf laughed with a sound like a metal rod pulled along a heavy picket fence. "Do it and you'll break your teeth."

RAHTAHA, RAHTAHA, RAHTAHA. "Where did you find this guy?" Wolf asked Denroe. "In a puppet factory?"

"Listen you big sack of Cro-Magnon crap, at least I don't go around licking my thumb and STICKING IT IN OTHER MEN'S EARS." Archie had heard about the disgusting form of greeting that delighted the Special Forces men in Vietnam. "Let's make a deal. You answer my questions and I won't swear." Wolf hesitated, then nodded agreement, and they shook hands.

"Sir, the trial begins in two minutes," Denroe tried to interrupt.

"Was the guy a double agent? Do you have any proof?" Gant demanded of Wolf.

"Yeah. No."

"Let's go," Gant said to Denroe.

Promptly at ten o'clock Major Jay Denroe prepared to present Mister Archibald Gant as the individual counsel for the accused to the president of the General Court-Martial Board – a full colonel from the Infantry branch – and to the law officer, a thin major.

The room was large, 40 by 20 feet. Denroe and Gant stood behind a table next to Wolf Lochert. The law officer, the LO, had a table by himself at the left side of the room. The LO, as with all general courts-martial, had to be an active-duty officer who was a member of the bar of a Federal court or of the highest court of any state. The LO ensured that the composition of the court was proper and qualified and that the trial was conducted in accordance with the MCM. To his left, at a long table in the center of the room, sat the six members of the court with the president of the court. Each man had a note pad and several pencils in front of him. There were two other full colonels – one infantry, one artillery, and three lieutenant colonels – all senior to Wolf, all from the Infantry branch, on the court-martial board. The president and members of the court were officers from the field without any special law background.

The court reporter sat at the LO's right; past him, Wolf Lochert sat at the table reserved for him and his counsel. At the far end of the room, directly opposite the LO, was the table for the trial counsel and the assistant trial counsel. Large air conditioners chugged in each of the three windows.

The law officer looked up. "Before the court convenes, I wish to state I have examined the appointing orders, I have determined the accused and a proper court are present, and that the appointed trial counsel and defense counsel are apparently qualified." He looked at Denroe. "You have an individual counsel of the accused's choice?"

"I do, sir." Denroe introduced Gant to the court and presented his qualifying documents. After a cursory examination the LO nodded at the president of the court. "You may proceed, sir."

Archie Gant stood up. "If I may present a pretrial motion," he interrupted. The LO nodded at him to continue. "I submit the United States Government has failed in its charges to allege an offense in accordance with Paragraph 68b of the Manual for Courts-Martial. Therefore, I request the law officer declare these proceedings are a nullity."

"Explain yourself, Counselor," the LO said.

Gant fished a copy of the charges from the stack in front of him.

"Colonel Lochert is on trial under Article 118 for murder. Under that very Article, I contend he is *not* guilty, and, in fact, no offense has taken place." He opened the MCM book. "Article 118, Paragraph b, titled 'Justification,' states that a homicide committed in the proper performance of a legal duty is justifiable. Among the justifications listed is 'killing an enemy in battle.' Additionally, Paragraph c, titled 'Excuse,' of Article 118 states a person may be excused for a killing on the grounds of self-defense."

The trial counsel jumped to his feet and addressed the law officer. "Sir, I will prove beyond any doubt that a murder was committed, that the defendant Wolfgang X. Lochert committed the murder, and that the defendant Wolfgang X. Lochert had criminal intent at the time of the murder."

"Sit down, Counselor," the LO said.

Gant continued as if he hadn't heard the objection. "*And additionally*," he enunciated, "the charges should be quashed due to certain defects in the pretrial Article 32 investigation. To wit: violation of Articles 33, 35, and of 42b." He listed the time factors and press-release reasons as he had for Denroe.

The president of the court looked at the law officer, who spoke up.

"I assume you can prove what you say. I will examine the apparent irregularities. However, in any case they are not sufficient to dismiss the charges against the accused. Unless you have anything further – "

"All right then," Gant interrupted. "I want a one-year continuance on the basis of the following paragraphs from the MCM: Paragraphs 69b, 'Defects in Charges and Specifications,' and 69c, 'Defects Arising out of the Pre-Trial Investigation.' Under 69b I charge the offense is inartfully drawn. There was no murder. Under 69c, the defects in the pretrial Article 32 investigation are as previously enumerated. To wit: violation of Articles 33, 35, and 42b; grounds as previously entered."

Wolf Lochert stirred. He leaned toward Gant. "I don't want a one-year continuance. Let's get this over with," he rasped.

Gant ignored him. "Further, as counsel, I request continuance because I have not had adequate preparation time for the trial. Further, there is the absence of a material witness I wish to call. I need time."

The president of the court looked to the law officer and said, "I have no objections to a continuance if it is a legal request." Of course he had no objections. He was a field officer who wanted to get back to his unit.

The law officer studied Archie Gant, then turned to Wolf. "Colonel Lochert, Mister Gant is correct. I will grant you a continuance of six months."

Wolf Lochert glowered. "You didn't hear me. I want to get this over fast. I have a war to get back to."

"Fast, you say," the LO said. He studied his notes, then stood and faced the members of the court. "Gentlemen, you are dismissed. This court will reconvene five weeks from this date on fourteen March." He faced Wolf. "Colonel Lochert, you will remain confined to the grounds of the MACV Studies and Observation Group in Saigon to perform such duties as your superior officers desire, excluding carrying a weapon of any sort."

0930 Hours Local, Sunday 11 February 1968
Da Nang Air Base
Republic of Vietnam

Captain Toby Parker reported to Lieutenant Colonel Charles Annillo in his office as ordered. Annillo told him to sit down.

"You're looking mighty fit for a guy who was so puny just three weeks ago. I heard you went on an eating and workout binge in the gym. Lifting weights, too. Right?"

"Yes, sir." Since his return from Lang Tri, Toby had used every moment of the day to get back in shape. He was up to 140 in a bench press, and could do a mile on the track in just under six minutes. He had been put back on flying status within a week of his return.

"Great. How many missions you got now, Toby?"

"Hundred and twelve, sir."

"What would you think of a change of scenery?" his commander asked.

"Sir?"

"This came in this morning." He tapped a copy of a TWX message on his desk. "It seems it's a by-name request for you to go on temporary duty to Ubon in Thailand."

343

"Ubon, sir? What for?"

"To help set up a night-FAC operation in F-4s. You know the area of the Trail they're interested in. They want to use your expertise."

Toby sat forward. "Does this mean I'll get checked out in F-4s, sir?" He had wanted to fly F-4s all the time he was in pilot training. He had lost the assignment due to a massive error in judgment on his part: out of boredom he had barrel-rolled a T-38 during an instrument descent on a training flight as a student pilot. His instructor, Chet Griggs, had wanted him washed out. Because he had earned so many medals as a nonpilot in his first Vietnam tour, the USAF had wanted Toby Parker to complete pilot training successfully. That he was an exceptionally gifted pilot was not in question, he was tops in everything. But Griggs had felt Toby did not have the maturity or judgment to be awarded Air Force pilot's wings. A compromise had been reached. Griggs had withdrawn his washout report on Toby and gotten the assignment to fighters he had always wanted. Toby Parker had lost his fighter slot but graduated from pilot training on time and gone to FAC school.

"No, no checkout," Annillo said. "But you will do some F-4 flying from the backseat as you help them set up the program."

Toby smiled. "Sounds great, Colonel. When do I leave?"

"In two days."

"By-name request, you said, Colonel. Who made the request?"

"The TWX is from the Seventh Air Force DO, but the man setting up the program is a Major Bannister, Court Bannister. You know him?"

1530 Hours Local, Monday 12 February 1968
The Oval Office, White House
Washington, D.C.

Major General Albert G. "Whitey" Whisenand sat at his desk in his office in the White House. He wore a dark civilian suit, a pale blue shirt that was in reality USAF standard, and a dark tie. It didn't pay to walk around Washington these days in military uniform. One risked an egg or worse thrown at him. Not just by the bearded ones, either. A housewife-looking woman had splattered a Navy friend of his in uniform with an overripe tomato while the friend had been waiting in Shirlington for a bus to the Pentagon.

Whitey had just returned from the small office he maintained on the Fourth Floor E Ring in the Pentagon. He took the last of the reports from his ancient satchel-type leather briefcase. He was fond of the old case; it had been issued to him as a second lieutenant in the thirties.

For two weeks the Tet battles had raged. Now, in the third week, victory for the allied side was assured. Collated intelligence sources put the count of enemy casualties at 37,000 killed and 5,800 captured during the first two weeks of the offensive. On the free forces side, 1,001 U.S. soldiers had been killed and 2,082 allied and ARVN soldiers killed. The offensive had been likened to the last desperate effort Adolf Hitler had made in 1944, when he had thrust into Belgium and been soundly defeated in what came to be known as the Battle of the Bulge. Any massive sudden attack can cause initial casualties. When the attack is not sustained, nor the people rally to the cause, as had been expected by General Giap, then costly failure is the result. The Tet offensive was proving a tactical disaster for Giap's forces. Not only had his troops not gained their objectives, the South Vietnamese Army had not revolted, and few civilians had rallied to their side.

The press, however, had made the Tet offensive into a

stunning victory for the communists. The American public was in an uproar. Told for months the war was nearly over, told that the Viet Cong were on their last legs, told there was light at the end of the tunnel, they were appalled by what they saw each night on their flickering TV sets. Clearly, somebody in Washington had been lying.

A cascade of death and destruction in living color flooded the living rooms across America with vivid reality of what war truly was. No John Wayne Iwo Jima attacks here, where death was heroic, painless, and, above all, neat. No clean *Twelve O'Clock High* command decisions. Instead, it was grim and bloody street-fighting, dead soldiers' arms outflung, crumpled civilians, burning and crushed houses, ambush interviews with battle-weary soldiers saying it was hell out there. Death, blood, screaming, savagery, destruction. Real war.

Cameramen could not get on the other side to show the incredible losses of the Viet Cong and North Vietnamese Army. And what they did film on the American side had to be compressed and visually dramatic or they would not gain air time, which sooner than later would lead to someone with more of an eye for bang-bang replacing them.

Much of the public, knowing nothing of tactics or strategy, nor being given any in-depth background on what was happening, hearing only the comparison of Khe Sanh to Dien Bien Phu – a great loss for the French – but not hearing that the Tet offensive compared to Hitler's defeat at the Bulge, was upset and quick to lose what remaining confidence they had in their government leaders. Never had American leaders satisfactorily explained the value of trying to keep South Vietnam free, so there was nothing to offset the cost of the war as shown so vividly on the television sets in millions of homes.

The light from the President's secretary lit up as Whitey's intercom buzzed. "Yes, Ethel," he responded.

"General Whisenand, the President would like you in his office immediately." Her voice sounded cool and remote. She was a longtime Johnson employee from Texas, whose reputation for efficiency and for never revealing privileged information was legendary. She had, for example, told no one except the President himself when a certain senator from Wisconsin threw up on her carpet as he left the Oval Office after finding out exactly what Lyndon Baines Johnson thought of him. It was LBJ himself who reveled in telling that story, both to humble the senator and to brag about his faithful closed-mouth servant. Whitey picked up a note pad and his blackboard as he went out the door.

He sat next to Ethel's desk for twenty minutes before LBJ's press secretary came out and said he could enter.

The six-foot, three-inch President stood by his desk, watching the three TV screens built into a large white cabinet. He wore bulging black trousers and a white shirt rumpled and loose at the belt.

It was now two weeks since the Tet offensive had begun, and five weeks since LBJ had renewed the Rolling Thunder bombing campaign against North Vietnam. He had stood down the Air Force and Navy for nine days, from December 24 into early January, hoping Ho Chi Minh got the message that he should capitulate or at least come to the negotiating table in Paris. The pressure to stop the strikes up north and get out of South Vietnam had become more intense each month. Only under the urging of Whitey and other members of the military had LBJ grudgingly resumed the strikes.

One of the three teletype machines next to the big TV cabinet started to clatter. They were wire services from AP, UP, and Reuters. Abruptly President Johnson's expression changed from scorn to rapt interest. He smiled, his earlier rampage forgotten.

"Those tickers," he said, waving his arm, "they're like friends tapping at my door for attention. I love having them around. They keep me in touch with the outside world. They make me feel I'm truly in the center of things. I could stand by them for hours and never be lonely." He stood up and made a sly grin. "And soon they're going

347

to have a lot more to tick about than they could possibly know." He waved at a chair in front of his desk.

"That Nixon, you know, says he's going to run against me for president. Bah. He didn't make it against Kennedy in sixty and he won't make it against . . . well, whoever runs this year."

"Whoever runs this year?" Whitey echoed. He was startled. It wasn't like LBJ to be equivocal about something as obvious as his running for re-election as president. "You *will* run, of course."

"I've made up my mind. It's Clark Clifford," LBJ said abruptly. "He's the man I'm naming as the new Secretary of Defense. He'll be here in five minutes. I want you to meet him, brief him on what you do for me, and give him all the assistance you can whenever he asks. He replaces Bob McNamara the first of March."

Whitey nodded, not too surprised. He had guessed correctly some time ago that Clifford would be the next Secretary of Defense. Nor was he surprised at LBJ ignoring his question about running for a second term. By now he was used to the President's rapid mood changes. The war was wearing the big Texan down.

Whitey turned his attention to what LBJ had just said. Whitey thought highly of the Democrat, Clifford. Anything but an Ivy Leaguer, Clifford had been born in Kansas in 1906 and earned a law degree from Washington University twenty years later. He had played poker with Churchill, helped Truman upset Dewey, and helped author the National Security Act of 1947 which had set up the CIA and the NSC. He had been a major force molding the Truman Doctrine – the containment policy – which had successfully stopped Soviet expansion in Greece, West Berlin, and elsewhere. Later, he had been JFK's personal attorney. He had directed the transition from the Eisenhower administration to Kennedy's New Frontier.

Ethel buzzed in Clark Clifford. He was lean, over six feet, and a very fit sixty-year-old man. His features were chiseled elegance, his hair wavy and golden. He wore a double-breasted dark suit, white shirt with a high starched collar, maroon tie, and black wingtip shoes.

"Mister President," Clifford said as a greeting in his cultured voice. "And General Whisenand. How good to see you again." They shook hands. "Still betting into ace-high draw?"

"Of course," Whitey guffawed, "when I'm sure there's nothing behind it." Clifford was referring to a quarter-limit poker game played years before, when he had lost four dollars trying to bluff Whitey into believing he had a pair of aces.

LBJ walked over by the fireplace. "Tell me and the general here exactly your views on Vietnam."

Clifford stood next to the sofa. He pinched an earlobe for a moment, cleared his throat, and began to speak in a quiet voice.

"I've lived and slept Vietnam for a long time now. It's clear to me we entered this war with the noblest of motives. We were coming to the rescue of a beleaguered South Vietnam, which was resisting aggression from North Vietnam, which is supported by two great communist powers. We said if we can defend South Vietnam we can stop communist aggression from spreading throughout Southeast Asia. Later we got into it more and more, trying to defend the freedom of these brave people and also to look out for our own national security. Even *that* relevance and accuracy is in doubt now. Maybe we have misunderstood or exaggerated. It all goes back to the failure on the part of France and England to face up to Hitler and the threat of the Third Reich. It's clear to me if Hitler could have been stopped, the Second World War could have been prevented, with the millions of people who lost their lives. And after the Second World War was over and the Soviets started their aggressive stratagems, Mister Truman and the others had a clear example of what happened if we didn't face up to aggression. So NATO, and the Marshall and Point Four Plan, and the Berlin Airlift, stopped Soviet aggression in

349

its tracks. So there we have two dramatic illustrations: we could have prevented the Second World War had we moved, and we did move against Soviet aggression and did stop it. And when they began to move in Southeast Asia, we said 'By God, not again.' And it was noble. Remember, it was JFK himself who said that neither the United States nor Free Vietnam was ever going to be a party to an election obviously stacked and subverted in advance by the communist North and its agents. Free Vietnam will be a proving ground of democracy, and the cornerstone of the Free World in Southeast Asia. Yes, it was noble. But other factors are intruding now."

Johnson was silent for a long moment. "What do you believe now, this very day?"

Clark Clifford looked his President in the eye. "Exactly the same as I wrote in my letter to you three years ago. That our ground forces should be kept to a minimum, that Vietnam could become a quagmire. Later, I said we could lose as many as fifty thousand men, and that the whole Vietnam effort could become a catastrophe for the United States."

"Do you still feel that way?" Johnson barked.

"Let me say this. In 1965, as the head of the Foreign Intelligence Advisory Board, I visited Southeast Asia and was greatly impressed with the spirit of our military men and that of the Vietnamese. I would like to visit again."

"You will, you will," LBJ boomed. "But do you feel the same way?"

"Yes, yes, I do, Mister President," Clifford said after a short pause. Clifford turned to Whitey Whisenand and noted the black-bordered poster he held. "I've heard of your pilot's casualty blackboard. Is that it?"

"Yes," Whitey said.

"May I see it, please?"

"Oh migawd," the President said.

Whitey held out the blackboard on which he tallied the current aircrew casualty figures.

	MIA/KIA	POW	Aircraft
	Aircrew		
USAF	404	206	879
USN	226	129	374
USMC	73	15	206
USA	160	58	454 (Helios)
TOTAL	863	408	1913

"I might add, Mister President," Whitey said, "that the overall casualty count for last week is the highest ever. In one week we lost 543 killed and 2,547 wounded."

"It's that damned Tet battle, isn't it?" the President exploded. "And Khe Sanh. We're losing men there, too, aren't we?"

Whitey answered him. "While it's true we are losing men in the Tet battles, particularly where the Marines are retaking Hue, we are not losing many men at Khe Sanh. The casualty rate there is minimal. The men are well bunkered in and the enemy shows signs of pulling out."

"Well, then, it's that damned Ho Chi Minh," the President raged. "He just won't fight a war like a good Christian should."

19

1345 Hours Local, Tuesday, 13 February 1968
Hoa Lo Prison, Hanoi
Democratic Republic of Vietnam

The pain never went away. It was endured, relegated to life itself. Pain from his ankles where the stocks closed on them met with the pain from his badly healed left arm. The dull numbness where his hips lay on the cold concrete was merely a buzz in the background that would spike every hour to wake him and force a slight shifting to a new position. To feel pain meant to live, to live was to survive. Survival was everything. To survive was to win over his captors who were so intent on breaking his spirit. They had broken his body, and – in the ropes – they had taken away his mind for a time, but the flame of his spirit still existed. From a bare flicker while in the ropes to a raging exuberance when in contact with a fellow American prisoner, the flame existed. They would never totally possess him. He knew now how he was inside, he had measured himself. And what he found gave him pride. By trying to debase him, they debased themselves. By torturing him to breaking, they formed a hot-steel core they would never understand. He knew now they would have to kill him to extinguish the flame. And he was convinced that for the time being they did not want to kill him. He was worth more alive than as a corpse. Alive, they could maybe make propaganda use of him. Yet they could not see that the figures in pajamas they presented to communist pressmen were mere robots performing in jerky, programmed ways that fooled no one except their captors. Or that his misspelled and badly written "confession" was worthless except to the vanity of the imbecilic man who had beaten it out of him.

Flak Apple had been having reoccurring dreams of either flying or walking the streets of his old neighborhood with his mother. In the flying dreams he rarely flew an airplane. Usually it was effortless soaring and rolling around huge white clouds. Although in his dream with his mother he was full-grown, he seemed to speak to her as a child. But so far she had never answered. Every time when he awakened from the dream he would keep his eyes shut, trying to go back. Fragments would flicker, but he could never regain the feeling of reality the dream provided. His eyes would sting, ineffable sadness would sweep over him like a wave that could drown him. He was back in the despair of a prison camp in Hanoi. He fought back with prayer. "Dear God," he would begin. "I ask only for enough to bear this burden." And his mind would tell him he was given enough to start the day. He knew that was God talking to him because God had given him his mind in the first place. Then he would begin his day.

The guard would never enter and release him to perform his morning toilet; he had to pull the waste can over to the slab and lift it next to himself.

He had great joy twice a day. Right after noon, when the guards were somnolent in the heat, he would tap code through the wall with Ted Frederick, and late in the afternoon he would be taken to a filthy cesspool to empty his waste bucket. Even then he could communicate. Frederick had taught him that coughs, sneezes, throat-clearing, sniffs, spits, finger-snaps, even how one walked spelled out tap-code letters. Sometimes he found secret messages written on scraps of coarse toilet paper stuffed in a drainpipe. Maybe Julie Andrews thought the hills were alive with music, but Flak knew the camp was alive with communicators. It was time now to talk with Ted Frederick.

TAP TAP TI-TAP TAP, he rapped.

TAP TAP. Frederick was on line.

HOW U, Flak asked.

COPING. N U.

SAME. HARDEST PART IS AFTER DREAMS.

YEAH, Frederick rapped back. CIDS. WIFE. ESCAPE.

HOW BIG YOUR SHIT CAN. HOW WIDE, Flak tapped.

BUCET SIZE. WHY.

MY LEGS HURT. CANT SQUAT. RIM CUTS BUTT.

PUT SANDALS ON RIM.

There was a long pause while Flak digested this important piece of news. He was ecstatic. Simple things became earth-shaking to a POW. Sitting comfortably on the crapper was one such.

JOY. JOY. JOY. MEGA THANX.

DE NADA.

They spoke of home, various squadrons, and mutual acquaintances.

HOW POW NAMES GET OUT, Flak asked.

WILL TELL WHEN WE CAN TALC NOT TAP. Then the guards started stirring. Time to sign off. Frederick made two raps and a GBU.

They came for him early that evening. Crazy Face unlocked his stocks with heavy, fumbling hands that sent sharp pain shooting up both legs. When he rolled off the concrete slab and fell to his knees, Crazy Face drooled and kicked him in the ribs. A second guard standing outside the door barked something in Vietnamese, causing Crazy Face to scuttle away. The man, wearing a uniform, told Flak to put his clothes on, meaning the maroon-and-gray pajamas. Then he escorted Flak out of his cell and into a courtyard toward an iron gate within the prison complex he had never been through. As he approached the gate, Flak heard a quick spate of coughs and sneezes from behind one of the boarded-up cell windows. ICU, they spelled out. That meant that some POW had seen this movement of an American and would put the word into the central memory that Major A. A. Apple had been seen at this time on this date being led through that gate. Flak was comforted to know someone was watching.

Once through the gate they were in a courtyard Flak had never seen before. It was neater; what looked like Vietnamese prisoners were tending rows of flowers in raised beds twenty and thirty feet long. He was led into an administrative building, down a dark hall, up a flight of stairs, and into an office that overlooked the POW compound. The walls of the office had been freshly whitewashed. The floor was wood lath, waxed and clean. A ceiling fan stirred the air that came through the tall windows.

A broad-shouldered Caucasian stood near the window. He had dark brown hair cut short, a large Zapata mustache, and stood about five-ten, Flak judged. He was tanned, had crow's-feet around eyes as dark as coal, a roughly handsome man in his mid-thirties who wore an American field jacket. He flicked a finger as dismissal for the guard and stared at Flak for a long time. Then he turned to a small table by the window and poured a glass of yellow liquid from a plastic bottle.

"Have an orange juice," he said in unaccented American English. He held the glass out to Flak. Flak accepted, sniffed to make sure it wasn't urine, and drank it down. He and Ted Frederick had decided long ago to eat or drink anything offered if there weren't any strings or trickery involved. It was a weak and sticky orange soda. He handed the glass back to the man, who did not take it.

"Put it on the table," he commanded.

Flak did as he was told. On the table were plastic bottles with water and other juices, a half-full bottle of vodka, and a tray of nuts, raisins, and apples. On the wall, under pictures of Fidel Castro and Ho Chi Minh, was a map of Hanoi. He lingered, trying to study the map and compare it to recce photos he had seen of downtown Hanoi.

"So. You are Algernon Apple. I am Alvaro Ceballos," the man said. He held out his hand. It was quite large. When Flak ignored it, he said, "You *will* shake my hand." Reluctantly, Flak offered his hand. Immediately, Ceballos caught it above the knuckles and began to squeeze. He looked full into Flak's face as he applied tremendous pressure. Caught unawares, Flak at first tried to withdraw his hand, but Ceballos held firm and grasped his wrist with his other hand. Flak remembered a trick from grade school. Instead of trying to return the pressure, or even contend with it from such a painful position, he curled his hand inward, trying to make his thumb meet his little finger. That caused his knuckles to roll out from under Ceballos' grip. Flak stared back at the man. He knew better than to do anything other than passive physical resistance. "Hunh," Ceballos snorted and released Flak's hand.

"Eat," he said, and pointed to the snack table. "Eat, and we will talk. I've heard a lot about you. I think I can help you."

Keeping an eye on the sturdy man, Flak ate from the trays. He crunched on the nuts and raisins. Without asking permission, he poured another glass of the orange soda. Who is this guy? he asked himself. What does he want? What's the trick here?

Ceballos walked over and sat behind his desk. He watched Flak eat for a few moments, then spoke.

"Sit over here," he said, and pointed to a chair in front of his desk. Flak put handfuls of raisins in his pajama shirt pocket and sat down. There were no pockets in the pajama pants.

"You want to know why you are here, don't you? Of course you do," he said without giving Flak a chance to talk. "I'll tell you why you are here. You are here so we can talk about your life. Yes, your life in that so-called land of the free, that United States. We will just talk. I am an educated man. You can talk to me. How about that? Algernon?"

Stall, Flak told himself. This guy wants to play mind games, and there's no way I can win. I need to figure out what he's after. Stall. "What did you say your name was?" he asked Ceballos.

"Alvaro Ceballos," the man said with a frown.

"Where are you from, Mister Ceballos?"

"You don't ask me questions, Algernon. I ask you questions." He spoke in a mild voice. He took a pack of Marlboro cigarettes from a drawer, lit up, inhaled deeply, and offered a cigarette to Flak, who took it and put it in his pocket.

"Don't you smoke?" Ceballos inquired pleasantly.

"No."

Ceballos smiled. "Give it back. Put it here on the desk." When Flak did as he was told, Ceballos folded his hands in front of himself and leaned forward, an inquiring expression on his face. "Why didn't you talk to that Robert Williams?"

Flak shrugged. "He did all the talking."

"Didn't you agree with what he said?"

"No."

"Tell me, then," Ceballos said, "how was *your* life in the United States?"

"Fine."

"Didn't you ever have any problems?"

"No."

"Didn't you ever have trouble in school?"

"No."

"Listen, Algernon, you can tell me. I know how it is. Let me tell you something. You want to know where I am from. I am Cuban. Yes, Cuban. But I lived in the United States many years when I was younger. And I even was in New York and Washington after the revolution." He stood and said with great pride, "I was Fidel's closest aide and interpreter." He shook his finger at Flak. "We stayed in Harlem, Fidel and I. I know how it is to be a Negro in America." He pronounced it "nay-grow," revealing for the first time a Spanish accent. "And look here." He slid

357

some *Time and Life* magazine copies across the desk. Flak could see the cover stories were about the Detroit riots of last summer.

"Pick them up. Tell me what they say," Ceballos commanded, his voice imperious. Flak haphazardly thumbed through the pages. "Tell me what they say," Ceballos said in a louder voice.

Flak stopped at a page. "Right here it says that 'Ode to Billie Joe' was one of the top songs of the year." He turned a page. "Here it says you can buy a new Chevrolet sedan for thirty-two hundred dollars complete with radio and heater."

"You're a smart guy, hunh?" Ceballos said. "Won't admit the murder of the Negroes in Detroit. That killer Johnson couldn't kill enough people in Vietnam so he has to use your Army paratroopers to kill Negroes in Detroit. Don't you see how you are being exploited?" Flak said nothing.

"Look," Ceballos continued, "don't you even know how many Negro men are in the Army? I'll tell you. In the Infantry, twenty-five percent are Negro. In the Marines, thirty percent, even fifty percent. You don't have more than ten percent of Negroes in your whole population. So Johnson puts them on the front lines to be killed. Or kills them in Detroit. What do you say?"

"Nothing."

"Listen to this," Ceballos said. "He is one of your own, this Stokely Carmichael. He broadcasts for us." He switched on a tape recorder.

Flak heard a man tell of the Imperialists' unjust war against the peace-loving people of Vietnam, of how black men were forced to fight their Asian brothers. He ended his harangue with the words, "There is a higher law than the racist McNamara. There is a higher law than the fool named Dean Rusk. There is a higher law than a buffoon named Lyndon Baines Johnson."

"And this," Ceballos said. The next tape played the words of Olympic gold medal boxer Cassius Clay. "I am Muhammad Ali. My religion forbids me to fight. I ain't got no quarrel with those Viet Cong. They never called me nigger." Flak heard Martin Luther King say the war was a "blasphemy against all that America stands for." Doctor Benjamin Spock said he felt "nothing but scorn and horror for Lyndon Johnson's Vietnam policy. In the rest of the world, our ruthless actions are being compared to the Soviet Union's suppression of the Hungarian revolt and Hitler's murder of the Jews." Flak had a hard time keeping an impassive face when he heard these famous men tearing down the country he loved. Ceballos switched off the machine. "Doesn't that mean anything to you?" he asked.

Flak Apple didn't answer. Mean anything, he thought. God in heaven, it meant so much he was afraid he would break down in front of this man, his enemy. Rage, he thought. Let the rage build. Use it. Rage against those Americans who were trying to destroy his will to resist. He stiffened.

"Answer me," Ceballos thundered.

"Ali is a good boxer, Spock is a good baby doctor," Flak said in a voice without inflection, wondering if he was being taped.

"Listen, Algernon. I'm trying to be reasonable with you. Help me help you and you will live better. You may even go home very soon. All I want you to do is tell me how badly you were treated in the United States. Tell me that you were exploited. I can understand. You are not a criminal like the rest of the prisoners. All you have to do is talk to me. Come on, talk to me."

"It's raining outside," Flak said.

Ceballos slapped his desk with a sound like a pistol shot. "Listen, smart guy. You keep this up and I'll turn you over to the men who interrogate you, the ones who punish you. If you do not cooperate, they will perform severe punishment. If that punishment causes you to lose your arm or your leg, they will dispose of you. They would not send you home a cripple." He lit a fresh cigarette. "Now tell me, what do you want? To cooperate with me or to be a cripple? You must make a choice."

"Let me think about it," Flak finally replied.

"No. You must talk to me now." Ceballos slammed the desk.

"How can I talk to you when I am in pain, when I haven't slept for months, when I am starving? How can I make a decision under those conditions?" Flak passed a hand over his face.

Ceballos got to his feet and came around to Flak's side of the desk. "On your feet," he barked.

When Flak stood up, Ceballos lashed out with both hands and slapped him a dozen times fast and hard. Flak swayed and fought to keep his balance. His ears roared and his vision became blurred.

"You must decide," Ceballos roared into Flak's face. "You must decide."

Flak blinked and tried to focus. "Okay," he said. "I decide. I decide I want to go back to my cell."

Ceballos ripped off the pocket that held the raisins, then punched Flak in the stomach, knocking him to the floor.

Holding his stomach, Flak struggled to a sitting position. "So you are an educated man, Ceballos," he said, breathing hard. "Educated men don't have to use their fists. They use their minds."

"Yes, I am educated. You are the stupid one. It is only my fists that get your attention. You cannot see how much better life would be for you if you would cooperate with me." Ceballos strode to the door and threw it open. He signaled the guard and turned to Flak.

"Now listen to me," he said. "I will let you go back to your cell. I want you to think about what I said about cooperating with me. I will arrange for special food. Then I will send for you."

"Will you arrange for special food for everyone?"

"Of course not."

"Then I don't want any."

"I said you were a stupid man, Algernon. Now go. I will arrange the food anyhow. We will talk again, very soon."

"I need medicine," Flak said. "I need a doctor." He held out his bent arm. "Look at this." He pulled up his pant leg and pointed to the open sores from the stocks.

Ceballos' face clouded. "You have committed crimes," he shouted. "You are lucky to be alive." He pushed Flak out the door to the guard.

When Flak was let into his cell, the guard did not fasten the stocks on his ankles, nor was Crazy Face anywhere to be seen. That night, the bowl a new guard brought to Flak contained a warm, thick vegetable soup and a banana. Flak stared at the windfall. After a moment's indecision, he slowly drank all the soup, savoring the flavor, and peeled and ate the banana. Then he ate the banana skin. Late that night he contacted Ted Frederick.

WHAT U HAVE ON CUBAN CEBALLOS.

WE CALL HIM FIDEL. MEAN GUY. SUPPOSED TO GET US TO DO THINGS WITHOUT TORTURE. SUPPOSED TO SHOW THE V HOW IT CAN BE DONE. STARTS OUT NICE BUT WINDS UP HITTING.

HE SENDING ME SPECIAL FOOD.

SRO SEZ EAT. SEND ME SOME.

WISH I COULD.

GN GBU.

GN N GBU. "Good night and God bless you." Flak arranged his blanket and for the first time in twelve weeks fell into a deep, uninterrupted sleep.

1230 Hours Local, Thursday 15 February 1968
Catinat Hotel, Saigon
Republic of Vietnam

"I don't care if it is two-thirty in the morning. I'd have got you at midnight if it didn't take so long to get this damn call through." Archie Gant propped the phone on his shoulder and pawed through his notes. He had circled in red a statement made by Wolf Lochert about the CIA's knowledge of Buey Dan. He sat at the small desk in his hotel room.

"I'm not complaining," Michael LaNew said, "merely remarking." He spoke from his apartment on Hill Street. Gant's phone call had awakened him moments before. The connection was not good.

"So you're not complaining. You should. You don't have anything to do."

"The hell I don't. I'm putting in twelve hours a day on the Dunston case." LaNew grinned. He was used to the brisk and sometimes brutal repartee from his boss.

"Well, drop it. No, don't drop it. Do what I tell you in addition to Dunston."

"Do what?" Some of the words Gant spoke never made it to San Francisco.

"Do what I tell you. Now listen. I remember when you first joined the firm. When I covered points on your resume, you spoke of being the man who apprehended Shawn Bannister in Thailand last year on spy charges."

"That's correct, but they were dropped."

"I know, I know. That's not the point." Gant stabbed a finger at Wolf's words that the Agency knew Buey Dan's code name. "I remember you talking about your interrogation of Bannister and you said he used the name Lizard about someone he had seen. Tell me that part again."

"What about lizards?" LaNew yelled over the line.

"TELL ME WHAT SHAWN BANNISTER SAID ABOUT A MAN CALLED THE LIZARD." The line cleared in the middle of Gant's shouted response.

"Okay, okay," LaNew said, holding the phone from his ear. "Sometime during the interrogation Bannister said he went many places to get information for his articles. Not just to an American base in Thailand. He had, he said, been in the VC tunnels under Cholon and met the commander of local VC forces. He had also seen a man he was told later was a top official known as *than lan*, which is Vietnamese for lizard."

362

"AH HA," Gant trumpeted over the line. "What I want you to do is this. Find Mister Shawn-the-spy Bannister, show him the pictures I am going to send the office by satellite of Buey Dan. See if he identifies him as the man he saw in the tunnels with the VC commander. When he does, get a sworn statement to that effect. Airmail it back to me."

"Easier said than written, Mister Gant."

"What do you mean?"

"Shawn Bannister is running for a state assemblyman slot from Berkeley. One of his major platforms is, and I quote, 'To stop the wanton racist killings of Asians by Americans.' To that end he is using the Wolfgang Lochert case as a media springboard. Every day he's on the TV or the radio or front page of some newspaper calling for Lochert's imprisonment. Even said he would for once advocate the death penalty, that Lochert should be shot as a murderer to pay for his crime. I don't think Shawn Bannister would do a single thing to help Lochert."

"Find a way, LaNew. Find a way."

20

1930 Hours Local, Friday 16 February 1968
8th Tactical Fighter Wing
Ubon Royal Thai Air Force Base
Kingdom of Thailand

It was raining and there was very little wind. Water fell
straight and hard from the night sky and splashed up
silver from the lighted flightline ramp, the airplanes, the
black asphalt streets of the air base. It streamed down the
Ubon control tower windows, it hammered the ponchos
of the Air Police walking perimeter guard, M16s muzzle
down. Rushing streams filled runway drainage ditches.
Blue maintenance vans moved slowly down the ramps and
around the revetments, low bow waves spreading from their
tires. Pilots and crew chiefs huddled under the wings of their
glistening Phantoms, waiting for a lull to finish preflights
and to open the canopies. Soon the core of the storm passed
and the business of the 8th Tac Fighter Wing resumed in
the light warm rain that remained.

Court Bannister cracked the door of his BOQ room to
let the tranquil rain sound mix with that of The Mamas
and The Papas *(. . . go where you wanna, wanna go . . .)*
he was playing on his Akai tape deck. The roar of an
F-4 taking off into the heavy rain on a night mission
vibrated in his gut for a few moments until the fighter
was swallowed by the heavy black overcast.

Two nights before, Court had flown with Howie Joseph,

a highly experienced instructor pilot from the 497th Night Owl squadron, in his backseat. Court had been building up his night-combat proficiency under Howie's expert tutelage. The AAA had been thick and the mission very dangerous. Court had had to use both his flares and his CBUs to destroy a truck park. Howie had performed the duties of a backseater, but had let Court figure out the attack problems by himself. At the end of the flight, Court had asked Howie Joseph if he would like to be the operations officer for Court's new night-FAC outfit. Howie had responded, "Does a bear shit in the woods?"

Court's BOQ room was small but private. All lieutenants and captains and most majors had to double up. As a commander of a unit, he did not have to share with a crew member of equal rank. His room was in the same long, one-storey building as the crewmen of 497th Tactical Fighter Squadron, the Night Owls. The squadron whose aircraft took off only after the sun had gone down, and whose pilots and navigators fought the war only in the dark.

The rooms were side by side and opened motel-style onto a long, screened walkway which led from one end of the building to the communal bathroom and a covered breezeway at the other end. In the breezeway the pilots had built a bar with ceiling fans, papasan chairs, music from a tape deck and the local USAF radio station on the base, and a government refrigerator for which they had traded a dozen aviator sunglasses. Thai housekeepers kept the rooms clean and did the men's laundry for a few dollars a week from each of them. Court's 10-by-12 room held a bunk with a real mattress, a small wood desk, and a tall steel locker with drawers. In the back wall was fixed an air conditioner that ran full-time. There were no windows. All the Night Owl rooms were completely blacked out so the crews could sleep in the daytime.

At the moment Court's room was illuminated only by the small circle of light from the lamp where he sat at his desk. He took some paper and an envelope from a leather stationery folder and addressed the envelope to Susan at her

Manhattan Beach apartment. The stationery was creamy and rich, a Christmas present from his father. He put his return address – his mail-room box number and APO San Francisco 96304 – and wrote the word "Free" where a stamp would normally be fixed to the upper-right-hand corner. Since airmail stamps cost eleven cents each, total postal savings per man per year in combat totaled around twelve dollars, depending on how much he wrote.

His cigarette in the ashtray sent up long spirals of smoke. He sipped from a glass of Australian red wine and thought of what to say to Susan. He tapped a finger on the glass, then wrote:

> Dear Susan,
> The trip back to Saigon was dull. Got a lot of sleep. Spent about a week flying out of Tan Son Nhut, then came back here to Ubon. Have to do some more training before I get the FAC program in gear. Can't believe two weeks have passed since we were together. Seems more like months.
> Had dinner the other night with an old friend, Doc Russell. Don't know if I ever told you about him, but I told him about you. Nice guy. Wanted to know when we were going to get married.
> Susan, I know you wanted me to talk more, to tell you how I was feeling, but I

He threw the pen down and crumpled the page. Christ, he thought, that's as insipid as a kid writing his mother from summer camp.

He took his wine and moved to the open door. The rain glistened off trees and grass and bushes. The cool breeze swirled around him. He saw the two empty lawn chairs, sodden in the rain, beyond the veranda where he and Flak Apple used to sit and commiserate with each other about the war. And now Flak was gone. Shot down up north. No one knew whether he was dead or captured. The North Vietnamese never gave out prisoner lists. The only way the American Government knew who was captured was by either the very few photographs released for propaganda purposes, the radio broadcasts made under torture, or through simple codes in the few letters that were allowed out. And Flak was gone. So many were gone. Lost another one from the 433rd today, he had heard.

He put down his wine and walked down to the Night Owl bar in the breezeway, where he found Toby Parker, wearing shorts and a T-shirt, sunk in a papasan chair in the corner. Toby lowered the notes Court had given him to study. He had arrived the day before from Da Nang to provide Court and his new unit with the latest Ho Chi Minh Trail information. They had spent most of their time together in Wing Headquarters.

"For a guy with a new command, you don't look very cheerful," he said to Court, "you look positively gloomy. You should be happy and all inspired. This is your big command. The first of many, I'll bet. What's up?"

With effort Court worked up an alert smile. "Everything is just fine. Ready for the big briefing tomorrow?"

"Sure. But I'll bet I can't teach you guys much."

"You can. You're down there in the weeds eyeball to eyeball with the bad guys. You see things we never will."

"Yeah. When you're tied to a tree you see a lot more than you ever wanted."

Court nodded agreement. "That must have been as rough as it comes. But you're looking great now, Tobes. You sure have come a long way since Bien Hoa."

"A lot's happened since then," Toby said. He held up a can of soda from the Night Owl bar. "A long way from Bien Hoa." He glanced at the door. "Speaking of Bien Hoa, look who's coming in."

Doc Russell, Baby Huey to his friends, marched through the screen door, shaking water from himself like a big, tubby hound-dog. He wore white shorts, a polo shirt, thongs, and was soaked. He waved at the men at the bar and walked over to Court and Toby.

"Like old times," he said.

"Just talking about that," Toby replied.

Doc Russell got two cans of soda from the bar, gave one to Court, and sat across from the two pilots. He and Court had an unspoken agreement not to drink around Toby.

"Last of the big-time drinkers, too. Cheers," Toby said. The three men took pulls at their sodas. Court lit a cigarette.

"Gonna kill you someday," Toby said.

Court laughed. "If I live long enough."

"You think we're still winning the war, Court?" Doc Russell asked without preamble. At Bien Hoa on his first tour, Court had been easily convinced the Vietnam war was soon to be won.

Court leaned back and made a sardonic grin. "Look, Doc, why don't you ask something easy, like explain the theory of relativity in twenty-five words or less." Court waved his hand as if to brush away a mosquito. "Next question."

"That was enough." Doc Russell laughed.

Toby looked up from his notes. "Court, I see you have a pilot named Chet Griggs on your roster. Is he a young captain from the Air Training Command?"

"Yeah. You know him?"

"Somewhat. He tried to wash me out of pilot training. When he couldn't, he prevented me from going into fighters. That's why I'm driving 0-2s around now."

"What happened?" Doc Russell asked.

Toby told them the story of how he had rolled a T-38 through a barrel-roll maneuver while making an instrument letdown with his instructor pilot, Chet Griggs, in the front cockpit. Toby didn't smile as he told the story. "I guess I was, how to put it . . . bored, maybe. Or shining my ass. Or something. I don't know why I did it. Chet put me up for elimination on the grounds of lack of discipline. I deserved it." He had a look of self-disgust.

"Bad judgment, Tobes," Court said, "doing it with your IP on board. You're lucky you're still in the Air Force. Seeing as how he couldn't get you flushed out of pilot training, how do you think he's going to react to you here?"

Toby looked at him. "Chet Griggs is a straight-up guy.

If his boss says something will or will not happen, he salutes and says 'yes, sir' and presses on. At Randolph he came to see me with the news in my BOQ room. We had a fight, but it was my fault. I was drunk. He was really nice about the whole thing. I guess he's accepted that I'm still in the Air Force and that I did get my wings. I think everything will be okay between us."

Doc Russell looked around. "Pretty dull for a Friday night."

"For the Night Owls, it's Friday morning," Court said. "They're all off to work. And I'm off to bed. Big day tomorrow."

"Not like the old days," Doc Russell said. "No more big nights at the O'Club."

"It's a different war up here, Doc. Much different from Bien Hoa. More losses. Down there we drank to party and have fun. Up here it's more . . ." He searched for a word.

"Survival?" Doc Russell offered. Court didn't answer.

The three men chatted a bit more about the new BX opening, the protesters in the States, and how much it rained in Asia. When the small talk trailed away, Toby said goodnight and went back to his room.

Doc Russell shook his head. "You pilots. You always make things so complicated."

"Complicated? What are you talking about? Pilots are the most uncomplicated and easygoing guys around. We're just simple line jocks."

"Simple? No career fighter pilot is simple, and you're more complicated than most."

"You sound like Susan."

"Do I now? I'll bet she thinks you're a bit complicated."

Court didn't answer right away. "Perhaps. She pokes around like you do, asking questions why I feel this way or what I think about that."

"What do you tell her?"

"Not much."

Doc Russell went to the bar and brought back two shots of a good scotch. "Sipping stuff," he said, handed one to

369

Court and sat down. "I've known you for a long time as far as air wars go. We're on our second tour together, first Bien Hoa, now Ubon. So I'm confident I can tell you what I think and not have you jump through your grommet. I've put a lot of thought to your being so, ah, moody-broody, and this is what I've come up with. First," he ticked off his finger, "you're pissed because you can't fly north and get that fifth MiG. Second, you're pissed because you don't think the government is doing a good job running this war. Third, you suspect Colonel Bryce isn't being so buddy-buddy anymore because you're suddenly a detriment to his career, not an asset. Fourth, one of the reasons you're in the Air Force is to leave behind all that Hollywood notoriety crap, and now your half-brother has his face and yours plastered over most of the magazines in the world. Fifth, you brood over a failed marriage that wasn't much of a marriage to begin with, and you brood over not finishing the test-pilot school when in fact you got your test ticket but didn't go on to the aerospace portion." His face softened. "And lastly, you've had some losses. Ev Stern, Flak Apple, maybe even that Russian pilot. There are others, I know."

Court tossed off his scotch. "Well, shit, Doc. You've been doing a lot of homework, or snooping, or something. Let's just say it's true. So where does it all lead?"

"It *could* lead to you giving up. You think you're the only one in the world carrying a lot of weight – "

"Now wait a minute – "

Doc Russell held up his hand. "Hear me out. You're pushing too hard. You want a perfect war, perfect government, perfect marriage, perfect test-pilot school. Yes, perhaps even a perfect enemy – one who remains a monster, not a human being like that Russian pilot. You saw too many J. Wayne movies where everything is in black-and-white simplicity. Real life ain't that way. You take your wars and your women too seriously, and yes, your government. You got to understand," said Baby Huey, happily married father of three, "life is just a handjob."

Court choked on his scotch. "Whaaat?"

Doc Russell laughed. "Got your attention, did I? Good. Unwind. Learn how to relax. I doubt you were this way as a lieutenant. I can point all this out to you, but only you can do anything about it." With mock severity he peered into Court's face. "Und you vas not like dis as a leutenant, so vy be dis way now, yah?"

Court gave a low laugh. "Okay, Herr Doktor Freud, your points are . . . listened to, if not well-taken."

"You'll put some thought to all this?"

"Sure," Court said. "I will." They said goodnight to each other and turned in.

Court smoked two cigarettes before he fell asleep. He dreamed he and Susan were on two different boats. Hers was pulling away and his was sinking.

0730 Hours Local, Saturday 17 February 1968
8th Tactical Fighter Wing
Ubon Royal Thai Air Force Base
Kingdom of Thailand

The chosen men filed into the main briefing auditorium and headed toward seats in the front rows. There were fourteen of them: lieutenants, captains, one major; pilots and navigators. The auditorium, first door on the left after the front door to Wing Headquarters, had movie theater seats and a large stage from which briefings were given for big strikes fragged for North Vietnam. Large 4-by-8 plywood pullout boards on rollers with maps, photos, and weather charts pinned to them stood in slots on each side. In the center was a movable speaker's podium with the 8th TFW plaque and motto, ATTACK AND CONQUER.

371

Court Bannister and his new operations officer, Howie Joseph, stood in the open area between the stage and the seats. They had set up a table with a large metal urn of hot coffee and paper cups.

"Gentlemen, come on down and have some coffee. I want everybody to meet each other." Talking and joking quietly among themselves, the men surrounded the coffee table and handed each other coffee. They wore their green K-2B flight suits with rank and name stitched in black thread.

"Most of you know each other because you're from squadrons here in the Eighth," Court said. "But I want to introduce you to some people you may have heard of but never met." He put his hand on Joseph's shoulder. "This is Howie Joseph. He got a MiG with a Thud on his first tour. It tasted so good he decided to upgrade into a real fighter, the F-4. We are lucky enough to have him on his second tour as our operations officer."

Court put his hand on Toby Parker's shoulder. "And this bright young man is Toby Parker. He is liaison from the 0-2 FAC outfit at Da Nang. He's an old friend, shit hot good pilot, authentic combat hero, and knows the Ho Chi Minh Trail area as well as the chin he shaves every morning." Toby grinned and ducked his head, his face flaming. He still had a hard time admitting to himself that the deeds he performed so automatically were worthy of military recognition. Never in his life before joining the Air Force had he been recognized for much, other than partying and casually skating by serious subjects.

"I think most of you know Tom Partin," Court continued. "He's been in the military since Christ was a corporal." Partin was a silver-haired taciturn Texan whose face was as leathery and worn as an old saddle. He nodded at those he knew, shook hands with those he didn't.

"And over here we have our resident swabbie, Lieutenant Rolly Grailson. As you can tell by his flight suit," Court continued, "the Navy does things different. Not as many zippers, and it is brown to go with his brown shoes, I suppose. Rolly is here with us from the mighty USS

372

America, CV 66, where he had been flying F-4JS with VF-33, the Tarsiers." Most of the men had met Grailson the night before at the Officer's Club. Grailson grinned and shook hands.

"Next we have a man who outranks all of us, Major Carlos Bretone." Bretone came forward. He was a husky man of medium height, with a thick chest, thick cheek-bones set high, and Mediterranean-dark coloring. He wore thick glasses. "Carlos has more fighter time than all of us put together. He's a navigator up from F-89s and F-10ls. He's spent more time running aircraft intercepts from the backseat than we pilots have total time up front. Carlos will probably be the first navigator in the Air Force to command a fighter squadron. He just finished flying ninety missions with the 497th Night Owls." Bretone nodded at the crowd. A quiet man, he wasn't given to small talk. Even though he outranked Court by a few months, he was assigned to him and subject to his orders – and efficiency reports. It was not uncommon for a navigator to be rated by a pilot of lesser rank. It was an anomaly as yet unsolved by the USAF. The Navy, on the other hand, did place Naval Flight Officers in command positions of flying units. An NFO was not a pilot but a radar intercept officer or bombardier-navigator.

Court turned and waved his hand in a circle. "Duckcall Donny Higgens, Pete Stein, Rail, Mitchell, Griggs, Docks, you all know each other." He vaulted to the stage. "If you gentlemen will take your seats, I'll get on with the briefing."

As they sat down, Court saw each man pull out a note-book and pencil. "Good. I never trust a man who doesn't take notes."

He pulled out the first board. Pinned to it was a 1:250,000 aerial navigation chart depicting western Thailand, all of Laos and Cambodia, and North and South Vietnam. The cities of Hanoi, Saigon, Phnom Penh, Vientiane, and Bangkok were highlighted. The dozens of USAF air bases suitable for recovery in South Vietnam and Thailand were circled and named.

There were three arrows pointing into Hanoi. "These are the supply lines running into North Vietnam," Court said. He traced the line from the east, from the Gulf of Tonkin. "This one is from the harbors of Haiphong, Hon Gai, and Cam Pha. These two, from the northeast and the northwest, are railroads from China. Red Chinese supplies exclusively come down the northeast rails, Russian and Chinese flow down the northwest line. Ships from both Russia and China plus from Sweden, Britain, and other countries including our own unload supplies in these harbors."

The men groaned and booed. They had flown many missions up north and had only occasionally been targeted by the White House against these vital supply routes. They had never been allowed to completely cut the rail lines and keep them cut, or place antishipping mines in the harbors. They couldn't even attack SAM sites and MiG bases under construction. It was worth a court-martial to attack a ship in the harbor even if it shot at a plane.

"What do you mean," one of the younger backseaters asked, "about ships of our own in the harbor? How the hell can we be attacking gook materials from the air while Americans are supplying them from the sea?"

"The boats I refer to are from various American anti-military groups such as the American Friends Service Committee and the Quakers. They ship medical supplies to the communists."

"And that stuff winds up on the Trail," the young man said.

"That's right," Court replied.

"And we lose pilots trying to destroy it."

"That's right."

"Geez. My mother never warned me there'd be wars like this."

Court continued his briefing. "From Hanoi the supplies go straight south along the rail and road lines, then on to Route 12 to the west into the Annamite Mountains, where they split the flow into Laos through the three passes. Most of you have flown the Trail, but this is the first

374

mosaic we have put together that shows the whole route structure. The North Vietnamese, by the way, call it the Truong Son Road because it goes though the Truong Son Mountains."

The maps filled an entire 4-by-8 plywood sheet. The black, hydra-headed Ho Chi Minh Trail on the acetate overlay stretched from the three passes into Laos, where it branched into Vietnam, looking like the trailing arms of a squid.

Court ran his index finger along the Trail. "From Hanoi down through Laos and on to the point where the supplies swing into South Vietnam is close to a thousand miles. Add the double trails, switchbacks, cat's eyes, truck parks, maintenance depots, resupply points, off-load and transfer points, and we have a system, in reality, which is three or four times as long. In most areas the Trail can be widened, switched, dualed, duplicated, or cut through a fresh new batch of jungle damn near overnight." He pulled out enlarged mosaics of the Mu Gia Pass area. "We have geographical points designated by Delta numbers. Delta 22 is here, Delta 32 there, Delta 69 here, and so on. Other places are known by specific terrain features." He traced prominent river features that wound and looped into many shapes and forms easily recognizable from the air. "This is the Bird's Head, the Dog's Head is down here by Ban Loby, here are the North Boobs, here the South Boobs. You must memorize all of these. You frontseaters and backseaters must be as familiar with this area as your own backyard." He faced the audience.

"Right now the slow 0-2 FACs and the fast F-4 FACs have been controlling the primary interdiction strike missions against the Trail, using Navy, Marine, and Air Force fighters. Right with them have been the Air Commandos from NKP, flying prop jobs day and night along the Trail. Ask Toby. He's been there. Those guys at NKP have the greatest collection of World War Two aircraft this side of the Confederate Air Force. They fly the twin-engine A-26, the C-47, C-119s, C-123s, and the biggest single prop job in the world, the Douglas A-1 Skyraider. Added to their effort is the Igloo White missions, which drop electronic sensors in an effort to locate trucks and troops. Then there is the radar-directed Skyspot mission."

The crewmen hissed. They called Skyspot "Sky Puke" because all they did was fly under the direction of a radar site to dump bombs "on a pile of sand."

"All those efforts, the Air Commandos, Igloo White, and Skyspot perform night missions to some degree," Court continued. "Unfortunately without great success. Supplies and troops are still moving down the Trail after dark. That's the main reason the powers-that-be have decided to form a dedicated night FAC unit. They hope we'll have better BDA." BDA was the acronym for Bomb Damage Assessment — what each airplane destroyed or killed on a single mission.

He walked to the edge of the stage and folded his arms. "The Wolf FACs here at Ubon, the Marine Playboy FACs from Da Nang, the Stormys, the Laredos, Falcons, Tigers, they've all done a great job stopping the flow of supplies on the Trail during daylight hours. As a result the trucks of the 559th NVA Transportation Division now have to run at night."

Court gave a broad grin. "And that, gentlemen, brings us to why you are here today. We are forming a new outfit, a special outfit. And you gentlemen weren't chosen from a bunch of names in a hat. You were chosen because I found you are all uniquely qualified in one way or another to perform this night FAC mission. I spent a lot of time going over pilot and navigator records and talking to your operations officers. Once we get everybody trained and on line, our mission will be to stop the nighttime supply flow down the Trail. We will do it by sniffing around for the trucks, the truck parks, the overhaul depots, the trans-shipment points, and anything else that makes up or protects the flow of supplies moving down the Trail at night."

There was a stir in the audience as Donny Higgens spoke

up. "*Protects?* Did you say *protects*? Like in *guns*? You mean we gotta go after guns?"

"Yeah, Donny," Court said. "Guns. At night."

"Me? Little old beautiful me?" Higgens said. "Marvelous me is supposed to fly at night?" He looked around, mock terror on his face. "If God wanted me to fly at night" – he was interrupted by a chorus from the audience – "I'd have been born an owl," they chanted. "Aw, howdja know?" Higgens replied. He had been flying as a Wolf on the day FAC mission for months.

"Yeah, Donny, fly at night. But listen to this. We will not go on the line until each man has at least ten day Wolf FAC missions and twenty Night Owl missions in his log book. That means you Night Owls got to aviate in the day when everybody can see you, and you day jocks got to learn how to flog around at night without killing yourselves. Furthermore, you all must be volunteers. If at any time before we are operational you want out, let me know. You'll just go back to your squadron."

"What if we want out after we are operational?" Docks asked.

"Then I'll find you a nice slot in Seventh Air Force at Tan Son Nhut. Of course if you get shot down twice and still make it back, I'll find you a slot anyplace you want to go."

"Shit, who gives a hoot about the Night *Owls*," Higgens said. "How about being a night *duck*?"

"Speaking of owls," Court said, ignoring him, "we need a name and a call sign for this outfit. The day FACs are the Wolfs, the night squadron is the Night Owls. So what should we be called?"

After a moment suggestions came from the crewmen. Night FACs, Owl FACs, Eagles, Night Strikers, Night Hawks. Higgens was booed when he proposed Night Ducks. Then a voice said Phantom FACs.

"Phantom FACs," someone else said. "That sounds good."

"Yeah," Higgens said. "If we can't be Night Ducks, let's

be Phantom FACs. What do you think, boss?" he asked Court.

"It's up to you guys," Court said. "Take a vote." Joseph organized the vote. It was 13 to 3 for Phantom FACs.

"Okay, we are now known as the Phantom FACs. How about a motto?" Court said.

After a lively discussion involving several scatological and reproductive terms, they decided on "We Get Ours at Night."

"Okay," Court said, "we got a mission, a name, a motto, all we need now is some organization." He pulled out a board with the crew roster taped on it. "And here we are." He took a grease pencil and wrote the new name and motto at the top.

Phantom-FAC Roster
We Get Ours at Night

Position	A/C	GIB
Commander	01A Maj C. Bannister	01B Lt Pete Stein
Operations Officer	02A Capt Howie Joseph	02B Lt John Martin
Intelligence Officer	03A Capt Tom Partin	03B Lt Mike Steffes
Maintenance/ Weapons	04A Capt Donny Higgens	04B Lt Horace Rhoades
Admin Officer	05A Capt Chet Griggs	05B Lt Neil Tallboy
Supply Officer	06A Capt Lynn Mitchell	06B Lt Matt Henry
Special Projects	07A Lt Rolly Grailson	07B Maj Carlos Bretone
Flying Safety	08A Capt Deacon Docks	08B Capt Toby Parker

The numbers and letters were each man's individual call signs. The Alpha and Bravo meant the position a crewman flew in the aircraft. If Phantom Zero Four was flying,

Phantom Zero Four Alpha would be Higgens in the front seat, Zero Four Bravo would be Rhoades in the backseat. However, when a frontseater flew in the backseat, he took a Bravo code after his call sign.

Court pulled out a board with aircraft and weapons pictures and diagrams. "We will carry a 600-gallon centerline tank, two SUU-42 flare dispensers with sixteen Mark-24 flares each, three CBU-24s, and ten Willy Pete marking rockets. The flares are to find 'em, the rockets to fix 'em for the strike birds, and the CBU is for us to use on a fleeting target, gun suppression, or on movers if no strike birds are available."

He walked back to the podium. "The missions will be single-ship, no wingmen on these missions. The crew will report two hours before takeoff time to check the weather, intelligence, and current strike reports. Get out to your birds at least thirty minutes before start engine time. Night preflights are tricky. Take your time. We're all new to the SUU-42 flare dispenser. Make sure the fuzes and timers are set correctly. A dud flare is a wasted pass. Taxi extra slow at night, all nav lights on Bright. Watch the armorers in the armament area just before you take the active runway. They will signal you with flashlights what to do. Both front- and backseaters, put your hands outside the cockpit so they can see them and know the cockpit is clear. The armorers will check the electrical continuity and stability of all the weapons under your wings, then pull the safing pins and signal that you are cleared. Do your standard pre-takeoff checks before taking the active runway, and standard runup checks once on the runway. Here are your radio frequencies. Channel eleven is for us to talk among ourselves." He pulled out a board.

Channel	Agency
2	UBON GROUND CONTROL
3	UBON TOWER
4	UBON DEPARTURE CONTROL
5	UBON DEPARTURE CONTROL
6	LION RADAR
7	LION RADAR
8	INVERT RADAR
9	INVERT RADAR
10	UBON COMMAND POST
11	FAC TACTICAL

"We go on line in two weeks. At 1800 on 1 March, as a matter of fact. I'll take the first mission. Howie Joseph will post the rest of the schedule. Meanwhile I want you Night Owl GIBs to fly with the day pilots, and you day GIBs to fly with the Night Owl pilots until each of you gets the ten Wolf and twenty Night Owl missions." He grinned. "These are all night missions, gentlemen, over extremely hazardous terrain, generally in bad weather. It's hairy stuff. You must get used to flying on the gages. Plan on instrument takeoffs every night. Once airborne, Ubon Departure Control will hand you off to Lion Radar. When you are far enough out, Lion will hand you off to Invert Radar, who will give you a vector for the tanker. We don't have far to go to the tanker. Once off the tank, stay in contact with Invert the whole mission, except when on tactical frequency conducting a strike. If you go down by yourself, only Invert will know where you are. They will tell you what SIF code to squawk." SIF was the Selective Identification Feature device that put out a coded signal preset by the pilot when challenged by a friendly ground or airborne station. The coded signal provided a burst of energy on the receiving radar screen unique to the code the pilot was asked to "squawk" on his "parrot" by the radar controller.

"After the tank, contact Moonbeam for clearance as you cross the fence into and out of Steel Tiger. Turn off your navigation lights when you reach the Lao border, which the radar controllers call 'the fence.' Just tell them you are 'blackout at the fence.' The frequencies for the tank and Moonbeam change every twenty-four hours. The Intelligence briefer will provide them each day on pre-printed cards." Moonbeam was the call sign for the night Airborne Command and Control Center. "Your flares burn three minutes, give or take a few seconds. In a light mist or cloud, they make you think you're flying in a bowl of milk with no up or down. Keep one man on the gages at all times." That meant one man in the two-seat F-4 should be looking at the flight instruments while the other was looking outside the cockpit.

Court continued with tactics and wound up the briefing by assigning to each man the extra duties that keep a unit functioning. "Note," he said as he walked from behind the podium, "we have no CFC officer." Cheers greeted this announcement that no one had to dun the others for money for the Combined Federal Campaign. Although the CFC was the USAF's answer to all the requests made on it for charitable donations, things had gotten out of hand, and each year the luckless officer appointed (usually a junior) had to do better than his predecessor the year before "because," his boss would say, "the amount you raise is a direct indicator of your organizational abilities."

"Now," Court said, "we'll have a briefing from Toby Parker, who knows the Trail from the air and the ground. He has flown over one hundred slow FAC missions on his trusty Oscar Deuce. Six weeks ago he was shot down and captured" – there were sounds of surprise from the audience – "and was rescued by the guys in Laos we can't talk about except to say they eat snakes and wear funny green hats."

Toby mounted the stage. He looked trim and fit. The rolled-up sleeves on his flight suit accentuated his new muscle development. He pointed to the large briefing board with the Ho Chi Minh Trail.

"Some of you may know some of what I am about to brief, and most of you have flown the Trail many times, so if at any point I miss something, speak up." He walked to the podium.

"You have been used to whipping along at Warp Nine, hitting a target clearly marked by a FAC, and hauling ass. But now, to successfully operate on the Trail, you have to completely change your way of thinking from strike pilot to Forward Air Controller. You are controlling, not being controlled. To control means being in charge. You are the main man. You send colonels home if they are not performing well or correctly. But before you can control anything, there is quite a bit of material you have to know. And it must be memorized. You have neither the time nor the light to review notes or maps." He smiled. "First off you have to find a target. You are not fragged for a target, as you have been used to, you have to find your own. This can be a serious problem, depending on the weather and the lighting conditions. During the full-moon phase it isn't necessary to flare a target unless the definition is poor. Ideal light is when the moon phase is between the second and last quarter. This gives you enough light to see the road network from the air, but not enough for the trucks to run without lights. This doesn't happen often. What you get varies from max black when you are under an overcast with no moon, to full-moon clear sky. Under a full moon the roads are readily visible but the trucks run without lights. Under these conditions you must learn to differentiate between stationary shadows that appear to move because you are moving and actual moving shadows.

"During moonless conditions you may pick up the glow of the truck lights, but not the roads. A word on the lights. They, of course, are not the kind of high-beam, low-beam lights we are used to on stateside highways. Instead, they are little narrow slit lights, sometimes blue, that themselves are not visible, but the light they cast is. They are attached under the front bumper and give the driver only a few feet of visibility. They often get ripped off or shorted out in streams. You can see the light from them better by crossing perpendicular to the road at random intervals. At difficult spots sometimes women carrying white marker-cloths line the side of the road to help the drivers. But when a truck is hit beyond repair, it is just pushed to the side or tumbled down the mountain. Often with the dead driver still inside. The political commissars are supposed to write the guy's name, home village, and date of birth on a piece of paper, stuff it in a penicillin bottle, and put it in his mouth. The commissars were issued a real French ballpoint pen to do this. Helluva way to run a railroad." He made a face.

"That's not all. We carry a heavy burden around here. We have three categories of rules. We have the ROE, Rules of Engagement. These are from the JCS and define what we can and cannot hit, harass, harry, or blow up. Then we have the ORs, Operating Restrictions. These are from CINCPAC and define what we can and cannot hit, harass, harry, or blow up. Finally, we have the Seventh ORs, Seventh Air Force Operating Restrictions from Tan Son Nhut that define what we can and cannot hit, harass, harry, or blow up. They tell us that all these rules are national policy translated for battlefield use. We lump them all together and call them the ROE. Every time the government talks to someone from North Vietnam, or every time McNamara has a new message to send to Ho Chi Minh, the ROEs change, usually for the worse."

"Heavy burden is right," Duckcall Donny Higgens said. "Like a lead parachute."

"Then there is the Basic Operations Order from the AIRA in Vientiane," Toby said.

"The BOO," Higgens said. "Sounds about right. What's an AIRA?"

"The AIRA is the Air Attache to the American Embassy in Vientiane. He has to respond to the Ambassador, who, by Presidential Directive, is responsible for supporting the RLG – the Royal Lao Government. That's in northern Laos, mostly the PDJ area, the Plaine des Jarres, code-named Barrel Roll. There are three armed recce zones there. It's another story in southern Laos, the panhandle area code-named Steel Tiger. First it was divided into seven recce zones, then three, now four. Each has its own BOO and ROE. Our area of operation, along the Ho Chi Minh Trail, runs through Steel Tiger. No one can hit anything over two hundred meters from the Trail without AIRA approval and FAC control. West of Steel Tiger no one can hit anything without AIRA permission, and then they have to be controlled by a Nail or Raven FAC."

"Jesus Christ," Partin said in disgust.

"Yeah, probably Him too," Toby replied. "You have to memorize all these and be tested on them before you are authorized to control strikes along the Trail."

He went on to explain No Bomb Lines – NBLs around suspected POW camps; restricted areas around RWTs – American Road Watch Teams on the ground in Laos to recce the Trail; what ordnance was restricted in what zones (no Mk-36 mines or M-28 Gravel without photo justification); a special operating area called Cricket West; restricted areas; Yankee Team ops; Chinese road builders in PDJ Zone 3 West: no Arc Lights (B-52s) in SALOA's (Special Arc Light Operating Areas) without AIRA permission, which could take up to fifteen days; the requirements under MACV Directive 525-13 and 7th Air Force Reg 55-49; Short Round (friendly fire) reporting; no strikes within 1,000 meters of shrines, temples, national monuments, places of worship, active huts or villages – none of which were in the Steel Tiger area anyhow.

"Magnificent! But it isn't war," Higgens said, in a heavy accent parodying the French general at Balaclava.

"One wonders," Toby said. "One fucking wonders." He pulled out a card. "Now let's go over what you must know and be prepared to brief the incoming strike pilots on."

384

ALTIMETER SETTING
WIND DIRECTION AND SPEED
HIGHEST TERRAIN ELEVATION WITHIN
    TEN MILES
BEST BAILOUT AREA DIRECTION AND
    DISTANCE
TARGET DESCRIPTION
TARGET ELEVATION
RUN-IN AND PULL-OFF HEADINGS
ORDNANCE TO USE
AAA SIZE AND LOCATION
FAC LOCATION

"You get the altimeter setting from Moonbeam, who gets it from some spook on the ground. You must estimate the wind at ground level by seeing what happens to your smoke, and at flight level by drift of your airplane. Everything else is self-explanatory except FAC location. You and the strike birds are flying blacked-out. It's not like the daytime, when each strike pilot is required to have the FAC in sight before he rolls in. You must either be over the strikers or well off to one side. Whatever the terrain and weather dictate.

"Use common sense when it comes to marking targets. Don't mark moving targets until you have the strike flight about ready to roll in. Serves two purposes: the targets might move too far away from the mark by the time the strikers are ready, and it tips off the enemy that ordnance is on the way. Try to have two prominent features to use as a yardstick. Telling a striker to hit one hundred meters north of your mark isn't as explicit as telling him to hit twice or half the distance between two objects, such as two smokes or your smoke and the river."

Toby rested his elbows on the podium. "As to whom and what is actually on the Trail, let's start with the North Vietnamese soldiers, your basic NVA. As minimum load each man carries a tubular sack of rice slung around his torso and a knapsack with thirty pounds of other food, medicine, extra clothes, a hammock, and a waterproof sheet. On top of that he carries his weapon and ammunition. When he arrives at the Laotian border, his North Vietnamese Army uniform is exchanged for that of a Lao neutralist. This is to maintain the fiction there are no NVA soldiers in Laos. He is supposed to give up all personal effects, but few do. We've found scads of personal stuff on bodies. A local guide takes him halfway to the first of a series of way stations, called *binh trans* in Vietnamese, along the HCT. There he is met by the next guide, until he is in South Vietnam. These posts are linked by telephone wire to keep radio transmissions down. In South Vietnam he receives a set of black civilian pajamas, two unmarked NVA uniforms, a sweater, a hammock, mosquito netting and waterproof sheeting, a rucksack, a water canteen, two cans of insecticide, and one hundred malaria pills. This weighs about sixty-five pounds. After being issued a five-day supply of food, he is assigned to an operational unit and sent on his way. They travel from dusk until midnight, resting ten minutes every hour. They stop every third day to hunt, fish, and rest. They walk at six-meter intervals in the forest and fifty meters in the open.

"Next we have the human pack animals. They can be men or women. They either tote a sixty-pound load or they push a bicycle. Along parts of the Trail many of these bikes carry three to four hundred pounds. They steer them by sticks attached to the seat and handlebars. In the mountain sections they press-gang mountain tribesmen as load-bearers. Their motto is, 'Walk without tracks, cook without smoke, speak without sound.' There are no villages along the Trail to replenish supplies. But there are hundreds of supply caches and manned outposts for truck repair, road repair, antiaircraft sites, and underground hospitals. This information, by the way, comes from controlled American sources and Special Forces teams on the ground, prisoners of war, and SI and SPARS, which is Signal Intelligence and Special Aerial and Radio Sources."

He pointed to a recce photo. "This picture looks like just

jungle canopy. Yet we know from a road-watch team there is really a truck park underneath. Truck drivers attach freshly cut foliage, palm fronds, and banana leaves to their vehicles. Jeep drivers weave leaves into nets stretched over their vehicles. Some of the maintenance people climb into trees and place fresh-woven green nets over the upper limbs that stretch over the entire park. They fabricate double- and triple-canopy jungle with fresh foliage every day. When they drive, they leave the nets over their vehicles to use at the next park." He tapped the photo. "The reason we knew so much about this particular park was because a road-watch team was spying on it for three days. They even took before-and-after pictures from their position on the ground. Based on their coordinates and time frame, we blew it away shortly after the recce photo was taken. Here is the poststrike photo. With all the camouflage torn and blown away, you can see clearly the burned-out truck bodies."

He pointed to other photos. "They have many ways to deceive the day FACs. They make papier-mâché trucks, phony roads and pipelines, bridges built just below the water level so they can't be seen from the air, fires to disorient infrared systems, and faked explosions near trucks to make the FAC think they have destroyed it. Or they'll build a fake bridge at the obvious point, then conceal the real one farther up or down stream under two feet of water. At night they might set off decoy fires or phony explosions to draw you away from the real storage place.

"The *binh tran* truck parks and stations are placed about every twenty miles or so. A station launches a truck convoy south, then calls the next station up north and says he's ready to receive. They leave after dark and try to be at the next *binh tran* before daylight. The same shift of drivers drive the same bit of Trail back and forth with the same vehicle. That way they know the road and its problems like their own village neighborhood." Toby indicated some pictures that looked like a sandy version of a moonscape. "These are a few of the choke points we blast every day and they repair every night. Based on intelligence reports, we estimate there are about 600,000 people on the Trail at any given time. The majority are support people, not movers. Of the support people, we estimate 200,000 are road-repair crews." There were expressions of surprise from the audience.

"Because of the daytime interdiction strikes, the open portions of the Trail, which comprise about twenty percent of the route structure, are closed. This causes most of the trucks to hole up. During that time loads are shifted, repairs are made, drivers rest. By the way, there are women drivers. It's also during that time the day FACs and the others look for those truck parks. They don't have much luck. A little hint from the FACs: look for small open areas that look like vegetable gardens. They probably are. Except for rice shipped to them, these drivers must live off the land and will try to grow food in gardens, and gardens need sunlight. Back to the trucks – and this is the point – the trucks do not drive one inch in the daytime in the open areas. Secondly, driving at night cuts about fifteen percent movement because it is dark and the drivers don't want to turn on even the slit lights if they hear an airplane. If the day FACs stop the movement in the open areas during the day, and you Phantom FACs stop it at night, then we'll put some real hurt on them." Toby pulled out some new charts.

"About defenses. Most are 14.7mm, 23mm quad-barrel ZSUs, and 37mm single-barrel guns. There is a rumor of a 100mm by Delta 32, but no hard intell as yet. So far they are not radar-directed, but they are plain mean. The gunners are good. In the daylight they can track an airplane at one-thousand-feet altitude flying five hundred knots. That's manual tracking by the Mark One, Mod Zero Viet nine-level gunner's eyeball. At night it's a different story. They actually have giant ears to pick up the sound of our engines. They have modified what the VC and the NVA do in South Vietnam. They dig bowl-shaped holes about six feet across and seat a guy in the center. Some are in hillsides, some on the flats. The ones on hillsides face different directions to give better azimuth readings

388

of the inbound fighters." Toby put his hands on his hips. "About those guns. You must protect your strike pilots. They need to know where the guns are. Since it isn't as easy as the daytime, when you might spot them even before they shoot, at night you must make them illuminate themselves." He grinned. "Only one way to do that – make them shoot at you. Believe me, sometimes they light up the sky like Times Square. Other times all you see is pinpricks of light on black velvet. You backseaters have got to log where those guns are. The only way you can do that is know the area like the back of your hand. It ain't easy, guys, but there is a way. There always is. In this case it's gaining experience, but gaining it the hard way. You just go out and do it."

Toby stopped and looked around. "That's about it for now. Any questions?"

"How many tons a day on the Trail?" Grailson asked.

"During the dry season, about two hundred tons per day in motion from one end of Laos to the other. Note I said dry season. Weather is a big factor. The dry season runs from October through May, the wet season from June through September. We've got three good months to stop those trucks before the weather does."

"Any SAMs out there yet?" Neil Tallboy asked.

"No. But that's not to say there won't be. They could be in place tomorrow." Toby scanned the crewmen. There were no more questions. Court took over.

"We have two rooms in this building we've got to fix up for ourselves. They were storerooms just off the big Wing Intelligence map room. Rolly, it's special-project time. Get some of the troops, scrounge up whatever you need to set up our Phantom FAC area." He looked at his watch. "It's nearly ten. You've got all day. Have the rooms ready for business by tomorrow night. Although we're on a training schedule with the Wolfs and the Night Owls, I want us to have our own squadron area. Meanwhile, you guys get your sleep schedules flip-flopped. Noon is now midnight and vice versa. One last thing. I'm having a long talk with the support people. I want us to have our own hooch, since

389

we're all on the same schedule. Right now you guys are scattered around the squadrons. I'm planning on getting us all together within a few days. Meanwhile get all your daytime personal stuff taken care of. Howie Joseph and I are flying tonight. It's time I get started on my twenty Night Owl missions. That's it. You're dismissed."

21

"Oh, baby, why won't you go to bed with me? You're
so cute. I'll bet you're a great lover. But, hey, let's have
another toke, what say?" The dark-haired girl pouted and
swayed on her feet as she spoke to Michael LaNew. LaNew
sat on the frayed couch in her apartment, which had once
been tastefully furnished. Now, rough wear and lack of
cleaning gave the rooms the appearance of a fourth-rate
flophouse. Dirty mattresses were scattered about, some flat,
some bent against walls. The cloying smell of the burning
incense didn't quite cover the ropy smell of marijuana and
stale vomit. Several couples were scattered about, crashed
in drugged stupor or arguing the merits of grass over
mescaline. Sitar music whined up and down, low lights
glowed. These were serious followers of Doctor Timothy
Leary's turn-on, tune-in, drop-out philosophy.

LaNew took a pull at a pint of brandy. He wore
sunglasses, blue jeans, a rough denim shirt, and a dirty
suitcoat two sizes too large for him. His quick but deep
research in response to the call from Gant on Shawn
Bannister had turned up the background on the founders of
the Peace and Power to the People Party. Alexander Torpin
was one founder; this woman, Becky Blinn, swaying in front
of him, was another. He discovered Torpin was still active

and powerful, a man very much in control of himself and his destiny. He was strong in the party, perhaps controlled it.

It was not the same for Becky Blinn. Through careful research, help from the neighborhood police precinct, and sly local questions, LaNew had found out she had become far too strung-out on drugs to be of any benefit whatsoever to herself, much less to the party. She lived now by charging the locals only handfuls of grass, and whatever pills they had, to use her crash pad. She was a dying woman and smelled bad.

LaNew took another swallow of his brandy. He wished he had some wintergreen to rub under his nose. "Sure," he said. "I'm a good lover. The best. You want some pot first? Okay with me." He patted a pocket in his coat. "But you haven't answered my questions about Shawn Bannister." He had been feeding her some good stuff for over six hours, ever since he had appeared, as nameless as the others, at her door.

"Why you so innerested in that bassar, anyhow?" Becky Blinn sat down suddenly in the center of the floor. "Come on, give us something," she said in a wheedling voice.

LaNew pulled some thick marijuana cigarettes from a box in his pocket. "Sure, babe, sure." He held one just out of reach. "All you got to do is tell me how you got it on with Shawn Bannister."

"You keep asking that," she whined. "Is that how *you* get off? Hearing about the others?"

"Maybe. Who cares? You want some more of this stuff, you got to talk."

"Come on, baby. Give me some and we'll get it on, you and me. The hell with him." She reached for the cigarette. LaNew pulled it back.

"Okay," she said. "Okay. You wanna hear about him? He was freaky, a real space cadet. Finally had to toss him out of here. Here's how it was." She started to talk.

LaNew slid his hand into a pocket of his coat and flicked on the tiny switch of the tape recorder. He was careful not to rustle his clothes and flood the mike, covering her

392

words. Using interrogation skills learned in the OSI, he led her along the paths and into the details he wanted.

"Yeah," she said after a long description of bizarre sexual events, "he wanted all that. An' we did it. Hey, he used to give us money too, you know. Lots of money, every month. Din' even have ta use the pichures," she slurred.

"Pictures? Tell me about the pictures." LaNew was very alert and solicitous.

"Good old Torp had a hin cam – " She belched. "Hin camera and took some ziz wow pichures. Ri' up his ass," she cackled. As she went on, she sank lower and lower onto the floor. LaNew had to get off the couch and kneel close to her. When she closed her eyes and began mumbling, he took the chance and pulled the microphone from behind his lapel and held it near her lips. He coaxed a few more details from her, made sure she reaffirmed they were talking about Shawn Bannister, and sat back when she lost all consciousness. Thin drool seeped from a corner of her mouth. He checked her pulse and heartbeat and sat back on his heels. Her face was the color of old rice. She would last a while longer: a week, a month, a year perhaps.

The music sawed and droned. LaNew pulled out a Minox, snapped a few very high ASA black-and-whites of her and the room, then got to his feet and started searching. Careful to leave no fingerprints, stepping over drugged bodies, leaving mumblings behind him, he searched the entire apartment and found nothing.

LaNew finally left the rancid rooms, carefully closing the door. A black man lurched against the wall as he went down the dark hall lit only by a pale bulb.

"Hey, bro, wha's happ-ning?" the man said.

"Not much, man. Not much," Michael LaNew replied as he went out the door to the street.

1000 Hours Local, Monday 19 February 1968
The Emerson Building, Haight Street
Berkeley, California

Michael LaNew stood across the street from the Emerson Building, the five-story brick structure that housed the office of the Peace and Power to the People Party. He wore the same clothes and was tired and dirty. He had been up all night clearing up the tape and working with the Minox negatives in his portable lab. It wasn't the first time his photography hobby had come in handy.

He stared at the office across the street. The building, sturdy and well-built, had been constructed at the turn of the century. As with the others, it had been designed with a storefront on the bottom floor and apartments above. The stores now were mixed. They sold nature foods, old-time clothes with beads, psychedelic trappings, and drug paraphernalia; others were launderettes, Zen churches, counseling services, and coffee shops. Drugstores, dry-cleaning shops, and small markets had moved out because they couldn't sell enough to stay in business and couldn't prevent shoplifting. All the apartments were shoddy, since rent control didn't allow landlords enough money to keep them fixed up. Several radios tuned to the same radio station flooded the streets with acid rock.

The windows of the shop on the ground floor of the Emerson Building were emblazoned with large pictures of Shawn Bannister, and with signs proclaiming his running for assemblyman as the candidate from the Peace and Power to the People Party. The picture was the blowup of one taken in Vietnam, where he had been wearing a tiger suit and holding a camera while crouched by a piece of shrubbery. LaNew thought he recognized the shrubbery as some located behind the Continental Hotel in Saigon.

LaNew checked his watch. It had taken several days to arrange a meeting with the man he had arrested for spying less than a year before. He had had less trouble seeing Becky Blinn the night before.

"LaNew?" Shawn Bannister had said on the telephone. "Michael LaNew? The cop who busted me on false charges in Thailand? Why should I see you?"

LaNew had prepared a noncommittal answer that he hoped would pique Shawn's curiosity. "It would be in your best interests to see me. I don't want to say any more on the telephone." With that, Shawn agreed to the meeting.

LaNew crossed the street and entered the office. It was crowded and bustling. Several people, male and female, in jeans and granny dresses, were using telephones, writing flyers, painting signs, working a mimeograph machine.

Shawn recognized LaNew and went to him without offering to shake hands.

"Is this an official visit?" he asked. "Because if it is, you'd better present your credentials." Several burly men with long hair stared with obvious hostility at LaNew as they looked up from their duties.

"I am no longer in the Air Force," LaNew said.

Shawn regarded LaNew's clothes. "Are you an undercover narc? Or with any government agency whatsoever?" he asked.

"No."

Shawn Bannister flashed his famous smile. "Then what do you want? A job?" He gave a short laugh. "Because if you do, I can always use a smart man like yourself. A man who has been there and who has seen the follies and failures of our policies in Vietnam." He smiled again. "Is that how it is? You want a job?"

"No, I don't want a job." LaNew looked around. "Let's go someplace where we can talk."

Shawn said a few words to one of the men and went out the door with LaNew. Moments later they sat on rugs at a table with sawed-off legs in a coffee house.

"Okay, LaNew, what is it that is in my best interests to hear?" Shawn spoke in a sarcastic tone.

"It pertains to the statements you made at Ubon."

395

"So? You let me go. You had to. I wasn't doing anything wrong. The Air Force itself admitted that."

"It was when you were talking about freedom of the press and how you reported on both sides. You said you were taken into the tunnels under Cholon to interview a VC colonel."

"That's right. They were a hell of a lot more polite and cooperative than you were. They're organized, they've got a plan, and, most important, they all know they are right. The Americans don't."

LaNew waved his hand. "I'm not here to debate the war or to listen to your views. You said you saw a man with the VC colonel who was referred to by your guide as the Lizard."

"I did?" Shawn looked both doubtful and defensive.

LaNew pulled a 3 × 7 black-and-white photo from his pocket. It was a blowup of Buey Dan's ID photo from the MACSOG file. He placed it on the table facing Shawn. Although Shawn barely glanced at it, LaNew saw his eyes flicker in recognition.

"Who is that?" Shawn asked.

"You tell me."

Shawn flicked the photo back to LaNew.

"Haven't the foggiest."

"I think you do."

Shawn glanced at his watch. "You don't have my interest at all. I've got to go." He started to rise.

LaNew grabbed his wrist and forced him back down. "Maybe I should have played this first," he said. He pulled a small tape recorder from his jacket pocket and flicked the on switch.

"Yeah," came the slurred voice of Becky Blinn, "I know that Shawn Bannister. Let me tell you what that basser likes." She giggled and began to recite some of the rank and raunchy exotic delights involving, among other things, peanut butter, fried eggs, and turkey feathers that made Shawn Bannister scream and cry out in joy.

Shawn's self-conscious grin faded to a scowl. "Gimme

that." He grabbed the recorder and slammed it onto the rug. The other patrons barely looked up. They were used to sudden and irrational behavior.

LaNew made a mocking smile. "I have more."

Shawn straightened his back and looked down at LaNew. "You don't have any plans to blackmail me, I hope. I might be running for office, but my constituents would find this quite amusing, actually." He didn't speak with much conviction.

LaNew grinned broadly and spoke in a mimicking voice. "Actually, yes. I do have plans to blackmail you."

"I'm leaving."

"As liberal as your constituency might be, I think they would be appalled to find you like to crawl around on your hands and knees with turkey feathers stuck up your ass while some naked girl with spurs on rides you like a horse."

"This is ridiculous," Shawn Bannister said in a thick voice, and swallowed twice. "Why should they care?"

"I think they would always wonder if you'd ever be found crawling around the Capitol halls with an assful of turkey feathers."

Shawn blinked rapidly. "You've got no proof. That tape could be a phony."

LaNew leaned forward and spoke in a voice so soft that Shawn had to lean forward. "Listen, turkey snot, you give me what I want or the *California Sun*, Democratic headquarters, and your public will get more than just the tape. They will get a blowup of this." He pulled a photo from his jacket and placed it on the table.

Shawn looked down at it and let out a little squeak. It was a blurry photo of a naked man on all fours in Becky Blinn's living room. He quickly looked away. Perspiration burst out on his forehead. "Who took that?" he moaned. He didn't see the gleam of satisfaction in LaNew's eyes. LaNew still felt strange from crawling around naked in front of the low tripod, holding his Minox on self-timer. It wasn't too difficult to superimpose the results on the shot of Becky Blinn's apartment.

"That guy Torpin was filming you all the time," LaNew said, and quickly took the picture back. His bluff had worked, and he didn't want Shawn to study the faked photo. Shawn Bannister saw what he had forced himself to see – himself, doing what he knew he had been doing.

"Okay, okay," Shawn croaked. "What do you want from me? Money. You want money? Is that it?"

"No, Shawn," LaNew said in a kindly voice. Once you broke them, you were nice to them to gain their confidence. "All I want is a little information . . ."

2000 Hours Local, Saturday 17 February 1968
8th Tactical Fighter Wing
Ubon Royal Thai Air Force Base
Kingdom of Thailand

Court Bannister and Howie Joseph met in the Intelligence Briefing room at eight P.M., the time shown on the big military wall clock as 2000 hours. They sat down across from Major Dick Hostettler, one of the Wing intelligence officers. Hostettler was a powerful man, who worked out at the base gym each day. He could bench-press 240 easily and run a mile in six and a half minutes. He had been a guard on the West Point team and a former assistant line coach at the Air Force Academy. He also had the extra duty as manager of the Ubon Officer's Club.

"Very little activity tonight, gentlemen. There was an Arc Light strike about twenty miles south of Mu Gia. No secondary fires or explosions counted. Some thirty-seven triple-A reported near Ban Karai by a Blindbat C-130 aircraft." Arc Light was code for B-52 strikes.

"No belches or farts tonight, Dick?" Court asked. Hostettler was known for his more-than-dynamic, positively scatological briefings for strike missions up in North Vietnam. He used belches to denote AAA; the louder and more

398

sonorous the belch, the higher the caliber. And he used farts for MiGs.

"Only for the hairy ones up north, partner. Takes too much out of me." He pointed to the Steel Tiger area. "We are getting much better intell from Special Forces teams on the ground as Trail watchers. Took them a while to get squared away, but now the info is accurate and fast. The guys are on what we call X-Ray teams. They get comm with some clandestine radio-relay stations in Laos and pass on what they have." He listed several coordinates in the WE (Whiskey Echo) grid and drew a red circle five nautical miles in diameter around the points. "These are NBLs – No Bomb Lines. Between information from the X-Ray Teams and recce photos, we think these are locations of POW holding sites."

"Think?" Joseph said. "Don't we know?"

"Good question. I don't think we know for sure. No one seems to be able to get close enough to actually see white faces in the caves at these points. All the photos depict are flight gear near the cave mouths, as if it had been washed and was laying out to dry. The photo interpreters definitely ID-ed flight suits and issue boots. Your guess is as good as mine. Is the gear worn by the North Vietnamese or Pathet Lao? Maybe some Russian Spetsnaz troops are running around up there. Sometimes we've heard perfect American English spoken on the radio, but the talker never identifies himself properly. Or are there really POWs in the caves? We don't know, so we don't bomb around there." He looked at Phantom One, the flight card for Court and Howie Joseph. "Speaking of bombing, what are you guys doing up there tonight? I don't see you fragged on any target."

"Just an orientation flight to exercise the system," Court said. "See if we have the right configuration of fuel tank and rockets, see if all the tankers are on station, see if we are taking on enough fuel for running around the Trail at low altitude, see if we can really see anything at night."

"See how badly we can scare ourselves and still do the job," Joseph said.

"And your job is to find trucks," Hostettler said.

"And guns," Court answered.

"Well, I bet you find a lot more guns than trucks," Hostettler said. "I think they've got gun sites up there we haven't even logged in yet because they won't come up until something big happens."

"What makes you think that?" Joseph asked.

"Part intuition, part hard intell. There are hundreds of big guns being towed down the Trail, but the AAA reports we get from the pilots don't seem to account for all of them. Particularly a hundred-millimeter gun I think is in the Mu Gia area. I saw on a recce photo what looked like the gun being trucked south through the Pass into the area."

"Trucked in?" Joseph said. "I thought guns that big were mounted on wheels and towed."

"That's true," Hostettler said. "That's why nobody else thinks it's a gun. The powers that be in the Twelfth Ritz in Saigon say the tube I saw is just pipe for a gas line to refuel the trucks. Although it's never been done before, I think they might have dismantled the gun and are bringing it down in segments. Some parts of the Trail in the mountains in North Vietnam are too narrow in the switchbacks and sharp curves to tow a long tube through."

"So," Court said, "we have a phantom hundred-millimeter gun and suspected POW sites out there. What else do we have?"

"Big black karst all along the Trail that rises up over a mile in the black sky and will BITE YOU ON THE ASS," Hostettler said, waving his hands curled in claws like an attacking demon.

"Thanks a hell of a lot, Dick," Joseph said. He and Court started picking up their flight gear. The two pilots started toward the door.

"Very fucking funny," Court said as they went out.

"Invert, Phantom One blackout at the fence," Joseph transmitted an hour later as they crossed from Thailand into Laos. He had the front seat, Court sat in back. They flew at 22,000 feet, full of fuel from the Cherry tanker.

"You're awful quiet back there," Joseph said to Court. "Remember, you said you *wanted* the backseat. Said you had to see the Trail at night from the GIB's point of view. Do you sleep on nails at night, too? Wear a hair shirt?"

"Nuts to you, Joseph. Since you're my ops officer, I'm really here to see if you can fly worth a shit." Court checked his map and the INS against the Tacan. "So far you seem to be doing okay. That should be Mu Gia down there dead ahead at twelve o'clock for twenty. Isn't that right?"

"Is the Pope a Catholic?"

Faint starlight from the sky supplied just enough contrast with the pitch black of the ground to provide a barely perceptible horizon. Below and twenty miles ahead of them, running north and south, crossing from left to right, rose the mass of the Annamite mountain chain. Court adjusted the radar set to paint the difference between the terrain and the few rivers that provided suitable contrast. The faint glow of the screen blossomed slightly as the nose-mounted antenna swept back and forth.

"Okay," he said, "that's Mu Gia. Let's start down. Switches on, cockpit lights off."

Joseph turned his weapons switches on, brought both throttles back to 85 percent RPM, lowered the nose, aimed the red lamp at his flight attitude indicator, and cut the cockpit lights off. In back, Court kept his instrument lights as dim as possible and monitored the navigation instruments and the flight instruments.

Court called out the altitude as they descended. His primary job was to keep his head in the cockpit to monitor safety of flight by checking the gages. His secondary job was to look outside and help the frontseater find a target. Smart front- and backseaters coordinated who was looking where, and when.

"Level at seven point five," Court called as Joseph leveled off. Because the elevation of Mu Gia Pass was 5,300 feet, they had selected a 2,200-foot safety margin above the ground to get oriented. They had to make sure they were where they wanted to be, then they could let down farther, even lower than the surrounding karst. Unless the guns went wild. Then they would re-assess – upwards. Quickly, very quickly. Court checked his radar screen.

"Okay," he said. "We're coming up on the Bird's Head. That's Mu Gia over there at eleven o'clock for five nautical." The Bird's Head was a series of prominent bends in the river that looked like a bird's head, beak and all.

"Tally," Joseph said, using the shortened form of the ancient Tally Ho that has never left the fighter pilot's lexicon since World War One. "Taking it down." He pushed the throttles to 92 percent and lowered the nose. Trading 5,000 feet of altitude for airspeed put the black Phantom at 2,500 feet above the ground at an indicated airspeed of 500 knots (575 miles per hour). They were below the mountaintops now, and were south of the milehigh karst at Mu Gia.

"Let's cross the Bird's Head, cut across the mouth of the Pass west to east, pickle three flares, then pull up north and fly back over the Pass heading west," Court ordered. "We'll see what we can see."

Mu Gia Pass opened like a funnel from north to south. The narrow end, a half-mile in width where the supply trucks entered, was in North Vietnam. The wide end, where they fanned out onto the Trail, was in Laos, and was three miles across. Under the current rules of engagement the fighters could fly only in Laos. They could not cross into North Vietnam unless specifically fragged to do so by the Secretary of Defense, Robert Strange McNamara. They could attack the trucks coming through the Pass, but not the trucks bunched up in North Vietnam waiting to enter the narrow end of Mu Gia Pass.

Joseph zoomed across the Bird's Head and punched the red button on his control stick three times as he shot across the wide mouth of Mu Gia. Then he pulled up sharply to the left and crossed the Pass from east to west. Court checked the gages, saw that Joseph had everything under control, and looked out of the left side of the canopy down at the Pass.

One by one, the parachutes popped out of the silver canister of each flare and opened. The tug on the shroud lines triggered the igniter inside the canisters, which set off the magnesium to burn so hot that the fierce white light registered at 200,000 candlepower. All three hung swaying in their chutes, dripping pieces of burning metal, etching white smoke trails against the black sky, broad-casting light like miniature suns.

Below, the Pass lit up in the intense white light like a two-dimensional photo negative. Narrow strips of dirt road hacked out of the mountainsides ran parallel along each side of the huge ravine. Three more strips meandered along the river in the Vee of the Pass. They saw black objects crawling along the strips like rectangular caterpillars.

"Hey, hey, hey," Court crowed in exultation. "Lookee what we have here. I count . . . ah, twelve, thirteen, fourteen of those beauties."

"Let's git 'em," Joseph yelled.

"Quick, before the flares burn out," Court said. "Never thought we'd be self-FACing ourselves. Too bad we don't have something a bit better than 48s."

Howie Joseph selected the CBU-48 on his weapons panel. The -48 was the clamshell weapon that opened at a preset altitude and flung CBU bomblets in a wide circle. It was a fine weapon for flak suppression against gunners in gun pits, but not too effective against hard targets like trucks. Joseph slammed his throttles forward, pulled up and around to make his run south to north, perpendicular to the flares but parallel to the strips of road.

"Twelve thousand feet, three-fifty knots," Court read from the instrument panel to let Joseph know where he was relative to his bomb run. The flares were close to the ground, near the end of their illumination time.

"Rolling in," Joseph said. He started down the chute of a 45-degree bomb run heading north.

"Ninety-five, eighty-five, ready, ready . . . PICKLE," Court said as they passed through 7,500 feet. He felt and heard the "chung-chung" as Joseph punched off two CBUs.

He grunted as Joseph pulled up and jinked left, right, then left again. By then each flare had hit the ground. All was pitch dark.

Suddenly the sky lit up above them as an explosive fireball blossomed over their heads, then two more, then a fourth, then a fifth.

"Oh Christ, that's 37 and they got our track," Joseph said with effort against the G-forces.

"Not for long," Court said. They looked down in the blackness from the turning plane as the bomblets of the first CBU began sparkling in a multibanded circle like a ring of fiery diamonds. Then the second batch hit the ground, overlapping the first. Immediately, several medium red fires sprang up, then scores of small, quick secondary explosions that flashed red and orange, then winked out. The red fires grew larger.

"We got a gun pit," Court said, "and some, ah . . . three trucks." He recognized the rectangular red fires as trucks, and the quick, sharp, yellow explosions within the red as ammunition cooking off.

Joseph pulled up to orbit west of the target at 15,000.

"Too bad we don't have a way to take a picture at night," he said. "Nobody will believe . . . My God," he said in an awed voice as a huge orange-and-yellow explosion lit up the sky in front and just below them. They heard the boom in the cockpit.

"Break left, break left!" Court yelled as they buffeted in the concussion of the huge antiaircraft shell. He thought he heard tings as pieces of metal banged against their Phantom. Another fireball exploded behind the first and to the right.

"Tighter, pull it tighter," Court said. A third exploded farther to the right, exactly where they had been.

"How 'bout that shit," Howie Joseph said. "I think we just found that hundred-millimeter gun."

"*Au contraire*. They just found us," Court replied.

22

1630 Hours Local, Tuesday 20 February 1968
Hoa Lo Prison, Hanoi
Democratic Republic of Vietnam

Flak heard tapping on the wall from Ted Frederick's cell. He lay flat on the floor to look under the door and check the passageway outside. When he saw nothing, he moved to put his ear to the wall.

HELLO, HELLO, he heard in the tap code. He didn't answer.

HELLO, HELLO, was repeated louder. Flak quickly lay back on his cot, hands behind his head. He listened for noise at his door.

HELLO, AL, LETS TALC. HELLO. Flak heard faint noise outside his door. He didn't move.

HELLO, HELLO. After a while he heard soft footsteps going away from his door and no more tapping on the wall. The trick to catch him communicating hadn't worked. The guards had never learned that all POWs signed on with the "shave-and-a-haircut" taps. No POW communicated without that secret challenge and response ever since one man had been caught tapping back when called up by a communist official who had learned the tap code.

He dozed, taking advantage of his sudden lenient treatment put into effect by Ceballos. Normally the POWs were not allowed to be on their sleeping devices until bedtime was announced around nine P.M. by a guard banging a metal rod on a piece of resonant metal hanging from a tree in the courtyard. Someone who rapped it was called a tocsin. The gonglike sounds controlled the life of the POWs in Hoa Lo: get up, eat, sleep. In between were the propaganda broadcasts from the loudspeakers hanging all around the camp, some hanging in cells.

Flak arose and slowly began his exercises. He had to ease through the pain layers. First he walked 300 round trips from the cell door to the rear of the cell and back. From the door to the wall took three strides, which Flak estimated at nine feet. Three hundred round trips at eighteen feet each meant at least one mile had been covered. He had gotten his mind to the point where it could automatically count paces and round trips and still be thinking of another subject. The only problem he had was turning around. He wanted to alternate turning left and right, but frequently forgot and kept turning one direction until a warning bell went off in his mind. The bell was getting less frequent, he noted, which meant he would soon be alternating exactly as planned.

After his mile, which he estimated required twenty minutes, he performed sixty situps. He had been increasing them at the rate of two more each day.

Then he rolled over for push-ups. They were extremely difficult. Without medical attention, his left arm had healed crookedly and had a bulge where the bone had been broken. He had to rely almost entirely on his right arm, and so far was able to do only twelve push-ups. When he finished, he flexed his fingers from full out, then back to a fist as fast as he could. His left fist would not completely close. He could manage 175 before his hands locked up.

Then he ran in place for 420 steps. That, too, was increasing – about thirty paces a day. As he ran, he performed isometrics with his fists and palms.

When he was finished, he paced his cell slowly to cool down and prevent stiffening. He was proud of himself. This was his second set of exercises for the day. He had eased into the exercises as soon as he wasn't locked in the stocks all day. He realized he had to do something constructive each day to make the time pass and to feel good about himself.

Then it was afternoon matinee time, as Flak called it. He climbed up on his concrete sleeping slab facing the rear wall. He leaned forward to rest on his hands and peer out the bottom of the boarded-over tiny window at the top of the wall. Through a crack, he gazed around a small section of the courtyard. Sometimes he saw POWs walking alone to and from the stone bathhouse, other times he saw POWs escorted for a quiz, as they called interrogations. Today he saw a lone man sweeping the yard. He was young, very thin, and swept with a peculiar rhythm. He coughed and cleared his throat so much Flak thought him to be ill. Then Flak caught on. This was the famed sailor who had fallen off his cruiser one night in the Gulf of Tonkin. Frederick had tapped about him. His name was Hegdahl and he was considered stupid by his captors. So much so, in fact, they had him frequently outside performing menial tasks. Flak listened carefully. Hegdahl was quietly whistling "God Bless America" while passing camp news with signals from his broom and throat. So many sweeps and a hack, more sweeps and a cough, then more sweeps, and Flak and all the rest who heard this amazing young seaman apprentice got a good portion of the news of the day.

Frederick had taught Flak that one cough equaled one tap; two coughs equaled two taps; clearing the throat was three taps; a cough and a spit four taps; clearing the throat and spitting was five taps. A hock-tooey and a cough was a V. Hegdahl transmitted the news.

GUARINO IN STOCCS AT ZOO BEARING UP.

STRATTON SEZ BACCUS.

NEW GUYS SAY US GIRLS WEAR VERY SHORT SCIRTS CALLED MINI.

Flak didn't know who Stratton was or what BACCUS meant. He knew Guarino was a tough SRO. When Hegdahl passed from sight and sound, Flak got down from his observation post. He lay on the slab and dozed until some hours later he heard the "shave-and-a-haircut" tap from Frederick's wall. He answered with two taps – "two bits."

HOW U, Frederick tapped.

GREAT. U HAD A V IN UR ROOM WHO TRIED TO TAP ME UP. The POWs referred to the Vietnamese as the V.

I WAS AT QUIZ. THEY WANT PEACE LETTER.

U DOING ALL RIGHT.

COPING.

WHO IS STRATTON AND WHAT IS BACCUS, Flak asked.

STRATTON IS NAVY GUY SRO. BACCUS IS STOCDALE POLICY. B NO BOW IN PUBLIC WITHOUT FORCE. A STAY OFF AIR NO RADIO NO TAPES. C CRIMES DONT ADMIT TO BEING CRIMINAL. C IS CISS DONT CISS ENEMY FOR FAVORS.

WHAT CISS, Flak interrupted.

CISS, CISS. U KNOW. U CISS A GIRL ON THE LIPS.

OKAY, LICE CISS MY ASS. Flak finally remembered the letter C could stand for a K.

YEAH. US IS UNITY OVER SELF. SRO MUST ASSUME COMMAND WHEN NEEDED EVEN IF TORTURED. THAT IS BACCUS.

I C SOME OF OUR GUYS IN BLUE AND WHITE PJS. WHO THEY.

EARLY SHOOTDOWNS. MAROON AND GRAY PJ NOT GIVEN OUT TIL 6 7.

WHAT U WEAR, Flak asked.

BLUE.

WHY CALL AREA WHERE ROOM EIGHTEEN N NINETEEN LOCATED HEARTBREAC HOTEL.

BECAUSE NEW GUYS PUT THERE THEN BEAT UP TO SEE WHETHER PROGRESSIVE OR NOT.

WHAT U MEAN PROGRESSIVE.

I MEAN BELIEVE THE COMMIE HORSESHIT. HOW THEY ACT DETERMINES WHERE THEY GO FROM HERE. ALL THE HEAVIES R IN SOLITARY.

WHAT HEAVIES.

THE SROS.

WHY YOU HERE, TED.

I THINC I LEAVE SOON. THEY BEAT ON ME MUCHLY.

YOU MEAN ESCAPE. EVER THINC ESCAPE.

ALL THE TIME. GOT ANY IDEAS.

NOT YET. WILL WORC ON IT. YOU WANTA BUST OUT OF HERE OR WHAT.

I WANT TO BUST OUT.

GOOD. THERE MUST BE A WAY. GN GBU.

THERES ALWAYS A WAY. GN GBU. Flak lay on his back and studied the glow of the dim bulb. There's always a way, always.

The glow seemed to dim and brighten as Flak stared at the bulb. It dangled from two wires. Flak stood on the slab to get a better look. The wooden-slat ceiling was one foot above his head. The wires were old and covered by crumbling black insulation. One bare wire was wound around the threads, the other was soldered to the base connection. It occurred to him that the bulbs he had seen in the torture rooms were hanging in the same fashion. The French must have really cleaned this place out when they left in '54, he thought to himself. Even ripped fixtures from the jail.

He looked at the round hole in the wooden slats the two wires came from. It was about four inches in diameter. Flak could see the tiny holes where the original fixture had been screwed to the slats. He stuck his fingers in and felt around, careful to keep away from the 220-volt wires. He felt a small pellet and pulled it out. It was a rolled-up piece of toilet paper. He sat down and smoothed it out, and read the words written in pencil:

Hey GI, why you look up here? This numbah ten place. 32 days stocks but hanging on. The V taking me elsewhere soon. GBU. Tuna, USN.

Tears sprang to Flak's eyes. He knew Tuna was the code name for Navy Captain Jim Tunner. What a guy, humor and hanging on. He'd heard that Jim Tunner was taking heavy torture for his attempt at organizing the Las Vegas area. He was now rumored to be out by some power plant as a human shield against possible bombing. If Tunner could hang on, so could he. Flak rolled the pellet, climbed up, and tucked it off to one side of the hole, then started testing the strength and fit of the slats. He tugged slightly at the concave edge of one and felt that it would come loose easily.

He stopped and listened carefully for sounds of the guards in the halls. When he heard nothing, he tugged harder at the slat and found he could slide it loose from its tongue-and-groove track. It was about four inches wide and three feet long, he estimated. The segment next to it came out easily, as did the next. Careful to avoid the bare wires, he bent the light bulb up and looked up into the rectangular opening a foot above his head. His heart jumped. He could see a crawlspace up there that was at least four feet high up to the apex of the tin roof, room enough to explore and hide if need be. The closest ceiling joist was a sturdy 2-by-8 board that looked dry and hard as iron. Probably the French used teak when they built this place, he thought. He could pull himself up into the space, maybe even cross to other rooms, look down the light bulb hole, make contact. Oh my God. His heart started pounding so hard he had to sit down.

After a moment he calmed, raised himself again on the slab, and tried to chin himself on one of the crosspieces. His left arm wouldn't support his weight. He sat back down. Dear Lord, he prayed, I'll give it all I can, would you take care of the rest? Please. Please, Lord?

Flak took a deep breath, willed the adrenaline to flow in his body, climbed on the slab, and chinned himself on the joist. A kick of the legs and he was up and into the crawlspace, heart pounding, muscles quivering. If we did it once, God, we can do it again. Squatting on a joist, he quickly glanced about, saw that he could step from joist to joist throughout the whole length of the eight cells in the building the POWs called the Mint. He saw the rusty sheets of tin forming the roof, saw the electric wires running parallel to each other, separated by round ceramic insulators nailed to the joists, saw that the end of the attic toward a street outside of the compound was of brick. He picked up a six-inch piece of leftover copper wire and dropped it through the hole onto the slab. Barefoot, he eased down a joist to the wall, peered through a triangular vent in the bricks, and saw a quiet street below. Then he painstakingly stepped across the joists to look down a corridor light bulb hole. He couldn't believe he was looking at his own cell door. Then across to the hole above Frederick's cell. He couldn't see in. He pulled a small string from his blue shorts and carefully hung it on the wire that supported the bulb. Enough for the first reconnoiter. It was awkward squatting on the joist, duckwalking about. His leg muscles quivered. He crossed back to his own hole, grabbed the joist, let himself down, pulled the light bulb to hang straight down, and quickly slid the slats in place.

He tapped the challenge to Frederick. When he got the response, he gave him the news.

U WONT BELIEVE THIS BUT I WAS IN ATTIC. WE CAN GET OUT.

YGTBSM. (Fighter pilot talk for "You got to be shitting me.")

DONT YOU THUD DRIVERS TRUST ANYONE. LOOK AT BLUE THREAD ON WIRE TO YOUR LIGHT BULB. There was a pause, then Frederick tapped: O MY GOD.

In a flurry of taps they exchanged ideas and information. They had to knock it off twice as they heard guards open doors into the Mint.

Flak told how he had seen the street. It had no streetlamps, just the glow from kerosene lanterns in the wretched houses and in small shops open to the cracked concrete sidewalks. No repairs had been done since the French had departed fourteen years before, in 1954. The two men discussed what to wear, how to act, where to go once they

411

got out. They never once doubted they could get out. That was the easy part; where to go from the prison was the problem.

GOT IT, Flak tapped. ILL WEAR TURBAN. ACT AS A SICH.

WHAT IS SICH.

SICH AS IN EAST INDIAN.

DO U LOOC AS A SICH.

NO, BUT ILL FROWN A LOT. U BE BRIT JOURNALIST. WE GO TO BRIT EMBASSY.

ILL GIGGLE A LOT AND TALC ABOUT BLOODY AMERICANS. SHIT MAN, WERE ON TO IT.

YEAH.

After the night gong and almost until daylight, they rapped out how they would do it. Flak would bend and snap the copper wire into two pieces, drop one to Frederick, and they would sharpen them into needles and make over their prison garb into street clothes. They would weave straw into what could pass for shoes and attach them to the rubber sandals they had been given. They would study the roof and the surrounding wall for barbed wire, electric fencing, and guard shacks. They would exercise to be in shape, particularly arms for chinning and legs for duckwalking. They were getting feverish with excitement. Just before daybreak Frederick tapped a question.

HEY FLAC. WHERE BRIT EMBASSY. There was a long pause.

ILL FIND A WAY TO FIND OUT. THERES ALWAYS A WAY. GN N GBU.

GN N GBU. They slept until the wakeup gong.

"So," Fidel said to Flak Apple, "you want to see me. They say you yelled 'bow cow' until someone would talk to you. Very good. Maybe you are learning, Algernon, maybe you are learning." *Bao cao* was the Vietnamese term the men had been taught to call for the guards. Flak stood at attention in front of Ceballos' desk. He was dressed in his maroon-and-gray pajamas. POWs were forbidden to wear their blue shorts anywhere but in their cells or to and from the washroom and waste tank.

"You wanted me to talk to you," Flak said. "You told me you were an educated man and that we could talk. You wanted to know about my life in the United States."

Ceballos nodded eagerly. Flak Apple looked around. His gaze lingered on the tray with condiments and plastic bottles of juices against the wall. The tray under the pictures of Castro and Ho Chi Minh. The tray under the map of Hanoi.

Ceballos followed his eyes. "Help yourself," he said.

Flak walked to the tray and slowly poured a glass of the sticky orange soda, his back to Ceballos. He drank very slowly, head bent toward the tray, but eyes raised up to range over the map.

He and Frederick had been studying and memorizing as much of the Hoa Lo area as they could see, and gleaning bits of information from all the POWs they could talk to. They had learned that the D-shaped prison had been built years before by the French to house Viet Minh and others who opposed French colonialism. Current leaders had probably once spent time behind these walls. Someone said Hoa Lo meant "fiery furnace." A massive sixteen-foot-high, thick gray stone wall surrounded the prison. The wall was topped by electrified barbed wire and six-inch greenish glass shards

413

set in concrete. The Mint, where the cells of Flak and Frederick were located, backed up to one of the walls.

Flak stuffed his mouth with peanuts and tried to read the tiny print of the *Mapa de Hanoi*. He had just found the D-shaped *Prisión Hoa Lo* when Ceballos spoke.

"What is it, Algernon? What do you wish to speak of? How you were mistreated in the United States? How you wish to write to Ho Chi Minh for forgiveness?"

Flak frantically scanned the city. He found the *Embajada Sueca*, which he guessed was the Swiss or Swedish embassy.

"Come over here, sit down. We will talk," Ceballos said in a soothing voice. "You can bring a glass with you." Reluctantly, Flak tore his eyes away from the map and walked to the chair in front of Ceballos' desk. God, what was he going to talk about?

"Ah, you said you were an educated man, Mister Ceballos."

"I am an educated man, yes."

"Ah . . . well . . ." Flak dug frantically in his mind for a subject. "Do you like mathematics?" he blurted out.

Ceballos frowned. "*Mathemáticas?* Yes, I like them. Why do you ask? Were you denied learning them?"

"No, not at all. Ah, look . . . can I get some more soda?"

"Yes. Hurry up. What do you want to talk about?"

Flak walked as casually as he could to the small table and put his eyes back on the *Embajada Sueca* as he slowly poured some more soda. He started a circular search pattern. The streets were small, the Spanish writing cramped. He had just spotted the word *británica* when Ceballos snapped at him. "Get over here. What about *mathemáticas*?"

Flak walked back. "One equals two," he said to Ceballos.

"What? You are a crazy man today."

"One equals two. Let me have some paper and a pencil."

"What do you mean?" He handed Flak a pencil and tore a page from a large yellow note pad.

Flak wrote some letters and figures. "See, 'a' equals 'b' equals one. You go along with that?"

414

Ceballos nodded, still frowning.

"Now," Flak said, "multiply 'a' equals 'b' by 'a' on each side of the equation and what do you have?"

"You have 'a' squared equals 'b' squared," Ceballos said, no longer frowning.

"Very good." Flak could see he was getting interested. "Now subtract 'b' squared from each side, then factor each side. What do you have?" He pushed the paper to Ceballos and walked back to the soda tray. He found the *Embajada Británica* and began mentally tracing the route back to the Hoa Lo prison, which he discovered was on avenida Hoa Lo.

Ceballos spoke in a proud voice. "Here. Look at this." Flak walked to the desk. He needed more time to imprint the map and exact route from the prison through the myriad of twisting routes and small streets. The general direction was north *if* the map was oriented to the north. Ceballos spun the yellow paper for Flak to see his equation.

$$a = b = 1$$
$$a^2 = ab$$
$$a^2 - b^2 = ab - b^2$$
$$(a+b)\,(a-b) = b\,(a-b)$$

"That is very, very good, Mister Ceballos. You are an educated man. Now let's divide each side by 'a' minus 'b' and what do we have?" When Ceballos slid the paper back under his pen, Flak walked back to the tray. He noted the map was oriented to the north. By now he was sloshing in soda, so he started filling his shirt pockets with peanuts as he memorized the streets and alleyways.

"Hey, man," Ceballos said. "This is no good." Flak stayed at the wall. He almost had what he needed. Just a few more seconds. "What is this?" Ceballos said in a louder voice. "Come here. You did something wrong. Come here."

As Flak walked back to the table, he kept repeating in his mind which street was which, what direction they should turn after how many blocks.

Ceballos tapped the yellow paper. "Come on now, what is this nonsense?"

"We agreed 'a' equals 'b' equals 'one,' didn't we?" Flak said. Under the factored remainder of "a" plus "b" equals "b," he wrote "one" plus "one" equals "one." Under that he wrote "two" equals "one," then casually put the pencil in his shirt pocket.

$$(a+b)\,(a-b) = b\,(a-b)$$
$$a + b = b$$
$$1 + 1 = 1$$
$$2 = 1$$

He pushed the paper to Ceballos and prayed Ceballos would react as he wanted. Ceballos did. He studied the equation, went over the points with his pencil, muttering about something being wrong. "Bah," he said, sat back, and flipped the paper to Flak, who casually put his hand on it.

"This is nonsense. Get on with it. What did you want to talk about? It can't be this." He waved his hand at the paper, which Flak desperately wanted.

"Yes, actually," Flak said after a pause, during which he ran over the streets and turns one more time in his mind. "Actually I wanted to talk to you about the Geneva Convention. North Vietnam signed it, you know. So did Cuba."

"What about the Geneva Convention?" Ceballos said, nearly grinding his teeth.

"I think you should be treating all of us in accordance with the Geneva Convention." As Ceballos erupted, Flak abstractly folded the yellow paper into squares.

"Geneva Convention?" Ceballos yelled in puzzlement. "You dare talk of Geneva Convention?"

"Yes. Treat us as prisoners of war are supposed to be treated under the Geneva Convention. You have our cards." Flak almost smiled. All USAF crews flew with their blue USAF ID cards and a small white card that said the bearer should be treated in accordance with the

416

Geneva Convention if captured. The card was a source of great cynical merriment to all. Flak casually pocketed the folded paper.

Ceballos burst out from behind his desk and slapped Flak across the mouth.

"You are insane!" he yelled. "You are not a prisoner of war. Your El Presidente Lyndon Shit Johnson never DECLARED war. You are a CRIMINAL. You have committed crimes against the peace-loving people of the Democratic Republic of Vietnam." He slapped Flak twice more. "Back to your cell," he bellowed. "Think about your crimes."

He pounded on his desk. "Guard," he yelled. "Take this criminal away."

23

0515 Hours Local, Saturday 24 February 1968
Main Briefing Room, 8th Tactical Fighter Wing
Ubon Royal Thai Air Force Base
Kingdom of Thailand

When Court and Howie Joseph had debriefed the location of the big gun that had fired at them, Hostettler had transferred the coordinates to a larger map, then checked his foreign-weapons book made up by the specialized Foreign Technologies Division at Wright-Patterson Air Force Base in Ohio.

"About like this," he said as he drew a circle around the point. "This circle represents the maximum range the gun could be from the bursts at 15,000 feet. There are certain areas within that circle we can discount because of terrain features. It couldn't fire from the backside of a mountain, for example." He pointed to a karst peak at WE84524475. "This is where I think it is. This peak is 4,900 feet high, and see here, just under the northwest tip, would be a perfect spot for a gun platform. It's level, firm, and big enough for a gun of that size."

Court and Toby examined the spot. "Okay, Toby," Court said, "here's your chance to show me what you know about the Trail." He pointed to the 1:50,000 map Hostettler had made up for them. He put his finger on the WE coordinate Hostettler had marked. It was at the southwest tip of a high karst outcropping called Rho Magna.

"Hell of a name for a hunk of karst," Toby said. He stepped back. "If we get there early enough we'll have light fog. We will be able to see through it well enough to avoid smacking into anything, but the gunners won't yet be able to see us until it burns off."

"Sounds good. Gives us a chance to get oriented." Court traced the name Rho Magna on the map. "Strange," he said. He felt a strange tickle at the base of his spine. "*Rho* is the funny 'p' letter of the Greek alphabet and *magna* means 'great' in Latin. No comparable meanings in Lao. *Pha* or *phu* means mountain."

They gathered their gear and headed for the door. "I've never seen it in the daytime," Court said. "Just flew around it at night. Flew down the river, past those bends that look like a hatchet, and there it was. Howie Joseph and I are positive the big gun is there. All I want to do today is make sure of its location, then we'll see about putting it down."

"Ah, Court, just how do you plan to make sure of its location?" Toby asked as they rode in the crew van to the airplane.

"We'll have to drag it a few times to make it come up."

"That's what I thought," Toby said with a sigh. "You know, in 0-2s all we dragged was the home drome before we landed. Anything more than that and we'd get sawed in half."

"That's not what I hear about you, Tobes old buddy. You dragged that SF detachment in South Vietnam with an 0-1, and then you dragged Mu Gia with an 0-2 last November when the PJs were fishing me out."

"Yeah, dumb, wasn't it? That's when I was young and foolish."

Forty minutes later, at first light, they were four miles above the light mist blanketing the area north of Rho Magna. Sharp brown-and-green karst peaks protruded through the gauze cover like moss-covered rocks through snow. Court checked in with Invert, their radar control, then took a second to examine his map. The universal code name for

419

this section of the Ho Chi Minh Trail was Delta 32. Their call sign was Phantom.

They were silent for a few miles, then Court spoke. "Okay," he said, "I think it's that odd-shaped karst south of us. Starting down," he said as he pulled the throttles back and told Invert they'd be on the deck for a while hence out of sight below their radar sweep.

"Cleared," Toby said in his official FAC voice. "INS readout agrees. Check gun switches on, fuel-tank selector set to external."

"Roger, switches on, tanks set."

Wind noise built up as Court lowered the nose of the big Phantom fighter. They were carrying a gun in the centerline station; a rocket pod and a fuel tank under each wing. They had topped off with fuel from the Peach tanker. Heading south now, Court leveled at 2,500 feet and followed the thin thread of the Xe Ban Fai River, barely visible below the mist. He pushed the throttles up to maintain the 500 knots airspeed he had obtained in his dive.

"There's the Hatchet under the right wing," he called to Toby.

"Tally."

"Let's check the doughnuts," Court said. On the ground before takeoff, each man had inscribed a circle with a grease pencil on each side of his canopy in the ten o'clock and two o'clock position. The small circles were drawn around their view of a preselected object at a distance of 1,000 feet. Whenever either pilot wanted to put the eyes of the other on an object too small to point out readily, and he had the time, he would take the controls and position his doughnut over it. Court dipped the right wing and put his doughnut over a river bend.

"Roger on the river bend," Toby said from the backseat.

The early mist flitted under the racing fighter as Court jinked from side to side while gaining and losing several hundred feet of altitude to spoil an eager gunner's tracking solution. While aware of his tall karst objective straight ahead at two miles, Court's eyes flicked all over the terrain on both sides of the aircraft, searching for muzzle flashes while at the same time logging in memory the dips and peaks of the rugged terrain. This was not a time to be consulting a map.

He was not even conscious of moving the flight controls. He was the airplane, the airplane was him: one entity. He desired to be one place and he was there, he desired another and he was in that place. A pilot, a good one, is always conscious of where the switches in the cockpit are positioned, what radio and navigation frequency he has tuned in, his fuel state, how his engine is performing, and what his heading, altitude, and airspeed are. The same pilot is not conscious of moving the controls this way or that. They get moved and that's all there is to it.

Court pulled tight over a karst outcropping. "Everything I look at seems a good place to hide a gun," he said against the G-force pulling at his body.

"Roger that. Glad none of them are shooting at us."

"They will be, soon enough," Court said. He swung his eyes forward. "Oh my God," he breathed.

Directly in front, Rho Magna towered black and green a half-mile above his head, like a crouching dragon. Court was in line with the razor-sharp karst ridge that ran north from the wide top of Rho Magna, then abruptly descended into the mist in front of Court's airplane like the crenellated neck of the dragon. Court stared with mesmerized horror at the dominating mass, his mind suddenly filled with a revulsion so primal it made his whole body recoil and try to shrink into itself, like an early hunter seeing his first charging dinosaur. With a reflex barely under control, he pulled the trigger and started firing his 20mm cannon at the neck of the dragon. He delighted in the sparkling of the high-explosive incendiary rounds as he marched them up the neck to the heart of the Rho Magna dragon.

"Pull up, pull up!" Toby hollered from the backseat.

In a flash Court released the trigger, rolled left, and pulled back on the stick, converting his hundreds of knots into altitude. He slammed the throttles into afterburner at the same time. In seconds they leveled at 15,000 feet, two miles above Rho Magna, in a left-hand orbit, circling the huge karst mountain. From the sides it looked even more like a two-mile-long dragon sleeping with its long crenellated neck stretching north, curving down to the low mound of its head, which was a rounded hill a few hundred feet in height. Court estimated the base width of the Rho Magna dragon at a third of a mile. The razor back of the dragon rose to nearly 5,000 feet, then sloped down to the south into a line of rock that could be taken as a curled tail. A section of the Ho Chi Minh Trail split at the nose, then ran along each side to rejoin at the rear.

"Sorry, Tobes. Guess I wanted a closer look at that rockpile. This is the first time I've seen it in the daylight. Had no idea it looked like that." Court spoke in as calm a voice as he could manage.

"That is one spooky place," Toby said. "Did you know you were shooting at it?"

"Ah, sure," Court said, barely aware he had pulled the trigger. "Sure. Indeed. Now let's figure out the best place to hide that big gun. Hostettler thinks it's under the northwest tip of the thing."

Court settled down and began varying his altitude between 15,000 and 17,000 feet and made varying angles of bank in his turns. He selected that altitude because the deadly twin- and quad-barrel ZSU 23mm rapid-firing guns were effective to 9,500 feet, and the 37mm could shoot its clips of 5 to 7 rounds up to just over 13,000 feet.

"See there," Toby said, taking the controls for a minute and placing his left doughnut over a plateau barely visible in the northwest corner.

"Got it," Court said. The small plateau commanded a field of fire to the north and west and appeared bare of vegetation. The mist had burned off and the whole area was clear. "Let's go down and take a closer look."

"Okay, but move it. It's too damn quiet around here."

In answer, Court rolled the big Phantom on its back and pulled the nose down in a Split-S maneuver that looked like the last half of a loop. He left the throttles up and was soon pointing straight down, with the airspeed needle approaching 550 knots, which was 630 miles per hour. Passing through 10,000, he eased back on the stick and brought the nose up to a 60-degree dive angle. He was west of Rho Magna, headed north to parallel the beast. At 7,000 feet he started back on the stick so as to flash past the plateau at 5,000 feet of altitude a few hundred feet off to one side. That way he and Toby could take a good look at the possible gun site from a slant range of less than 1,000 feet.

"Five seventy-five," Toby called out against the roaring of the 660-mile-per-hour wind outside their canopy. "That ought to give us zipper protection." A good ZPU gun crew could manually track an airplane indicating 500 knots at a range of 1,000 meters.

In seconds they were just off the plateau, staring down at a 20-by-40-foot clearing made brown by rocks and sand.

"No tracks, no ruts, no bent vegetation, no blast marks, no gun," Toby said as Court pulled west and started to jink and zoom to altitude.

"Toby, I saw – "

Suddenly four black-and-orange 37mm bursts bracketed the speeding jet, a terrific bang from underneath blew them into a vertical bank to the left, and the cockpit pressure dumped with a blasting roar, sucking the air from their lungs. Court righted the airplane, put his regulator to 100 percent oxygen, and did what every pilot whoever took a hit did immediately: he let someone know what and where as fast as he could in case he went down.

"Invert," he gasped against the pressure from his mask, "Phantom Leader is hit, five miles west of Delta 32." There was no answer. "Toby, you okay?" he asked as several warning lights came on in the cockpit.

"Yeah, I'm okay. Man, look at that right wing. We done took a solid hit." The right wing had a hole several inches in diameter through the trailing edge. "I think it blew the wing tank clean off."

"It sure as hell did," Court said, holding heavy right

rudder against the drag from the lone tank on the left. "And the tailpipe temp is climbing on the right engine. See any smoke?"

Toby looked through the rearview mirror mounted on the right of his canopy bow. "Yeah, a thin stream. Can't see any flames. How does she handle?"

Court did a rapid damage check by moving the controls while checking the hydraulic gages. "Number One flight control is a little low, but Number Two is full up. Right generator is out. The right-engine oil pressure is low." He pulled the throttle back to midrange. "But I've stabilized the temperature."

"No more smoke," Toby said.

Court leveled at 15,000 feet, heading west toward the safety of Thailand and Ubon. "I've got to punch off that left tank," he said. "Too hard to handle." He centered the needle and ball in an instrument on his panel that depicted the degree of bank angle and skid, and hit the button to jettison the left fuel tank. Immediately he could release right rudder pressure.

"That's better," he said. "She'll hold okay on just one engine, and we've got one and a half. Fuel level looks okay for the moment, but we need to top off on a tanker to make Ubon. How about trying to contact Invert for me?"

Toby made contact the first try as Invert picked them up immediately.

"Phantom Leader, steer 282, Phantom. You copy Invert?"

"Roger, Invert," Toby replied. "Phantom copies five by."

"Phantom Leader, what is the nature of your problem and what are your intentions?"

Nothing happened when Court tried to transmit. "You'll have to relay for me, Tobes," he said.

Toby relayed that Phantom had taken a hit in the right wing, no one was wounded, that things were under control, and they needed a drink from a friendly tank on the way home.

Invert Controller 42 said no sweat. Both he and the

Peach tank performed as advertised and Court Bannister made an uneventful straight-in approach and landing on the active runway at Ubon Royal Thai Air Force Base at 0740 hours. At 0820 hours he was at attention in front of Colonel Stanley D. Bryce, who drilled him with his piercing gray eyes.

"What's going on out there, Bannister? You're supposed to be setting up a night FAC outfit, not ginning along the Trail in broad daylight getting your ass shot off. Suppose you explain to me just how in hell this will help you accomplish your mission?"

"Sir, a large gun came up the other night on me and Howie Joseph. We pretty well fixed the location. Hostettler checked the records and said several planes have been shot down in the Delta 32 area near Rho Magna. No one was quite sure what kind of gun it was. We found out. I could tell by the bursts it was 100mm. I think I know where it is and how to kill it."

"How come you are the only one in Southeast Asia that knows the location of that gun?" Bryce demanded.

"Sir, Parker and I got down in the weeds and took a good look. I think I know exactly where it is and I request permission to go put a strike in on it late this afternoon."

"Why late this afternoon?"

"The best attack heading is to the west. I want the strike birds to sneak in from the east, then pull off due west to hide in the sun in case they don't get it on the first pass."

"You probably won't get any fragged fighters this late, but okay, get to it."

As Court started out of the office, Bryce spoke up.

"Say again when your Phantom FACs will be operational?"

"I estimate by the first of March we will be fully operational ready to handle fragged and unfragged strike aircraft."

"That's barely a week from now. Get with it. Damage any more of my airplanes while you train and I don't care who your daddy rabbit is in Saigon, I'll ground your ass. Dismissed."

At 1515 hours that afternoon, Court and Toby orbited
west of Rho Magna, trying to arrange for fighters from
Hillsboro. They were an unfragged mission, and using
valuable fighters to probe by fire for a suspected gun site
was not a high priority.

"Phantom, Hillsboro. Sorry, we can't do you any good
today. Get me a couple of live trucks and I might help
you out." The controller wouldn't say in the clear that
the first half of a big strike was on up north and all
available assets were in use. Hostettler had warned them
before takeoff that such might be the case.

They spent most of their remaining mission time learning
the Trail from Mu Gia to Delta 32. They explored over-
hangs, valleys, ravines, suspected truck parts, cat's eyes,
and open stretches of the Trail. Guns came up only twice
as they roamed the 100-mile stretch of territory. One sent
up a small, looping tracer stream that fell far short. The
shoot time was too scant to spot where it came from. Toby
identified the rounds as 12.7mm.

"That's about .51 caliber in size," he said. "The gunner
is practicing or is trigger-happy. He's just lucky we weren't
looking in that direction at the time he fired. He'll get his ass
chewed out. Normally their fire discipline is much better."

The other gun was a 37mm that fired three bursts straight
up in the air, seemingly without aiming at them. "That's
their warning to outposts and *binh trans* an airplane is
headed their way. Means their landline is cut someplace."

Court varied his time memorizing the landscape as he
oriented himself on his map. When they had fifteen minutes
remaining in the mission, Court headed for Rho Magna.

"Just as we got hit this morning," he said on the intercom,
"I started to tell you I spotted another clearing just east

426

up the slope from the one we were looking at. It's hard to see and not nearly as big. I think those 37mm gunners were after us because they think we saw the pit for the big gun."

"I sure as hell didn't see any pit," Toby said. "Did you?"

"No, no pit. But I'm sure that the big gunfire the other night came from right in that area. I want to go down and look it over again. You game?"

"Bannister, I'm locked on your tail in perfect trail. Let's go see. You insisted I take a camera. Put your doughnut on the site and I'll snap it."

"Good. I'm going to head south and run down there east of the Trail over the jungle. When we get close, I'll kick in the burners and pull west across the same spot as this morning, then pull up into the sun. The site will be off our left wing just before we go over the old one."

"Why don't you dive directly at it and strafe the spot, then you'll get some gun-camera film of it?"

"No. I want them to think we're still faked out and don't really know where it is."

In the afternoon sun, Rho Magna was lit up on the westward side and in deep shadow on the east. Court felt his breathing and pulse increase as he approached the roll-in spot. Again he felt the tingling in his spine. It wasn't the imminent danger from the gun, he knew, it brought about a different reaction. Apprehension before combat often made his left calf contract spasmodically. He was so used to the condition that it was almost welcome. But this was different. He felt he was responding to something so basic as to be nearly uncontrollable. It was as if Rho Magna were a living thing that had a pulsing nucleus deep inside, a throbbing arachnid core composed more of unearthly matter than of a physical heart. Did early man worship or hate at this shrine? Was something inside himself, something best left unstudied, responding to an unhealthy call? Court felt his lip curl in disdain inside his mask. This is crazy, he said to himself.

He sped over the jungle, moved the throttles outboard

to engage the afterburners, and turned west toward Rho Magna, knowing he had one pass to locate the gun. A second pass was out of the question.

He sped over the jungle, looking up at the mass. "Let's hope the gunners aren't expecting a low-level pass from the east," he said.

"Hope, hell," Toby said. "Let us pray. We've got 600 knots." At that speed, nearly 700 miles per hour, they would be upon the site before the sound registered with the gunners.

"And here it is," Court said. He lifted the nose slightly and the plane flashed up the shaded flank of Rho Magna and roared over the site where Court thought the gun was located. He dipped the wing a second, then pulled up into the hot glow of the western sun. He had seen nothing in the tiny clearing.

"Yahoo," Toby shouted. "I got it. At least I think I did. I just kept snapping from before you dipped the wing until after."

Court looked into his rearview mirror. The big gun had not fired. Streams of tracers from half a dozen guns vaguely followed his path like the aimless movements of spider legs. He half-expected the tail of the dragon to rise up and lash them out of the air.

It was dark by the time they landed and debriefed with Dick Hostettler in the intell room. They scrutinized Toby's negatives on the photo interpreter's light box with a magnifying glass.

"Damn, all I see is a clearing, no caves, nothing," Hostettler said with reluctance as he straightened up.

Court checked the photo once again against his map. "I'm sure that's the place. And look at this." He pointed to the lower open area. "Maybe they resupply that gun by helicopter and it lands right here."

"Maybe so, but we can't convince Seventh Air Force of that long enough to frag some birds on it to blow the top of that mountain off," Hostettler said.

"Hey," Court said, "you've just given me an idea. I'll bet there is a cave, but the entrance is camouflaged so well we can't spot it. All I need to do is go out there tomorrow and put a few bombs on where I think it is and we'll know for sure."

"Tomorrow is out, Court," Hostettler said. "We've still got a big push going on up north, plus the normal fighter stream into Khe Sanh. Big wing gaggle here and at all the other bases. Best you can get is the same FAC-configured bird you used this afternoon."

Court felt a twinge at not being on the schedule for the missions up north and maybe a chance for his fifth MiG. "Okay," he said, "I'll take it."

Hostettler examined him closely. "I'm not sure I like that look on your face."

Court gave him a cocky half-grin that bordered on slyness. "So okay, no bombs. I'll have rockets, won't I? And a gun. What else do I need?"

"A helluva lot of luck, a shit-hot good guardian angel, slow gunners, maybe a new backseater," Toby said.

"You mean that, Tobes, old buddy? A new backseater?"

Toby sighed. "No, not really. Wish I did, though." He turned to Hostettler. "You know, Court seems pretty obsessed with that thing."

"What? The gun or the mountain?"

"I think both. Maybe he takes his wars too seriously."

Dick Hostettler cocked his head at Court. "How about it? You taking this war too serious? You feel anything special about Rho Magna?"

Court laughed. "You guys are barking up the wrong mountain. It's just another job to me." Sure, he said to himself, sure it is.

The hotline phone from 7th Air Force rang. Hostettler strode over and answered.

"Court," Toby said, "we're going to get that gun. I know damn well we are."

Court studied Toby's face. It was lit up and his eyes were sparkling. My God, Court thought in revelation, here this guy has had all the troubles in the world and he's happy, he's optimistic. What a great attitude.

Hostettler made extensive notes and returned. The talk had been elliptical to confuse probable listeners on the Vietnam side, because no fighter wing in Thailand had a scramble phone. He spent a moment decoding what he had.

"Okay," he said, and looked up at Court. "Maybe you thought it was just another job, but it has suddenly become a very important one. A Navy A-6 just got blown out of the sky in the Delta 32 area by flying into what his wingman classified as huge explosions. They were at 30,000 feet. Nothing can reach that high with any accuracy except a hundred-mil gun. Seventh is now paying big-time attention to our reports. Still can't frag any birds to you because of the Khe Sanh and North Vietnam push tomorrow, but you are authorized your bird plus one other to be uploaded with all the thousand-pound bombs that beast can carry or any other ordnance you want. The written-authorization frag will come in tonight at the normal time."

It was very quiet in the room. Court held Hostettler's eyes for a few seconds, then looked away.

"This is what you wanted, Court," Toby said.

Court took a deep breath and slowly blew it out. "Yeah, this is what I wanted." Then he gave a mocking laugh. "But hell, do I always have to get what I want?" He stood up and slapped Toby on the back. "Tell Deacon Docks and Neil Tallboy they've got the early go with us. Briefing starts right here." He checked his watch. "In five hours at 0330. We've got a lot to cover with them, and then I want us to hit those gunners from out of the morning sun. You can turn in, Toby. I'm going down to the Armament Shop and see what kind of bombs and fuzes we can get. This is a one-shot deal and I want to be able to blow the top of the mountain clean off."

Their call sign was Phantom. The four of them, the two
frontseaters and their GIBs, had spent long hours that
morning poring over the maps and photos, discussing dive
angles, pull-offs, and tactics against the heavy defense the
big gun had. Toby had not turned in when Court suggested.
He had stayed up with Court, getting the M904 fuzes set
with the proper delay for the six 1,000-pound bombs Court
would carry. Then they arranged to have special ordnance
loaded for the second airplane. Because the 23 and 37mm
defenses were so heavy, Court had decided Deacon Docks
would roll in first and cover the area near the gun site with
CBU 49, the Cluster Bomb Units the size of grapefruit that
exploded and sprayed steel pellets in all directions. Though
they wouldn't necessarily destroy a gun, the varying times
the units exploded either killed the gunners outright or kept
their heads down for the vital moments it would take Court
to roll in with the earthmovers. They had choreographed
their movements to the split second and were now cutting
across the Ho Chi Minh Trail twenty miles to the south
of Rho Magna at 22,000 feet.

Court and Toby were leading in Phantom Leader, Deacon
and Neil followed in radar trail as Phantom Two. Without
words, they had topped off from a tanker in the gray dark
before dawn and set up their armament switches as they
crossed the fence into Laos. They had told NKP operations
with coded words before takeoff to alert Moonbeam, the
night ABCCC, where they would be and when, so Moonbeam would divert fighters through their area.

"Looking good," Toby said from the backseat. "All gages
in the green." He looked into his radarscope. "We start
north in two minutes."

"Okay, Phantom Two," Court transmitted. "Take the

431

lead." He dropped back to let Deacon Docks go in first.

Around them, the sun had risen from the South China Sea with a blinding brilliance that promised another blast-furnace day. They had planned to cut due north after they crossed the Trail south of Rho Magna, curve east slightly, then roll in, Court behind Deacon, from the sun. They hoped the surprise and intensity of the attack would keep the gunners from shooting, particularly during the vulnerable phase when they were pulling off. Court would be last, and it was usually the last man that got it. Rarely was the first man in on a target hit. It always took the gunners a few seconds to determine the direction of an attack. If the last man rolled in on the same heading as his leader, he was asking to get hammered. Same if he pulled off in the same direction as the rest of the flight. The gunners would have a sightline ready. Deacon had planned to pull north, Court would pull to the south.

"There he goes," Court said to Toby as he watched Deacon roll in from 22,000 feet. They planned a 60-degree dive with release airspeed of 450 knots at an altitude of 10,000 feet so they would bottom out 3,000 feet above the gun position. For safety's sake it was normal to bottom out 4,500 feet above the guns. But to be more accurate, Court had decided to take them lower, counting on surprise to add the safety factor.

Court checked the sun over his shoulder and rolled in ten seconds behind Deacon. He brought his gunsight pipper slowly up to the target as he stabilized his dive; needle and ball centered, proper dive angle, airspeed building. He rechecked the proper mils depression set into the sight mechanism. He could easily see Deacon's plane a few thousand feet below, its bentwing shape and lizard camouflage already making it blend into the mottled hues of Rho Magna.

"Eighteen thousand, seventeen thousand," Toby intoned as their airspeed built and they screamed down toward Rho Magna. "Dive angle approaching sixty."

Court felt the tension build as the roar of the wind

432

outside the canopy approached a crescendo. Rho Magna grew bigger in his windscreen; the mass once again outlined the sleeping dragon. Just as Court felt his teeth clench with resolve, the whole side of the dragon's neck lit up like Fourth of July sparklers and pulsing strobe lights. For an instant he thought he was seeing Deacon's CBUs. But Deacon's plane was still diving in, into the maelstrom of winking lights and streams of cherry tracers now flowing upwards like garden-hose streams. The cherry streams at first seemed random and uncoordinated, then they started to converge on a single point, setting up a wall of fire through which both fighters had to pass. Just as the dark CBU canisters left Deacon's airplane, he flashed through the wall of exploding antiaircraft fire, bottomed out the other side, and started his pull to the north. Court thought he saw a piece fly from Deacon's speeding jet. He bored in as the fire diminished only slightly and the CBUs started going off in fiery overlapping doughnut rings several hundred feet in diameter.

"One's hit," Deacon transmitted as Court had his gunsight squarely on the target. In reflex to the call, Court glanced up at the Deacon's Phantom, and when he looked back to his gunsight, it was too late to drop. At that instant he was in the fiery wall.

Black-and-orange balls of 37mm were exploding at 10,000 feet, 23mm was dotting the sky with basketball-sized puffs of white smoke at 9,000 feet, and wavering tentacles of 12.7mm were weaving an orange net below both layers of steel death. Two loud bangs jolted Court's airplane from the left.

"Pickle, pickle," Toby yelled, telling Court to release the bombs.

"Too late, lost my sight picture."

"Oh God. You mean we gotta go in again?"

"Yeah. Sorry 'bout that. Check for damage," Court said as he pulled sharply left to jink south away from the explosions. He struggled against the G-forces to check his instrument panel. All the gages read in the green. "Everything looks okay up here."

"Samo samo back here," Toby said, his voice high from excitement.

"Phantom Two, what's your status?" Court called when they were clear of the murderous fire zone.

"Ah, Lead. I think we're okay. Number Two engine is out, but no fire. All systems operating. We can hang around while you drop." Deacon Docks spoke in a faraway, almost detached voice, as if he were merely a dispassionate witness, not an embroiled participant.

"Okay," Court said. "Let's join up like we're leaving the area and check each other over for damage."

"Rog. Level at fifteen, indicating 350, heading 260." Minutes later Court was in formation. They took turns flying around and under each other, looking for holes.

"You've got a few holes in your right engine bay, but you're not leaking anything," Court said.

"And you're clean, Lead," Deacon said after his check of Court's aircraft.

"I think we're out of sight now. We'll circle north and I'll go in again," Court transmitted. He started climbing and led Docks to the north of Rho Magna, then started back south. He checked in with Hillsborough and Invert for flight monitoring and radar coverage.

They both knew it wasn't smart for Docks to fly a crippled airplane home without an escort. Nor was it good practice for Court to attack a heavily defended target by himself. Both cases required a witness to call for help in case the other went down. Therefore it was imperative they stay together, plus have Invert and Hillsboro monitor their progress.

"Okay, Toby, this time we'll surprise them and come down out of the north."

"Some surprise," Toby said. They both knew there would be no surprises to the alerted gunners below. "At least they'll have to replot their killing zone and we can pull off into the sun."

"I'm not going to pull east," Court said. "We just saw they're fused for that already. I'll pull west and hope for the best. Let's hope they figure I won't pull off in the same direction twice."

"Rog."

"It suddenly occurred to me why they were ready for our run in from the sun, and why they fired barrage instead of individual tracking."

"Why?" Toby asked.

"They probably do that every day just in case anybody ever had the idea to do a surprise attack out of the morning sun."

Court maneuvered to the attack position and called Deacon Docks.

"Okay, Phantom Two. Orbit high and dry. We'll pick you up when we come off target." Docks rogered, and Court readied himself and his airplane to roll in.

"I'm going to make this one different," he told Toby. "I'm going to roll in lower, from eighteen thousand, to keep our exposure time during the dive as brief as possible. I'll still release at ten grand. All bombs at once. There's no second pass."

"That's what you said last time."

Court chuckled and put them in a dive, slowly bringing the gunsight pipper to the target.

"Seventeen," Toby sang out, "sixteen – "

"Christ," Court said in surprise. "I see the big gun. It's rolled out on some sort of tracks that had been covered with sand. And a big camouflaged door is opened in the rocks behind it. Shit hot."

"Shit hot, huh? Who they aiming at?"

Court didn't answer. He concentrated on stabilizing the Phantom and compensating for the crosswind that had arisen since his last pass. He eased the pipper to the gun.

"Fifteen, airspeed 420. Dive angle sixty. Fourteen, airspeed 430 – " Toby intoned.

Court had his pipper placed such that just as his airplane would flash through 10,000 feet and he had his computed release airspeed of 450 knots, he could ripple off the bombs. He planned on marching them through the gun, then along

435

the track to the cave mouth. If he didn't get the gun, at least he'd get the track or the opening so the 100mm was trapped outside and could be destroyed by another flight. He rechecked his switches by feel.

"Thirteen, airspeed 440. Twelve, airspeed 450 – "

Then the sky lit up below them as the 37 and 23mm AAA guns opened up. This time the gunners were trying to track and shoot directly at him as well as set up a barrage at his release altitude.

"Toby, we got to go lower. They're barraging ten grand."

"Shit oh dear. We're passing through eleven . . . now."

"I'll pickle at nine." Court knew the shortest time in the barrage zone was to dive through it. To pickle higher meant they'd bottom out in it; to pickle in the zone would give the same effect. He had to release lower. He steadied the aircraft as a loud explosion went off behind them.

"Ten thousand, airspeed 450 – "

Suddenly, through the smoke and explosions in front of his gunsight, Court saw the big gun fire three times and start back up the rails to the opening. Shrapnel rattled off the side of the plane as three more 37mm shells burst on their left.

"NINE THOUSAND. PICKLE, PICKLE, PICKLE," Toby yelled.

In a split second Court had to place the pipper short of the gun, otherwise the bombs would fall beyond the target due to his releasing 1,000 feet lower than he had computed. He pressed the small red button on top of the control stick, felt the bombs ripple off as the ejector cartridges boosted them from the racks, then banked and yanked first left then right. Two cherry tracer streams played behind them, sending looping fireballs after their plane. There were no 37mm bursts. With a muffled bang that neither man heard, one 23mm shell tore a jagged hole in the trailing edge of their rudder.

Both men grunted to keep blood in their heads as Court pulled seven Gs on the big Phantom. Then they were west and out of the firestorm and able to lighten the G-load and look back at Rho Magna. Four huge dirt-and-gunpowder clouds were drifting down the hill, nearly obscuring tumbling rocks and an avalanche of earth from the plateau. Smoke and sheets of fire spurted from the mouth of the cave. The gun-carriage tracks were twisted and bent in the air like a wrecked roller-coaster.

"Yahoo," Toby cried. "Look at that gun, will you?"

The gun had been blown off the plateau and down the steep sides. The tube had separated from the carriage and lay like a section of black sewer pipe along the slope.

"Just another day at the office," Court said. "It's safe enough now. I'm going over the site at fifteen thou. Get some pictures."

Court flew over the smashed gun while Toby snapped pictures with his camera. Court called Deacon Docks.

"Phantom Two, what did you think of that action?" There was no answer. He called again. "Phantom Two, check in."

"Oh shit," Toby said. "Look back at four o'clock."

There in the morning sky were the residual puffs of the three 100mm shells and a long vertical streak of black smoke that led to a fireball on the ground.

24

0900 Hours Local, Friday 15 March 1968
MACV Headquarters
Tan Son Nhut Air Base
Republic of Vietnam

Lieutenant Colonel Wolf Lochert stood next to his chair
in the small room where he was to be tried for murder. He
wore his TWs, the Tropical Worsted uniform, because Gant
had demanded he do so. Gant felt the TWs to be neater and
more imposing than the TCUs (Tropical Combat Uniform)
or the tiger suits worn by some combat infantrymen and
almost all of the Special Forces soldiers. It was the only
"coat" uniform authorized in Vietnam. Wolf had made up
his uniform with all his badges, patches, and decorations.
Gant had demanded that also.

To Wolf's left stood his defense counsel, Major Jay
Denroe. To his right stood his assistant defense counsel,
Archie Gant. Denroe wore his khakis so as to not detract
from Wolf's TWs. Gant wore a white cotton suit, black
string tie, and carried a straw fan. He found that most of
the members of the court were from the South and knew
exactly how they expected their lawyers to look. Across
from them, behind the longest table in the room, stood the
seven members of the court: three full colonels, one of whom
was president of the court, and four lieutenant colonels. The
law officer and the court reporter were to their left. To their
right was the trial counsel, Colonel Bruno Rafalko, and his

assistant. The trial counsel in a court-martial is the man appointed to prosecute the accused. Two air conditioners chugged and hummed in the background.

In a dry voice without intonation, the law officer opened with the litany that all the papers, procedures, and legal qualifications of those present were in order. He nodded at the president, the full colonel so appointed on USARV orders, who called the court to order and said the attendees may be seated.

Colonel Bruno Rafalko rose. He was a tall, athletic-looking man with short brown hair. He had wide-set brown eyes and wore khakis with badges and decorations that showed he had seen combat in World War Two and Korea. Although he had the CIB, he did not wear a paratrooper's badge. He faced the court.

"The court is convened by USARV appointing orders G-6, a copy of which has been furnished to the law officer, each member of the court, the accused, and to the reporter for insertion at this point in the record." He turned to the seven members of the court. "The prosecution is ready to proceed with the trial in the case of the United States against Wolfgang Xavier Lochert, Lieutenant Colonel, 5th Special Forces Group, who is present in court."

Bruno Rafalko then swore in the reporter and introduced the two defense counselors to the members of the court.

"Proceed to convene the court," the law officer said.

"The court will be sworn," Bruno Rafalko said. "All rise while I administer the oath." He then swore in each member of the court. When he finished, the president took over and swore in Colonel Bruno Rafalko, then turned to Denroe and Gant.

"You, Major Jay Denroe and Mister Archibald Gant, do swear that you will faithfully perform the duties of defense counsel and will not divulge the findings or sentence of the court to any but the proper authority until they shall be duly disclosed. So help you God?"

"I do," Major Jay Denroe said quietly.

"I do," honked Archie Gant, thinking to himself that

439

these military guys do a lot of swearing-in of each other.

The court members turned to face the law officer, who said: "The court is now convened. You may be seated." The room resounded with the guttural barks of wooden chairs scraping on the wooden floor as the members sat down. The trial counsel remained standing. He addressed the members of the court.

"The general nature of the charges in this case is murder; the charges were preferred by Commander, USARV. So far, the records of this case disclose no grounds for challenge." He looked around the men in the room. "If any member of the court is aware of any facts which he believes may be a ground for challenge by either side against himself, he should now state the facts." When none of the members spoke up, he addressed Denroe and Gant. "Does the accused desire to challenge any member of the court for cause?" This offer gave Wolf and his defense an opportunity to give a reason why one or more members of the court should be replaced.

"We do not," Denroe said.

"Does the accused desire to exercise his right to one peremptory challenge against any member?" This allowed Wolf to request any one member be dismissed without stating a reason.

"We do not," Denroe said.

Colonel Bruno Rafalko continued the ritual of opening a general court-martial by reading the charges against Wolf.

"The charges have been properly referred to this court for trial and with their specifications are as follows. Charge: Violation of the Uniform Code of Military Justice, Article 118. Specification: In that Lieutenant Colonel Wolfgang Xavier Lochert, U.S. Army, Fifth Special Forces Group, Nha Trang, Republic of Vietnam, APO 96240, did, at Saigon, Bien Hoa Province, Republic of Vietnam, on or about 28 January 1968 murder Buey Dan, citizen of the Republic of Vietnam, by means of stabbing him with a knife." He looked over at the defendant's table.

Denroe and Gant arose. "The accused, Wolfgang Xavier

Lochert, pleads, to all charges and specifications, not guilty," Denroe said and sat down. Gant remained standing. Denroe tugged at his sleeve but Archie shrugged him off.

Ignoring him, the law officer looked at Bruno Rafalko. "Does the trial counsel wish to make an opening statement?"

"Excuse me," Gant said. "The defense has additional evidence which we would like to introduce at this time and perhaps save" – he bowed toward the trial counsel's table – "the prosecutor some time."

"Does the trial counsel have any objections?" the law officer asked.

Bruno Rafalko sucked at his upper lip and studied Archie Gant. "I do not," he said finally.

Gant fished a folder from his briefcase and waved it in the air.

"I am going to produce a sworn statement to the effect that the man named Buey Dan, allegedly murdered by the defendant, Lieutenant Colonel Wolfgang Lochert, was in fact a known agent, spy, and terrorist for the communist army from North Vietnam – "

"Objection!" Bruno Rafalko said as he jumped to his feet. "Counselor is making use of a political appellation by choosing the word 'communist.' "

"Sustained," the law officer said and nodded at Gant.

"I beg the court's pardon," Gant said in an overly polite voice. "Although North Vietnam avows communism, practices communism, is governed under communist principles, and is in fact supplied by the two separate communist governments of Russia and China, I will not refer to the North Vietnamese communists as communists. I will refer to them as 'the enemy army.' I trust that appellation, as the prosecutor puts it, will please the court?"

The law officer nodded. "Proceed," he said. The members of the court concealed grins. They were line officers whose job it was to kill communists. They knew very well what Gant was trying to do.

"To continue," Gant said. "I am going to produce a sworn statement to the effect that the Vietnamese known as Buey Dan was a known agent, spy, and terrorist for the communist army . . . oops, sorry, the *enemy* army from North Vietnam."

"Objection!" Rafalko said in a loud voice. "First off, it makes no difference if Buey Dan was connected in any way with the other side. He was an unarmed man murdered in broad daylight. Secondly, a sworn statement is not enough. The defense must produce the witness."

"Now, hold on there – " Gant started, but was interrupted by the law officer.

"Gentlemen," the law officer said, "the court is in recess for five minutes while I talk to the counsels in private." He crooked a finger at Rafalko and the two men at Lochert's table. They followed him to a small office down the hall. The LO did not want the members of the court to be influenced one way or the other by two squabbling lawyers. He realized he should have declared the recess when Gant first wanted to introduce the evidence. Presentation, and acceptance or rejection of additional evidence, should be performed away from the members lest they hear or see something prejudicial to the case.

"Clarify your objection, Colonel Rafalko. State what you want," the law officer said.

"I see no reason to bring in a sworn statement about Buey Dan. Even if he was an enemy agent or soldier – and I am not admitting he is – members of the armed forces of the United States are not permitted to summarily kill, execute, or murder members of an opposing force when said members are unarmed in a non-hostile, non-threatening environment. You don't just gun them down on the streets. Secondly, I do not stipulate to any sworn statements from anybody. I do not know anything about the writer or his testimony. He must be presented for deposition and cross-examination." A stipulation is an agreement by both sides that what is in a sworn statement is what the writer would present in person were he to be physically present in front of the court.

Gant looked at Rafalko with exaggerated contempt. "All

right, then, I won't ask you to stipulate. I ask you to produce the man to be a witness for the defense in this court."

"No way," Colonel Rafalko snapped. "You should have provided his name earlier."

"We didn't have his name earlier."

"Where is he?"

"He is in the U.S. He's critical to our case, and the government has to find him and pay for his transportation and room and board here in Saigon. And the government is you."

"What? Are you out of your mind?" Rafalko's face grew dark. "Look, Gant, we don't have the funds for that sort of thing."

Gant scrunched his face into the kind of smile that borders on a leer. "According to paragraph 115d of the 1951 Manual for Courts-Martial, the trial counsel – that's you – is authorized to subpoena a witness at government expense. Wouldn't the public like to know that the United States Army, while spending twenty million a day to kill VC, won't spend two grand to help one of its great heros who killed a VC in self-defense?"

"How do I know his testimony is material and necessary?" Rafalko said in a voice increasing in volume.

"Put it in writing, Mister Gant," the law officer interrupted in a weary voice. "Give me a synopsis of his testimony, full reasons why he must appear in person, and any other matter showing how his testimony is necessary to the ends of justice."

Gant dug into his briefcase. "I have something right here that fills requirements one and three. And I must state the full reason he must appear is because the trial counsel wants him to appear."

"I do not," Rafalko roared.

"You said you wouldn't stipulate to his sworn statement. Therefore you must want him physically present."

Rafalko ground his teeth and turned to the law officer. "I request a one-day recess to, ah, check the availability of

443

funds." The law officer agreed and the court was adjourned until nine the next morning.

"Who is it? Who is this on the phone?" Pinky Pulmer sat straight up in bed. He wore two-piece pajamas. Due to the thirteen-hour time difference, it was four in the morning Washington time, compared to five that afternoon in Vietnam. "Oh yes, General Farquell. Is the trial over? Is that why you called?" Pulmer fumbled and snapped on the small lamp next to the telephone.

"The trial is not over. It is in recess for a day." Farquell's voice was tinny and distant in Pulmer's ear. "I need to report something to you. And I need a decision."

"Yes, yes. Go ahead." Pulmer slipped on his glasses and took a sip from the water glass on the bed table.

"The defense apparently has a sworn statement from the very fellow that is supposed to be helping us gain public support against this murderer – "

"Who is it? Who is it?" Pulmer interrupted.

"Shawn Bannister," Farquell replied.

"Oh my God." Pulmer removed his glasses and pinched his nose. "The defense has it, you say? Does it hurt the prosecution?"

"From what I understand, the evidence is more than sufficient for the members of the court to vote for acquittal."

"What do you mean, vote for acquittal? You signed the investigation – Article 32, you called it – and said you recommended a court-martial. Furthermore, you told me the judge and the prosecutor worked for you. So what is the problem?"

"The judge, as you call him, Mister Secretary, is a law officer who oversees the proceedings for proper content and procedures. The prosecutor is called the trial counsel, and yes, both work for me."

"To remind you, General, this is the Office of the Secretary of Defense you are talking to." Pulmer's voice elevated a note each time he spoke. Oscar Nebals of California was his sponsor, and Oscar Nebals wanted this little job taken care of, for God knows what reason. If Nebals wasn't happy, then he would most likely be out of a job and back to being a clerk or administrative aide somewhere on Capitol Hill.

Even over the flawed telephone circuitry, Farquell's exasperation was evident. "Mister Secretary, while it is true those two men work under my jurisdiction, and perhaps even share my dislike for the actions of the accused, the fact remains that at least four of the seven officers who make up the court will most likely vote to acquit Lochert because they will feel the government cannot prove its case."

"But – but *you're* the government!"

"I may be the boss but I have to play by the rules."

"Can't you make, ah, *arrangements* with the seven members?"

"If you mean what I think you mean, I wouldn't even think about it, much less try it. To try to influence a combat-line officer to go against one of his own is like trying to get your boss McNamara to admit he is a nincompoop. I'm sorry. There is nothing more I can do."

Pulmer slumped. "You said you needed a decision."

"I can prevent Bannister from being subpoenaed by refusing to fund his trip. As Commander, USARV, I can do that. I want to know if you think I should?"

"Ah . . . do, do what you think is best," Pulmer said. He was not about to give a definite agreement that might someday tie him too closely to the Lochert trial. "Ah, what *do* you think is best?" Pulmer asked.

"Whatever the prosecutor wants," Lieutenant General Elmer Farquell responded.

The next day, having received the decision from Lieutenant General Farquell, Colonel Bruno Rafalko stood in front of the law officer. "All right, all right. I so stipulate." The problem was solved. He would not bring Shawn Bannister into this courtroom. It was Rafalko's studied opinion that there was no amount of cross-examination he could perform that would erase the idea

445

from the court's collective, liberal-hating mind that if a proven antiestablishment person like Shawn Bannister appeared to defend Wolf Lochert, then Wolf Lochert must definitely be not guilty.

The law officer stood up. "Gentlemen, can we get back to the court?"

Archie Gant was greatly relieved. He knew from what LaNew told him that Shawn Bannister would never have agreed to appear in court, because even if it was closed, the press would have seen him coming and going. Even though a subpoena would compel Shawn to attend, he could change or recant his testimony just enough to cast doubt that he had actually seen Buey Dan in the tunnel. As it stood now, Shawn's written word, properly sworn to, was more powerful than his actual appearance in front of the board.

Once back in the courtroom, Colonel Bruno Rafalko got on with his case. He established through a death certificate that one Vietnamese male identified as Buey Dan died on the date in question as the result of a knife wound. Rafalko entered into evidence the certificate and Wolf Lochert's stiletto. Archie Gant stipulated to each.

Bruno Rafalko then produced Mal Hemms as a witness for the prosecution. Hemms, dressed in a tan safari suit splendidly cut to minimize his portly frame, introduced his TV film of Lochert and Buey Dan and testified to its authenticity. Rafalko played it again and again in both slow motion and stop motion until, he hoped, the sight of Wolf Lochert's plunging a knife into Buey Dan's body, then flinging the dead man into a tree, was deeply imprinted into each court member's mind. Archie Gant cross-examined after Colonel Rafalko finished his presentation.

"Mister Hemms," Gant asked, "at what point did you see Colonel Lochert and the communist terrorist fighting?"

"Objection!" Rafalko said. " 'Communist' and 'terrorist' are inflammatory words inappropriate and inadmissible in this court."

"Sustained," the law officer said. "The court is advised to dismiss those words." He looked at the seven officers who made up the court-martial board. It was obvious they weren't dismissing anything of the sort. The law officer addressed Archie Gant.

"Mister Gant, you will refrain from using such words to describe the deceased. Rephrase your question, please."

"When did you first see the defendant and the deceased?" Archie asked Mal Hemms.

"When I directed the cameraman to roll the film. When the colonel stuck the knife into the man." Hemms spoke with the enunciation and studied earnestness of the practiced TV reporter. His small eyes looked concerned, his bushy brows were furled with concentration.

"You must have seen some earlier activity in front of the church that day or you would not have told the cameraman to begin filming. What did you see?" Gant asked in a friendly voice.

"Activity. Just activity."

"I see. Would you describe the activity as two men talking?"

"No."

"Two men arguing?"

"No."

"Were they in contact?"

"Yes."

"Dancing, perhaps?"

"Of course not."

"Well, just what were they doing?" Gant moved closer to Hemms.

"They were moving around."

"You said they were in contact. Were they scuffling?"

"You could say that."

"Could I say they were fighting?"

"Unh, yes. I guess so."

"But according to the film and the charges of this trial, Colonel Lochert murdered without provocation a Vietnamese civilian. Yet you say they were fighting – "

"Objection," Rafalko said. "Witness did not say that they were fighting. The defense counselor did."

447

"Sustained," the law officer said, and told Archie to continue. Archie moved closer to Mal Hemms. "You agreed to my use of the word 'fighting,' so I ask you this: If they were fighting *before* you had the camera on them, is it not possible the deceased Buey Dan *could* have thrust a knife at the defendant during that time? The very time you did not see them?"

"Unh, yes, I guess so."

"So Buey Dan *could* have thrust at Colonel Lochert the same stiletto he took from Colonel Lochert so long ago?"

"I just said yes," Hemms replied with asperity.

"No further questions," Archie Gant said and turned away.

Archie then introduced Shawn's sworn testimony as evidence that Buey Dan was in the army of the enemy in some capacity, either soldier or spy. There was a quickly suppressed stir as they recognized the name of the famous writer and his article about the Viet Cong tunnels of Cholon.

Gant put Wolf Lochert on the stand. Wolf told of the actions and attitudes of Buey Dan in the past and his attack with the missing stiletto in front of the Catholic church. The members of the court exchanged frosty glances when he told of the missing C-130 after a night HALO into Laos. The plane just disappeared from radar control without any radio transmissions over territory that had no antiaircraft weapons to bring it down. Buey Dan could easily have left a bomb on board, Wolf said.

After a recess the court was bused to the site in front of the church to watch Wolf walk through the events of that morning. He said the stiletto Buey Dan had pulled was the one he had lost during a VC attack on his patrol on 13 December 1966.

Back in the courtroom, USAF Captain Toby Parker was called by Major Denroe as a defense witness. Denroe felt evidence as far back as two years about Buey Dan maybe setting up Wolf Lochert would be a big plus for the case.

Toby was sworn in. He said on 13 December 1966, during

448

the helicopter rescue mission of Wolf's team, he had seen Buey Dan pick up a knife near the unconscious body of Wolf Lochert.

"A knife, not a stiletto?" Bruno Rafalko asked.

"It could have been either," Toby said. "I was too far away to see the blade width."

"So you cannot positively state the stiletto present in this courtroom, the stiletto that was used by the defendant to kill Buey Dan, was the weapon allegedly stolen from the unconscious body of Colonel Lochert by Buey Dan?"

"No, I cannot," Toby said with great reluctance.

When the time came, Gant summed up the defense by saying that Wolf Lochert had committed an act of war, one for which he should be decorated. It assuredly was not murder, any more than you would try an MP for shooting a terrorist who had tried to attack him. It wasn't criminal to kill an enemy in time of war, he maintained.

Colonel Rafalko wrapped up his case as the prosecutor by playing three times in slow motion the film portion showing Wolf pulling Buey Dan onto the knife.

With the closing arguments concluded, the law officer addressed the members of the court.

"The court is advised: First that the accused, Lieutenant Colonel Wolfgang Xavier Lochert, must be presumed to be innocent until his guilt is established by legal and competent evidence beyond reasonable doubt. Second, that if there is a reasonable doubt as to the guilt of the accused, the doubt should be resolved in the favor of the accused and he should be acquitted. Third, that if there is a reasonable doubt as to the degree of guilt, the finding must be in a lower degree as to which there is no reasonable doubt. Fourth, that the burden of proof to establish the guilt of the accused beyond reasonable doubt is upon the Government." The law officer drew a breath and continued. "You must disregard any comment or statement made by me during the course of this trial which may have seemed to indicate an opinion as to the guilt or innocence of the accused, for you alone have the independent responsibility of deciding this issue. Each of you must impartially resolve the ultimate issue – whether or not Colonel Lochert did murder the Vietnamese Buey Dan – in accordance with the law, the evidence admitted in court, and your own conscience. I will now close the court and you may vote on your findings."

The makeshift courtroom cleared, the seven members went for coffee and returned to their table.

"Any problems or questions?" the president asked. The two other colonels and four lieutenant colonels said no. Each man then wrote either "guilty" or "not guilty" on a square of paper and folded it in half. The junior member, the newest lieutenant colonel, collected the papers, tallied the votes, and wrote the results on a piece of paper which he handed the president. The colonel glanced at the result.

"That's it," he said. "Let's call them back."

Wolf Lochert, flanked by Archie Gant and Major Jay Denroe, sat stiff as a statue. The two lawyers were astounded at the speed at which the verdict had been rendered. They exchanged apprehensive glances.

"The court will come to order," the president said.

"All parties to the trial who were present when the court closed are now present," Colonel Bruno Rafalko said.

The president nodded and continued. "Lieutenant Colonel Wolfgang Xavier Lochert, it is my duty as president of this court to advise you that the court, in closed session and upon secret written ballot, has found you not guilty of the specification and charge. This court is adjourned."

1830 Hours Local, Saturday 16 March 1968
Officer's Club
Tan Son Nhut Air Base
Republic of Vietnam

The club was smoky, crowded, and humid from the usual

450

afternoon thundershower that drenched all of Saigon and the sprawling Tan Son Nhut Air Base next to it. No attempt had been made to air-condition the huge room. Big floor and ceiling fans moved the air about in sodden drafts heavy with the smell of sweat, beer, and abominable cigars. Green cardboard shamrocks hung from the walls. The Vietnamese waitresses wished one and all a "Happy Sane Patty Day."

"It's not until tomorrow," some would say.

"Happy Sane Patty Day," the cute little girls would repeat. "Happy Sane Patty Day."

There was a small crowd gathered about the piano in one corner. In that crowd was Wolfgang Xavier Lochert, and Wolfgang Xavier Lochert was tight. Pleasantly, gentlemanly, tight. It was well known that Wolfgang Xavier Lochert rarely touched alcohol, and certainly never got tight, at least not since many years ago in Korea and twelve years ago in Heidelberg, Germany. Assigned then to the 10th SFG (Special Forces Group) at Bad Tolz, he had been detached for a few weeks as liaison officer to a bunch of legs from the 4th Armored out on maneuvers in what they had nicknamed the Sunshine Forest near the Neckar River. At the end of the exercise, he and a Norwegian army officer had visited the Roten Oxen university beer hall (one drank beer from a glass boot) in Heidelberg. At that venerable establishment (called the rotten ox by the troops, the Red Ox by the officers; it had been in business since the 17th century) Wolf had been neither gentlemanly nor pleasantly tight. He had been stinking, knee-walking, bar-wrecking drunk.

As it had been reconstructed, Captain Lochert, Wolfgang X., had been listening to his Norwegian friend tell how the Nazis had lined up most of the people from his town against a wall one sunny day and shot them. They had been shot because a small German patrol had been ambushed and slain. His friend's father had led the ambush. His friend's father had been shot that day, and so had his mother.

The Norwegian officer handled himself well as he told Wolf the story. Well, that is, until a table full of cute

451

American leg lieutenants, who had spent World War Two in grade school, thought the German oompah band should play the "Horst Wessel Lied." The song had been a rallying piece for the Nazis and had been banned since 1945. The young Americans thought it all a joke.

Two of the lieutenants still wear bridges, the base drum and its thumper along with the accordion player still shudder as they walk along the broad Neckar into which they were thrown, and Wolf Lochert has a small scar on his ankle from the chains his friends had had to use to pin him underneath the bridge and away from the Military Police. That was Wolf's second and last big drunk.

Now, twelve years later, he stood by an old upright played by the pie-eyed San Francisco lawyer Archie Gant and sang Irish ballads. He was neither a tenor, soprano, or basso profundo. Hard to tell what he was. Even though his face was creased in a beatific smile, his "Too ra Loo ra Loo ra, that's an Irish lullaby" defied description, almost.

"Hacksaw," said Court Bannister, who had arranged some official business at 7th coinciding with the victory celebration, "a dull hacksaw on plywood." His business at Tan Son Nhut was to brief Commander, 7th Air Force, and his staff, on Phantom-FAC operations. The short but intense session had broken up an hour earlier.

"File on glass, I'd say," said Toby Parker, who had a Coca-Cola can in his hand. He was due back at Da Nang the next day.

"Gravel," Jay Denroe said. "A car skidding on gravel." He was drinking Ba Mui Ba beer from a large bottle. He was due back at USARV on Monday.

"Wolf's a grunt," Court said, "and grunts don't sing, they grunt. That's why they're called grunts."

"You men are so mean," said Greta Sturm. "Vulfgang has a wery manly voice." She wore a flowing cotton shift and sandals. She sipped a soda water. Greta now had an apartment in Saigon on a tree-lined street near the West German Embassy.

Court and Toby moved off to one side when Archie

swung into "Danny Boy" and Wolf lurched along a mere half beat behind.

Three weeks had passed since the two pilots had attacked and killed the 100mm gun. There had been no chutes, no beepers, no contact whatsoever with Captain Deacon Docks and Lieutenant Neil Tallboy, who had been apparently shot down by the big gun. Repeated recce of Rho Magna and the surrounding area turned up no clues as to the fate of the missing men, but neither was the big gun heard from again, or any other that size. The USAF had declared the two men MIA, Missing in Action. The pain of their passing had been brief. Those men removed from Docks and Tallboy by rank and experience filed their faces among the many that disappeared each month. Those men who were close held short, private requiems within themselves, filing away their grief for expungement at a later date, a date they suspected would never come. The men knew instinctively that combat was neither the time nor place to mourn. Death due to distraction awaited mourners. Court had moved up another crew into training from his volunteer list to replace them. Life in the fighter wing moved on, while back in the States two families were forever shattered.

The Phantom FACs had been on line and operational at night for the last two weeks. Their flying schedule was heavy, and they were still shy one backseater. So far they had taken no hits, but neither had they killed any trucks. They had, however, killed three or four guns a night.

Toby Parker had returned to Da Nang after spending his time with the Phantoms. He had flown several uneventful missions in the DMZ before being subpoenaed for Wolf's trial.

"How did it go today at Seventh?" Toby asked Court.

"I know we're stopping traffic, because agent reports say we are," Court said, "but Seventh is getting pressure from the Pentagon because we aren't racking up truck kills. They're glad we are killing guns, but they say trucks are our targets, and why aren't we getting any?"

453

"What did you tell them?"

"I said the statistics of supplies moving down the Trail should eventually prove we have cut traffic dramatically, but we'd have to wait. Even so, the method of finding out how much material comes out of the pipeline isn't all that accurate. Then I said that if they wanted more night truck-kills, we'd have to have night eyeballs."

"Meaning what?"

"Get a few of the new AC-130 gunships to be stationed at Ubon to work the Trail with F-4s. Hostettler worked out a plan where we could suppress flak for them as well as augment their fire-power." The gunships, call sign Spectre, were huge four-engined (turboprops with over 4,000 horse-power each) transports that carried 7.62mm, 20mm, and 40mm side-firing guns. Future plans called for a 105mm gun to be mounted in the plane.

"Think they'll go for it?"

"Probably. If they want to *kill* trucks. About all we've been doing is keep them off the road. So far we haven't killed any. We've dropped a lot of flares, dumped a lot of ordnance, caused a few secondary explosions, but no positive truck kills. We come humming over, dropping flares, giving the gomers plenty of advance warning to pull over and watch us make little karst rocks out of big ones. Meanwhile we lost one strike bird into the karst. Not a very good return."

The songfest broke up when Archie tried to sing one of his early Navy songs. Something about some limey broad's fundamental orifice brought Wolf protectively to Greta's side. He put his arm around her waist, his big hand resting just above her ample posterior.

"It sounds very clinical," she said to him, a disapproving frown on her face.

"Now just don't worry. You don't have to listen to him," Wolf said with soothing affection. "I'll be glad to sing some more." He weaved only slightly as he held her.

"Nein, danke," Greta Sturm said. She took his big hand in

454

hers. "Come, take me home now." She seemed determined to have her way.

"One moment, *Liebling*," Wolf said, and disengaged. He pulled Archie Gant to his feet and maneuvered him over to Major Jay Denroe.

"You guys did a fine job. And I just want to say something to you both." He paused and put an armlock on each man's neck and gently butted their heads together. He had to bend Denroe to Gant's level. "I just want to say that for a leg" – he tightened up on Denroe – "and a squid" – he tightened up on Gant, nearly popping both men's eyes – "you guys are okay." He gave a final squeeze and released them. He said goodbye to Court and Toby. Everybody shook hands. Gant was quiet. This was Wolf Lochert's show. Wolf went back to Greta Sturm.

"Okay, we go now." He put his arm around her and steered her toward the door, clearly in charge, maybe even in love. A final wave and he was gone.

"He's right," Court said. "You guys did a hell of a fine job. You helped him beat it all."

"No, what he beat was going to jail," Denroe said. "His career is ruined. He'll never rise above lieutenant colonel. Somebody, someplace, wanted just that to happen. This never should have gone to trial. Somebody was pushing."

"Yeah, maybe so," Archie Gant rasped. "But I was glad to do this for him. For a grunt, that is."

Court looked at him, well aware it was his money paying the lawyer's substantial fee. "You hinting you waive payment?"

"Waive payment?" Gant honked in smiling delight, as aware as Court who was paying. "Waive payment? Hell, no, I'm a lawyer, aren't I?" He slapped Court on the back. "But your brother might not be too pleased to know it's your money that squeezed that deposition out of him." He gave Court a synopsis of Michael LaNew's blackmail activities that forced the statement from Shawn Bannister. "Does that bother you?" Gant asked, studying Court's face.

Court was silent for a moment. What Gant mistook for

contemplation of a difficult question was in fact Court's efforts to keep a grin from his face over his half-brother's self-inflicted tribulations. He succeeded, and with a straight face answered, "Not one bit."

"How about this, then? Came this morning from my office." Gant took out his large folding wallet and handed Court a newspaper picture from the *California Sun*. "Does this bother you?"

Court studied the picture. It showed a clean-shaven Shawn Bannister in the foreground of a crowd of bearded protestors carrying antiwar signs. On one side of Shawn was a heavily bearded man wearing Army fatigues sitting in a wheel. On the other side was a scowling and warlike-looking Richard Connert. The headline stated that combat pilot Richard Connert was the latest member of the VVAW – the Vietnam Veterans Against the War.

Court laughed. "It doesn't bother me one fucking bit."

Gant barked approval and turned to Denroe, who looked at his watch and said, "Time to go." The two lawyers departed on a pre-arranged tour of Saigon bars. Toby and Court stood by the silent piano.

"I got some good news from Colonel Annillo today," Toby said. He had a broad smile on his face. "He called this morning and said he had fixed an upgrade slot into F-4s for me at George Air Force Base."

"Toby, that's great," Court said in pleased surprise. "You've got the fighter-pilot attitude, now you get your fighter. Try to get Ken Tanaka as your instructor."

"I will."

"You know you'll come right back to the war, don't you?"

"I know that."

Court regarded him steadily. "I hope it's what you really want."

Toby Parker looked off in the distance. He thought of Phil Travers, the pilot who had introduced him to the sheer joy of flying. Travers had been killed in front of Toby while rescuing Wolf Lochert and a Special Forces

456

unit. The roar of afterburners from a fighter taking off drowned the club noise for an instant.

Toby nodded and grinned. "It's what I really want."

Toby took a long pull at his can of Coca-Cola. "Court," he said, "mind if I ask you a question? It's kind of personal."

Court took a sip of his own Coke. He still didn't want to drink in front of his Toby. "Sure," he said, "go ahead."

"Well," Toby said, slowly, "you seem so *serious* these days. You don't seem to laugh as much anymore. Is everything okay? Phantom FACs doing okay? Your dad all right? I don't mean to pry, but . . ." He trailed off.

Court slammed his Coke down on the piano top. "Goddamm, Tobes, you're getting just like Doc Russell. What's with you guys, anyhow? Just cause I don't go around ha-ha-ing and ho-ho-ing all the time you think I'm a candidate for the couch of the closest shrink."

Toby looked concerned. "Court, I'm sorry. I shouldn't have brought it up . . . but, well, you're my friend and I want to help you. I think I know what your problem is."

"You what?"

"Yeah, I know what your problem is."

Court's eyebrows went up. "Okay, Doctor Parker, what is it?"

Toby looked around conspiratorially; his glance swept by two Air Force nurses at a corner table.

"Lackanookie," Toby said.

Court drew back. "Parker," he said with an explosive laugh, "you son of a bitch, you're probably right."

Toby nodded his head toward the two nurses. He had seen earlier that the two girls seemed to have noticed Court, as if they knew who he was. Court followed his glance. One of the nurses, a tall brunette, nudged the other, who looked up and smiled.

Toby turned to face the girls. He spoke to Court out of the corner of his mouth. "Tally ho, eh what, old chap?"

"Tally ho it is," Court said.

The two men started for the table.

25

It was set. Conditions were right; it was raining. Tonight was the time they would go. Frederick had learned how to slide his ceiling slats out. They had made their needles and sewn the pajamas in such a way that at the last minute they could attach pieces of the blanket so that from a distance the clothes would appear to be civilian garb. At the last minute they would dunk the whole maroon-and-gray ensemble into a vile mixture of beet juice and mud they had been hoarding. First they had to pee into the can for moisture, then rip and crush the beets they had stolen from the pitiful garden the guards kept, then blend in the mud. Then they were to poke their newly formed civilian clothes into the mess and hope they would come out dark enough to camouflage the stripes. They knew it would be a stinking mess that wouldn't fool anybody at twenty feet in the daytime. But they were going out at night and wouldn't pass within ten feet of anybody. They hoped.

At what they guessed was one in the morning, they tapped and said, "Let's do it." They both had actions to perform while the other kept watch under the door. If a guard was spotted, the watcher would give a loud sneeze and a kick on the wall. Frederick would take the first watch.

The preparations had been painstaking. As soon as Flak was clubbed back into his cell after his visit with Ceballos, he pulled out the pencil he had stolen and the yellow paper with the "one equals two" equations on it. He drew quickly and accurately the map portion of Hanoi that led from the Hoa Lo prison to the British Embassy. The last two blocks were a muddle. He hadn't quite had the time to pinpoint the exact streets from Ceballos' map. He tore a piece off and made a second copy. That night he had climbed into the attic and dropped a copy to the waiting Ted Frederick. Memorize the map, Flak had tapped to him. They still hadn't seen each other's face. The moving of the slats was practiced and easy now. They had agreed Ted wouldn't touch his slats until it was time to go. Then Flak could help him from above. They both had taken to sleeping on the floor, so the guards were used to looking in during night inspections and not seeing them on their bunks.

Flak had held water as much as he could and now peed with vigor into the waste can. He was naked. Sweat gleamed on his black skin, accentuating the muscles he had developed for the escape attempt. Then he shredded the meager beets he had stolen, mixed some dark dirt into the mess, and set about staining his pajamas. He heard a sneeze and a light thump on the wall. They had practiced for just such an event. He quickly seated himself upon the waste can as if he had to use it. The guard strode the hall, opening flippers at random. He looked in at Flak and quickly passed on. The V abhorred such sights. Two thumps from Frederick and he knew he was clear. He finished the dye job and tapped for Frederick to begin. Minutes later, when Frederick tapped he was ready, it was time to climb to the crawlspace and escape.

He stood on his slab, quickly took out each ceiling slat and piled them up inside the attic, pulled himself up, wiggled, and was crouching on the ceiling joists. Off to one side, he was aware of Frederick wriggling through his opening. He replaced the slats, which cut the light considerably. As he had learned from his practice runs, just enough light came up from holes to fill the crawlspace with a dim glow. The two men duck-waddled toward each other. As agreed beforehand, they did not speak. They stared at each other's face in the gloom and clasped hands, then embraced.

To finally see each other, after becoming so familiar with each other's thoughts through the tap code, was strange and disconcerting. Though they had shared pain and sorrow, joy and humor eked out of the harshest of conditions, neither man looked as the other had imagined. There were no familiar contours and planes of recognition, nor hair color or profiles of well-remembered physique. In the gloom, Flak could see Ted Frederick had thick black hair, a square jaw, and broad shoulders. It was almost like starting an acquaintance with a stranger.

Flak whispered into Ted Frederick's ear. "You smell like shit."

"So do you," Frederick whispered back. "We'd better not get too close to anybody. Where's your turban?"

Flak pointed to the cloth he had wrapped around his arm. He motioned to the triangular wall near the street and the two men waddled to the bricks. Flak peered out the louvered vent. The street was black, deserted, and rain-swept, barely lit except by flashes of lightning from the west. The vent came loose in his hands when he tugged at it. He and Frederick began dismantling a portion of the wall downward from the vent hole. With a little tugging back and forth, the mortar yielded and the bricks came loose one by one. As they widened the opening, they looked down at the top of the huge wall surrounding the prison. The sharp glass pieces looked thick, as if from champagne bottles. How French, Flak thought. They piled the loose bricks inside and stopped removing them when the hole was big enough to climb though.

Flak picked up the ten-inch piece of bare copper wire he had found earlier in the crawlspace and stashed at the base of the wall. As planned, Frederick held him by the waist and he leaned out and gingerly wound one end of the wire around the top strand of barbed wire. Holding it up in the rain, he looked back at Frederick with a question in his eyes. Frederick gave Flak a reassuring squeeze and nodded his head. Flak released the wire. It swung down and shorted against the bottom strand with a popping crack and flash as 220 volts blew the ancient fuse someplace in the circuit. Half the lights in the prison went out, and now it was pitch black in the crawlspace. The illumination from the street barely provided an outline of the top of the wall.

Operating more by feel than sight, the two men stepped across the open space to crouch on top of the wall, careful to place their feet between the glass shards, one leg on each side of the barbed wire. The rain enveloped them, chilly and persistent. They helped each other balance, then, as planned, Frederick steadied Flak as he let himself down to hang over the street side of the wall and let go. He fell the remaining ten feet and landed in a heap, head buzzing, feet hot through the rubber sandals from the hard landing. He staggered to his feet, leaned against the wall, and looked up at the dim outline of his fellow pilot.

"Ssst, ssst," he hissed in the pre-arranged signal signifying he was ready to cushion Frederick's fall. A large mass suddenly materialized above him and struck him to the concrete sidewalk where he lay stunned.

"Hey. Hey, Flak," Frederick said in his ear as he untangled himself. "Come on. We got places to go and people to meet."

Flak sat up, blinked in the rain, unwound the cloth from his arm, and fashioned it into a turban on his head. Frederick looked at Flak. "You look about as much like an East Indian as the Creature from the Black Lagoon."

"Yeah, thanks. *You* look as much a journalist as Genghis Khan."

Two minutes later the men were darting down the black street in the direction they had memorized from Flak's map. The streets were sparsely lit by one lamppost per block with a low-power bulb. Their sandals made soft slapping and splashing noises as they ran.

Frederick pulled Flak to a halt. "Sandals too noisy, hard

to run." They took them off, held them in one hand, and ran on, silent as ghosts, darting from shadow to shadow, elusive as smoke. The streets were lined with shops, their metal doors and grillwork pulled into place. The rain slowed, then stopped. Thunder rumbled to the west, somewhere a dog barked twice, the subdued whine of Vietnamese music sounded from one of the windows over a shop. The dim glow of oil lamps made shadow outlines on a few windows. Each time they came to a corner, they flattened against a building. One of them would drop to the ground and slowly poke his head to look around the corner. Seeing no one, they would continue. They counted the corners and made the turns they had memorized.

As they lay flat before the sixth turn, something scrambled on a small balcony over their heads, and a small dog started to yap. Flak crawled to the corner and slowly inched forward, his nose almost in the angle between sidewalk and building. It smelled of dog feces and something rotten. He was soaked with the accumulated water from the streets. He cautiously looked around the corner and froze, every nerve jangling. From the ragged light of a small lantern, he saw two militiamen strolling toward him, casually chatting in the empty wet street, AK-47s slung muzzle-down over their backs. They were fifty feet from the corner.

Flak slowly worked himself backwards. "Two soldiers," he whispered in Frederick's ear, "with AKs."

Their eyes glistened as they looked at each other. Lightning flashed, closer. Then crashing rolls of thunder. Each knew what the other was thinking. If we take them, we at least have weapons and maybe uniform parts that might be a better disguise. But what to do with the bodies? Worse, if we are captured we will be executed for murder, never mind the escape.

Each shook his head no at the same time. They both crawled backwards, hoping to find a doorway. They had only seconds. There were no doorways among the shop fronts, just shutters and grilles pulled flush to the face of the ancient concrete building. They could hear the murmur as the two soldiers approached the corner. The dog on the balcony set up a constant yapping. A muffled voice from inside snapped a few Vietnamese words.

"Make like street sleepers," Flak whispered in Frederick's ear and assumed the position of a person curled up in sleep in an inhospitable environment. After a heart-stopping instant, Frederick did the same. Then the soldiers were at the corner. They barely glanced at the sleeping forms on the sidewalk and continued on.

"What took you so long?" Flak whispered. They lay there, looking at each other.

"What did you say to do?"

"Make like street sleepers."

"I thought you said 'street sweepers.' "

Flak burbled a giggle and had to bite his tongue. "Oh God, Ted. There you are, laying in a street in the middle of downtown Hanoi in rags, smelling of your own piss, and you think we should sweep the street."

"You should talk – you're covered with dog shit."

Flak punched him lightly on the shoulder. "Let's press on."

For the next hour they slowly and cautiously worked their way toward the British Embassy. They came to a cemetery. Large and small croissant-shaped structures of concrete were set amidst square and rectangular headstones, many with crosses. In front of several stones were small lacquer bowls and sticks of incense. A few military trucks with blackout lights rumbled down the large street bordering the far side. The two men crouched outside the wrought-iron fence.

"This isn't on the map," Frederick said. The cemetery stretched off in both directions for several blocks.

"This is the area I couldn't memorize without Fidel becoming suspicious. I do know we must cross that big road on the other side. The Embassy isn't far beyond."

"Then I guess we better cut through the cemetery," Frederick said, and glanced up at the fence. "We can climb this easy enough." They started to climb. Frederick reached the top, started swinging his leg over, and looked down. Flak was clinging to the fence halfway up, a look of agony on his face.

"What is it?" Frederick hissed.

"My arm, it's . . . it's killing me. Hurts like hell, won't function."

Frederick locked his legs on the top of the fence for balance and reached down to help Flak up next to him, then helped him climb down to the inside of the cemetery. They scuttled in among the stones and settled in the rounded vee of a concrete-and-plaster tomb halfway between the surrounding streets. They both were sweating in the misty rain. They sat with their backs to the tomb, facing the darkened street they had just come from. There was a tiny door into the tomb next to them. Flak massaged his left arm.

"How does it feel?" Frederick asked.

"It's okay," Flak said, knowing he was lying. It hurt like hell, but he didn't want Frederick to be alarmed.

Frederick lay flat and peered around the corner of the tomb toward the big street visible through the trees and beyond the small grave markers and rounded vaults. There was no civilian traffic. One after the other, about twenty-five meters apart, a convoy of military trucks splashed through the wide, rain-covered boulevard, blackout lights dim and low to the ground. After a moment Frederick pulled back. The two men could barely see each other.

"Do we have to cross?"

"If we want to get to the British Embassy we do."

"We'll have to wait for a break, then dash across," Frederick said and lay back against the tomb. "You know what these are?"

"The tombs?"

"Yeah, the shape. They're shaped like the thighs of a woman . . . and her crotch. They're called *hùyet* in Vietnamese."

"From the womb to the womb," Flak said. He sat back next to Frederick. "It's going to be daylight soon." They spoke in hushed tones.

"God, I'm hungry," Flak said.

"Let's send out for a pizza."

Frederick felt around the small door to the tomb. Something clattered. "Here," he said. He produced a bowl with what felt like hard bits of rice in it. Something scurried under the pressure of his thumb. "I also read where the Buddhists leave some food out by the tomb for the spirits of the departed." The two men split the contents, teeth cracking the dried rice like small chips of candy.

"Agh," Flak said, "it's like trying to eat sand."

"Let it soak in your mouth for a while," Frederick suggested. The splash and roar of trucks continued. "Looks like we might be here a while."

"At least until that convoy passes." Flak settled back. "You flew Thuds from Tahkli, didn't you?" he asked, naming a USAF base in Thailand.

"Yeah. Up until one of three SAMs fired at me ripped most of a wing off. How about you?"

"Ingested MiG debris that slowed me down, then I was hit by antiaircraft near Vinh. Eighty-five mil, I think."

"Your backseater get out?"

"I don't think so. But you never know."

"No, you never know."

"Ted, you tapped through the wall that our names were getting out. How?"

"Right now in letters home. The V allow a few guys to write and receive letters. They make oblique references like 'I miss going with Bobby to the lake and sailing boats.' That means Navy man Bob Lake is here. I guess our intell guys study those letters pretty thoroughly. And some writers use the dot code. That's where they make a tiny dot or prick a hole in the paper under a letter. Others emphasize or raise certain words and letters."

"Sounds too slow and unwieldy to me. Who's allowed to write? They never said I could."

"The way we figure it is just those guys whose shootdown was publicized for propaganda purposes or whose pictures were shown by an East German or Japanese camera crew.

Maybe the V think that shows their 'humane and lenient' policy. Anyway, each of our writers is assigned so many names. But you're right. It's too slow. So we have a man who is memorizing names. The wheels have ordered him out on an early release."

"Early release. Can something like that happen?"

"You didn't know? Some of our guys cave in without torture and write letters to Uncle Ho begging forgiveness for their 'crimes against humanity.' If they do that and 'show a good attitude' by making broadcasts and meeting with the so-called peace delegations, they might get an early release. Now, I'm not talking about the guys who are tortured to do these things. I'm talking about guys who cooperate the minute they are captured. So far six of those bastards have gone out with Americans from the peace groups."

"Who is the guy ordered out?"

"Hegdahl. So far he's memorized two hundred fifty names by service and rank. He's only nineteen and he really plays the village idiot around the V. They have him out there sweeping sidewalks and emptying slop buckets and all the time he's communicating. He's also sabotaged some trucks."

"Go on. How'd he do that?"

"When he was over at the Zoo, Stratton saw him sweep up some dirt and pour it in truck gas tanks."

Flak sat up. "Listen," he hissed.

"I don't hear anything."

"That's it. I don't either. The convoy has passed."

They crawled to the sides of the tomb and looked over at the wide boulevard. They saw the last truck disappear out of sight.

"Okay," Flak said. "This is it. Time to cross over."

"I'm not sure I like the sound of that."

The two men got to their feet and darted through the tombs and mausoleums to the black iron fence. The boulevard was deserted in both directions. The shop fronts across the wide avenue were closed, the shuttered windows above presented dead eyes. With a quick glance in both directions, Ted Frederick sprang halfway up the fence and reached for the top. The fence shook, and he heard a clatter behind him and looked down. Flak Apple was in a heap at the base, his face a mask of pain in the shadows.

"It's my damn arm again," he moaned softly. They heard a truck approaching.

"Quick," Frederick said, clinging to the top and reaching down for him. The truck noise grew louder. There were several. "Christ," he said. "It's another convoy."

"Press on," Flak almost shouted. "Don't wait for me. Move it, goddammit. Move it!" The noise grew louder. Frederick made a motion up to the top of the fence, then dropped back down to the ground next to Flak. "Nah," he said. "We go together or we don't go at all." They scuttled back to the sheltering arms of the tomb as the first of the trucks roared past the cemetery. The moist air deadened the sounds. Flak pressed his arm to his side and eased himself down to rest against the tomb.

"Why in hell didn't you go on?" he asked.

"I forgot where the Embassy was." More trucks accelerated past the cemetery.

"Forgot, hell." He looked to the east. There was a faint grayish glow. "I think we are going to have to spend the day here."

Frederick looked around. "Let's crawl in one of these womb tombs."

"Yeah, a big one. Real big."

They found one near the fence. It was as large as an automobile. The plaster was crumbling; parts of the rounded corners were missing. They knelt at the two-foot-square door in the vee of the angle and pried it open with their fingers. Pieces of the wood came off in their hands when the wood-and-leather latches snapped. The door fell to the ground. Musty and fetid air oozed out heavy as smoke from a greenwood fire. They looked at each other. The gray of the wet and overcast dawn diffused the cemetery in moist gauze.

"After you," Ted Frederick said, his mouth twisted in a lopsided grin.

"YGTBSM," Flak Apple said and crawled in. Something scurried away in the blackness in front of him. He wiped a hand in reflex as cobwebs draped his head and face. He nudged big stone jars that scraped the concrete floor with gritty noise. He felt around in front of him, found a wall, and stopped. He touched the blank face, then backed out.

"It's about five feet deep and four wide," he told Frederick. "Let's back in, then pull the door shut after us."

"Unh, Flak, is there anything . . . unh, *anyone* in there?"

"Only in the jars."

One after the other they backed through the narrow door and lay facing each other, knees drawn up to squeeze into the confined space. Flak reached out and pulled the fallen door to the front of the opening and wedged it in place, shutting out the dim gray light that had given them form and substance. A round dot of gray on the door marked a missing screw.

"Cozy," Frederick said. Their faces were six inches apart.

"Too cozy for words," Flak replied. "Your breath is . . . well, *imposing*."

"Yours isn't exactly eau de cologne."

"It's all that damn pumpkin soup and rotten rice."

"Just don't fart. Whatever you do, don't fart."

"Don't you." Flak started to giggle. "We'd never make it through the day."

"We'd be outta here like corks from a bottle." Frederick had a hard time suppressing his laughter. "Say," he said, suddenly serious. "You don't have diarrhea or anything, do you?"

"No, thank God. Not anymore. How about you?"

"Yeah," Frederick said, glum now, "I've had some trouble."

Flak Apple sniffed. "Personally, I don't think it would make any difference. These clothes smell like shit anyhow." They lay still a few minutes.

"You think we're going to make it to the Embassy? What about the guards? They're probably Viet," Frederick said. They spoke in low voices.

"We've made it this far. Damn near twenty blocks. Only a few more to go. As for the guards, we'll create a diversion. Throw a rock or something. Then climb over the wall into the compound. POC."

"POC? What's that?"

"Piece of cake," Flak said.

"I'll tell you, this is it for me. I'm not going back into jail. I'm going to make it out of here one way or the other." Frederick's whisper was a harsh rasp.

"What do you mean?"

"I mean I get away, completely away, or I'm dead. Simple as that. I'm not going back. I can't take anymore."

Flak had heard on the fighter pilots' grapevine that Ted Frederick was a hard man, a resister. A man of Maine toughness who gave no quarter and asked none. He had been surprised Frederick had been so compassionate and understanding with him, especially his shame and misery at signing the statement. But they had spoken through the tap code for long hours on the wall and Frederick had, Flak thought, revealed himself as a gentle man whose toughness had come through in his abiding faith in his God, his country, his fellow POWs, and himself. Frederick had given Flak guidance and tender succor as he had come to grips with the harsh facts of his shootdown, his wounds, his captivity, and – worst of all – the reality that Americans both at home and in Hanoi were siding with the enemy to condemn him and his fellow POWs as, if not war criminals, at least as dupes of a fascist government.

"Sure you can," Flak said. "You can take anything. You're too tough to give in."

"Who said anything about giving in?" Frederick snapped. "If I'm caught, I'll fight the bastards and take as many with me as I can."

Flak checked the screwhole. It was bright as a tiny bulb. "We've got about fifteen hours of daylight to go, O mighty warrior. What say we log some Zzs?" Frederick agreed. Flak had to turn away to face the wall so they could squirm and double up spoon fashion and be moderately comfortable. A jar scraped the rough concrete.

"Hey," Frederick said behind Flak's back. "One of us should stay awake. Sort of pull guard duty. Wouldn't do for both of us to be crapped out at the same time. I'll take the first watch."

"Good man," Flak said over his shoulder. "Wake me in a few hours with some tea, will you, old boy?" He folded his hands together under his cheek and tried to sleep. The gray eye of the screwhole above his head glowed like an electric eye.

First the hard concrete bit into his hipbone. He wriggled slightly to take the pressure off. Then the mold of the crumbling walls assailed his nostrils. It reminded him of the damp and mildew he had found as a child when he used to play under the front porch of the home where he had been raised in Washington, D.C. "Allie," he heard his mother call as he fell asleep. "Allie, where are you? Dinner's ready." He slept, seeing the mounds of food on the Thanksgiving table before him. Food he could see but not touch.

He awoke with a start. He guessed it was close to noon. Frederick was nudging him. He tilted his head back.

"Somebody out there," Frederick whispered into his ear. "Take a look."

Flak raised up on his elbow and pressed his head to the tiny gray hole. Something was moving just outside the tomb entrance. Something close, too close to focus on, a black-and-brown blur. Then he heard snuffling and a whine.

"Oh God," he breathed to Frederick. "It's a dog. I can see it now. Damn near a puppy." They heard the dog whine and make scratching noises with his paws as it dug at the door. "Oh shit, it smells us."

"See anybody with it?" Frederick hissed.

"Can't tell. It's too close. Blocks the hole." The dog made impatient yips as it pawed and clawed the door.

"We've no choice. We've got to open the door and pull

470

it in here and hope to hell no one is out there with it."

"Then what?" Flak asked.

Frederick didn't answer. He rolled over on his belly and raised to his elbows. Flak did the same. In the dark they felt for the small door and slowly tilted and eased it down. Gray light flooded the small enclosure. The dog backed away and began yapping at the two men more from playful invitation than aggressiveness. It was a terrier, runty and full of mange. Frederick lunged through the opening like a striking snake, grabbed a front leg, and pulled the startled dog into the tomb and under his body.

"Quick – close the door," he said, his whisper grating with strain. Flak quickly pulled the door in place. He hadn't seen anyone outside in his narrow field of vision. In the sudden darkness, the dog was squirming and scrabbling under Frederick and making a series of sharp yips. Frederick made a quick motion and the noise was choked off. There was the sound of labored breathing, then the crunching and snapping of cartilage and frantic scrambling that slowly stopped. Then one small convulsive movement. Then silence. Frederick made a keening noise in his throat.

"Ah God," he said quietly. "That was awful." He swallowed. "I think I'm going to throw up." His body convulsed twice, then subsided. "I'm okay now," he said, and took some deep breaths. He paused. "You hungry?"

Flak couldn't contain himself, and giggled. "God, Frederick, but you are rotten."

"To the co-wah," Ted Frederick said in a thick Maine accent. Rotten to the core.

They both froze as a knock sounded on the small door, then another. Before they could move, the door fell open, revealing a figure looking in.

The gray overcast formed a backdrop for a little Vietnamese girl in the white blouse and blue skirt of a schoolchild. Short black hair and bangs framed her quizzical face as she squatted, arms on knees, peering in.

"Dũa bé?" Puppy? she asked in Vietnamese. "Puppy?" She seemed undaunted by the presence of two foreigners

471

in a *hûyet*. Maybe she thinks we're friendly spirits, Flak thought insanely as he stared at her tiny feet encased in thongs. Then he felt the still-warm body of the puppy pressing against his side. He twisted his head suddenly to look at Ted Frederick. Frederick met his gaze with a sudden wild look, his round pupils black and unreadable in a sea of white, mouth contorted in a rictus of fear and loathing, lips drawn back in a silent snarl. Frederick snapped his head around toward the little girl. He bunched his legs and arms under himself. Flak gaped at him in horror.

"Ted, oh my God, you're not – " He was cut off as Frederick bolted out of the *hûyet* and snatched up the little girl in his arms.

"Run," he shouted as he spirited the little girl away from the tomb and toward the side of the cemetery farthest from the boulevard. "Run, Flak," he shouted over his shoulder. "It's your only chance. Haul ass."

Flak sprang from the tomb, his mind working. As he turned to flee, he saw in a tableau that Ted Frederick had stopped with the now-crying girl near the far fence and was trying to soothe her terrified sobs. Pedestrians were gathering outside the fence, yelling in singsong voices and waving at armed men across the street. So far, in the confusion, Flak hadn't been noticed. He spun around the crumbling *hûyet*, leaped another, and all but ran up the fence separating him from the boulevard. Arm pain deadened in the shock of adrenaline, he vaulted down from the top, scattering pedestrians and bicycle riders, and dashed across the wide street. He darted behind a military truck, almost collided with a pedicab, and splashed through the gutter parallel to a sidewalk, heading toward a corner. Small people plucked ineffectually at his sleeve as he ran by. Singsong voices rose in an excited babble. On he ran in long strides. He turned up the side street he was sure headed toward the British Embassy. Here the sidewalks were even more crowded with scurrying Vietnamese. He ran to the middle of the road, dodging the bicycles and pedicabs. His breath was coming hard now, and he heard himself panting as he sucked air into his burning lungs. Two armed men, soldiers, came around a corner and aimed rifles at him, screaming something in Vietnamese. He veered toward a knot of people as a screen and ran on. Another corner and he knew he was close to the Embassy. His turban started to unravel and he snatched it from his head and flung it away.

"About here, about here, about here," he started to chant in time with his thumping footfalls. Then a sandal tore loose and he went down, tumbling and rolling through civilians that were frantically trying to get out of his way. He tore the other sandal off and ran barefoot, sprinting on his toes and the balls of his feet. He was weakening. Pain stitched his side. Then he saw a high wall with a polished brass plaque on the corner where the bricks came together. He barely caught the word EMBASSY as he dashed around the corner, surprised a Vietnamese guard lounging against the wall, and flung himself past the small wooden guard shack into a cobblestone compound fronting a gray stone villa. A flag flew next to the large double doors. Behind him, the guard screamed in Vietnamese as Flak flung himself on the doors, beating them with his fists. Sweat was streaming down his face and body.

"Open up," he yelled. "Let me in. Open up!" He looked behind him as he hammered his fists on a panel. The guard was leveling a long rifle at him. The pain in his side and lungs caused the apparition to blur as he stared down the huge gun barrel, barely ten feet away. He felt himself graying out in the first dizzy fog of a faint. It got worse. The world turned gray as he fell to his knees. "Open up," he mumbled. "Open up." The last thing he saw was one of the huge doors opening. He tumbled forward into the blackness.

He awakened to a feeling of incredible softness. Softness without definition. And coolness. Blissful coolness beyond compare. This can't be right, he thought. This can't be right. Then awareness flooded his body. I made it, he thought. I made it. He blinked his eyes open. He could tell he was on a couch. Two men stood staring down at him, white men. Caucasians. He struggled up on his elbows.

"I'm Major Algernon Apple, United States Air Force. Is this the British Embassy?"

The two men glanced at each other. "No," one said in heavily accented English. He was thin and had a narrow mustache. "I am Colonel Beaudreaux. This is the Embassy of the Republic of France."

Flak broke into a broad smile. "Hell, Colonel. France, England. What difference does it make? I made it. I'm safe." Then he remembered Ted Frederick. "How long have I been here? Do you know anything of another American?"

The colonel with the mustache spoke rapidly in French to his companion, then answered at length.

"You have been here for about eight hours. Asleep. He cleaned you. The doctor" – he indicated the man next to him – "injected you. The other American, it was reported to us he was shot."

Flak Apple slumped back. "He saved me. He let me get free." He sat up abruptly. "Look, I've got to contact the American forces. I've got to let them know I'm safe. They'll get me out of here."

Colonel Beaudreaux drew back. "I am afraid, Major, that is not possible," he said in a stiff voice.

"Not possible? What do you mean, not possible? I'm an American. I've escaped from a POW camp. You've got to help me. I need protection."

Beaudreaux looked pained, like Maxim's headwaiter at a badly dressed patron. "It is as I said. It is simply not possible to give you any help or protection. We are under diplomatic protection, and under diplomatic agreement with the Democratic Republic of Vietnam. We cannot jeopardize these arrangements by taking in criminals – "

"Criminals," Flak exploded. "Criminals! How dare you say that?" He jumped to his feet, head swimming. "You sound just like them. You sound just like the V." He swayed. The doctor took his arm and said soothing words in his ear. Beaudreaux barked at him and took Flak by the elbow. Flak could see they were in a parlor furnished with couches, and chairs, and elegant tables. The colonel led him to the door at the far end. The doctor stood back. Flak saw a look of inestimable sorrow on the doctor's face as Beaudreaux opened the door to an anteroom and pushed Flak in where six armed Vietnamese soldiers were waiting.

The beating started immediately. They asked no questions, said no words. They simply took him to the knobby room, put him in the ropes, hung him upside down, and started beating him. Two men, one with a leather strap, the other with flayed bamboo, beat him, on and on. When he began screaming, they poked a filthy rag in his mouth and continued beating. First one would strike, then the other. On and on.

Inside, deep inside, it was only the flame of hate that kept him alive. He felt calmness flood over him. His pain, his screams, slowly faded. He knew he was losing consciousness. His last thought was if they hadn't killed him by now, they never would.

He would survive, and to survive was to triumph.

DAVID MACE

SHADOW HUNTERS

In the Cold War there was a ritual: the big Russian Bear lumbering into British airspace. A Nato interception, closing to escort it away.

Now suddenly there's something more: satellite photos, half-sightings. A radar-invisible Russian intruder?

US Colonel Oliver Lutwidge, for whom the Cold War has never ended, is ordered to put together a top-secret F-15 team for a mission near-impossible. Test fly the new sight-vision sensors. Search the moonless skies. Total radio silence.

Find the invisible Red Wraith . . .

Shadow Hunters seethes with tension, rivalry, sexual politics and betrayal, and features some of the most exciting air sequences ever written.

RICHARD HERMAN JNR

THE WARBIRDS

When Libya provokes a world crisis, the 45th Tactical Fighter Wing is relocated to a base in East Anglia to prepare for combat. Pilot Jack Locke and Colonel Anthony "Muddy" Waters must find a way to turn conflicting personalities into a team in record time.

And when the combat starts, it is terrifying in its intensity.

Combining the hard world of power-politics with phenomenal air-war sequences and nail-biting tension, *The Warbirds* is the flying novel of the decade.

'*The Warbirds* is an imaginative action story told to perfection'

Clive Cussler

HODDER AND STOUGHTON PAPERBACKS

RICHARD HERMAN JNR

FORCE OF EAGLES

Prisoners of Iranian fundamentalists: 281 men of USAF 45th Tactical Fighter Wing.
And one woman.

Brutalised and half-starved, they were held in a military prison deep in Iran. Intelligence confirmed that within days they were to be parcelled out among rival terror groups and dispersed throughout the Middle East.

Any rescue mission had to come in fast – and work first time.

Colonel Rupert Stansell headed up an unrivalled fighting team: F-111s and the latest F-15E Strike Eagle fighter bombers, C-130 transports and an AC-130 gunship, air superiority fighters and an AWACS eye-in-the-sky.

But ranged against him were a fanatical enemy, hostile terrain – and Pentagon inter-service rivalry and incompetence.

Force of Eagles is a superb human drama and high-tech thriller.

HODDER AND STOUGHTON PAPERBACKS

CHARLES RYAN

THE CAPRICORN QUADRANT

Sabre was the future.

Soviet stealth technology, artificial intelligence and cold fusion beam weaponry interacted in an ultra-high level, anti-satellite plane years in advance of any US project.

Sabre was down.

Somewhere in the Pacific, drifting, crew dead but a living entity: its systems scanning, sensing, ready to react to any approach, innocent or hostile.

Sabre was the ultimate threat.

With Soviet hardliners nerving themselves for a coup, a vulnerable French research platform nearby and nuclear-armed naval task forces from East and West, closing fast, *Sabre* was beyond human control, preparing to trigger off a global holocaust . . .

'A technothriller that brings to life all of our bad dreams . . . a pulse-tingling scenario'
New York Times Book Review

'Charles Ryan is a true master of adventure'
Clive Cussler

HODDER AND STOUGHTON PAPERBACKS